W9-AWQ-591

SLEEPLESS CITY

BOOKS BY REED FARREL COLEMAN

REED FARREL
COLEMAN

SLEEPLESS CITY

A NICK RYAN NOVEL

**BLACK
STONE**
PUBLISHING

Copyright © 2022 by Reed F. Coleman, Inc.
Published in 2022 by Blackstone Publishing
Cover and book design by Kathryn Galloway English

The characters and events in this book are fictitious.
Any similarity to real persons, living or dead, is coincidental
and not intended by the author.

Printed in the United States of America

First edition: 2022
ISBN 978-1-9826-2747-8
Fiction / Mystery & Detective / General

Version 1

CIP data for this book is available
from the Library of Congress

Blackstone Publishing
31 Mistletoe Rd.
Ashland, OR 97520

www.BlackstonePublishing.com

I don't know if my being there in that place and at that time makes me a bad person, but on most days I think it means I do not get to claim to be a good one.

—KEVIN POWERS

PROLOGUE

JUNE 25

He'd torn off the name patch above the right pocket on his camo jacket. Tonight he wasn't Nick Ryan. He was an anonymous guy, an invisible face in the crowd marching down Church Street toward the Brooklyn Bridge. Invisibility was one of his talents. In that way, he was like the jacket he wore, patterned to blend into the brown color palette of the Afghan dust and mountains. These were different mountains he walked among.

He disdained using his invisibility this way, but he did as he was ordered. Duty was a matter of blood to the Ryans. He'd pleaded and cajoled, ego-massaged his target for three weeks to set up the buy-and-bust for tonight in Red Hook. Now that was history. Gone like his name patch.

"No way, man," the wannabe drug kingpin had told Nick when he tried delaying the takedown. "I like you, and maybe we can do business in the future, but I got this Apache sold three times over. First come, first serve."

Apache, Dance Fever, Murder 8—fentanyl had a hundred street names. Getting a kilo of it out of circulation might not have sounded like much to the women and men marching with him. Nick knew better.

Listening to the blaring car horns and cursing of frustrated drivers at every intersection, he looked around at the patchwork quilt of Black, brown, yellow, and white faces—young and old—and did the math. A million milligrams in a kilo. Fatal dosage two to three milligrams. But there was only one death these people cared about: Vincent Merrimack's. And they let the world know as they chanted his name.

"Vincent was innocent. No justice, no peace. Vincent was innocent. No justice, no peace. Vincent was innocent . . ."

Nick had listened to this chant for the past ninety minutes as the throng, squeezed between barricades and row after row of impassive cop faces, slowly made its way downtown from the staging area. His job wasn't supposed to be about feelings. His opinions were for off duty. He'd been ordered to seem a part of the demonstration while really being apart from it. Nevertheless, he had seen the body-cam footage of the shooting. The protesters were correct. Vincent *was* innocent.

In the early morning hours of June 22, Vincent Merrimack, a sixteen-year-old African American kid, was shot to death by four cops on Flatlands Avenue, in the Canarsie section of Brooklyn. Vincent, who was on the autism spectrum, became disoriented after his Aunt Marta suffered a stroke. Unable to rouse his aunt, Vincent began screeching and banging his fists into the wall. Marta's neighbors, misinterpreting the noises, called 911. When no one answered repeated requests for entry, the responding units broke into the home. Totally beyond his stimulation threshold, Vincent shouted at the cops and took a step toward them, shaking his fist. That fist shake would prove to be the last act of Vincent Merrimack's too-short life.

Nick looked at all the makeshift signs, many bearing likenesses of Merrimack. Vincent had been a handsome teen, his expression as beatific as any saint's. That was what he had become for the marchers: a martyr they could rally around. But Nick turned away, instead focusing on the other marchers, looking for the people he'd been briefed about.

He wasn't so much studying faces as looking for long sleeves, closed hands, loose-fitting clothing, backpacks. In Afghanistan a clenched fist and long sleeves meant a detonator and hidden wires. Backpacks and loose-fitting clothing could conceal explosives. It was a cool night for early summer—perfect for long sleeves or loose jackets like the one he was wearing. And while no one was anticipating anything as extreme as a bomb, Nick knew that if you looked only for what was expected, you were already beaten.

The first inkling of trouble came as his part of the march neared Duane Street, two blocks before the crowd was to turn left down Chambers Street, in the direction of the Dinkins Municipal Building, One Police Plaza, and the Brooklyn Bridge. A group of four white men in street clothes slipped into the crowd through a convenient gap in the metal barriers. Nick recognized one of them from the academy, though the name escaped him. The others were strangers, but they carried themselves like cops. You know your own kind. There was something else he recognized: a pack on the hunt.

Thinking he needed to keep an eye on them, Nick moved closer, zigzagging unnoticed through the demonstrators. He didn't register as police. That was part of his talent for undercover work. Then the pack showed its hand. Three of the four cops worked their way between the demonstrators and a Black man in his late twenties. The man was now isolated between the barricades on his left and the three men—one walking behind him, one to his right, and the last in front of him. Nick had marched near the man the entire way from Herald Square. The man had been less vocal than most of the other marchers. He didn't carry a sign, hadn't even chanted, and ignored the few counterprotesters shouting as he passed. Though he was surrounded, he seemed unaware of anything outside his own thoughts.

Something wasn't right. Arresting an African American man in the midst of this protest was tone-deaf bordering on stupid. But if this guy was a threat or was wanted for a serious felony, Nick was in no position to judge. Maybe they were following orders same as he. There was a commotion to Nick's right. The fourth member of the pack stumbled hard to the pavement, drawing the crowd's attention away from what was really going on. Nick wasn't fooled by the sleight of hand.

At the precise moment of the fall, the other three pack members came together around the Black man, shoving him through the barricades at the corner of Church and Reade Streets. The uniforms lining the barricades closed ranks, vanishing the hole as quickly as it had appeared. Nick was pushed along by the surging crowd. He looked back and saw the three cops dragging the man down Reade Street. Turning right, he saw that the cop who stumbled had conveniently disappeared.

"Excuse me," Nick said to the woman next to him. "The man who fell—where did he go?"

"It was really weird. He got right up and ran ahead."

There it was, the familiar pull in two directions—to follow orders or his gut. Nick never needed long to decide. He had lived through two tours in Afghanistan by trusting his instincts. Hopping the metal barrier, he worked his way back to Reade Street. He tugged on the chain around his neck and took his detective shield out from under his T-shirt. At that point, he ceased being invisible, and people stepped aside.

Reade Street was eerily quiet. City quiet, not country quiet. The chanting from the crowd became a muted, indecipherable echo as he walked away from the march. The block was closed off to vehicular and pedestrian traffic down to Park Row. Nearing Broadway, he saw two unmarked NYPD SUVs parked in a V formation on the sidewalk. His view was obscured by the vehicles' height and their dark tinted windows. As he approached the SUVs, Nick heard the unmistakable sounds of a beating. Fists pounding flesh, grunts and moans. He heard something else too. Footsteps coming up quickly behind him.

"Hey, you, asshole, didn't you see the street's closed off?" a breathless voice called to him.

He turned to see the cop who had taken the pratfall. "I noticed."

The cop saw Nick's shield and slowed, but his attitude didn't change. "Look, Detective, we all got enough on our plates, right? Why don't you go back to whatever it was you was doin'? This don't concern you."

"When people tell me not to be concerned, it concerns me."

The cop shrugged. "Still not your business."

The sounds of the beating stopped.

"Get rid of that guy, Jimmy," growled a voice from behind the SUVs.

"He's a detective, Robby."

"I don't care if he's the pope. Get his ass outta here."

Jimmy made a face, not a happy one. "You heard him. C'mon, just go. Everybody's happy that way. Nobody gets hurt or nothin'."

"I'm already pissed. That guy you're kicking the shit out of . . . he's hurting. So, no I'm not moving."

Jimmy wasn't tall, but he was sinewy. The kind of guy that always gets underestimated. Nick turned, baiting Jimmy into making a move. It didn't take long. As soon as Nick about-faced, Jimmy came charging. Nick heard him coming, saw his reflection in the SUV's side window. As Jimmy got close, Nick dropped to one knee and swung his left elbow up into Jimmy's solar plexus. He didn't have to swing hard; Jimmy's momentum supplied all the power. The cop tumbled into the driver's side door of the SUV with a loud bang. Jimmy was red-faced, struggling for breath. Nick cuffed him to a vent pipe.

"Yo, Jimmy," Robby called out. "What the fuck?" When Jimmy didn't answer, Robby called out again, this time with worry in his voice. "Yo, Jimmy, everything okay?"

Nick jumped up onto the hood of the blue SUV. "Jimmy's having too much trouble breathing to answer."

The victim's hands were strapped behind him with a plastic tie, and two cops were propping him up for a trimming. The man's mouth was bloodied, and his eyes were swelling shut. Robby, the guy Nick remembered from the academy, was wearing a pair of brown leather gloves, keeping his hands unmarked as he delivered the beatdown. Nick jumped off the hood of the car and stood only a few feet from him.

Robby was thick all around, legs to neck, with a cruel smile, which he aimed at Nick.

"You're a detective, so what? You're not my CO. Get the fuck outta here and let us do what we gotta do." He reached out, giving a derisive flip to the left pocket on Nick's camo jacket, "Booyah, Semper Fi, and all that rah-rah bullshit." He gave a dismissive salute. "Now, go fuck yourself. I owe this nig—"

"Don't even say it, not in front of me. It's *oorah*, by the way, and I was army, shithead. See, it says it right here in big letters."

Robby squinted his eyes, wagged his gloved finger at Nick. "Wait a second . . . I know you—"

"Hey. Robby, let's get on with this, man," one of the other cops said. "We're exposed out here."

"Shut up, Tom. I went to the academy with this prick. This is Nick Ryan. The guy whose father ratted out his precinct to the Argent Commission."

Nick snapped his fingers. "Yeah, I remember you now. Robby Rasmussen. You were a prick back then and that hasn't changed."

"Yeah, Robby, forget him," the third cop said. "Let's get Jimmy and split. It's getting dark, but we're out in the open here."

Nick pointed at the injured man. "He's coming with me."

As the last word came out of Nick's mouth, Rasmussen threw a left. Nick slipped the punch, but the leather grazed his jaw. Nick stepped to his right to get a good angle and, using the top of his foot, kicked Rasmussen twice in the left calf. The vicious, short chopping kicks jellied Rasmussen's leg, collapsing him. Nick took a quick peek at the other two cops to see if they were going to be a problem. He needn't have bothered. They were busy deciding whether to court any more trouble than they already had.

Nick returned his full focus to Rasmussen, who had managed to get to his knees. Nick thrust the heel of his palm to the underside of Rasmussen's nose. He didn't hit him hard enough to break the nose, but he wished he had. Rasmussen went back down, temporarily blinded by tears, coughing out blood.

Nick pulled his Glock and got back to the issue at hand. "You two, cut the tie and step away from him. Now!"

They did as they were told. When they had freed his hands, they raised their own, palms out. "Look, we got no gripe with this guy," Tom said. "It's Robby's gig. The guy made a complaint against Robby's part-ner, and Robby just wants to convince him he made a mistake, is all."

Nick ignored him. "You . . . Sir, what's your name?"

"D'Anton Waller," he said, wiping the blood off his mouth with his sleeve.

"Mr. Waller, do you need medical assistance?"

"I been worse."

"Then please step over here behind me."

As Waller stepped behind Nick, Rasmussen tried gathering himself again. Nick kicked him in the ribs to dissuade him.

"We're leaving, and if you try to stop us, I *will* shoot you and worry about the fallout later. Don't doubt it."

"Whoa, whoa," Tom said. "Easy. Easy, Ryan. We're not gonna do nothing, but can't we keep this thing between us? You know, brother to brother."

"You're not my brother. What to do about this is up to Mr. Waller, not me." Nick nodded to Waller. "If you can, climb over the hood. I'll cover and follow you."

"I'm good," Waller said. Then a few seconds later, "I'm over."

Nick didn't have anything else to say, but Rasmussen did, his voice thick from the blood and mucus. "Watch your back, motherfucker, 'cause I'm coming for you."

"Get in line."

Nick climbed over the hood, looped his arm through Waller's, and walked him quickly back toward Church Street. As they got close, Waller shook free of his arm.

"Fuck them guys and fuck you. You ain't no hero. You all the same."

"'Hero.' What does that word even mean anymore? But we're not all the same."

"You go on thinking that," Waller said. "Even if you are good, so what? What's one cop gonna do against a rigged system? One good man don't mean shit." Waller spat blood on the ground and walked away.

Nick understood how D'Anton Waller could see it in that light. To Waller, the barrel was all rotten apples, not just a few. There wasn't much Nick could have said to change the man's mind. Something Waller said resonated. *What's one cop gonna do against a rigged system?* Nick didn't dwell on it. He holstered his weapon and put his shield back under his shirt. As he rejoined the march, his posture changed and he once again became some anonymous guy, invisible.

ONE

Never goodbye.

Goodbye was an omen of dark permanence. That was what Nick's mother used to say. A superstition come from Ireland, stowed away in steerage with his great-grandparents, or something his family had adopted when it bubbled up from the stew pot of ethnicities that was and is New York City. The stew recipe changed from time to time—Guyanese and Bangladeshis instead of Irish, Ukrainian Jews, and southern Italians—but the pot boiled. Always! Sometimes, it boiled over. Another man—gazing down from the high windows of his Bay Ridge condo at the cruise ship cutting the water white beneath the Verrazzano Bridge, or at the glass-and-steel prickles of the lower Manhattan skyline glowing orange in the dawn light—might have been able to fool himself that the stew pot was at a low simmer and all was peaceful in this sleepless city.

Nick Ryan did not deceive himself that what lay spread out before him was anything resembling peaceful. Quiet was often the preamble to deadly. Since 9/11, crime in this city had been tamped down. Three generations of the Ryan family had helped make it so. But the vibe on the street was changing, and the summer just past had been a restless, ugly one dominated by three stories splashed across the front pages of the failing tabloids. Stories that fed the infernal lifeblood of social media.

The stories dominating the media were very much on Nick Ryan's mind. Disparate stories of power, money, race, sex, and violence, bound together by an invisible blue thread. There was the arrest of Aaron Lister, a hedge fund guru whom the *Post* dubbed "Baby Bernie," and the *News* labeled "Mini Madoff" for his swindling of a billion dollars. Most cops wouldn't have given Lister a second thought but for the fact that a significant amount of the pilfered funds had come from investments sponsored by all the New York City law enforcement unions. The dream of windfall payoffs from private investments meant to supplement their civil service pensions had, with the click of handcuffs around Lister's wrists, swirled down the drain. Every penny burned away like fog under the glare of the sun.

Then, there were the shootings. Three-plus months had passed since Vincent Merrimack's death. The Brooklyn DA had so far resisted charging the cops in that case. Worse, another Black teenager, Shawn Bannister, had been killed in Queens during a confrontation with the police. What started as an intoxicated Bannister relieving himself in public had escalated into a shouting match, a drawn knife, and three shots in the back. As with everything else these days, people had taken sides. Stoking the flames of racial tension was Roderick Ford, the alt-right conspiracy nut, Holocaust denier, and racist who used his media platforms to espouse the notion that the dead teenagers were deserving of their fates.

After the Bannister shooting, there had been three weeks of candlelight vigils and protests, sit-ins blocking traffic on the Brooklyn Bridge, rallies on the steps of city hall and at One Police Plaza. Despite tensions, there hadn't been any violence—not yet. Nick, who understood the street and could read the creases in its palm like a Coney Island mystic, knew that the lid was this close to blowing off. One more shooting, no matter the circumstances, and there would be no holding back the rage. But the third story mattered to Nick Ryan in a way the others couldn't. It was personal—very damned personal—and he meant to do something about it.

He turned his attention away from the window, back to Angeline, the woman sleeping in his bed. He marveled at how the soft folds of the blue linen sheets conformed to the curves of her naked body. He noticed how the air smelled vaguely of bourbon, sweat, and sex, and of her crushed-sage-and-grated-lemon-peel perfume. At certain points last evening, he'd had trouble remembering her name. Nick tried to make himself care about his occasional moments of absentmindedness. He didn't try hard. He had since moved on from the vagaries of petty guilt. Although Afghanistan had supplied him with all the perspective a man could endure, Nick was already wise to the truth of the world. There was the storm and there was the eye of the storm. Nick was in the eye. While chaos swirled around him, he was calm. It had always been so.

His teammates on the basketball team at Xaverian had called him "Chilly" because nothing on the court rattled him, and also because his blue irises had that crystalline, cracked-ice quality about them. Whether it was playing in the Catholic high school championship game at Madison Square Garden, working undercover, or on night recon, the moment was never too big, the pressure never too much. He was the one who anticipated trouble, who knew before anyone else that things were about to go sideways.

War changed people. It had changed him. While many of his army brothers had come home as cracked and scrambled as Humpty Dumpty, Nick had come back hard and focused. Most people's moral code featured flexible boundaries, their dos and don'ts defined in a situational shade of gray. Nick's lines were sharply drawn. That clarity led him to decide to kill Ricky Corliss—clarity, accompanied by the suicide of Pete Moretti.

Pete was Nick's best friend and the detective who had shown Nick the ropes when he got the bump. It was more than a debt of love or gratitude that led to the decision. That was another thing war had taught him: killing wasn't something to be done capriciously. Every life had its own intrinsic value and it was only the people who didn't understand that who deserved to lose their own. Ricky Corliss badly needed killing. Every decent living soul in New York City had come to the same conclusion. Thing was, no one seemed willing to do it. Nick didn't need someone to shout, "Simon Says."

Nick came back into the moment as Angeline rolled over onto her back. He studied her in sleep. He supposed she was on his side of thirty, the age when living had stripped away any last hints of girlishness. The age when lovemaking began to morph from youthful ferocity to the threshold of solitary desperation. What people feared second to death was loneliness. He'd given up worrying about either a long time ago.

They'd met at McCann's, his local watering hole in the shadow of the Verrazzano Bridge. While McCann's wasn't exactly a "cop bar" in the traditional sense, it had the reputation as a place where badge boys and bunnies were known to start or finish their pub crawls. Nick didn't waste too much energy wondering why some people were attracted to men and women in uniform. People had their reasons. With his stark blue eyes, cleft chin, and dark-blond hair, he had never needed to lean on the allure of the job for companionship.

Angeline's shoulder-length blond hair and light-brown eyes had gotten his attention. She had been dressed in a low-slung blouse, white and satiny, and wore her tight black jeans over ankle boots. It was more than her looks that got his attention. McCann's was packed, some of the women more attractive than Angeline, some less. Behind her good looks, beyond her *Hey-I'm-over-here!* outfit, was a distinctive lost quality. While Nick would never be mistaken for St. Jude, he did have a soft spot for the lost.

She was nervously drumming her pointed silver nails on the bar top when Nick approached. She was looking everywhere and nowhere—a defense mechanism New Yorkers learned at an early age. You never wanted to be caught making eye contact on a subway.

"First time?" he asked.

The drumming stopped. She flushed. "Is it that obvious?"

He laughed. "Like Kabuki, it takes time and practice to learn the steps."

She smiled a neon-white smile. "I hope it's less complicated."

"You'll catch on." He put out his hand. "Nick."

"Angeline." She shook his hand.

"Drink?"

"Sure." She cleared her throat. "Are you—"

"Detective third."

"Divorced?"

"Nope."

The air went out of her. "Married?"

"Came close once."

"What happened?"

"Depends who you ask. How about that drink?"

She pointed to the bourbon shelf, the bottle with the drippy red wax seal. "On the rocks."

He shook his head, smiled, and said, "No. Not for you. Not tonight."

Nick waved to the red-faced Irishman behind the bar. Mack, a man in his sixties, wore his ginger-and-gray hair in a ponytail. The tip of his long, unruly beard flirted with the second button of his flannel shirt.

"Evenin', Ryan. What'll it be, boyo?" Mack's gruff voice blended the old-country lilt with harsh notes of Brooklynese.

"My bottle." Nick held up two fingers. "Glasses for Angeline and me."

Mack returned holding a tall bottle with a tapered neck, one-third full of honey-colored liquid. Below the distiller's label featuring an older bearded man smoking a cigar, "NICK RYAN" was written in black marker across a piece of masking tape. Mack poured a finger's worth in each glass. When he turned to go, Nick grabbed his thick wrist.

"Leave the Pappy's."

Surprise was as obvious as the beard on Mack's pitted face. "Whatever you say, son."

Angeline frowned. "I like mine on the rocks."

"Not this stuff," Nick said, pushing a glass toward her.

She held the bourbon up to her nose, and her eyes got wide. "It smells like caramel and vanilla and . . ."

He clinked his glass against hers. "Smells great. Tastes better. Cheers."

"Oh my God! This stuff is better than sex."

"Still want ice?"

"This all part of your Kabuki? Impressing the woman by calling for your own bottle?"

"Do you think I need to do that?"

"No." The word caught in her throat.

"I don't share this with anyone, and we'll see about the sex."

She laughed at that, the tension going out of her. "Why me?"

"Why *not* you? Besides, there's too much left in the bottle for me to finish alone." He stroked her cheek with the back of his left hand. "And I don't want to be alone tonight."

"What's special about tonight?"

"I met you." It was a deflection, one that made her blush. He wouldn't tell her the truth about why her or why tonight.

Now, as he watched her tossing in his bed, he considered climbing back in and peeling off the sheets to rouse her. Instead, he sat at the edge of the bed, running his fingers through her silken hair. Squeezing his eyes shut to concentrate, he gave her hair a final stroke to remember the feel of it on his skin. Yet, as much as he had enjoyed being with her and luxuriated in the feel of her hair on the ridges and whorls of his fingertips, Nick knew one other woman he had to see before tonight. Unfinished business was one of the few things that disquieted him.

T W O

Nick parked his GTO on the street in front of the ten-story prewar building on Sutton Place. He had never gotten used to the forbidding black wrought-iron-and-glass entrance. It was as welcoming as a cemetery gate. The wind blowing hard off the East River toyed with the sidewalk-imprisoned trees, their leaves fading from vibrant summer green to terminal shades of red, yellow, and brown.

Before Nick got both legs out of the car, the doorman was out on the street, screaming and wagging his finger. He was a young Latino in a long gray tunic with gold buttons and ridiculous maroon piping. The matching hat was even sillier.

"Not here! No good, my friend." His tone was anything but friendly. He pointed at the red-and-white No Parking sign swaying in the breeze.

He didn't know this doorman. Years had passed since Nick left for basic training. Once things fell apart with Shana, he hadn't looked back. No reason to revisit chapters in a closed book—until today. He didn't know why, but he felt there were pages still to be written.

Nick asked, "What happened to Bill?"

The doorman cocked his head. "Bill? No Bill here."

"Bill Dougherty. Retired cop. The old daytime doorman."

"*Muerto.*" The doorman crossed himself. "Heart attack."

Nick flashed his shield, pointing at the NYPD parking permit on his visor. "I won't be long. What's your name, *jefe?*"

"Felix. Who you want to see?"

"Shana Bla— Mrs. Carlyle."

Felix's smile was short-lived, replaced by a familiar look, one Nick had seen from the day he and Shana Black became a couple. It was what Nick had come to think of as the "different worlds" expression. An expression that said, *Men like you don't have anything to do with women like her.* Felix didn't need to give it a voice. Nick heard it quite loud enough.

"Don't bother calling ahead," Nick said. "I know my way." It wasn't a request.

Felix was worried. On Sutton Place, a doorman could be fired for neglecting to say good morning to a resident's Shiba Inu.

"Relax." Nick patted Felix's shoulder. "Police business, right? I'll cover for you."

The doorman tried and failed to smile. Nick walked down the walnut-paneled hallway toward the elevators, his footfalls echoing on the pink granite floors.

On the fifth floor, the corridor had been freshly painted and the old floor covering replaced with sage-and-maroon-patterned carpeting so plush, Nick felt as if he were walking on the moon. The carpeting smelled as new as the paint on the walls. In a building where even the smallest units cost several million dollars the hallways didn't smell of crushed allspice for jerk chicken. Nick remembered that they smelled of only one thing: money.

As he turned the corner, he saw that where there had once been doors for apartments 5A and 5B, there was now only one. The work was flawless. Of course it was. He rang the bell.

"Who is it?"

He recognized the raspy impatience in Shana's voice. Before he could answer, the door swung open, and there she stood. The sight of her brought it all back. Nick's breath caught in his throat, as it had the first time he saw her.

He had held the door for her as she walked into the memorial service for his uncle Kenny and the other Three Ravens Equity employees killed on 9/11. Uncle Kenny's death was cruel irony. The lone male Ryan in three generations who had forsaken a police career was the only family member to perish at Ground Zero. It was Kenny who had willed his condo, car, and motorcycle to Nick.

With that recollection of Shana came the memories of a city in shock and mourning. Financiers and firefighters were the same that way, death being the great equalizer of all living things.

Although barely sixteen at the time, Nick wasn't too young to appreciate the choking sense of grief in the air or the ungodly beauty of a girl who split the wind like the curved blade of a saber.

"Nick!" There was considerable freight in that one syllable: joy, excitement, anger, suspicion, disappointment, a thousand other things. Something else too. Something unspoken in her expression. Something unexpected and out of place. Fear. It vanished as quickly as it came. "What are you . . . Come in. Come in," she insisted, pulling him by the wrist.

Her touch was electric. He felt the surge. He was sure she felt it too. Her hand lingered. The memory of fear on her face lingered as well. He could not make sense of it. Still, he drank in the sight of her dressed in a navy-blue cashmere sweater, tan slacks, and brown lizard-skin boots. Her beauty was dark and brooding, her movements balletic. She might have been Mila Kunis's green-eyed sister. Depending on the light falling on it, her shoulder-length hair could appear any shade from deep red to black. Backlit by the sun streaming into the apartment, it shone auburn.

Forcing himself to look away from her, Nick saw that the remodeling had only enhanced the views of the river, Roosevelt Island and the Ed Koch Fifty-Ninth Street Bridge. Shana followed his gaze.

"As an engagement gift, Bradley bought 5B and had the place remade for . . . us."

"Nice."

"Nick Ryan Jr., Mr. Effusive." She laughed.

He loved that laugh and, despite everything, supposed he still loved her. "Don't be pissed at the doorman. I flashed my shield and told him not to call ahead."

"You haven't changed." She was disappointed. "For you, it's still about the little guys and the losers."

"The lost, not the losers."

It had been the persistent rub between them. Everyone in Nick's world *was* the little guy. Everyone in Shana's was moneyed, powerful, or both.

She asked, "How's your dad? Sean?"

"Dad's the same. I don't see him much. Sean's a fuckup, same as ever."

"You look tired, Nick."

"Long night. You look perfect."

Shana had never been falsely humble. Marriage hadn't changed that. "Thank you. Pardon my bluntness, but what are you doing here? You were always the man who didn't look back."

"Now that I am here, I'm not sure. I thought I came for answers."

Her laugh was sharp and joyless. "Answers! That's easy. I never lied to you about who I was. I wasn't a character out of *Little Women* who was going to sit patiently by the hearth, pining away for you as you went to war. I begged you not to go, and you went. You made a choice. I wasn't it."

"What bothered you more, the war or that you weren't my choice?"

"Does that matter now?" She turned, walking around the bend into the huge living room.

"Today, yes, it matters." He followed a few paces behind her.

"What's to explain? You went away."

"And I came back."

"It was too late the day you left," she said, opening the door of an elaborate wall unit. The exotic hardwood's reddish grain was spotted like a jaguar's coat. She poured herself a short glass of single malt that had the peaty smell of a doused campfire. "I see you're admiring the cabinetry. Snakewood, and before you ask, yes, it cost your annual salary and then some. The money we spent on things always seemed to matter to you. I never understood it. We could afford it." She sipped her scotch. "You still a bourbon man?"

"Not today. Thanks."

Her mood turned angry. "What incredible chutzpah! You don't get to show up here after years of zero contact and question me like a suspect. Our story is a common one. A mutual teenage crush that grew into love that everyone except us knew was doomed. A love that persisted longer than either of us had reason to believe it would. But you and me against the world lasts only so long. It ended because things end. The mechanics of how . . ." She shrugged, finishing her drink but not her sentence.

"Sounds like a story you've recited to yourself so many times, you almost believe it."

She leaned in close to Nick, putting her lips softly to his. It was much like their first kiss, tentative and gentle. This time it tasted of whiskey.

She pulled back, turning away. "I'm sorry, Nick."

"Why did you do that?"

Before she could answer, the planet wobbled on its axis.

A little girl bolted into the room, squealing with joy. She held three paper flowers in her hand. She slammed into Shana's leg, grabbing her thigh with her free arm. She held the colored-paper-and-pipe-cleaner bouquet up to Shana. "Mommy, Mommy! Look what Odile and I made for you."

"Thank you, honey." Shana took the red, blue, and orange flowers, sniffed them as if they were roses, and smiled proudly. "They're so beautiful, and they smell wonderful."

"You're silly, Mommy! They don't smell."

Nick felt light-headed. But for her crystalline blue eyes and dirty-blond hair, the little girl looked like photos of Shana at the same age. When he looked up from her face to Shana's, he saw it again—fear. Nick's gaze shifted back to the small face whose eyes and hair were a reflection of his. He didn't speak. He couldn't. The girl was staring at Nick, her expression ripe with suspicion and curiosity.

Shana broke the spell. "Becky, I'd like you to meet Mommy's old friend Nick."

Nick smiled, found his voice. "Hello, Becky."

Becky giggled, burying her face against Shana's thigh.

Shana called out, "Odile, please come get Becky."

A petite brunette woman in her early twenties came into the room and took Becky by the hand. She bowed her head slightly to Nick. "Come, Becky," she said in French-accented tones. "We make more flowers for your father."

"Bye, Becky." Nick waved.

She waved back, giggling.

"She's beautiful, Shana."

"She's amazing." A moment of awkward silence came and went. "The kiss . . . You asked me about the kiss."

Still distracted, Nick said, "Yeah, what was that about?" But the sight of Becky had made the kiss feel as if it happened a million years ago.

"We never had a real goodbye. I don't owe you explanations, but I owed you that. I owed *me* that."

"I'm going." He about-faced, moving to the front door.

"Nick!"

He stopped but didn't face her. "What?"

"Never come back, please."

"Don't worry. I won't."

He let himself out. If he had any second thoughts about killing Ricky Corliss before the visit, they had evaporated at the first sight of Becky. Even if the little girl wasn't who he knew in his heart she must be, Nick had to remove the possibility of a man like Corliss from her life.

THREE

A passing N train threw an alternating series of shadows and lights across Eighty-Sixth Street at Ricky Corliss's feet. He stood statue-still, a wide-brimmed fedora squashed down low on his forehead, and dark sunglasses covering his eyes. He waited for Montez to wave him ahead. Montez, Corliss's personal security, waited for the noise of the subway to subside before letting his client take another step. Being out in public was a huge risk and one that Montez had argued against. But the safe-house isolation was driving Corliss up the wall, and he craved Lenny's Pizza beyond all reason. As calculating and careful as he was, Ricky Corliss was a man who could resist his cravings for only so long.

Corliss had been a meticulous predator. A man who left few traces in his wake, a man who cremated the bodies of his young victims until they were memories written only in ash and charred bone. It was his attention to detail that made the original case against him so paper-thin. The prosecution had a collage of circumstance and inference, of area sightings by semireliable witnesses, suggestive CCTV footage, and wishful thinking. The case so weak, the prosecutor felt fortunate to get a hung jury the first time around. The DA might have felt lucky to get a hung jury, but it was also what compelled Pete Moretti, the lead detective on the case, to plant blood evidence.

———

Standing between cars at the edge of the shadows, Nick Ryan felt a strange sense of liberation in the knowledge that any criminal act was more easily managed if you were at peace with getting caught. It was the way he mentally prepared for his UC work. He didn't worry about what would happen if he were found out. Worrying meant you weren't paying attention to what mattered. Although he had every intention of getting away with what he was about to do, he was at ease with the consequences. Unlike Pete Moretti, he'd been careful not to let anyone in on what he was planning. A secret shared was no secret at all.

"Once the words are out of your mouth, you are no longer their master." Thus spake Kathleen Ryan, Nick's late mom. "Everybody in the world has a friend they can trust with their deepest, darkest secret. Every one of those friends has a trusted friend, and every one of those trusted friends has a trusted friend too. So it goes."

Pete might still be alive if he had heard that advice. It was a trusted friend who had been his downfall. It wouldn't be Nick's. He thought about Pete and how the law of unintended consequences had put the gun in his mouth and the scapegoat bull's-eye on his back. Because when his evidence tampering came to light, not only did the judge declare a mistrial, but it put the stink on *all* the evidence against Corliss. The case and Pete's career got flushed down the toilet with a single flick of the handle. And while the Bronx DA was making all the right noises about having a third go at Corliss, it was a well-known secret that another trial would be a waste of time and money. Enter Peter Moretti, serving up his own head on a silver platter. Moretti was labeled a renegade cop and his disgrace became the river in which everyone from the DA to Corliss himself washed away their sins.

Nick's last conversation with Moretti echoed in his head as the train racket abated.

You should've come to me, Pete. We could have figured something out, something a little less . . . obvious.

No way, Nick. I wasn't gonna risk jamming nobody else up. What did I have to lose except alimony payments? Joking was Moretti's way, but neither of them had laughed. *I gotta go.*

The next day, Pete did just that. He went to a place where he was free, a place where not even words could ever harm him. It had been a month now since Pete swallowed a bullet at a motel across from MacArthur Airport. A little more than three weeks had passed since they planted him in the ground. Fired, stripped of his benefits, and awaiting trial, Pete really had nothing else to lose. Yet even in death, the department denied him any shred of dignity. No flag-draped coffin. No Emerald Society bagpipes playing for a man who had given twenty-six years and sacrificed two marriages to the NYPD. The only music that day had been the song of pelting rain against the glossy wood of the flagless casket. In the time since, Nick had been busy.

Spotting Corliss and his protection rounding the corner, Nick receded fully into the shadows between the rear of the stolen Ford van and the crystal-white Escalade parked behind it. Nick couldn't let them get to the black Suburban parked farther up the block. He had to make his move.

———

Montez walked on the curb side of the pavement, keeping himself between Corliss and any drive-by threat or attack from the street. The security man noticed that the Ford van's sliding door was open and the cargo compartment was empty. He slowed. Halted. Threw his right arm out to stop Corliss.

"What is it?" Corliss sounded more annoyed than frightened.

Sensing the threat without seeing it, Montez turned his body to face the shadows, putting himself squarely in the line of fire.

"Shut up and get back!" Montez shouted at Corliss, reaching for his H&K.

It was already too late.

———

Nick squeezed the Taser's trigger. Montez's muscles seized as the voltage pulsed through him. He went down face-first, his head making a sickening, hollow thud as it hit the pavement. Nose broken, chin bloodied, body in total spasm, and grunting in pain, Montez was helpless. Corliss was paralyzed by fear and confusion. He hadn't heard the pop or seen the spray of particles explode out the front end of the Taser. The darkness camouflaged the thin wires extending from the weapon's power generator to the barbed hooks that had attached themselves to Montez's shirt. Corliss didn't know what to make of the sizzling and crackling noises.

It finally dawned on Corliss to move. He ran, but he was a short, corpulent man with heavy, unmuscular legs that no doubt moved much faster in his dreams than in reality. He didn't make it more than half a car length before the sweep of a metal baton came out of the night, cracking across the back of his knees and sending him sprawling. Nick cuffed Corliss's hands behind him.

"You won't get away with this." The man's voice was a breathless whisper.

"Aw, Ricky, that the best you can do?"

Nick dragged the struggling man through the van's open door and slid it shut behind them. He laid a leather-covered sap to the back of Corliss's head and Corliss went limp. Nick took the cell phone from Corliss's pocket and dialed 911 to get Montez some help. Then, he climbed into the driver's seat, wiped the phone, and tossed it out the window. Nick pulled away from the curb and headed toward a condemned house on the other side of Brooklyn.

FOUR

Nick had killed before. Killing at a distance was an abstraction. Most of the time, you couldn't hear the screams of the dying. Close up was something else. Tough to fool yourself when you made a man's chest explode and stood in the crimson mist of his atomized blood, when you breathed it in knowing that the coppery taste in your mouth was the vaporized remnant of a dead man's soul. This was different. This was an execution. A pale deliverance. No orders from above. No kill-or-be-killed.

There was justice and there was right. They weren't always the same thing. Cops learned that the first day on the job. When he looked down at Corliss, naked and on his knees, Nick didn't know whether what he was doing amounted to justice or right, both or neither. What he knew was that it needed to be done. Nick had dealt with murderers on the street and in war, but very few had earned killing the way Corliss had. He had kidnapped, tortured, and raped five eight-year-old boys before burning their wrecked bodies.

Perversely, the folds of Ricky Corliss's pink, nearly translucent flesh reminded Nick of a newborn's. Having spent the past half hour alternating between denial and defiance, Corliss was running out of both. Executing him wouldn't be enough. Nick understood that vengeance was inherently disappointing. Death couldn't undo things. It didn't blot out an evil man's existence. It didn't erase him from the pages of history or cleanse the people whom he had touched. What it did was stop one evil man. That would have to suffice.

He had made Corliss confess his crimes in exacting detail. He would send the confession to a journalist he knew at the *Times*. It might give the families some sense of closure, whatever that was. The way Nick saw it, closure was more unsatisfying than revenge. Something better in the yearning than in the receiving. Nick hoped that once the facts got out, Pete Moretti's kids could once again remember their father with pride and not shame. They would know that he hadn't tried to frame an innocent man but instead tried to save the next little boy.

"My confession ain't worth shit in court," Corliss said one last time, his throat raw.

For Nick, all of Corliss's attempts at manipulation were as insignificant as the beating of mosquito wings. He racked the Taurus 9 mm's slide with his gloved hand, shoving the muzzle into the back of Corliss's bruised head.

"You're right, but I'm going to do what a court couldn't."

Corliss shifted tactics, turning on the tears almost as if he were human.

"Please, man, don't do this. All that shit I just told you—it wasn't me."

More denial. Nick slapped him across the face and bloodied his mouth. "You just made that stuff up off the top of your head, right? Names, places, where you snatched the kids from—"

"No, no," Corliss moaned, blood dripping down his chin. "Mulvahill did it. I swear."

Francis Mulvahill was himself a nasty piece of work. A registered sex offender and convicted pedophile who shared Corliss's predilections, he had served two long stretches in prison that hadn't done a thing to mitigate his bent nature. Corliss and Mulvahill had met online on a dark site and developed a real-world friendship. Mulvahill hadn't been seen since the last of Corliss's victims disappeared. During his first trial, Corliss's lawyers had pointed their fingers squarely at Mulvahill.

Nick once again pressed the muzzle to Corliss's head. "You're lying. You smell like a liar."

"All right, all right, I burned the bodies. My lawyers told me to deny it, but I did it. I had no choice. Mulvahill would've killed me too. Look at me. I'm a fat little man. Frank—he was a beast."

Nick was tempted to beat Corliss, but he hadn't come here to brutalize the man. Beating him would have turned this into something else, something less. Only seven minutes earlier, Corliss had finished describing the things he did to each of his victims in such detail that it was impossible to believe he had been a mere observer. What sealed it for Nick, though, was the unconscious smile that formed on Corliss's face as he relived his crimes. Even in his current situation, the man found it impossible to disguise his perverse delight.

Finally, he resorted to the tactic that Nick knew would come in the end. He abandoned any attempt at disguising his true self—gray eyes narrowing and predatory, expression smug and superior, crooked smile underlined in his own blood.

"The cops were right, you know, about there being others. Lots of eight-year-old boys in the world with their perfect, unspoiled skin." He snorted, his smile broadening. "The world is like a salad bar for someone like me. So many options to choose from."

"So Mulvahill had nothing to do with the murders?"

"Sometimes I let him watch."

"Is he dead?"

Corliss made the little barking sound that was his version of a laugh. "What do you think? I couldn't afford to leave any witnesses."

Now that Corliss had mentioned other victims, Nick hesitated. This was what serial killers did. They bargained. It was their last line of defense, an expression of what was at the lightless core of their compulsion: power and control. Corliss was enjoying himself. Nick had seen many faces of evil, but this was something else. In Corliss, evil seemed almost anatomical or molecular.

Serial killers had real leverage. Where police were involved, they always believed there were more victims than had been discovered. Nick knew it, and Corliss knew he knew it. That was the point. But the cops hadn't been able to connect Corliss to any other reports of missing boys in New York or surrounding states. More victims meant more tortured families wondering about the fate of their children.

Nick was decisive but not impulsive. If there were unknown victims, he was willing to stay the execution. But Corliss had to earn his stay.

Nick put the Taurus down at his thigh and said in as relaxed a voice as he could manage, "Give me the name, description, and location of one of the victims we don't know about. You make me believe it and you'll buy yourself some time."

"Robert Danziger . . . King of Prussia, Pennsylvania," Corliss answered almost as smoothly as when he was confessing his known crimes. "He was . . . redheaded with green eyes."

"What was he wearing when you took him?"

"Catholic school uniform. Maroon and gold were the colors."

It wasn't there, the joy in the reliving. His eyes didn't roll back. No physical response. He was making it up as he went. "No sale, motherfucker."

Panic set in as Corliss realized he wasn't going to talk his way out of it. He came apart at the seams, pissing himself. A sheen of pungent sweat, visible even in the dimly lit basement, covered his body. Nick had smelled fear before. It smelled like Corliss. If it were possible for Nick to make himself forget the damage this man had done, he would have found Corliss a pitiable creature. Corliss seemed to read Nick's mind and transformed himself before Nick's eyes. The smug grin returned.

"Go ahead and kill me. It won't make a difference. I've made my mark. I've done everything I wanted to do. You will be forgotten. The boys' names—people have already started forgetting them. What were any of them to other people? Nothing. Oh, and their poor families. Boo-hoo." He shrugged and made a sad face. "Kill one and they remember the victim. Kill three or four or five and they remember *you*. My name will live on." He snickered. "So go ahead, make me immortal."

Nick was disgusted, imagining how that voice, so cold and devoid of humanity, must have terrified those poor little boys. But he knew Corliss's game. Even here, even now, it was about holding on to any vestige of power and control he could salvage.

"That's not how this works," Nick said, walking past him. "I'll decide when."

Just as he drew abreast of Corliss, the fat man sprang up from his knees in a laughable attempt at knocking Nick off his feet. Nick easily sidestepped him. The preliminaries were over. The time had come. He had the confession. All the proof of evil anyone could ever want. He yanked Corliss back onto his knees and raised the Taurus from his side. He took his finger from the trigger guard. Then, everything changed.

"Drop the weapon. Now!" The voice came out of the darkness at the foot of the basement stairs. "Now!"

Nick held on to the Taurus, keeping it aimed at Corliss. "Who the fuck are you?"

Corliss said, "Thank God, you're here. This guy's trying to kill me."

A man stepped out of the shadows, pointing a black semiautomatic pistol straight at Nick's chest. He ignored Corliss, keeping his full focus on Nick. "Drop it now. I won't ask again."

Nick had a decision to make. The gunman hadn't identified himself as law enforcement. He wasn't displaying a badge and that foreign-made pistol in his hand was anything but standard NYPD issue. As he emerged into the light, Nick looked closer at what little of the gun was not covered by a thick white fist. Something about the inwardly tapered slide, the small iron sights, and the stepped profile from trigger guard to muzzle. Nick knew the gun, a 9x18 mm Makarov. As common as cheap vodka in Eastern Europe.

"And if I don't drop it?" Nick didn't move.

"I was told not to do this in front of you, but what the hell . . ."

The man shrugged, swung the Makarov away from Nick, and fired three shots into Ricky Corliss, one blowing off a sizable chunk of his head.

The noise in the basement was deafening. Nick didn't have to hear to understand what would come next. He dropped the Taurus and waited to be cuffed, but the shooter motioned for him to leave.

Ricky Corliss was dead. Still, the ground had shifted under Nick's feet. Where there had been answers, there were now only questions. Nick would concern himself with that later. Even in a neighborhood where gunfire was not uncommon and cops were often seen as enemies, someone would call it in.

FIVE

The acrid smell of gun smoke was still in Nick's nostrils when he got outside. The van was gone, in its place an unmarked Ford Fusion. Running wasn't an option. He hadn't run from the Taliban, and he wasn't going to run now. And where would he run to, exactly? He wouldn't have made it down the block of condemned row houses.

The ringing in his ears had quieted to a low hum. Walking to the Ford, he heard the subtle whine of the electric motor sucking the passenger side window down into the door. A Black man with a shaved head and a boxer's nose turned and fixed Nick with a cold, unblinking stare.

The back door swung open. "Get in."

"Who are—"

"Get in."

Nick stood his ground. "No frisk? No cuffs?"

"Get in."

Nick shook his head very slowly from side to side.

The Black man aimed a Colt Python at Nick. "Get in and shut up . . . pretty please."

Nick found the Colt much more persuasive than the good manners.

He had barely sat down when the driver put the gas pedal to the floor, momentum slamming the door shut and pushing Nick back in his seat. The driver, much like the man who had killed Corliss, was a white man with no neck and powerlifter's shoulders. He was taller in the seat than the Black man beside him—younger too. Neither turned to look behind them.

Nick tapped the Black man's left shoulder. "Makarovs and Colt Pythons—what's the deal? The car's NYPD; what about you and your friend here?"

No response.

The driver shifted his eyes to the rearview mirror so that Ryan could see their reflection. "What part of 'shut up' didn't you understand?"

"The 'go fuck yourself' part."

The Black man's laugh was as cold as fish on ice. "We're just deliverymen. We don't know shit about shit. So sit there and shut up."

Nick sat back. He didn't start paying attention to where they were going until they exited from the Jackie Robinson Parkway onto the Grand Central and were heading over the RFK Triborough Bridge, into the Bronx. They got off the Major Deegan by Yankee Stadium, the lights of northern Manhattan at their back. The neighborhood was quiet but for the rumble of the elevated subway. The Ford zipped past the darkened ballpark, under the el, and made a series of tire-squealing turns. The last took them onto a lifeless street, lined on both sides by squat beige-brick industrial buildings with shuttered delivery bays and soot-dulled glass-block windows. Nick peered out the rear window at the stadium behind him, looming over the South Bronx. The Ford crawled along as the driver strained to see the addresses.

"This is it," the Black man said.

The Ford pulled over in front of a ragged storefront shouldered between a shuttered warehouse and an auto body shop. The storefront's bricks were painted over in faded lime green. The hand-painted sign read, Used Tires—Flats Fixed. Below that was something written in Spanish, which, Nick surmised, meant Used Tires—Flats Fixed. Two full sheets of plywood covered the spaces once occupied by plate glass.

The plywood on the left was painted with a Dominican flag. On the right, the US flag. The corrugated-steel gate protecting the tire store's entrance was pulled halfway down.

"Out," the driver said, gesturing with his thumb.

Nick didn't bother asking questions that would receive no answers. He did as he was told and watched the Ford's taillights recede into red pinpricks before vanishing in the night. Although the body shop was closed for the night, the sharp chemical tang of urethane and Bondo seeped out into the crisp early-autumn air. Nick was unsure what would come next. He understood that the future held no promises, but none of the scenarios he had imagined unfolding this evening involved a ride to a used-tire shop in the Bronx.

The shop door creaked open and a disembodied voice came out of the night. "In here, Ryan."

SIX

Nick ducked under the half-closed gate. The front door was open. Standing behind a grimy counter was a big man cut from the same stock as the men who had driven him here: muscular, well-groomed, and expressionless. Like his escorts, this guy was no one Nick had seen before. With thirty-five thousand cops on the job in New York City, it didn't surprise him.

His new minder gestured for him to turn around. "You know the drill."

Nick leaned forward, palms flat against the wall, legs spread. The big man unburdened Nick of the off-duty Glock 26 strapped to his ankle. He took Nick's phone and voice recorder too, but left his wallet and shield.

The guy pointed behind Nick. "Through that door, Ryan."

"What'll I find in there?"

"Used tires?" The big man shrugged. "Your future? Who can say?"

It was more of an answer than he'd gotten during the car ride with Ebony and Ivory. Nick stepped through the door. The place smelled of rubber, glue, and grime. Ill-matching tires and rims were stacked all around the shop. Shelves were piled high with wheel covers—some matching, some not; some dented, some not. There was a beat-to-shit tire mounting machine and a galvanized half-moon tub of water off to the side. Scattered around the shop were all manner of car jacks: scissor jacks, pneumatic bottle jacks, even old-style stick jacks that used to come beneath the full-size spare in your grandpa's Oldsmobile 98. But what caught Nick's eye were the two wide corrugated-steel doors built into the walls of the grubby tire shop. They didn't make any sense. Nothing about the past hour made much sense.

Seated at the center of the room on a green plastic chair was a tanned white man in his late fifties with wisps of white hair pinned to the sides and back of his balding head. He was well-fed but not fat and definitely not NYPD. His blue pinstriped suit was tailor-made. The French cuffs of his white shirt were held closed with diamond, gold, and black onyx studs, and the clear lacquer of his manicured fingernails shone under the softly thrumming fluorescent light. His left wrist was adorned with a rectangular Piaget watch that cost more than the car that had gotten Nick to the Bronx. *Definitely a lawyer.* Nick hadn't survived this long without being able to read people.

When Nick opened his mouth to speak, the lawyer shook his head, gave a windchill smile, and placed a manicured index finger across his lips.

"Shh, Detective Ryan," he said, patting the seat of another plastic chair to his right. "Please sit."

Nick sat. He pointed at the steel doors. "Where do those lead?"

"You may someday find out. For now, enjoy the quiet."

The lawyer's cologne, like his attire, was something expensive and subtle. They sat silently for a long few minutes. The fluorescent light overhead had a nervous tic, flickering every fifteen seconds. The lawyer crossed his legs and closed his eyes. The man from the outer office came in carrying two plastic evidence bags. He handed them to the lawyer.

The guy smirked at Ryan, cop to cop. *Welcome to the machine, asshole.*

"Thank you. You may go," the lawyer said, dismissing the man. When the big man left, the lawyer dangled the evidence bags at Ryan. "Recognize these?"

Nick was unfazed. He was already resigned to the possibility of doing twenty-five years in Dannemora or the Southport supermax.

"My Taurus and voice recorder."

The lawyer removed the voice recorder from its bag, slipping it into the pocket of his suit jacket. Then he removed the Taurus from its bag and ejected the cartridge from the chamber. It pinged against the shop floor. He dropped the magazine out of the handle and ran his fingertip along where the identifying numbers and marks had been filed and burned away.

"Untraceable. Very good, Detective Ryan. No doubt purchased in the parking lot at a gun show in a state with, let's say, a more relaxed view of the Second Amendment than we have here in the Empire State. No fingerprints on the ammo or magazine, if I were to venture a guess."

"No doubt."

"I would have expected nothing less given your meticulous nature. I confide that if my clients hadn't had their eye on you, you would have gotten away with killing Corliss."

"Clients?"

"We'll get to that." The lawyer had a different agenda. "Satisfy my curiosity. Why do you think the man who executed Corliss used the weapon he used?"

"The Makarov?" Nick smirked. "Easy. A Makarov points to the Russian mob. Corliss's third victim, Ari Rosen, was the grandson of a Ukrainian-Russian immigrant from Brighton Beach who came over to the States with the first wave in the seventies. A lot of those guys have ties to the Mafiya."

"Just so."

"The confession won't turn up in the *Times* or the *Post*, will it? No, it'll be in the Brooklyn edition of the *Russian Bazaar*."

The lawyer applauded. "Very good."

"Enough with *Jeopardy!* What is this?"

"May I call you Nick?"

"How about you tell me who you are and then—"

He held up his palms. "First, we're going to have to develop a degree of trust if you're going to work for us."

"Us?"

The lawyer ignored that. "A level of trust that will cut against your instincts."

Nick stood. "I'm walking out of here. I was willing to go to prison when the sun went down. You think a ride to the Bronx has changed that? Either you can talk to me or I'm leaving."

The lawyer smiled.

Nick took it as a challenge. "You think I wouldn't?"

"On the contrary. That I believe you would is one of the reasons we're here. The other reasons are more prosaic but, for our purposes, more valuable."

"Other reasons?"

"Your talents and your willingness to use them. Some important people have had their eyes on you for a while. Those people took note of how you saved D'Anton Waller from your fellow cops in spite of the personal cost to you. And this evening, you proved yourself fully worthy of their interest."

"With Waller, any good cop would've done what I did."

"I think we both know better."

"Tonight I was willing to kill a man. If I had been left to it, I would have."

"The elimination of Ricky Corliss should indicate to you that if my clients wanted killers, they would have no need of you. Violent men are never in short supply. Now, please, sit back down."

"First, give me your name."

"Pick one."

"It's like that?"

"Precisely like that."

"Satan?"

The lawyer laughed. "If you like. From your perspective, it's not entirely inappropriate."

"No," Nick said, shaking his head. "You're just somebody's flunky. 'Joe' fits better."

"'Joe' it is." He thrust out his hand. "I'm Joe, pleased to meet you."

Nick left the lawyer's hand hanging. "I'm listening."

"My clients have had their eyes on you since your return from Afghanistan. We know all about your . . . how shall I put it . . . troubles there."

Nick's expression hardened. "You're full of shit. No one's got access to that."

"On the contrary. Access is limited only by wealth, power, and leverage. My clients, your potential future employers, have huge reserves of all three. But that is beside the point for now. Suffice it to say that we know about what you did to avenge the girl's death."

"You can't—"

"But we do, Nick. We are aware that you disobeyed direct orders. That you organized a nighttime raid with volunteers from several units at your firebase. A raid involving human recon, drone surveillance, armored backup, and snipers. We know you wrangled AK-47s to make it seem as though your patrol was fired upon by enemy combatants. This to give cover to the men who volunteered. We know that when the battle began, you alone, in native dress, infiltrated a Taliban-controlled village and single-handedly killed six of Azmaray Dawi's bodyguards before killing him yourself. What was Azmaray called by his followers?"

"The Lion. *Azmaray* means *lion* in Pashto."

Joe said, "It wasn't 'the Lion' you carved into his abdomen after you slit his throat, was it? It was the girl's name. Amazing."

"Is that what you call it? Amazing?"

"Yes, Nick. Both your military and police exploits indicate that you possess a rare combination of talents that uniquely qualify you for what we are about to discuss. You are unafraid to act despite the potential personal cost to you, yet you make sure those who help you are protected from fallout. Others will follow your lead, but you are fearless when you are alone in a deadly situation. You can be invisible or a chameleon, a drug dealer or a Taliban warrior. You are a careful planner but are utterly adaptable when things go wrong. You have a powerful sense of duty and an equally powerful sense of right and wrong."

"Qualities that got me discharged from the army."

"Qualities that got you awarded a Bronze Star with Valor on the way out the door."

Nick stood. "Enough. Why exactly am I here?"

"I could be metaphorical and say something like, 'I represent your fairy godparents.'"

"I'd advise against it."

Joe smiled with seemingly genuine warmth. "I'm acting as a conduit between you and some very special people. That they accessed your military records should indicate as much. What I'm about to offer you isn't something that will come around again. So if you want your answers, please listen carefully."

"And if I don't like the answers?"

"Come on, you're far too intelligent not to understand the consequences of your own choices. Do you really want to work undercover your entire career with negligible impact? And please, Nick, don't bother arguing that all the good work you've done, all the danger you've put yourself in, has amounted to anything more than a very temporary pause in the machinery of crime in this city. You've taken how many tons of drugs off the street? Put away how many violent men? And to what end?"

D'Anton Waller's words rang in Nick's head. *What's one cop gonna do against a rigged system? One good man don't mean shit.* Nick said, "I do my job. I let other people worry about the impact."

Joe seemed to be reading Nick's mind. He leaned in close. "That incident with the other cops at the demonstration for the shooting of the Merrimack kid."

"What about it?"

"You risked your life and career for what? Yes, to save their prisoner, but Rasmussen and the others got slaps on the wrist. They lost some pay, some vacation time, and they're back on the street. Your entire career is an exercise in spinning your wheels. What if you could make a meaningful impact? What if the things you risked your life doing meant more for the people of this city?"

"You haven't answered my question. What if I say no? When do you get around to threatening me?"

"If you choose to leave, I won't stop you. No one else will stop you. The people I represent have no desire to coerce you into a job. What was it you called me before . . . a flunky? These people have all the flunkies they need. No, Nick, you have to want this because it's what's needed. They want you to accept it for the same reason you were willing to act against orders in Afghanistan and willing to execute Ricky Corliss: because it needs doing."

"I'm supposed to believe you'll just let me walk?"

Joe stood and fussed with his suit, smoothing out the front of his slacks and the sleeves of his jacket. He replaced the magazine in the Taurus and handed it back to Nick. "Take it as a gesture of good faith. You'll find your phone and off-duty piece on the counter outside when you leave."

Nick holstered the 9 mm on his hip. He headed toward the door but didn't make it five feet before Joe called after him.

"I said it was a gesture of good faith. You have my word that once I'm done explaining things, you can walk."

"What's your word worth?"

"To you, maybe everything."

Nick sat. "Okay, talk."

SEVEN

Joe handed a brown folder to Nick. "Please take a moment and look it over and tell me what you see."

Opening the folder, Nick saw a photo of Aaron Lister. His face had been all over the TV screen and the front pages for months.

"What do you see?" Joe asked.

"Trouble."

"Trouble is the point. Easy wouldn't require the services of a man like you."

"I won't bother asking what you think that phrase even means."

"Let's talk about Aaron Lister."

"What for? He's going to prison."

"Prison is inherently disappointing because it seldom leads to the intended result."

Joe was right. Cops knew better than anyone. The only goal prison was guaranteed to deliver as intended was punishment. The prison system chewed people up and spat out meaner, more resentful, more highly motivated criminals.

Nick asked, "What's this got to do with Lister?"

"Forget Lister for the moment. We have your new position to discuss."

"You talk a lot and don't say much."

"You'll get an immediate bump to detective first. You'll be reassigned to the Intelligence Bureau with a full-privileges backstage pass. When needed, you'll be able to get hold of any equipment, any intel, any CCTV camera, any database, any personnel, go anywhere you want whenever you want. There won't be a door in this city closed to you. You want to cut a Viper Room feed, no problem. You'll have whoever's phone number you require. You need to talk to the mayor at three in the morning or some guy you put in Attica, no problem. Done."

"And this largesse comes in return for what, exactly?"

"For cleaning up the messes that can't be resolved any other way."

"Messes?"

Joe looked directly into Nick's eyes. "There are things in this city that need doing that can't be done out in the open. It was true yesterday. It's true today, and it'll be true tomorrow. The messes will be ours. The solutions will be yours. You do whatever it takes to make things right. You'll be given whatever resources you require to make that happen."

"I'm not an assassin."

"Ricky Corliss would have begged to differ. Let me reiterate, killers are cheap and plentiful. Our employers don't want an assassin. While only a naive fool would say that killing never accomplishes anything, it isn't the answer to most problems. Messes come in all varieties. That's why I showed you that file on Lister. What a disaster. Killing him might give people momentary satisfaction, but it would be the worst possible thing. With him dead, none of the funds could be recouped. There's no interest in you having to bloody your hands. If it ever came to that, the decision would be yours."

"Why me? Lots of cops do good UC work."

Joe shook his head. "Weren't you listening earlier? We know all about you. If it were only your undercover work, you wouldn't be here. It's your psych degree from Brooklyn College, your military experience, and your decisiveness. You would have killed Corliss on your own initiative, but it's beneath a man of your talents. You're also quite inventive. I've heard you're as adaptable as a Swiss Army knife when you have to be. And then there's your ability to move freely in different circles. Being good on the street isn't good enough. All those years spending time with your old fiancée's family and friends makes you the proverbial rara avis, a—"

"Rare bird."

"Just so. There are apt to be occasions when you'll need to know which fork is for salad and which little plate is for the dinner roll."

Nick formed the fingers of his left hand into a *b* and the fingers of his right hand into a *d*. "Little *b* is for bread. Little *d* is for drink. The bread plate is on the left. Water glass on the right."

Joe mimicked the trick with his fingers and laughed. "Who taught you that?"

"The nuns. I can also diagram the shit out of a sentence, and I have neat handwriting."

Nick understood. The mention of his former fiancée was both a veiled threat and an indication of how deeply they had researched his life. He wondered if they knew about Becky.

"So, do we have an understanding?" Joe glanced at his Piaget. "It's getting late. I have a full schedule tomorr—later today—and you have a rather long subway ride home."

"You can get all those things? All that access? All that freedom?"

"Anything can be done, Nick. All it takes is the will and the power. If you possess the will, we possess the power. Access to any safe house, any crime scene, any witness—anything. But know this: what you do, you do for our employers. No more freelancing. No more foolish risks." Again Joe leaned in close. "Between us, I am glad there are men and women in this city like you. People who act. Whoever killed Corliss, one inarguable truth comes out of this: that cockroach will never hurt another little boy or destroy another family. The things you will have to do may not be that cut-and-dried, but they will be just as necessary and maybe more important. Do we have a deal?"

Nick stood. "No."

"Let's discuss Pete Moretti."

"What about him?"

"Pete Moretti was a sloppy, impatient drunk who acted rashly. His fate was of his own making."

"He was a good cop who taught me—"

"Please, Nick, spare me the lecture on his sainthood and good intentions."

"Why bring him up if you're just going to bad-mouth him?"

"A little patience, please."

Nick smiled in spite of himself. "I'm listening."

"What I have just said about Moretti notwithstanding, we will see to it that his families get his full pension and benefits restored."

"And you issue an apology for—"

"Stop there, Nick." Joe's expression was as stern as Nick's old parish priest's. "What there will not be is a public statement of exoneration."

"The answer's still no. I already know where I stand, whether I make a difference or not. I don't much like secrets."

"Says the best undercover cop in the city. You lie for a living."

"But those lies are mine, not someone else's."

"This is a negotiation, Nick, not a capitulation. But as another gesture of goodwill, we will restore Moretti's benefits whether you agree to do this thing or not."

"That's good for his families. The answer is no."

Joe's face was reddening in frustration. "One last thing."

Now Nick laughed. "Here's the part where you threaten me, huh? I figured you'd get around to that eventually."

"No threat, just a word of caution."

"Sounds like a threat to me."

"Perception is reality, no?"

"We'll see about those good-faith gestures you promised. I'm leaving. Thanks for the offer."

Joe shook his head. "You are an annoyingly frustrating fellow, Ryan."

"I pride myself on it."

"The door's right there." Joe nodded.

There was no further wheedling from Joe or turning back for Nick. He left, but he harbored no illusions that leaving meant this was over. He had trouble believing a lot of what Joe had promised. But the man had spoken one indisputable truth: Ricky Corliss would never hurt another child. Regardless of what might come, that was enough.

———

When Nick was gone, Joe dialed the one preset number on his burner phone. The voice on the other end of the phone spoke a single syllable.

"Well?"

"He said no. It was always a possibility."

There was silence, hostile silence.

Joe heard it. "He said no, but when it comes down to the moment, he will do it."

"How can you be sure?"

"If ever there was a man who could not turn away from the face of trouble, it is Nicholas Ryan Jr."

"That's not what I asked you."

"Nevertheless, that is the answer."

"We need him. You, on the other hand, are an easily replaceable, convenient luxury."

Joe clicked off.

EIGHT

Martellus Sharp was pacing the sidewalk in front of the Quarterdeck when Nick pulled up. The 'Deck was a losers' bar in Gerritsen Beach that stank of fish and disappointment. Cigarette smoke too. Nobody gave a shit about the law in places like the 'Deck. The fish smell was attributable to the crews from the charter boats in Sheepshead Bay. The disappointment was from the gray-stubbled old men who wore their defeat like Purple Hearts. There were also the neighborhood regulars, younger men but no less disillusioned, finished at the start. No one came to the Quarterdeck to hook up. You came for the kinship of sorrows and to nurture them with two-dollar beers and three-dollar shots.

"Thanks for the heads-up," Nick said, shaking Sharp's hand.

Gray-haired with a gaunt triangular face, Martellus Sharp was a lean African American man in his early fifties. At six two, he stood eye to eye with Nick. With thirty-plus years on the job in uniform, he had a long and unique history with the Ryan family. He had partnered with Nick Sr., served with Nick Jr. at the 111th in Bayside before Nick got the bump to detective third, and was now partnered with Sean Ryan.

"I left your little brother at a table by the jukebox."

"Sounds like a country song. 'A Table by the Jukebox.'"

Sharp shook his head. "Sean's life *is* a damned country song. He's sober—barely."

"I heard he was doing okay in AA. What the fuck happened?"

"He's your brother and you're asking me?"

"Exactly. You're his partner."

"Don't remind me."

Every good precinct had a uniform like Martellus Sharp, a cop who loved the street and wanted no part of a detective shield or brass on his epaulets. The kind of experienced cop who could be the voice of God for problem cases—knuckleheads like Sean Ryan. He could lend a sympathetic ear or dispense tough love, be a friend or a father figure. If you couldn't partner with Martellus Sharp, your next stop was a one-man Highway Patrol unit or the door. Sean was on a fast track out the door.

"He was doing good. Took him out for dinner last week to celebrate his sixty-day chip."

"What's he saying?"

"Man, I can't figure him out. Sometimes he talks to me and sometimes he don't. He's got rabbit ears. He overhears shit. Maybe somebody bad-talked you or your daddy. Who knows what sets him off? Life's a minefield for your little brother."

"Okay, Marty. Thanks."

Sharp wasn't finished. "What's goin' on with you, Nick? I haven't heard from you since that shit with Moretti went down. A shame, him eatin' his gun like that."

"Same old bullshit. Job's like swimming in mud."

"Well, something's goin' on with you. I can see it. You wanna talk, let me know." Sharp reached into the pocket of his bomber jacket. "Anyway, here's his car keys. You need me?"

"Thanks. I'll handle it."

"You better, for his sake, Nick. Nobody at the Six-O got any more patience for him. That cat in there—he's just about used up his nine blue lives."

"Understood."

———

Nobody bothered checking Nick out as he walked the length of the bar. To them, he was just another loser. One of their own. Sean was staring down a half-empty beer glass. Two empty shot glasses stood upside down on the tabletop. Nick slid onto the seat across from him.

"Talk to me, Sean."

"I'm not in the mood for a lecture."

Sean lifted his gaze. He was handsome in a different way from his brother. His face was less rough-hewn, with dark hair and hazel eyes. His looks favored their mother. He was two inches shorter, thinner, and lacked Nick's ever-present cool head. What Sean lacked in cool he compensated for with rage. Nick trod lightly.

"No lectures."

Sean raised his glass and smacked his hand down on the table. One of the empty shot glasses rolled off and disappeared in the darkness. "To small victories!" He finished his beer. "Martellus call you?"

"Who else?"

"Son of a bitch!" Sean grabbed his jacket off the seat back and rifled through his pockets.

Nick dangled Sean's keys in his fingers. "Looking for these? He was being a good partner, but that's between you two. What happened, Sean?" he asked, girding himself for his little brother's customary display of defiance. He didn't get it. Sean seemed to collapse into himself.

"Marie kicked me out."

"She catch you fucking around?"

"Nah, it's not like that. For all my baggage, that's not me. A collection service called, and then she went looking and found the late notices."

"Late notices for what?"

Sean laughed, defeated. "For everything. The cars, the mortgage, the credit cards—everything."

"How much?"

Sean was confused. "How much what?"

"How much do you need?"

That pushed the button. Sean was red-faced and angry. "I don't need you to rescue me."

"Then why am I sitting here?"

"Don't ask me; I didn't call you."

"You're right." Nick raised his palms. "Sorry. Tell me what happened."

"Aaron fucking Lister happened, that's what!" Sean flagged down the waitress. "Two Buds and two bourbons."

The waitress, a heavyset woman with bulldog jowls, looked to Nick. Nick nodded his okay. She gave him a one-shoulder shrug.

Nick waited till she was out of earshot. "What about Lister?"

"I invested all of Uncle Kenny's money that was left over from when I bought the house in Massapequa."

"That sucks, but you have lots of company. Half the guys on the job got taken in by Lister's scam. That doesn't explain—"

"Two beers, two bourbons." The waitress clanked down the glasses without an *excuse me*.

Nick reached for his billfold. "What's the damage so far?"

"Ten for the round. The Black dude paid for the others."

"Thanks." Nick put a twenty on her little tray.

Sean drank his bourbon, slammed the glass upside down on the table, and was into his beer before Nick put his billfold back in his pocket. Nick drank his shot. He grabbed Sean's wrist and forced him to put the beer back down.

"That's enough liquid courage, little brother. First, explain what's going on. You're still getting paychecks. Marie's still teaching, right?"

"I borrowed against the house and against the investment before it was exposed as bullshit."

"For what?"

"I still owed some people."

"What people?"

Sean wrenched his hand out of Nick's grasp and chugged the beer. "Who do you think? The kind of people who don't send late notices."

"Jesus Christ! You borrowed money off the street?"

"It was an old debt from when I was gambling. I had no choice."

"There's always choices."

"I knew it. You couldn't go five minutes without lecturing me. Go the fuck away. I'll figure it out."

"Yeah, sure. You'll figure it out. That's why you're sitting in this dump, drinking yourself stupid. How's that working?"

"The old debt is satisfied."

"It's going to cost you your wife and your house. And if you keep drinking like this, you won't have a job."

Sean didn't seem to hear. "If I could get the investment money back, I'd be ahead of the game even after I paid off all the bills and late fees."

"That Lister money's gone."

"How's it feel being a saint *and* a war hero? The air must be thin up there, huh?" Sean came back into his angry self. He waved for the waitress. "Just gimme my keys and leave me alone."

Nick stood and threw another twenty on the table. "That's for a cab whenever you're done feeling sorry for yourself. I'll drop your keys at the Six-O. You're welcome to crash at my place. Otherwise, I'll be in touch."

Sean flipped his brother the bird, but Nick had already turned his back.

NINE

Nick was in limbo. He didn't much like the experience. Joe had kept his word. Pete Moretti's pension and benefits had been restored. Nick had checked with both Pete's ex-wives. His first wife, Miranda, admitted as much, and then only in person. There were strings attached to the deal. Of course there were. In New York City, nothing was ever free and clear. Nothing. Ever.

"I could lose it all for telling you," she whispered to Nick at a Starbucks around the corner from her house in College Point. "They wouldn't even let me keep a copy of the NDA."

"Deniability." He stroked her graying black hair. "But don't worry about it, Miranda. They wanted you to tell me."

She clutched Nick's hand. "Did you have anything to do with this? This feels like you—I mean, something you would do. What did you have to give the bastards? How big a piece of yourself? Pete gave them everything. Everything. And what did he get in return? They couldn't even let him be buried with a little dignity." Then she noticed people were staring and that she had raised her voice well above a whisper. "Don't do it, Nick. Don't. I know you think you owe Pete because he was your friend and he taught you how to be a good detective, but you paid that debt a hundred times over with your love and loyalty."

"I could never repay what Pete gave me."

She laughed. "Do you think I don't know you paid for the funeral?"

"He deserved better from the job, from his old friends, from everyone."

"We were divorced for a long time, but I could never get past him."

"I don't think I ever will either. He was the best friend I ever had."

"I think of him dying alone like that in a shitty motel room and—"

"I know, Miranda. I know."

Nick stood up from the table, squeezed her hand, and let it go. "Enjoy your latte, and make sure those boys stay in school or Uncle Nick's gonna come by and kick both their asses. You need anything, you call me."

Hushed tears flowed out from the corners of her eyes.

"What is it?"

"I could never make Pete love us enough. The job was always more important to him."

"It's hard to explain, but Pete . . . he saw the kind of evil in the world from men like Ricky Corliss, and it ate at him. It was because he loved you and the kids so much that he got obsessed with protecting you from that kind of evil. It happens. Sometimes it hollows a man out, or, like with Pete, it focuses him. He was willing to sacrifice everything, including his own happiness, to make sure evil never touched you."

"But he sacrificed our happiness too."

"I guess he did. He had a choice to make. Maybe he made the wrong one."

"You're not like that, Nick. You wouldn't throw away the people you loved."

She was wrong. That was exactly what he'd done. Having seen Becky, he knew he had thrown away more than he ever could have imagined. Nick kissed Miranda's forehead. He left without looking back.

After meeting Miranda, he had intended to visit his dad. Nick hadn't seen him in months and this time in limbo seemed as good an opportunity as any. Miranda's words about throwing people away rang loud in his head. He decided to head back home. Seeing his dad would change nothing. His dad was committing slow-motion suicide, drinking himself into oblivion in a dumpy Bayside apartment. Nothing had been right between them since his dad appeared before the Argent Commission, testifying against cops and superiors in his own precinct for protecting drug gangs. On the job, regardless of how pure one's motives, a rat was a rat was a rat. The son of a rat wears the rat's shame as his own. It was a cross he and Sean would have to bear their whole careers. There was only one place for him to go.

TEN

Two weeks had passed since his long, strange trip to the Bronx. Without explanation, his CO had taken him off the street, handing his cases off to other detectives. He hadn't been reassigned. *Joe giveth and Joe taketh away.* The carrot-and-stick routine. The carrot: Moretti's benefits were restored. The stick: Joe was letting Nick know there was a price to be paid for his refusal to take the job. So he had sat around the precinct house, shooting paper clips at Styrofoam cups. It only served to emphasize what both Joe and Waller had said about Nick's relative insignificance in the grand scheme of things. During his absence from undercover work, crime in New York City had neither skyrocketed nor plummeted. The world still spun on its axis, and God was in His heaven. *What did one cop matter?* According to Joe, the right cop in the right job might matter a lot.

Even if he changed his mind, Nick had no way of contacting Joe. It was a test of wills. Everything in life was a test. He had been tested by his fellow cops, drug cartels, street gangs, the Taliban, and the ego-crushing penthouse snobs on Park Avenue. Nick had the least patience for the snobs. Poverty, violence, and ignorance helped explain criminality. It was much easier to comprehend the cruelty of people who came from a world of privation and abuse than those who wanted for nothing. For the rich, cruelty was a sport. Once he had come to know the moneyed class, Nick got what foxhunting was all about. In Shana's world, he had been the fox.

The key to passing any test lay in defining the parameters and requirements. And the answers to this one were manifest: patience and resolve. Eventually, Joe would get the message that Nick didn't want the job and he would move on to the next candidate. Then, Nick could move on with his life. If not, that was Joe's loss. Nick possessed enough patience and resolve to wait out Rip Van Winkle if need be. There were plenty of paper clips and foam cups in New York City.

He walked into McCann's, hoping to see Angeline. The place was already crowded and noisy. That suited Nick just fine. He was ready to leave Joe's head games behind for the weekend.

———

As the sweat glued his T-shirt to his skin and his vest to his T-shirt, Patrol Officer Joon Jae-In regretted having had a full traditional Korean meal with his family before his shift. The scent of garlic and chilies was strong on his breath and in his perspiration. But his father had insisted on the meal, and a loyal son did not disobey his father, especially when his father was the first Korean American NYPD Chief of Detectives. No, especially not then. Nor did he disobey his father when the chief demanded his son abandon any notion of attending the Fashion Institute of Technology.

Even now, as he unholstered his weapon, JJ—that was what everyone on the job called him—was consumed with intensely conflicted feelings of love and hatred for his overbearing father. He tried unsuccessfully to clear his head as he shouldered open the heavy metal stairwell door. The dented door was layered with spray-painted gang tags, each obscuring the last. Some of the paint was so fresh, JJ worried that he might roll his ankle on a rattle can as he moved forward. The battered door moaned and screeched, its corner dragging against the concrete floor. The noises echoed down the now eerily silent hallway.

Stepping onto the stairwell landing, he caught the whiff of stale urine and marijuana smoke. His heart thumped hard in his chest as he eased the door shut behind him.

———

Mack spotted Nick at the end of the bar and came over to greet him, right hand extended. "How's the boy?"

"Thirsty," Nick said, shaking the barman's hand.

Before Nick could say another word, Mack turned on his heel. He came back holding an unopened bottle of Pappy Van Winkle.

"Got your new bottle right here." Mack patted the bottle, broke the seal, and poured. "Jesus wept! Coppers' wages must have taken quite a fookin' leap in recent years."

Joe. Another carrot. "It's a gift."

"Introduce me to your mate, will ya? I'm in dire need of friends like that."

"I said it was a gift. I didn't say it was from a friend. Pour yourself a glass."

Mack obliged. Before he could ask Nick to explain who, other than a friend, might gift a man a thousand-dollar-plus bottle of bourbon, there was a chorus of calls for the barman.

"Hold on to your skirts, boyos," Mack said. "I'm coming." He lifted his glass to Nick. "*Sláinte mhaith.*" Mack drank the bourbon and sighed. "Lovely. Lovely. Okay, you lot, what'll ya have?"

Nick sipped his Pappy's, focusing on the large flat-screen hanging over the opposite end of the bar. Archival footage of Ricky Corliss surrounded by his legal team flashed across the screen. Corliss's fleshy face displaying that familiar condescending smile. Nick recognized the footage from the press conference held outside the Bronx courthouse after Pete Moretti's evidence planting was exposed and a mistrial declared. Since the night of Corliss's disappearance, speculation about his fate had been a hot topic in the media.

In the past several days, the ground had shifted. As Nick predicted, the transcript of Corliss's recorded confession had appeared in a local Russian-language newspaper. The story could not be contained. Once the voice on the recording was confirmed as Corliss's, redacted excerpts appeared everywhere. It wasn't long before the complete recording, minus Nick's voice, went viral. The prevailing view held that Corliss was such a narcissist, he simply could not bear the thought of being unable to take credit for his deeds. People at the fringes believed his abduction was a scam, an elaborate way for him to escape to some tropical island.

Nick figured Corliss's decomposing body would eventually turn up in some dump site connected to the Russian mob. With the Makarov bullets extracted from the corpse, and the confession going to a Russian-language paper, no one was going to suspect the NYPD's involvement. The Russkaya Mafiya would wear it as a badge of honor. He turned away from the TV, knowing that somewhere in the city Joe and his employers were watching. Smiling because they were confident Nick was watching too.

———

Joon looked up at the useless stairwell light fixture, his shoes crushing frosted shards of the shattered fluorescent tube. He wished he hadn't let his partner, Dennis Byrnes, go back to the car ahead of him. But Byrnes was hungover and barely making it through their shift. As the elevator doors were closing on Byrnes, JJ laughed to himself because elevators in NYCHA buildings were renowned for their disrepair. In the last year alone, five residents had plunged to their deaths after stepping into vacant elevator shafts. JJ wasn't laughing now. The partners had responded to a report of a domestic dispute. It turned out to be a hearing-impaired woman named Sharon Karsten, playing her TV at full volume. It seemed to JJ that a lot of the job was responding to bullshit calls.

Just as the doors closed on Byrnes, he had heard something coming from the adjacent stairwell. *A woman screaming?* JJ froze, listening, sorting through the creaking elevator noises and his own rapid breaths. *There it is again, muffled screams.* Now, on the darkened landing, he refocused, pushing back against his own suffocating panic and the memories of his father's implacable disappointment. The screams were louder on the landing, but because the sound bounced off the concrete, steel, and tiles, it was difficult to discern whether the screams were coming from above or below him.

He walked up a quarter flight, his compact flashlight still attached to his belt, forgotten in the consuming effort to hold himself together. The smell of urine was stronger, but the screams and the smell of pot were less intense. He reversed course. Heading down the stairwell, he realized he should have called for backup. Too late. He couldn't risk letting his voice give away the element of surprise. Besides, he had something to prove to his father, to the other cops, to himself.

JJ took tentative steps, keeping his shoulder to the wall as he descended. With each step down, the screams grew louder. It was all he could do not to run away. Despite his efforts to ignore the panic, it was enveloping him, overpowering his training and good sense. A trickle of sweat ran out from under the band of his hat, into his eyes. He lifted his hat off with his free hand, wiping away the sweat with his sleeve. When the stinging eased, he saw he was almost at the next landing.

———

Nick came back into the moment with a tapping at his shoulder. *Angeline.* He recognized the citrus-and-crushed-herb fragrance of her perfume.

She threw her arms over his shoulders, kissed him on the cheek. "Hi, Nick.

He turned and kissed her cheek. "Hey."

She took her arms off his shoulders and stood back. Her smile belied her disappointment. She pointed across the bar at a group of two women and three men. The women were younger than she. The men were brash and chesty, the way young cops could be, their voices loud even in this din. Their gestures broad, faces falsely confident. *They'd grow out of it.* The ones who didn't were trouble. They were the ones like Robby Rasmussen, who got off on the power of the gun and the badge.

Nick read Angeline's expression but wisely didn't say any of those foolish things men always said. *I was going to call you, I swear. I've been busy. I lost your number.* He had thought about calling her, right up until the moment he saw Shana. That visit to Sutton Place had reordered the world. Until Joe took no for an answer, Nick wasn't going to risk involving himself in anyone's life, and maybe not even then.

"You haven't been around," she said. "I was hoping . . . never mind. Are you okay? There was something about that night we were together . . . about the way you were."

"I'm fine." He smiled up at her. She was right. There was something about that night, something not she nor anyone else would ever know about. He stuck his chin out at the group across the bar. "I see your Kabuki lessons are coming along."

She blushed. "I'd rather be with you," she whispered in his ear. He could feel the heat of her breath on his neck.

"Maybe next time," he said, feigning disinterest. "Your friends are waiting."

He didn't look at her expression. He didn't have to.

———

JJ wanted none of this. Not the badge. Not the uniform. Certainly not the gun. It was only the first time he'd had it out of his holster since graduation, except to qualify at the range. He kept gripping and regripping it in his sweaty palm. After the academy, he had asked his father to get him a tit job at 1PP or working community relations in an easy precinct like the 112th in Forest Hills, or in the hinterland of Staten Island. Even now, in his panic, he felt shame at the memory of his father's expression. If he lived to be a hundred, he would never get over the disgust written there. He saw it painted against the black canvas of the stairwell.

His right foot hit the landing, then his left, grit crunching beneath his shoes. The earthy, burning-rope smell of marijuana was intense. The woman's screams had become louder, urgent, insistent. He took three deep breaths but was inert, stuck. He took three more, his father's chiding voice and his own shame urging him on. He swung his SIG P226 out in front of him, around the wall, and stepped into eternity.

———

Ninety minutes and two glasses of expensive bourbon later, Nick's cell buzzed. He considered ignoring it. Instead, he looked at the screen. *Unknown Caller.* Maybe it was the bourbon or just his natural curiosity. He took the call.

"Yeah?"

"You can thank me for the Pappy's later." It was Joe.

"Thanks for keeping your word about Pete's pension and for the Pappy's. The answer is still no. Bye."

He pressed the red dot on the screen and ended the call.

Thirty seconds later Mack placed an old style landline phone on the bar in front of Nick. "For you, boyo."

Nick looked across at Angeline, drunk and laughing too loudly, one of the young cops over her like an octopus. She caught Nick's stare and looked back in defiance, but her hurt and disappointment showed. There was nothing to be done about it.

"Nick Ryan," he said, pressing the phone to his ear.

"Don't hang up, Ryan." It was Joe again. "Please."

"So you know where I am. So what? Here's where I say goodbye again."

"Don't do it, Ryan. You don't like me. You don't trust me. Fine. But don't turn your back on the city; you'll regret it for the rest of your life."

"A little heavy on the drama, Joe." Nick moved to put the phone back in its cradle, then stopped. Something in Joe's voice had gotten his attention. Nick's bullshit meter was reliable. Joe wasn't lying. Nick brought the phone back up. "I'm listening."

"You care if this city burns?"

"Don't get overdramatic with me again, Joe. It doesn't suit you."

"I'm not fucking with you, Nick. There's a situation that, I guarantee you, will tear this city apart."

"You trying to audition me?"

"If we were to do an audition, this wouldn't be it. But if you're who I believe you are, you'll do this. As a soldier, you know that people don't always get to choose."

Nick thought about Osman, the little girl in Afghanistan he had avenged. He thought about how he had stayed on the job even though his father had made him a pariah. He thought about how his blood ran blue and that he never turned his back on his duty.

"Okay, where?" Nick relented.

"Stillwell and V."

"That means one of two things: pizza at Spumoni Gardens or trouble at the Scarborough Houses."

"It's not pizza," Joe said. "You're wasting time no one can afford to waste."

"That bad?"

"Worse."

ELEVEN

Gravesend had been a predominantly Italian neighborhood wedged between Bath Beach, Coney Island, and Bensonhurst. In recent years, it had seen an influx of Asian and Russian immigrants. Despite its ominous name, Gravesend wasn't nearly the deadliest neighborhood in Brooklyn. And the Scarborough Houses were far from the most dangerous of the New York City Housing Authority's projects. As Nick downshifted, he cleared his head. Whatever the test, he would figure it out.

Above him the grinding wheels of a subway threw sparks like shooting stars into the night. The sparks paled in comparison to the dizzying array of flashing colored lights projected against the red brick of the Scarborough Houses. A hundred yards away from where he parked was a massive collection of emergency response vehicles: NYPD cruisers, a command truck, fire trucks, ambulances, and Con Edison trucks. Huddled around the vehicles and behind police barricades were people dressed in everything from pajamas and ratty bathrobes to gym shorts, nightgowns, and tuxedos. One sniff of the air explained it all—gas! The skunky rotten-egg stench filled up the night. Joe hadn't gotten him here to do plumbing. Or maybe he had.

Turning away from the light show, Nick saw the familiar though unwelcome face of a man walking his way. It was the shaven-headed African American detective who had ridden shotgun during his ride to the Bronx. Adding to Nick's confusion, the man was dressed as a firefighter—helmet, bunker coat, bunker pants. Except for one detail, he could have passed as the real deal.

"Forgot your boots," Nick said, pointing at the man's loafers.

"Fuck you, Ryan." He threw spare firefighter's gear at Nick's feet. "Put that shit on and follow me."

Nick picked up the bunker coat and pants. "So what's going on?"

"You'll see."

Nick pushed his legs into the heavy pants, slipping the suspenders over his shoulders. "Doesn't answer the question."

"They didn't get you here to fix a speeding ticket."

"Or to shut off the pilot light." Nick slipped the bunker coat over his sweater and put on the helmet. "Gas in the air. They needed an excuse to evacuate the buildings."

"Einstein got nothing on you, huh?"

"Guess not. What's the deal?"

"If Clusterfuck and Shitstorm had a baby, it would look like this."

"I get the picture."

"Believe me, you don't. Now, follow me. Anyone stops us, I talk."

"You got a name?"

"What?"

"I've got to call you something."

"Call me Ace. C'mon."

———

A cordon of uniformed cops stood in long, straight lines, boxing in the central courtyard between the eight buildings of the Scarborough Houses. Their indistinct chatter could be heard above the silence of the now-deserted buildings.

Standing next to his sergeant, one of the uniforms asked, "What are we doing here?"

"Our job."

Then the uniform spotted two firefighters walking their way. Neither was wearing boots.

"Who the fuck are those guys, Sarge?"

"I don't know, and I don't wanna know."

"But—"

"You like your job, kid?"

"Yeah."

"Then shut your mouth and turn your head when they pass. You're not gonna wanna remember much about tonight, especially about them."

———

Ace and Nick passed between two buildings. As they broke the line of uniforms, all the cops turned their heads away.

"What was that about, Ace?"

"Easier to forget what you don't know and don't see."

They stopped at a metal door below a pitted black-and-white porcelain sign—Bldg. #6 Mechanicals. Two other faux firefighters stood guard on either side of the door. Ace nodded. One of them unlocked the door; the other pulled it open.

Once inside, they shucked off their costumes. With the furnace shut down and all the tenants out of the building, the concrete-walled maintenance room felt like a tomb. While the telltale noises of Building Six were gone, the odors were not. The stale funk of apartment life lingered in the stagnant air. Nick recalled the fresh carpeting in Shana's building, the expensive sterility of the hallway.

Ace gloved up and gave Nick a pair. He handed Nick a flashlight, switched his on, and waved for Nick to follow him. They made their way up a staircase, the scraping of their footsteps echoing in the silence. As they approached the landing between the second and third floors, new smells—nothing to do with bacon fat or burnt coffee—scented the air. Marijuana. Urine. Feces. And something more subtle . . . blood. Nick Ryan was intimate with death. He didn't have to see it to know it.

Sprawled out on the third-floor landing was the body of a young Asian man in a dark-blue NYPD uniform. His head was turned to the left, eyes open, unseeing. His hat lay upside down on the step above him. Inside it were a wallet, a badge, and a college graduation ring. Nick knelt beside the body. The bullet had blown out a chunk of the young cop's skull. The black hair around the exit wound was bloody and matted. There was a nasty contact wound on the underside of the cop's chin and a 9 mm SIG Sauer on the landing near his lifeless right hand.

Nick noticed the nameplate on the dead cop's chest. He turned to Ace. "Joon as in Chief of Detectives Joon?"

"His son."

"Killed himself."

"He did. The kid is only half of it. He's Shitstorm. Clusterfuck's on the next set of stairs. Look for yourself."

Nick didn't hesitate, moving slowly up the stairs, making sure not to leave footprints in the blood spatter. He nearly stepped on a clump of material that shone under the flashlight's beam—satiny black panties. He swung the beam away from the panties, aiming it up the stairwell. There, lying awkwardly across several steps, was the body of a petite girl. Maybe seventeen, white, pretty, her long brown hair falling almost all the way to Nick's feet. She had been prettier before the small hole in her left cheek, when the right side of her neck was still intact. Her bloodied skirt was pulled up over her waist. Her right arm was thrown over her head, index finger pointing at Nick.

Three steps above her was the body of an African American teenager, pants and boxers bunched around the tops of his classic Air Jordans. He had three obvious wounds in his chest, arm, and shoulder. A cell phone beside the body buzzed and shimmied along the step. Nick looked down at Ace. Ace opened his mouth to speak, but Nick held up his palm for silence.

"Joon's in the building on a call. He smells the marijuana, hears something in the stairwell. It's the girl screaming. Stairwell's dark," Nick said, pointing his beam at the broken fluorescent lights on the landing. "By the look of him, the Joon kid's been on the job, what, a year?"

"Less."

"But the kid's trying to live up to his old man's hard-ass rep. Wants to be a hero, make Daddy proud. Weapon drawn, he turns the corner, sees the Black dude on top of the girl. She's screaming in pleasure, but Joon's scared shitless, drowning in adrenaline, and can't distinguish between pleasure and pain. He announces himself. Black kid gets pissed, either says the wrong thing or reaches for his phone. Joon panics, empties most of his magazine before he knows it. Kills them both. Sees what he's done, goes down to the landing, and pulls the plug. Better to be dead than to shame the family."

Ace nodded, impressed. "You got the easy part right. Hard part is what to do about it. This city will explode when it comes out that a cop shot another unarmed Black kid. Add in some innocent white girl, and things will get ugly. And don't even think about putting a drop piece in the Black kid's hand. No one's going to buy that shit, not after the other shootings."

A plan was already percolating in Nick's head. He never needed to think hard or dive deep. It was as if the difficulty of the situation initiated some mechanism in his mind. Before answering Ace, Nick went back down to where Joon was. He removed the dead cop's body cam and pocketed it.

"Where was his partner?"

"Apparently, Officer Byrnes was hungover. Joon sent him back to the car."

"Where is he now?"

"Stashed at the Six-One. He won't talk. He knows what he's facing if he opens his mouth."

"Promote him and give him a medal," Nick said. "The threat of punishment has its limits, especially if he starts feeling guilty over Joon. Complicity, on the other hand, makes it tougher."

"Done."

Nick moved on. "Give me your burner phone."

"What?"

"Give me your burner. I know you guys don't use your own phones."

Skeptical, Ace handed Nick his phone. "What are you doing?"

Nick smiled, "Calling the *Times*."

TWELVE

Nick scrolled through the contact list on his personal cell phone, then punched in a number on the burner. He slipped his own cell back in his pocket.

Ace didn't like it. "What are you playing at?"

"Playing? I'm not playing." Nick put his finger across his lips. "Keep quiet and listen." A few seconds later, Nick said, "This is a representative of the New Panthers Liberation Front. I'm informing you of an action taken this evening as a warning to the imperialist, corporate white power structure of this city and to any people of color who cross the lines of integrity and turn on their own. The blood spilled tonight is only a trickle compared to the blood of our own, spilled by our oppressors. We possess the dead pig's body camera. Power to the righteous peoples of color and their true defenders."

Nick clicked off, waving the phone at Ace. "Does this thing text?"

Ace grabbed Nick's sweater, twisting the green wool in his fists. "Are you crazy! You trying to start a fucking race war?"

"In a way."

"What?"

In one graceful movement, Nick moved his hand to his waist, slid the Glock out of the holster he had fashioned to keep it hidden during UC work, and pressed the muzzle to Ace's neck. "Let go of me, motherfucker. I can make killing you work for the narrative I just laid out."

Ace didn't look scared, but he didn't look pleased either. He relaxed his fists, the bunched material of Nick's sweater sliding out of his hands. "Take it easy."

Nick kept the muzzle right where it was. "I just bought us some time to fix this mess by muddying the waters."

"How's muddying the waters gonna help?"

"You let me worry about that. It's my test to fail."

"But it's the city you're gambling with. If you fuck it up, other people are gonna die."

"And what would happen if I did it the old-school way, tried to fix up the Black kid as a shooter? There'd be no holding the lid down on the city then."

Ace nodded. Nick holstered the compact Glock.

"Okay, when I'm done, wipe the phone, destroy it, but leave the pieces where they can be found. Then, make sure no one has access to footage from Joon's body cam that might've gotten uploaded."

"Where you going when you get done?"

"To undo the lies I just told."

"Hope you know what the fuck you're doing, Ryan."

"Me too, Ace. Now, give me five minutes; then clear out of here." Nick checked his watch. "Fifteen minutes after you leave, give the all clear and let the bodies be discovered as if no one had been here. One more thing."

"I can't wait to hear this."

"Dip your gloved finger in Joon's blood and write the letters *NPLF* on the wall next to his body."

"I've done some sick shit in my time, but . . ."

Ace didn't finish the sentence. What was the point? He knew he was going to do it. Nick knew it too.

———

Back in Building Six's maintenance room, Nick considered dispensing with the firefighter camouflage and getting to his car as fast as he could. He didn't have much time to make his plan work, and there was no guarantee it wouldn't go to shit anyway. All he knew was what would happen if he walked away from things now. Ace was right. The city would explode and more people would die needlessly.

Nick had taken a big risk setting things in motion the way he had, but there was no unfiring Joon's bullets. There was only moving forward. Nick slipped the bunker coat and pants back on, put on the helmet. His success on the street had been based on his ability to improvise. Now the city's fate rested on it.

Nick could feel eyes on him. He didn't need to see them to know. When he was close to his GTO, he spotted the two men in suits parked in a beat-up Mustang across Stillwell. The Mustang's dome light clicked off, but not soon enough. *Weak!* Nick didn't break his stride, didn't change his behavior in any way that would indicate he was onto them. He simply walked to the GTO, opened the trunk, and put the firefighter garb inside. So Joe and his new bosses were willing to trust him, but only to a point.

Nick pulled out of the spot directly into a U-turn, heading straight toward Coney Island. He didn't try to shake the Mustang. He needed to see how he was being followed, so he could formulate a plan. His next steps would vary if the Mustang were all he was dealing with rather than a multicar switch and pickup. Either way, there was no chance Nick would let them know where he was headed. He needed to protect the man he was going to see. Joe's promises of power and autonomy sounded great, but this wasn't an encouraging start. If Nick were to have minders, Joe could find someone else.

It was nearly impossible not to drive over the twenty-five-mile-per-hour city speed limit, but he didn't drive so fast that his tail would know he was aware of their presence. The Mustang hung two blocks back. At times, the gap grew half a block longer. When the tail car got caught by a red light at Stillwell and Avenue Z, the driver didn't blow through the light or seem in any rush to catch up. At that time of night, the streets were deserted enough that Nick could tell, no other cars were picking him up. A single-car follow with no switch-offs meant only one thing: they had planted a transponder on his GTO. It was attached to his electrical system somewhere, feeding off its juice. He didn't have time to stop and search for it.

The past few hours were about buying time for the city. Now, he needed to buy some for himself. Nick pressed the gas pedal to the floor, smoking the rear tires. Shifting through the gears, the nearly four hundred horses under the hood let out a throaty roar. He had to put distance between himself and the Mustang as fast as he could. He was doing a hundred when he hit the Stillwell Avenue Bridge over Coney Island Creek. The rim of a pothole sent the front end airborne. The car thumped down, nearly bottoming out.

Over the bridge he shot into the heart of the darkened amusement park. His screaming engine drowned out the sound of ocean breezes whistling through the ancient bones of the dormant rides. The only sign of life was the crowd gathered like moths around the red, yellow, and green neon of Nathan's Famous Hot Dogs. The Mustang's headlights were very dim in the distance. Downshifting, tires squealing, he hung a sharp left onto Surf Avenue. The Mustang was no longer in his rearview mirror. Thirty seconds was all he needed. He checked his rearview again. *No Mustang.* He shut off the GTO's headlights and turned right onto West Tenth Street, parking in the broken moon shadows of the Cyclone roller coaster. Nick turned off the ignition, locked the door, and bolted.

From the boardwalk, he could see the Mustang pass West Tenth then back up and turn. He didn't wait around. He ran along the wooden slats of the boardwalk toward Brighton Beach, climbed down by Second Street Park, and sprinted to Brighton Beach Avenue. Three minutes later a driver named Ahmed picked him up in a black Toyota Camry that smelled intensely of artificial pine.

"*As-salaam alaikom,*" Nick greeted Ahmed reflexively.

"*Wa alaikom as-salaam,*" Ahmed answered with a note of surprise in his voice. "You are going to the address on Ocean Parkway?"

"I am."

They didn't speak again until they arrived.

THIRTEEN

Calista Barrows had run the two- and four-hundred-meter races for the University of Kentucky Wildcats. As a reporter for the *Kings County Crier,* the farthest she had to run was to the corner for coffee to keep herself awake during speeches by the borough president. That man could put crystal meth to sleep. She was pounding the sidewalk at full tilt now, though. To avoid getting towed, Calista had been forced to park her beat-up Honda Civic four blocks away from the paper's storefront offices on Flatbush Avenue, near where it intersected with Nostrand. She burst through the door and sagged back against it.

"Murray . . . Murray," she said, taking in big gulps of air, "I think I've got something big."

"I hope so, kid, and it better be good. Old men don't enjoy getting dragged out of bed, because old men don't sleep. And for once, I was sleeping."

At seventy-eight years of age, Murray Kleinman saw everybody as a kid. True to his name, he was a little man, though he had once been a big deal. As a reporter for *Newsday* in the seventies, he'd won the Pulitzer Prize for a series on the human costs of the declining aerospace industry on Long Island.

Calista pulled her cell phone from her pocket, hit the photos icon, and handed the phone to her boss. "Scroll left."

Murray scrolled through about thirty shots she had taken at a distance in the dark, without using the flash. Shaking his head, he handed the phone back to her.

"For *this* you woke me up? Shitty pictures of firemen. Not for nothing, Callie, but it's not exactly a revelation to find firemen at the scene of a gas leak at a public housing project in New York City. Did you cover what I sent you to cover?"

"Murray, they're not firefighters. At least, I don't think they are."

"Really? So what are they, trick-or-treaters?"

"Look at their feet." Calista tapped one of the photos and used two fingers to enlarge it. She turned the screen to Murray. "See, they're wearing shoes. Even the guy getting out of the old car—he puts on the fire gear but doesn't wear boots."

"I should fire you for this, but then I would have to do even more work." He didn't mean a word of it. "So let me ask you again, did you even cover the story about the leak?"

"I did. I'll write it up in ten minutes, but I don't think you're understanding what's going on in the photos."

"I love you, kid. You know I do, and if I have anything to say about it, you'll catch on with one of the big media organizations. But explain what I'm not seeing because hunches don't fly. Proof. Sources. That's what you need."

"Okay, I just got done getting statements from the Con Ed rep, the NYPD Emergency Services spokeswoman, and the fire captain in charge of the scene. I'm walking back to my car and I spot this African American man in fire gear, and he's carrying another firefighter suit and helmet in his arms. The white guy who just got out of the shiny black muscle car puts on the gear and they head into the project. A half hour later, only the white guy comes out. He throws the fire gear in his trunk and splits."

"So what? Basically, this still comes down to them not wearing boots."

"I think they were cops, Murray. They carried themselves like cops.

You know the walk. I haven't been at this as long as you, but something's not right. I smell a story."

Murray laughed. "I know what that feels like. It's the thing that gives a reporter a rush like nothing else, the notion that you've found something no one else is onto. Unfortunately, most of the time when I thought I smelled a story, it turned out I'd stepped in dog shit."

"This isn't dog shit. This is the real thing."

"Write up what you have on the gas leak. I'm going home to chase sleep I won't find."

"I'm sorry, Murray."

He patted her cheek. "Don't be. I admire the burn you feel in your belly. Me, since Miriam died . . ." He shrugged. "You and this stinky little paper, you're all I got. I'll see you tomorrow. When you're done writing it up, go home."

Calista Barrows went to her computer and watched her mentor leave. She loved and admired Murray, but she knew what she knew. There was a lot more going on at the Scarborough Houses than a gas leak, and she meant to find out what. First, she went to a database she sometimes used when tracing car registrations. While she had only a partial tag number on the old black car, it was a start.

Waiting for results, she stared at the photo of the white guy's profile. *Handsome. Very handsome.* "Who are you?" she whispered aloud.

When she turned back to the computer screen, the results were disappointing.

FOURTEEN

Nick was in uniform in December 2007, before Afghanistan, before his father testified. He had been on the job a little bit longer than the Joon kid when he saw the flames lighting up the sky over Albemarle Road in Ditmas Park. His partner, Charlie Allyson, was half asleep in the passenger seat.

"Charlie, you see that?"

"Chill out, kid," his partner said between yawns. "Let New York's Bravest deal with that shit. That's what those humps get paid for."

But Nick could see that the ground floor of the three-story Victorian was fully engaged. Fire was pouring through the front windows, flames flicking the tips of their tongues at the shiplap ceiling of the wraparound porch. Then, the fire spread upward as if guided by a malign intelligence. Before he could get out of the cruiser, the second-story windows blew out, raining hot glass shards and burning splinters on the front lawn.

He screamed to Allyson, "Call it in!"

Nick took off in a full sprint. Seeing no possibility of getting in through the front, he veered around the left side of the house. Cutting through the stench of melting plastic, charred wood, and smoke was a heavy chemical odor—the unmistakable smell of nail polish remover.

Acetone! He didn't need to be Smokey Bear to know that acetone was an accelerant, an arsonist's best friend. The smell of it was so pronounced, even an amateur could recognize that this fire was no accident and that whoever started it didn't care who knew it. The arsonist wanted the fire to spread fast. The malice belonged not to the fire but to the fire starter.

The metal bulkhead doors to the basement were flung wide. They had initially acted as a feeder tube to the fire, the heat sucking in cold, oxygen-rich air from the outside to grow the flames in the house. Now, the accelerant's initial job done, flames shot out the open doors as if from a dragon's mouth. Nick swerved, but the intense heat singed his hair. Sweat soaked his uniform. His stomach reacted badly to the smell of his own burned hair. Above the roar of the flames, he heard the rear storm door slamming shut. *Someone got out.* But when he made it around to the small rear deck, no one was there. *Shit! They didn't come out. They went in!*

Nick didn't hesitate. He climbed the deck stairs, opened the storm door, and stood to one side. Using his shirt cuff to protect his hand, he turned the back doorknob. He nudged the door inward with his shoe and stood aside. When no flames greeted him, he dropped to all fours and crawled into the house. The place was shrouded in thick smoke. There was a wall of flame about twenty feet ahead of him and smaller pillars of fire to his left and right.

He shouted, "NYPD. Is anyone . . ." But hot smoke rushed into his lungs, burning his throat along the way.

He tried sealing his lips tight, to no avail. He couldn't stop coughing, his eyes tearing as he moved forward. Deeper into the house, the heat grew more intense as his path ahead narrowed. Just as he came to the point where the needle on his bravery meter was crossing over the red line into stupidity, his right hand hit flesh. He couldn't tell whether it was a man, woman, or child. Couldn't tell if he or she was even alive. It was time to get out.

Nick grabbed whatever cloth his hands could get purchase on and dragged the dead weight toward the back door. Dragging someone by their clothing was difficult enough under optimal conditions. In the midst of a raging fire, it proved impossible. Nick stood, his breathing ragged and shallow between coughs. He scooped up the limp body, hoisted it over his shoulder, and ran.

He stumbled out the back, through the storm door, onto the deck. Sirens blared at the edge of his hearing. His legs gave out as he made it off the deck, onto the dormant winter grass. Gravity and the weight of the body over his shoulder conspired to pull him to earth. He didn't remember falling, but he was looking up at a sliver of moon playing peekaboo with the clouds. His coughing was the only thing standing between him and unconsciousness. Even that couldn't last for long. He turned his head and saw that it was a man he had carried out. A living man—dead men didn't cough. As Nick's eyes fluttered shut, he caught a whiff of burnt flesh and hoped it wasn't his.

———

When Nick returned to duty, he was promoted to detective third, in part for his heroism. Lenny Feld showed up at the precinct house asking after him. Nick knew at once who he was—a man that disfigured needed no calling card. There were audible gasps from the other detectives in the squad room.

Nick shook his hand. "It's good to see you."

"I doubt that." They both laughed. "My right eye still works. I am glad to finally talk with you."

"Does it hurt?"

"My heart, always. My face, my eye . . ." He shrugged. "Not really. Severe burns can cauterize nerve endings, though I wouldn't suggest it as a cure for pain."

Nick changed subjects. "Are you back to work at the magazine?"

Feld was surprised. "You know about me?"

"You save a man's life, you want to know who that man is."

"Just as I was curious about the man who saved me. I suppose we're bound together, Nick, for better or worse." Feld wheezed a few short breaths. He asked if they could sit. "My lungs. The doctors tell me they're in worse shape than my face. You wouldn't think that possible."

Pete Moretti got up without being asked and gestured for Feld to take his seat. "I'm going for coffee. You guys want some?"

Nick looked at Feld, who shook his head. "None for us. Thanks, Pete."

When Moretti had gone and Lenny settled into Pete's chair, he said, "To answer your question, no, I've quit the magazine. I can't find it in me to do what amounts to intellectual exercises that only the wrong people pay attention to. I want to devote my time to something else."

"To finding who was responsible?"

"No, Nick, I already have that answer. I was responsible, or rather, my work was. I just want to ask the person who did it what sin I had committed that was so terrible it merited burning down my house with my family inside. I need to know why, and I need to see some form of justice done. On that day, I will lie down and die."

There was little to say after that. A few moments of uncomfortable silence passed between them before Feld stood. Nick walked him downstairs. In front of the precinct, Feld patted Nick's arm.

"Thank you again. If you ever need my help with anything, please don't hesitate to call on me. I owe you my life, such as it is."

Nick watched Feld walk down the street. He could see people wincing as the man passed.

"So that's the guy whose ass you pulled out of the fire?" Moretti said, coming up behind Nick. "Christ, the Phantom of the Opera got nothing on him. You didn't do him any favors."

"I don't think he agrees with you."

"You said he was loaded."

"Two MIT PhDs. Holds seven patents having to do with computer chip design and digital engineering."

"So what the fuck was he doing living in Ditmas Park?"

"Grew up there."

"It was arson, right?"

"There was enough accelerant used to fill a swimming pool."

"What he do, piss off some antitechnology wing nut like the Unabomber?"

"That's the working theory. As a hobby, Feld worked for an online magazine called *No Myths*. It's dedicated to disproving all kinds of woo-woo bullshit like conspiracy theories, miracles like people seeing the Virgin Mary in their breakfast cereal, or the Sphinx on Mars—stuff like that. He specialized in recreating 'proof' by digital manipulation. Say a guy claims to have footage of Bigfoot or UFOs. Feld would recreate the footage without ever leaving his house. Apparently, the thing that really agitated people was his debunking a lot of the conspiracy theories about 9/11."

"Who cares about that shit?"

"You'd be surprised. I checked with the homicide guys handling his case. Feld got a crazy amount of threatening emails and snail mail. Packages with fake ricin, fake anthrax, even a few fake bombs. They showed me some of the letters. Lots of death threats to him and his family. People get worked up about this stuff. Once people invest in a belief system, they fight like hell to protect it because they're really protecting themselves."

"That's nonsense."

"You think so?" Nick said. "How about if I substituted the word 'religion' for 'belief system'? What do you think the Holocaust, Rwanda, and Kosovo were about? If it's easy to see a whole group of people as worthy of slaughter, merely burning a house down with a family inside doesn't seem like a big deal."

"Homicide making any progress?"

"None. They interviewed as many of the letter writers as they could trace, but nothing solid."

"I got you a coffee anyways." Moretti handed the white-and-green cup to his partner. "Well, now you guys have talked, so that's that. I'm heading up."

Nick stood watching Feld until he turned the corner. As Feld himself had said, they were bound together, for better or worse.

FIFTEEN

Ocean Parkway was a tree-lined boulevard that cut a straight black line through the guts of the borough. Nick got out of the Camry on the service road two blocks away from his destination to make certain he wasn't being tailed. Even at that late hour, the boulevard buzzed with traffic, wailing sirens, and the loud rumblings of restless dreams. There was no quiet in Brooklyn, ever. As the Uber driver left, Nick stared across Ocean Parkway at the rusted green cemetery gates.

Poetic. He and Lenny shared a connection that only a savior and the saved could comprehend. When Nick wasn't availing himself of Lenny's insights and technical expertise, he would check in to make sure the man hadn't succumbed to the walls of his room closing in around him. This time, though, Nick hadn't come to do right by his friend. He was here to have his friend do right by him.

The synagogue was dark, its brutalist concrete facade even less welcoming than the granite-and-marble crypts and headstones across the way. Around back, in a corner of the basement, was where Lenny Feld hid himself away. Nick trotted down the steps to the basement entrance and rapped on the metal door. He studied the thin, oblong, colored-glass-and-silver box affixed at an angle on the doorjamb. *A mezuzah.* He knew from his time with Shana. It held a tiny scroll with a biblical verse—a kind of contract between Jews and God. A reminder of each one's obligations to the other.

After his first visit, Nick abandoned questions about why a man whose fate argued against the existence of God lived in the basement of a synagogue. It made even less sense given that Lenny had dedicated a good portion of his life proving humanity was a product of cruel happenstance, not the whim of an omnipotent being. To be an adult was to accept irony and contradiction as the way things were.

No one said kaddish or eulogized Lenny Feld. He wasn't yet dead, though he might just as well be. As he once confided to Nick, "The philosopher Berkeley proposed '*Esse est percipi*'—to be is to be perceived. If you don't see me, I don't exist." Lenny had spent all his time since the night of the fire vanishing himself, shrinking his footprint down so small that a mirror and survivor's guilt were the only things that proved he existed. "My life is all glass shards and burning coals. Everything cuts through me, Nick. Everything."

"Nick!" The surprise in Lenny's voice was tempered by drowsiness. "I was sleeping."

Compared to some of the horrific wounds Nick had seen in Afghanistan, Lenny's scarring seemed like a scraped knee. Fifteen years Nick's senior, he had once been a handsome, athletic man. Nick had seen photos on the net. Lenny may have been asleep when he knocked, but he was fully clothed. His pilled black sweater and rumpled jeans looked as if they had just come out of the wash with him in them.

Lenny read Nick's expression. "Something's wrong. Come." He walked down the dank, barren hallway, Nick following. Lenny said over his shoulder, "I heard chatter on the police scanner tonight about bodies at the Scarborough Houses."

"That's why I'm here."

Lenny opened the door to his room, gesturing for Nick to enter. "Quasimodo doesn't solve murders."

Nick ignored the comment. He was always amazed at the array of computers, scanners, and unnamed and unrecognizable handcrafted equipment Feld managed to cram into such a small space. Like the man himself, it was a contradiction. The room was as spare as a twelfth-century monk's hovel—unadorned walls, a cot, a metal folding chair, no window— yet, at the same time, as brutally efficient as an NSA monitoring post.

Lenny cupped his hand around the ragged stump of cartilage that was once his right ear. "I'm listening."

Rather than speak, Nick took out his phone and tapped the photo icon. "Scroll left."

"This is real?"

"Doesn't get more real." Nick explained what he assumed had happened in the stairwell.

"Why come to me?" Lenny said, handing the phone back. "I couldn't even save my own family. I may be Lazarus back from the dead, but I'm a little short on miracles."

"I don't need miracles."

Lenny was perplexed. "What, then?"

"Videos."

"Say again?"

"Complex lies, really. The kind that only a man with access to MIT's supercomputing network and unfiled patents can create."

"Is this what the world has come to?"

"It's what the world has always been. You know that better than anyone. When I was in Afghanistan, I read a lot to fill up the time— mostly noir and hard-boiled stuff."

"Fascinating."

"It is," Nick said. "Lotta great observations about the world in that stuff. You know what the darkest theme is in noir?"

"You're no doubt going to tell me."

"That the truth never makes anything better and usually makes everything worse. If the truth ever came out about what happened tonight, everything would get worse."

Lenny wagged his finger at Nick. "Telling the truth! This isn't about detective novels. This is about your father and what happened when he told the truth."

"You gonna help me or not?"

"Wait here. I'll boil some water for coffee."

After Nick explained what he needed, the abject disappointment was impossible to miss, even on Lenny Feld's wrecked and ravaged face. Nick wasn't surprised.

"Can we do what I'm asking?" Nick asked, ignoring Lenny's disappointment.

"The pinhole camera is easy. I can program it to upload anywhere you want it to go. The other things . . . They can be done, of course. *Should* it be done? That's a different question. Once something exists in a digital state, it's only a matter of manipulation—of will and skill and tools. I invented the best tools, which is why you're here. I regret the day I told you about the software I never dared patent." Lenny rested his head in his palms. "Nick, do you know why people believe in wild conspiracy theories?"

"I know, Lenny. A cat doesn't wonder why grass grows or how birds fly, but humans need to know how and why. We need narratives to explain things. If there's no obvious explanation, we create one. It's how we're wired. It's our blessing as thinking animals—and our curse."

"Precisely."

"You've given me this lecture before."

"Have I?"

"Many times. To paraphrase, when there's a big imbalance between an event and the person or thing given as the cause, we tend either to grab on to a supernatural explanation or to create a narrative based on shreds of disconnected or coincidental evidence. So when there was drought early in human history, we believed the rain gods were angry with us. When Oswald killed JFK, we couldn't accept that one single loser brought down the most powerful person in the world. When nineteen guys with box cutters destroyed the World Trade Center and nearly destroyed the Pentagon, conspiracy theories ran amok. Conspiracy theories are perversely comforting."

"You may have heard, but you didn't listen." Lenny smiled with the working half of his face. "Yet, there is another reason people cling to these crazy theories."

"And what's that?"

"Because sometimes they're true."

The words hung in the air between them like a time bomb on a parachute.

Nick broke the silence. "I know what I'm asking."

"Do you? Circumstance made us a pair. We had a deal: you help me find the person who destroyed my family, and I would help you. I've been happy to teach you how to apply bits of my software, to use some of my techniques, to assist you with some tricks meant to cause friction between rival drug dealers, and other little things. But this . . . this goes against everything I believe in. I spent years proving we *did* land on the moon, that those children in Connecticut really *were* gunned down, and that the Towers collapsed for all the reasons engineers have given. Now you want me to create lies that feed the crazy machine. You're playing with people's lives here, Nick. That is no small thing. Whole communities—the whole *city* is at risk."

"It's already at risk. That's the point. The truth will light a fuse no one can stomp out. That's on me, not you."

Lenny snorted, shaking his head. "The people who created the atom bomb didn't make the decision to drop it, but Truman couldn't have dropped what didn't exist. Whether history remembers the names Szilard, Oppenheimer, and Groves or not, they made the thing."

"I'm not asking you to destroy a city. I'm asking you to help me save one."

"If truth is the price, why save it at all?" Lenny asked.

"Because someone very special lives here—someone I need to protect."

"Shana? I thought you two were over."

"Not Shana. Someone more special. A little girl named Becky."

Lenny seemed on the verge of pushing Nick about the girl but stopped. "What of the man you want me to implicate? He will be hurt."

"Bad man."

"The difference between bad and guilty isn't a matter of degree."

"Somebody's always hurt. Three people are already dead who shouldn't be. I'm trying to stop the bleeding there."

"You've changed, Nick."

Lenny Feld was the smartest man Nick had ever known, also the most perceptive. He was right. Something *had* changed him, but Nick never talked about what happened to the girl, not with anyone—though if anyone would have understood, it was Lenny. And now, after seeing Becky . . . Nick played the one card that he knew would work.

"If we can make this work, I'll be promoted to detective first, Lenny."

"What's one thing to do with the other?"

"Nothing and everything."

"Riddles are beneath you."

"I think I knew even before the war that nothing is beneath anybody. If I told you that tomorrow I could get you the name of the man who tore your life apart, what *wouldn't* you do to get that name? So please, Lenny, let's you and me stay off the moral high ground. It's full of land mines and neither of us is armor-plated."

Lenny dropped his head. "But what does your promotion have to do with—"

"I'm being assigned to the Intelligence Bureau. I'll be able to investigate whatever unsolved crimes I want. I'll have at my disposal the full resources of the NYPD, the resources of all city agencies. The homicides of your wife and your girls will no longer be kicked around from one retiring detective's desk to the next."

Lenny opened his mouth to speak, but the words seemed to catch in his throat like a wad of cotton.

Nick understood what he was asking. He felt for Lenny, but purity couldn't survive in a world of shit. All men were compromised sooner or later. Nick had seen what happened to men who clung too tightly to their ideals.

"Get the coffee, Nick," Lenny said, dejected. "This is going to take a while."

———

When they were done—Nick having completed the purposely faulty video while Lenny perfected the other two—the sun was still barely tucked behind the frowning lip of the earth. For the first time since Nick's arrival, noises were coming from outside the basement room.

"The black coats are coming to pray." Lenny pointed at the ceiling.

Nick asked, "Did you send the video like I asked you to?"

"Not yet. Are you sure you want to do this, Nick? I dealt with this man years ago, when he was just beginning to spew his lies and appeal to people's worst impulses. He was even a suspect in the fire that killed my wife and kids, but he had an alibi. He is empty of everything except evil."

"I didn't think you believed in things like evil."

"Not in the biblical sense of evil." He pointed up toward the temple on the floor above. "If the devil made you do it, there is no responsibility. This man is fully responsible for the hate and anger he puts in the world. It's a calculation."

"I've seen evil, Lenny."

Feld smiled that haunting half smile. "Evil is like the wind. You can't see it, only its effects."

"I'm confused. A few hours ago, you were arguing against me hurting this man, even though he is evil."

"You asked for my help. I helped. The thing is done now, Nick. I'm only giving you a chance to breathe before the consequences are unleashed."

"No need."

"You know this man won't be easy to get to. I'm sure he's got plenty of security."

"Let me worry about that, Lenny. For your sake, make sure he can't trace the email back to you."

"Try to remember that you're here because I'm what people around here call a 'fucking genius.' The man won't have a clue where the email actually came from or who sent it." He patted Nick's cheek. "I understand your instinct to keep me safe, but I don't need protecting either."

"Then do it. Press send. I need him to sweat for a few hours before I contact him."

Lenny tapped the computer key. Once Nick Ryan decided on an action plan, there was no turning him back.

SIXTEEN

Nick climbed over the fence behind the synagogue, into the backyard of an adjoining house, hopped that fence, and zigzagged his way along side streets to Coney Island Avenue. Coney Island Avenue, running parallel to Ocean Parkway, was as ugly and commercial as Ocean Parkway was lovely and residential. To Nick's thinking, this was the ugliest street in Brooklyn. He flagged down a lime-green boro taxi.

His first thought was to have the driver leave him by the handball courts on Surf Avenue, and then to approach his car from the boardwalk. His NYPD parking permit ensured that the GTO would still be there. Any other vehicle would surely have been towed by now. Permit or not, Joe wouldn't have wanted the car touched. Nick had little doubt that when he finally got back to the car, someone like Ace would be waiting for him. At the moment, he was more concerned with food and sleep than anything else.

"Where to?" the cabbie asked.

"Drop me at Neptune and West Fifth."

———

The sun was low in the sky and it hurt Nick's eyes when he turned to face it. He looked away, then pushed in the deli's door. The smell of frying eggs and bacon made him glad he had decided to grab a break-fast sandwich. He needed to get something inside him before heading home for sleep. The next twenty-four hours promised to be trying ones. In line ahead of him were two hard hats and a bent old man. Waiting to order, Nick scanned the newspaper rack.

He picked up a copy of the *Times*. Local crime stories were usually reserved for the front pages of the city's two remaining tabloids and almost never for the front page of the *New York Times*. Local crime, like dirty fingernails and Bud Light, was beneath the *Times*. There were occa-sional exceptions, and Nick smiled when he saw that today was one of them. More than half the *Times'* front-page columns were dedicated to stories related to the murders in Building Six of the Scarborough Houses.

One story was straight reportage of the crime. A second piece was about Joon Jae-In and his father's rise to prominence in the NYPD. Another piece discussed the coincidence of the gas leak and how the evacuation of the Scarborough Houses delayed the discovery of the bodies. The paper refused to print the statement that had been phoned in by someone claim-ing to be a representative of a previously unknown radical group, the New Panthers Liberation Front. Instead, the journalist gave the gist of what the group's representative had claimed. And reading between the lines, there was confusion and skepticism about the NPLF's authenticity. Most impor-tantly, the incident was not being reported as another police shooting. He had bought himself and the city some time. How *much* time was unclear.

Nick didn't turn around when the string of bells attached to the deli's door handle jingled and a rush of air ruffled the newspapers. Whether it was a faint whiff of body odor, the sound of constant sniffling, or the nervous shuffling of feet, Nick couldn't say what alerted his sixth sense. Whatever the cause, he trusted it. He gave a sideways glance. The two men who had come into the deli behind him were all wrong.

Both were skeletally thin. Their hair stringy, unwashed, and plastered to the sides of their heads. Neither of them could stand still, looking every-where but straight ahead. They couldn't have called more attention to themselves if they were on fire. The one to Nick's right was madly scratching his left arm. The other guy kept rotating his skinny neck and wiggling his fingers as if playing an invisible piano. Nick smiled at them, even as he noticed the waist-high gun bulge beneath Itchy's untucked shirt.

Nick went through the scenarios of how this might play out, most of which had blood potential. He had seen enough blood for the time being, thank you very much. He had to control the situation because once Itchy went for the gun, it could turn ugly. Just standing back and letting these schmucks rob the deli wasn't an option. Once they demanded that the customers go into their pockets and Nick was forced to pull out his shield, things would deteriorate. Nick also had a flash drive in his pocket that was, at this moment, the single most valuable thing on earth to the immediate future of New York City. There was no way he would risk losing it. Even if he took down this pair of junkie clowns bloodlessly, the arrest paperwork alone would take hours he didn't have to waste.

Still smiling, the newspaper still in his hands, Nick nodded at the bulge at Itchy's side. "I'll give you forty bucks for it."

Itchy went still. Piano Man's eyes got wide. Nick's offer confused the shit out of them, each looking at the other for answers neither had.

"Okay, sixty!" Nick said.

"What the fuck are you talking about?" Piano Man said, his face reddening.

That got the other customers' attention. They about-faced away from the counter as it dawned on them what was happening.

"I'm talking about giving you sixty bucks for the piece under your partner's shirt."

Itchy moved his right arm toward his beltline. Nick dropped the *Times* to the tiled floor with a loud thud. Reflexively, Itchy and Piano Man looked down. When they looked back up, they were staring down the muzzle of Nick's Glock 26.

"You!" Nick shouted at Itchy. "Don't even think about it. Trust me when I tell you you'd both be dead before you had time to contemplate the afterlife."

"What are you, a cop?"

"What I am is doing you a favor. The offer stands. Sixty bucks." He waved the Glock at them. "Take it or leave it."

Itchy and Piano Man looked at each other again. Piano Man nodded.

"Give me three twenties out of the register," Nick said over his shoulder. "I'll reimburse you as soon as these two assholes are gone."

When a disembodied woman's voice from behind the counter protested, Nick politely but forcefully told her to shut up and to do as he said.

The cash register drawer opened. A few seconds later, Nick felt a tap on his left shoulder. He turned his head enough to see the old man waving three bills in the air. Nick held out his left hand.

"Turn around, put your hands on the wall, and spread your feet. You know the drill."

"I thought you said we had a deal." Piano Man sounded hurt.

"Just do what the fuck I told you to do."

They assumed the position. Nick reached around Itchy, yanked the short-barreled .38 from his waistband, and stuck it in his hip pocket. He patted them both down. Finding no other weapons, Nick shoved the three twenties into the front pocket of Piano Man's smelly jeans.

"We're almost done." Nick got his cell phone with his free hand. "Turn around and stand shoulder to shoulder."

They did as they were told.

"Smile," Nick said, taking their photo. He slid the phone back into his pocket. "I've got your prints on the gun, and I've got your pictures. I hear you try shit like this again, I'll hunt you down. If I have to do that, I'll make sure you won't walk away next time. Understand?"

They nodded.

"Now, get the fuck out of here."

As the door jingled shut behind them, Nick turned around. The other customers just stared at him, stunned. He holstered the Glock and took out his wallet. He put three twenties on the counter.

"You got a bag back there?"

The fleshy woman in a white apron was as stunned as the customers. She handed him a small brown paper bag. He put the .38 in the bag and put the *Times* back on the news rack. He left without getting breakfast.

SEVENTEEN

Nick broke down the revolver, dumping its component parts into various sewer grates on the way to retrieve his car. There was no need to toss the bullets, because there weren't any. *Dumbass junkies.* Drugs and alcohol—take them out of the equation and crime would be cut in half. Nick started learning that lesson his first shift on the job. You suppress impulse control and suddenly a stupid idea blossoms into genius. He had seen those genius ideas turned into bodies. Though he had given Itchy and Piano Man a reprieve, those two had a date with the coroner in the near future.

Tired, hungry, burnt, he no longer cared about who might be waiting for him at his car. All he knew was, he needed food and a few hours' sleep. Anything that stood between him, food, and his bed was bullshit. Since getting the phone call at McCann's, Nick realized there were some guarantees he needed before he took the job. He intended to share them with Joe the next chance he got. He suspected that the opportunity would come soon enough.

Turning off Surf onto West Tenth, Nick looked up at the Cyclone, a ride he had enjoyed on many a summer night. Shifting his gaze, he saw Ace's blue Ford parked beside his GTO. He ignored it, focusing instead on the GTO and the way its starlight-black paint glistened in the morning sun. God, how his uncle Kenny had loved that car, and how he had loved his uncle Kenny. The hurt of his uncle's loss had never left him.

"First real money I make, kid, I'm buying one of these," Kenny had said, showing his nephew a photo of a '69 GTO in an old *Car and Driver*.

And that was exactly what his uncle had done. Then came the old Norton Commando and the penthouse condo in Bay Ridge. Much of Nick's life had been shaped by Uncle Kenny's life and death. Although Nick physically resembled his dad, he was more like his uncle.

"When you walked into the memorial that day, it was as if you had a spotlight on you. In spite of all the grief in the chapel, all I could see was you," Shana had once confided to him. "My dad says your uncle Kenny was like that too."

At the moment, he wished the spotlight were shining somewhere else.

Ace got out of the car and opened the back door.

"Get in."

"Déjà vu all over again, huh?"

"Just get in and shut up."

He got in and shut up. The trip was a short one, less than ten city blocks.

———

The Ford stopped on an ugly stretch of Neptune Avenue, in front of Totonno's.

"Get out."

"Little early for pizza."

"Get out."

"Get in. Get out. You're good with two-word sentences."

"Fuck you."

"Exactly my point."

Nick got out and Ace drove away before he made it to the sidewalk. Totonno's coal-oven pizza was world-famous. The black-painted facade and the large plate-glass windows with their gilt lettering were very familiar to Nick. He'd been here many times, but never before seven thirty in the morning. Just as with the tire-repair shop in the Bronx, the security gate was halfway down. Nick ducked underneath.

Joe was seated at a booth, facing the front door. As in the Bronx, he was dressed in several thousand dollars' worth of tailoring and accessories. He looked annoyed. Although the lights were off, the oven was on. Mike, the pizza maker, in his white apron and squashed sailor's cap, was spinning a pie in the oven, checking for doneness. Satisfied, he shoved a peel beneath the pizza, pulled it, tossed it on a metal tray, and rolled a slicing wheel over it with the skill of a surgeon. He brought it over to the table.

"Thank you, Mike," Joe said. "Now, please leave us alone. Your tip will be on the table."

"Sure thing."

Nick slid into the booth, a bottle of Coke and a paper plate in front of him. "You really do have some pull. They don't usually turn the oven on until eleven thirty."

He took a steaming hot slice off the tray, folded it in half, and inhaled it. He demolished a second slice and moved on to a third. Joe feigned interest in the framed old newspaper articles, photos, and memorabilia on the walls. He stared up at the white-painted tin ceiling.

"Aren't you having any?" Nick asked between bites.

"I prefer Di Fara's, frankly, but this place had the advantage of proximity."

"Why am I here?"

"Why do you ask questions to which you already know the answers?"

"Look, Joe, I told you I don't want the job. I couldn't have made it any clearer. Then you put me in this shit. You had a problem you needed fixed. I'm fixing it."

"By making things worse?"

"I saw today's papers. That huge mess you had on your hands last night—it's not being reported as another police shooting of an unarmed African American kid. If it had been, a third of this city would already be burning, and justifiably so. You think I liked doing that? That poor scared Joon kid killed two innocent people, but I don't hear any sirens and I don't see any smoke."

"Your job is—"

"I did it for my own reasons. If the job is mine, it'll be for those same reasons and those are my own business."

"It's your job now, like it or not. You haven't prevented the explosion. All you've done is delay it. You've set things in motion that you might not be able to control."

"You want me for the job. You want me to do things my way." Nick leaned across the table. "So leave me the fuck alone and let me do it."

"What's your next step?"

Nick wagged his right index finger. "Uh-uh. It doesn't work that way. No buyer's remorse. Let's see what tomorrow morning brings. If there's still no smoke and sirens, it's my job and my conditions."

"Conditions?"

"More like guarantees."

"No such thing. You know that."

Nick stood.

"Sit down," Joe said. "What are these guarantees you need?"

Nick slid back into the booth. "You might want to take out a pen and pad."

"I'm blessed with a good memory. Let's test it."

"Okay, Joe. I'm nobody's dog."

"Everybody is somebody's dog."

"Even you?"

"Even me."

"Leashes chafe my neck."

"Fair enough. What else?"

"No one follows me, ever. Ever! I'll remove the transponders from my car. Don't bother trying to deny it. You don't interfere with my sources. You don't help me unless I ask for help. I'm going to buy some burner phones. One is for you. That's how we're going to stay in touch. No more surprise calls to show me how omnipotent you and your employers are. I get it."

"Anything else?"

"No more fetching me off the street. Ace shows up again and orders me into a car, we're done. You want to see me, call me. I need to be able to access every confiscated weapon in the city. If I need to act, I can't wait around for you to have someone deliver things to me or have me go pick them up. I need carte blanche to use any impounded or confiscated vehicle. My car's just a little too flashy. Remember, you promised anything I wanted, anything I needed. I want the freedom to shadow cases between assignments. Cases I want to work because they interest me. We'll start there."

Joe made an unhappy face. He looked at his watch and placed five crisp hundred-dollar bills on the table. He slid out of the booth. "Until tomorrow morning, then."

Nick finished another two slices before walking back to his car. Joe might never know that his choice of meeting places had given Nick inspiration for what was to come later that day.

EIGHTEEN

Nick checked his watch. In a very few moments, Roderick Ford would be finished recording his podcast. Roderick Ford—king of the crazies—the man who claimed on national TV that the Las Vegas shooter was a surgically altered foreign assassin, hired by the gun control lobby, who was dying of cancer.

"Don't believe it when the press tells you the police couldn't discover a motive. The motive was the fascist gun control lobby willing to murder innocent Americans to push their radical agenda. Remember, the first thing the Nazis did was take away people's guns. What do the lives of fifty-eight citizens mean when your plan is to rule us all?"

In a world without social media, Ford would have been dismissed as a self-aggrandizing charlatan. Until they banned him, he had thirteen million Twitter followers. His being banned from Twitter, Facebook, and the rest only enhanced his credibility with his legion of conspiracy lovers, fascists, and haters. It energized and grew the audience for his weekly syndicated TV broadcasts and podcasts.

"They conspire, but the truth will out!"

The truth will out! Roderick Ford's battle cry. As far as Nick could tell, Ford wouldn't know the truth if it swallowed him whole.

"The more outrageous the lie, the more convoluted and arcane, the better," Lenny Feld had said during one of his private lectures on conspiracy theories. "The more difficult for reasonable people to accept, the tighter true believers cling to the lies. It's a supremely effective, if cynical, strategy. The harder something is to prove, the harder it is to *dis*prove. And whatever you use to disprove it is false on its face because it's just another piece of the conspiracy. It's *Catch-22* in reverse."

Nick checked his watch again. No one had to prove to him that time was fluid, because the past twenty-four hours had passed as quickly as the lapse between two heartbeats and as slowly as the decades between birth and death.

On September 10, 2001, the teenage Nick Ryan could have strolled into the Abraxas Media building, or almost any other Midtown Manhattan office tower, without being questioned. But there are before and after dates. Dates like December 7, 1941; November 22, 1963; and September 11, 2001—dates on which the world went from being one thing to being another. In a post-9/11 Manhattan, Nick's task was considerably more difficult. These days, you needed either a scannable photo ID or a verifiable reason to pass through the security turnstiles and access the elevators.

Getting past building security didn't usually require Nick to do more than flash his gold-and-blue-enamel detective shield. This wasn't *usually*—not even close. Since nothing about what he was doing was official, he couldn't afford to be traceable or recognizable. The reflective aviator sunglasses, the beard and mustache, the unruly black wig hanging out the sides of his sweat-stained Mets cap—that was the easy stuff. He had long ago learned how to "decop" himself. The problem with most plainclothes officers was that their body language still screamed, "Cop!" They were still cops on the inside and carried themselves as such. Nick, on the other hand, became the role he was playing. Once the disguise went on, his posture changed. His attitude changed, and when need be, he spoke differently.

"I got pizzas here for . . . I can't never read dis shit," Nick said with a slight Nuyorican accent. He put the slip of paper on the counter in front of the security guard. "All I know is, it's on the twenty-second floor."

The guard looked over the counter at the red thermal bag hanging from the straps in Nick's right hand. Then, he looked at the slip of paper. "Pi-Gem Logistics." The guard picked up the phone. "Who you supposed to see up there?"

"How de fuck I'm supposed to know dat shit? Lady at the front desk, maybe. Don't it say on de slip?"

The guard looked at his watch. Nick had timed it near the end of the guard's shift. The square badge peered over the counter, eyeing the thermal carrier. "Open up. Let me see inside."

Nick didn't hesitate, unzipping the top. The aromas of baked tomato, oregano, melted cheese, and charred crust filled the air. Nick showed him there were at least three pizza boxes.

The guard put the phone back in its cradle. "Okay, suite twenty-two eleven. Here." He handed Nick a temporary pass. "Put that on your jacket where people can see it."

Acting annoyed and impatient, Nick zipped up the bag. He headed to the turnstiles without thanking the security guard.

Nick got off at the twenty-second floor, stopped to read the sign opposite the elevator doors, and turned left. He was on camera. New York City, especially Manhattan, had been turned into Surveillanceville. Cameras, seen and unseen, were everywhere, many running facial-recognition software. Radiation, chemical weapon, and explosive detection sensors were hidden in plain sight on corner lampposts.

The receptionist at Pi-Gem Logistics was friendly but confused. "I'm sorry, but I don't think we ordered any pizzas. Let me check."

"Don't worry. Dey already paid for, you know, and I ain't carryin' 'em back."

She pointed at a coffee table covered in magazines. "Okay, leave them there."

Nick made sure the camera in the hallway caught him stuffing his five-buck tip into his hip pocket. He got into the elevator but rode it down only three floors, to nineteen. There he got off with seven other people and fell in with four of them heading to the Abraxas Media offices and studios.

The receptionist at Abraxas was a slender young man with a model-handsome face and perfectly manicured stubble. His good looks were matched only by his impatience.

"What is it?" he barked, looking at Nick as if looking at a turd.

"Roderick Ford." Nick dropped the empty thermal delivery bag and the accent.

"What about him?"

"I have to speak with him."

The receptionist rolled his blue eyes. "You and several thousand other people. Do you have an appointment?"

"What you think, man?"

"I'll take that as a no. I suggest you leave."

Nick shook his head. "Just tell him I'm the guy who emailed him the video early this morning. He'll want to see me."

"Listen, José, take my advice and *vamoose*!"

"Call him."

The receptionist punched in a number on the console in front of him, whispering while cupping his hand over the mike on his headset. Nick knew it wasn't Ford on the other end.

A door opened on his right and two men dressed in expensive but oversized suits emerged. That meant they were carrying sidearms, maybe even MP5s. In their midthirties, they were clean-shaven white men with military brush cuts. The one in the black suit was six feet tall. The other, in a light-blue suit, stood no more than five nine. Both had square jaws and shoulders and wore dark sunglasses and Secret Service–style earpieces. Nick was familiar with these ex–Special Forces Blackwater types who honed their skills in Afghanistan—private security contractors who liked the action the military afforded them, just not the pay.

The thing was, this wasn't Afghanistan, and these two were no longer battlefield ready. They thought they were dealing with some sketchy pizza deliveryman they would shoo away like a stray puppy.

"Aw, man," Nick whined at the receptionist, "why'd you go and do me like that? I told you, Mr. Ford will want to talk to me. I'm not here to cause trouble."

Nick was still facing the receptionist when he saw the security man in the black suit coming straight at him. He waited until the man had built up some forward momentum, then side-kicked him in the right knee. Black Suit gasped and went down hard. Before Light-Blue Suit could react, Nick got on his knees behind Black Suit, squeezing his left forearm across the man's throat. Reaching under Black Suit's jacket, he pulled a .40-caliber Beretta out of his shoulder holster and pressed the muzzle under the helpless man's chin.

"Listen, I can either crush this fuckface's windpipe or put a .40-caliber round through the entire length of his skull and redecorate the ceiling with his brains. Anybody tries to zap me or be a hero, it's his life, then yours. If you haven't figured it out yet, I'm not a pizza delivery guy. Now, you, receptionist, call Ford's studio and tell him I'm the man who sent him the video this morning. Tell him I want to talk to him. Just talk."

Light-Blue Suit wasn't happy, but neither was he stupid. "Do what he says, Justin. Call Mr. Ford."

Thirty seconds later the receptionist, with a shocked expression on his handsome face, said, "Mr. Ford says to let the man wait in his office."

Nick released Black Suit from his grip. The man fell face-first to the red carpeting, gasping for air. Nick stood, released the magazine from the Beretta, and cleared the chamber before dropping it on the floor. "You'll live. The knee's only hyperextended. Get some ice on it." He patted Black Suit on the back, then turned to his partner. "You'll want to pat me down."

The frisk was less than friendly, Light-Blue Suit making sure to rough Nick up a little with a kidney punch. The guy may have been compact, but he had rock-hard hands. Few things hurt like a kidney punch, and for a brief moment, Nick saw more stars than at the Hayden Planetarium. "He's clean. I'm going to escort him to Mr. Ford's office."

The receptionist buzzed them through the door that led to the offices and studios. After a winding trip down several hallways and through two more security doors, Light-Blue Suit stood at a retinal scanner outside a large glass-walled office. The door clicked open. It was 3:50 p.m.

At 4:04, the lock clicked again.

NINETEEN

Like most evil men, Roderick Ford displayed none of the signs of the gnawing ugliness contained within his tanned flesh. Nick had seen him on TV, online, on subway and bus ads, but it was difficult to put him in proportion. Nick remembered how frightened the two-year-olds at Pete Moretti's kid's birthday party were when they caught sight of the guy dressed up in the Big Bird costume.

"On TV, he's this big," Pete said, holding his hands a foot apart. "He doesn't seem that big to them. But in real life, jeez! It's like when you see NBA players close up for the first time and you realize the guy who seemed short on TV is half a foot taller than you."

It was the inverse with Ford. In print ads and on TV, he was always made to seem as large as his bluster. In person, he was a slight, smartly dressed man in khaki pants over cordovan loafers, a pastel-blue Oxford shirt, and a navy blazer. The outfit was as much a disguise as the beard and wig Nick was wearing—all, no doubt, meant to lend him a semblance of normality while spewing hate. *See? I'm just a regular guy.* If there was one chink in his false preppy armor, it was that he wore way too much cologne. The room smelled like happy hour at the Bronx Botanical Garden. Ford came in wearing a wry smile.

The smile never reached his sparkly brown eyes. They were too busy assessing Nick.

"Great chair, isn't it? Not very comfortable, though." Of all the first words Nick imagined coming out of Roderick Ford's mouth, those hadn't been among them. "Cost me twelve thousand bucks."

"This isn't your office, not your real office. This is for show, just like your Ivy League wardrobe. Your office is back there somewhere," Nick said, gesturing with his arm. "I bet it's messy and smelly and dark and you love it."

The corners of Ford's lips turned up even higher, the smile now climbing up to his eyes. "I won't insult you by asking who you are, because you won't tell me." He sat opposite Nick in a curvy blond chair that looked like a sculpture. "Let's talk about the video."

It was Nick's turn to smile. "I figured you'd get around to that."

"It's perfect in every way. I had it checked out by my technical staff, and believe me when I tell you my people are very, very good."

"Good for them."

Ford ignored that. "The lip and tongue movements, the facial expressions, are flawless. The phrasing and vocabulary, the intonations, all perfectly matched. Looks like me. Sounds like me. You can't tell it was cobbled together out of old clips and sound recordings. I know it took supercomputing to do it. Amazing. Let's watch it together?"

"If you'd like."

Ford clapped his hands once, sharply, and said, "Theater." The three glass walls went from clear to opaque, the lights lowered, and a huge flat-screen emerged from the wall on their left. "Impressive, isn't it? This may not be my real office, but it has its uses."

"Almost like being in an episode of *The Jetsons*. The rubes must love it."

Ford's laugh was an edgy staccato bark. He was used to people who fawned over him and wilted in his presence. Nick was reminded of *The Wizard of Oz* and the weakling hiding behind the curtain.

"Ready?"

"As I'll ever be."

"Queue video one. Play."

(A waist-up shot of Roderick Ford, taken at an undetermined distance, appears on-screen. The camera is somewhat shaky and is slightly above Ford, to his right. Ford seems unaware he is on camera. Ford is dressed in a white Oxford shirt opened two buttons down from the collar. The shirt is visibly soaked through. His face is shiny with perspiration. Some of his eye makeup has run onto his cheeks. He mops the sweat and makeup off his face with a towel. The background is the set where he records his broadcasts. Heavy footsteps are heard approaching. Ford's eyes widen. He turns his head to his left.

"Is it done?" (Ford asks the unseen person who has just approached him.)

"It's been seen to. Yes, sir." (A deep male voice answers.)

(Ford smiles.) *"You have the patsy?"*

"We do, sir."

"And he's prepared to do as I say?"

"He's assured me he will, and I believe him, sir. He would punch his head through a window and eat the glass if that's what you wanted, sir."

"He's prepared to kill?"

"He's locked and loaded, sir."

(Ford winks, nods in pleasure.) *"We're going to blow this jungle of a city to pieces."*

"Yes, sir, I do believe we will."

(Ford frowns.) *"Watch it, son. Don't take the 'we' too literally. When I say 'we,' I mean me."*

"Yes, sir. Sorry, sir."

"The New Panthers Liberation Front indeed! It'll be war between the government's blue-uniformed gestapo and our African American friends." (Laughter is heard in the background.) *"All we need is one dead cop, preferably of Asian heritage. We—I can't afford to have this be just a black-white thing. It can't look like the setup it is."*

"May I make a suggestion, sir?"

"Talk."

"Jae-In Joon. He's the son of the first Korean chief of detectives."

"Excellent idea." (Ford claps.) *"This is what I want our boy to do. Get*

this cop to kill himself or stage it to look that way. Easy enough to accomplish. It is beside the point how he manages it. Then, have our patsy use Joon's weapon to kill at least one of our dark-skinned friends and a white girl. I don't care how you manage that, but make it happen. When he's done . . ." (Ford reaches behind him. A sheet of folded paper appears in his hand.) *"When he's done, have him phone that into the* Times. *The number is there at the top."*

"Yes, sir."

"This fucking shithole of a melting-pot city is going to burn. Halle-fuckin'-lujah!"

"Amen, sir."

(Camera shakes. Goes dark.)

A few seconds later, Ford clapped and said, "Office settings."

The walls turned back to glass. The lights came up. The flat-screen receded.

"Remarkable work for a pizza deliveryman. Remarkable. Like I said before, flawless." Ford vanished his smile. "You've passed your audition. Let's move on to business. How much?"

"No."

"No what?"

Nick stood up, walked out of the office, and headed toward reception.

Ford, caught by surprise, trailed behind. He shouted, "Security doors lock."

Nick stopped, turned. "We're not talking any place else you've got monitoring devices."

Ford was a lot of things. Thick wasn't one of them. "Security doors open."

Nick and Ford walked into the reception area. The two Blackwater types were waiting for them there.

"How's the knee?" Nick asked Black Suit.

"Fuck you."

"Don't follow us," Ford said without prompting.

In the hallway, about halfway to the elevator, Nick stopped at the men's room. "Please punch in the door code."

Ford stepped forward and tapped in six numbers, and the lock clicked open. They stepped in. Nick checked to make sure they were alone.

"Can we talk now?" Ford asked.

Nick nodded.

"How much?"

"How much what?"

Ford was impatient. "Money, of course. Money is the answer every time someone asks how much."

"Thanks for clearing that up. I think you misunderstood. What is it you think I'm here to sell you?"

"The software, of course, and for you to teach my people how to use it," Ford said as if it were self-evident. "Why else would you have gone through so much trouble? I have the best available digital video–sound synchronization software and the most skilled people at my disposal. I have enough influence to get supercomputing access. I'm sure you've seen the results on my broadcasts. They produce good work, but this . . . this is five generations ahead of where I'm at. Do you have any idea how valuable this process is?" He laughed that barking staccato laugh again. "Sure, you do. That's why you're here. My faithful listeners would make a formidable army if—"

"You mean the lame, thoughtless fools who take your word as gospel?"

"Your words, not mine," Ford said, sneering. "In any case, if I could supply my followers with flawless videos of my enemies conspiring against the common man by taking away his guns, turning his country into a brown-skinned menagerie, and letting women emasculate us, I could destroy my enemies as easily as snapping my fingers. I could get elected to any office I want." Ford's eyes glazed over, and he seemed lost in his megalomaniacal fantasies.

Nick let him bask in them before breaking the spell. "You've got me all wrong, Mr. Ford. I'm not here to sell you anything."

For the briefest moment, shock and disappointment flashed across Ford's face. "Then why are you here?"

"To blackmail you."

"What do you want? A job? Power? Influence? Women? Men? What? I can give you anything."

"I'm counting on that."

Ford was losing patience. "Make yourself clear or leave me the fuck alone. I can get where I need to go without your technology. It may take me longer, but—"

"Check your personal email in-box from three days ago, and"— Nick looked at his watch—"check your latest messages when you go back inside. You'll know which two I'm talking about when you see them. They will give you the blueprint for what I require you to do."

"Require me to do! No one *requires* Roderick Ford to do anything."

"Until today."

"Listen—"

"No, you listen, you walking, talking pile of shit." Nick got up in Ford's face. "If you don't do what I say, that video we watched will start appearing on the dark web. It won't take very long for it to cross over and see the light of day. Maybe twenty-four hours. Maybe less. From there, the news media will pick it up, and it will go viral. You have a lot of talents. Chief among them is making enemies. No one is going to feel sorry for you. Sure, you'll scream it's a fake and that it's a conspiracy, but no one will believe you. You said it yourself, the video is flawless. Even your followers know you're a hateful bastard who's capable of anything. How long before those outlets you still have will cut you off? Even *they* can't support a cop killer and murderer of innocent people— at least, not openly. You'll become a curiosity like Charlie Manson, but you won't be nearly as popular with your fellow inmates and you won't last nearly as long."

"Why are you doing this?"

"That's my business."

"Why me?"

"Because you're perfect. You'll understand when you read the emails. You're smart. You'll figure out what needs doing. Do that and we won't ever need to see each other again. The video will vanish into the ether, and you can go back to making a cottage industry out of hate. If not, that video will be only the beginning. And there's this: I'll owe you a favor, and I always pay my debts."

"But I don't know who you are."

"I'm Kareem Abdul-Jabbar. Great disguise, isn't it?"

"Talented and funny."

"About my identity . . ." Nick smiled. He pinched his right wrist, raising a peak of transparent latex. He let it snap back in place. "You won't have my prints. Facial recognition software won't work on me, and I'll be pretty upset if you try to have me followed. You don't want me angry with you. I know you're pissed underneath the veneer of civility, but trust me when I tell you to do as I ask. The favor alone will be worth it."

Nick was under no illusion that this warning and promise would dissuade Ford. Men like him, men who deluded themselves that they were actually kings of the universe, didn't take orders couched as advice.

Ford said, "We'll see."

Nick walked out of the men's room and through a series of maneuvers meant to scrub off anyone who might be shadowing him, gradually disappearing the pizza deliveryman. Thirty minutes later Nick Ryan, wearing a black motorcycle helmet with a darkly tinted visor, drove his Norton Commando out of the Hippodrome Parking garage and into westbound traffic.

TWENTY

Roderick Ford was beside himself. Not with phony outrage meant as meat for the masses who saw him as their messiah—a man who martyred himself weekly, not for their sins but for their anger at being abandoned and forgotten. His current fury was the real thing.

"What do you mean you lost him, Powell? How the fuck could you lose him before he even got out of the building? Remind me, what is it I pay your employer for?"

Powell, angry himself, spoke with a distinct Texas twang. "What do you want me to say, Mr. Ford? The man was wearing a disguise. And he—"

"You really are a fucking moron, aren't you? Of course he was wearing a disguise. He told me as much."

"And he is a pro. He knew exactly what to do and how to do it in order to lose anyone who might have eyes on him. See here." Powell clicked the mouse. "He's calm, doesn't run, doesn't do anything to draw any added attention. He understands he's on camera. He rides the elevator down to the third floor, exits, uses the southeast corner staircase to go to the basement. Again, there." Powell pointed at the top right corner of the monitor. "Once he gets down into the second subbasement, he just seems to vanish. Before you ask, Mr. Ford, he's no longer in the building's confines. We've done a thorough check using sound detection and thermal imaging equipment."

"You'll have to forgive me if I don't have complete confidence in your assurances."

"Understood."

"Can't we obtain CCTV footage from surrounding buildings and—"

"Some, but not all, and we have no access to the city's cameras. Let's say that the NYPD isn't very motivated to help you with anything, since you're given to calling them the 'blue gestapo.' Even if they were disposed to help, we would inevitably lose him again because of the holes in the footage we would be able to obtain."

"You said he's a pro."

"I did."

"What type of pro, a pro what?"

Powell hesitated before answering. "Someone who knows how to defeat a system is usually someone who understands how to use the system, someone who himself has employed the system."

"Goddamn it! Did you assholes assassinate Afghanis and Iraqis by speaking gibberish until they killed themselves? Speak English to me. If I have to repeat this question, I am going to fire your entire team and have a long talk with your boss. When I'm done, you won't get a job shining pointy-toed boots at DFW."

"Intelligence operatives, private security operatives such as myself, special forces military who have to operate in urban environments, private investigators, some law enforcement types with specialty training . . . He could have been any of those, or more than one."

"Specialty training?"

"For undercover work. He didn't get excited at all. I bet his pulse was under sixty from the minute he stepped into the offices until we lost him."

"You sound like you admire him."

"I do."

Ford moved on to keep from completely losing his mind. "He was good with voices, our friend with the fake beard. Brits are great at American accents. Was he American or was he just putting on an American accent?"

Powell smiled for the first time since Ford began his tirade. "We ran his voice. Definitely a native speaker; eighty-nine percent likelihood he was a New Yorker."

"That leaves us only eight million current residents to sort through." The sarcasm in Ford's voice cut like a serrated knife. "Now, let's consider how many former New Yorkers there are roaming about and how many of them might have special training and . . . I don't know, a quantum supercomputer might take only a thousand years or so to find our guy."

"Probably not more than a hundred years."

"Was that meant to be funny, Powell? Is that some form of shit-kicking cowboy humor that's lost on me?"

"Sorry, Mr. Ford. Forgive me, but I don't understand the urgency in finding this man. You agree that by doing what he said to do, you'll actually come off enhancing your reputation and credibility. Isn't that what you want to help broaden your audience?"

Ford stood up, his face red with fury. He put his nose close to Powell's "Don't you ever tell me what I want. It's bad enough you let some man stroll in here off the street and dictate to me . . ." Ford slammed his fist onto the desk. "I'm Roderick fucking Ford. No one dictates an agenda to me. No one, whether it's to my benefit or not. Now, get out of here."

Powell left as quickly as he could without running.

After the office door clicked shut, Ford pressed the intercom for his personal secretary.

"Yes, Mr. Ford."

"Call Ms. Bayles at Proctor and Stanhope and have her call me back. We need to set up a press conference for tomorrow morning."

"It's after seven, sir. She's probably—"

"I don't give a shit if she's on her way to Mars. Get her ass on the phone and hold the call until I tell you."

"Yes, sir."

Ford punched in a security code on the lock attached to the bottom right-hand drawer of his desk. When the light at the top of the lock turned from red to green, he fished out a cell phone hidden under a false bottom, beneath a pile of meaningless papers. He hit the one preset number and waited.

"Speak," said the electronically distorted voice at the other end of the phone.

"I have need of your services."

"At the agreed-upon price."

"Of course."

"You'll receive an email within the next thirty seconds detailing how and where to deliver all pertinent information to help successfully complete the mission. Be prepared to write it down."

"Why?"

"Look at your in-box now."

Ford looked up at his monitor and saw a new email appear. He opened it. All it contained was one sentence: Count to fifteen. He did so. At fifteen, the sentence vanished as he watched. When he rechecked his in-box, there was no record of the email ever being there. He checked his "deleted" box. Same thing.

"Now do you understand?"

"I do."

The voice disappeared. As it did, Ford picked up a pen and readied himself to write.

TWENTY-ONE

Nick was spent, exhausted in a way he hadn't been since Afghanistan. If he had been asked to recount his movements from the time he parked the Norton Commando behind the GTO in the basement garage of his building, he wasn't sure he could have explained how he made his way upstairs and into bed.

Now there was buzzing. Was he dreaming of bees? No. He wasn't dreaming. The buzzing wasn't in his head at all. Seconds before, he had been in a dreamless black well, a pit so deep he hoped it was what death held in store. He knew better. He had seen the worst forms of death—bodies blown apart so that their constituent pieces were scattered about the battlefield like fleshy red confetti, men and women torn apart, in excruciating pain, and knowing that death would be their only reward. The best he could hope for in death was nothingness. He had never yearned for death, though he understood the men he served with who did.

Still in that netherworld between sleep and waking, Nick swung his feet off the bed. With the shades drawn and the room dark, he had no idea of the time. Regardless, he had to stop the buzzing. He dragged himself to the intercom panel and saw his brother's face on the screen. He pressed the entry button, holding it down until he was sure Sean was inside the lobby. He wasn't up to speaking. Turning to his right, he saw through the rain-beaded living room windows that it was night. The tower tops of the Verrazzano Bridge were smothered in a thick layer of low clouds.

The pounding at his door was insistent.

"Christ, Sean, what the fuck?"

Sean smelled of beer and was as angry as he had been at the Quarter-deck. Anger was the prism through which he filtered his other feelings. That was why he expressed everything from love to grief in shades of rage. Anger was easy, but it took a toll on Sean and everyone close to him.

"What do you mean, *what the fuck*? I was pressing your apartment buzzer on and off for five minutes."

"You ever think maybe I was out or sleeping?"

"I checked your spot in the garage. Saw the Goat and the bike were there."

"Or that I walked over to McCann's?"

"First place I checked."

"From the smell of you, you stuck around to have a few. How about if I was entertaining?"

"If you were, you woulda got outta bed and told me to get lost."

"You got all the answers, huh, little brother?"

"No, Nick, you're the man with all the answers."

"Okay, now that we got that out of the way, what's up?"

"You look like shit, by the way."

"Thanks. Come in. You want water or something?" Nick asked, walking into his kitchen.

"How about something stronger?"

Nick shook his head. "You want to drink, go back to McCann's."

"Fuck you!"

Nick poured two glasses of seltzer and lime. He brought the glasses into the living room. Sean was seated on the distressed brown leather couch, looking out at the rain and the cloud-covered bridge. Nick put the glasses down on the kidney-shaped glass-and-brushed-steel coffee table. Sean ignored his and kept his eyes fixed on the world outside.

Nick said, "Cheers."

"What's to be cheery about?" Sean pushed the glass away. "Yeah, Uncle Kenny did pretty good by you. This condo, the Goat, the Norton, the money . . ."

Not that Nick's brother needed help finding things to be pissed about, but their individual inheritances from their uncle Kenny were one of Sean's top ten hits. Resentment fed his anger.

Nick wasn't in the mood. "This shit again? You were ten years old when Uncle Kenny died. He wasn't going to leave you a condo, a car, and a motorcycle. I mean, come on, Sean, you got three-hundred-and-fifty grand. I can't help it if you blew it."

"If I could only get that Lister money back . . . I'm out of the house. Marie doesn't want to hear from me."

"My offer to front you the money still stands."

"Shove your money. I'm not here about that."

"Then why *are* you here?"

"This morning—yesterday morning—what was that stunt you pulled in Trump Village Deli on Neptune Avenue? Did you think I wouldn't hear about it? About how Nick Ryan did his magic with two junkies. It's my fucking precinct, for chrissakes!"

Nick had already forgotten about Piano Man and Itchy. All that seemed very long ago. "It wasn't a stunt. I stopped a robbery before those two assholes could pull a gun and get themselves dead."

Sean shouted, "Don't ever do that to me again!"

"I didn't do anything to you."

"No more stunts in my precinct. It's hard enough fighting off Dad's rep." Sean's face turned deep red with rage. "The truth is, even though you're stuck as a detective third, everyone knows about your UC work and about you being a fucking war hero. I'm tired of carrying your shit and Dad's shit on my back."

Nick didn't think this was the time to tell Sean about the potential bump to detective first and his transfer to Intelligence. "All right, I consider myself warned. Any other shit you want to get off your chest?"

"Fuck you, big brother," he said and stormed out, slamming the door behind him.

This was how it always went between them. Nick figured either Sean would someday wake up and snap out of it or not. He dead-bolted the door behind Sean and stripped down. He needed a shower and a shave, but first he swallowed a mouthful of Scope to wash away his sleep breath and the bad taste of his brother's resentment.

He was just done washing his hair when he thought he heard knocking at his door.

"Oh, fuck this!" Nick said aloud. "Round two."

It seemed his brother had a never-ending litany of gripes that had only gotten worse since he was drinking again. He thought about ignoring him, but ignoring Sean only made things worse. Nick got out of the shower, mopped himself off, and tied the towel around his waist. He barefooted it to the bathroom door.

"I'm coming. I'm coming! Jesus Christ, Sean," he screamed, padding across the apartment. "Couldn't you do your whining all at once?"

But by the time he got to the door, it was already open and the person standing at his threshold wasn't Sean at all.

TWENTY-TWO

Shana Carlyle's unmistakable silhouette filled the space. She wore a long black trench coat cinched tight at the waist. Her rain-darkened hair glistening in the hall light seemed nearly as black as her coat.

"I thought it was Sean. He was here a little while ago. I thought he was back to bitch at me some more."

Shana jangled keys in her fingers. "You never asked for them back."

"Then why knock if you were just going to let yourself in?"

"Why?" she asked, stepping into the condo and placing the keys in her coat pocket.

"Why what?"

"That day you came to my apartment—I need to know why."

"I told you. I thought seeing you again would—"

"Don't lie to me." Her voice was raw and brittle. "You never lied to me before, though I used to wish you sometimes would."

"What are you talking about?"

"God, Nick, just shut up."

She uncinched the belt, dropped her wet coat to the floor, and closed the door behind her. She stepped close to Nick, threading herself into his arms. Neither of them seemed to notice or care about the water puddling around their feet. He pressed his lips to hers. There was nothing tentative or gentle about it. She pressed herself into him, arching her back to trace the curve of his body. Although it had been years since they were together, the taste of their mouths, the feel of their tongues sliding against each other, was as familiar as if it were yesterday. Years of mutual yearning made it something it had never been before.

Her breaths were rapid and urgent. She sighed but pushed herself away from him. He let her go. Shana knew her own mind. She was not a woman to be forced or cajoled into anything she didn't have the will to do. Her self-possession was one of the things he had loved about her.

"I need a drink, Nick, please." She sat where Sean had been sitting, the leather cushion still warm. She stared out the window as Sean had. "Do you think it means anything that we both live with views of a bridge?"

Nick handed her a glass of Laphroaig. "I think it means you and Brad and my uncle could afford places with expensive views. But you didn't come here to discuss bridges."

Shana turned away from the window and took her drink in a swallow. Nick refilled her glass. He knew she had something to say. He was sure he knew what it was, and since his visit to Sutton Place, he had hoped she would come to him and tell him the truth. He would make it easy for her, but he would not say it for her. She looked back at the bridge through the raindrop-streaked windowpane.

"She's yours, Nick."

"I know."

"Is that why you came that day? To claim her?"

"No," he said, standing close behind Shana. "I didn't even know you—we—had a little girl. I knew the moment I saw her. The eyes and hair . . ."

Shana smiled, relieved to have the burden of the secret lifted from her shoulders. "Her name is Carlyle, but she's a Ryan. She can be so stubborn, but she always knows her mind."

"Sounds more like you."

"She has a penchant for the lost. She wants to rescue every cat on the street, birds fallen out of their nests in the park."

"Does Brad know?"

"No." She took a drink. "Maybe . . . Well, he's never said anything."

"You didn't tell him I was there that day, at your place."

Shana swiveled around to look up and face him. "You know me so well, don't you?"

"Nobody knows anybody. We tell ourselves we do to get through the day, but we don't."

"We do know things about each other."

"Give me a for instance."

"I knew you would never come back."

"You asked me not to."

"That's why I came to you. You wouldn't come back because you're so damned honorable."

He laughed. "My honor's more flexible than you think."

"You're all I've thought about since that day."

"Because of Becky?"

Shana seemed not to have heard him. "What happened to us, Nick?"

"You said it yourself. We were kind of a cliché. Two kids from opposite sides of the river who lasted longer than we had a right to expect."

"You don't believe that any more than I do." She finished her scotch. She stood, placing her empty glass down on the coffee table. She leaned against him, resting her head on his bare shoulder.

"No, I don't believe it. I'm going to get dressed and get you a towel."

She reached out and grabbed his forearm. "Don't you dare! I mean, please don't. We have to talk about Becky, but first, there's something we both need to see to." She moved her hand from his forearm into his hand and pulled him toward the bedroom.

"Your hand's shaking," he said, reaching to flick off the bedroom light.

"Leave it on, Nick. We can't hide in the dark, not tonight.

He let the towel fall away and sat at the edge of the bed. Shana came and stood between his bare legs. As she pulled her camel-colored sweater over her head, he undid her belt and unclasped her jeans. He slid them and her thong down over her hips to her ankles. She slipped out of her shoes and out of the clothes bunched at her feet. Her skin was smooth, her muscles twitching at his touch. His fingertips and palms pulsing at the feel of her skin. He rested his cheek against her hard, flat abdomen. She encircled his head in her arms, stroking his still-damp hair.

Breathing her in, feeling her touch again, he understood Shana's demand that the light stay on. They needed to be responsible for this, each in their way. This couldn't be a makeup for missed opportunities. It couldn't be something they could pretend was an itch that needed scratching and from which they could simply walk away. With the truth between them, there could be no walking away. Not really.

Nick stood slowly, unhitched her bra, and let it fall. He lifted her in his arms, spinning her around and placing her on the bed. He straddled her, kissing her softly on the mouth, moving down her body, kiss by kiss. He flitted the tip of his tongue over her hardened left nipple—the more sensitive one—and rolled the right between his fingers. She tensed, sighing. He urged her legs apart and put his mouth against her. He sighed too, at the silky wet feel of her on his lips and tongue, at the scent and taste of her. No one had ever tasted as sweet. And tasting her was like coming home—a place he could never again turn away from.

A few moments later, she clamped her legs around his head, tugged his hair, and arched her back. Once the shudders subsided, she relaxed her legs and let go of his hair. She maneuvered Nick onto his back and licked herself off his lips, sending a small series of tremors through her body. Then, she straddled him.

An hour later they lay shoulder to shoulder, staring up at the ceiling. Even knowing that their conversation was unfinished, they didn't speak for what felt like a very long time.

Noticing the time on the cable box, Shana broke the silence. "What are we going to do?"

"Is Brad a good father?"

"A wonderful father."

"Becky loves him?"

"More than she loves me, I think."

"Is she happy?"

"That day you saw her. That's her. She's very happy." Shana rolled over onto her elbow, looking Nick in the eye. "This is the part where I say I love Brad, but I'm not *in love* with him, right? Where I say he's a good man and he's loved me since we were kids. The thing is, while all that's true, I married him to punish you."

"It worked."

"It was all okay until you showed up—even hiding Becky from you. Now what am I supposed to do?"

Nick sat up. He cupped Shana's chin in his hand. "Nothing. Nothing's going to change. No one can ever know Becky's mine. No one. Ever."

"But why? Why keep up the charade? Let the truth free us."

Nick put his fingers across her lips. "It won't free us. I know about Becky. We know. That's enough. I won't risk putting her or your family in danger."

"What are you talking about?"

"You trust me, don't you?"

"From the first time we caught each other's eye, I knew I could trust you."

"Then trust me now. Leave it there, Shana. Please. Go back to your life."

"But what about me? Us?"

"Us?"

"Don't shut me out, Nick. I can't do it again. I married Brad to punish you, but you weren't the only one to suffer. Let me come back."

"I did notice you put my keys back in your trench coat pocket. Keep them, but you can't just show up here unannounced anymore. We don't have to plan it, but I need to know."

Shana's face reddened. "Is there someone else? I don't like thinking about you and—"

"Don't think about it."

"As if that ever works."

He leaned over and kissed her hard on the mouth, sliding his hand along the inside of her thigh. Fifteen minutes later, when their heart rates had settled down, he said, "Please don't spoil her. That's all I ask. Show her the real world, not just *your* world. Show her what the world looks like at ground level and not just from above. Take her to Flushing, Coney Island, Harlem, the Grand Concourse—to places where real people struggle to get by."

Shana kissed him and got out of bed. Collecting her clothes and heading for the bathroom, she turned and said, "I'll do whatever it takes. You know, Nick, I came here tonight thinking I might never go back home."

Nick ignored her. "One more thing."

"What?"

"Next time, bring pictures of her. Of the things I've missed."

He watched her think about a hundred answers before she said, "I will."

TWENTY-THREE

Life was twisted up in sad, inexplicable ways that sometimes resulted in magic. If he hadn't decided Ricky Corliss needed killing, he would never have visited Shana that day, and last night wouldn't have happened. That was what Nick thought about over his first cup of coffee, but he didn't go to the next step. He didn't beat himself up with guilt over things out of his control, didn't bend himself into a pretzel asking endless whys or what-ifs that were as incalculable as the grains of sand on Brighton Beach. One thing led to another, but you couldn't know for sure what *another* would be or where it would lead.

The bridge towers had been freed from their cloud prison. The sun rose into a sky so blue, it was painful to look at. He looked away. He sat down on the sofa, turned on the TV. If things went as planned, the fireworks would begin any moment. What he got instead of fireworks was the last fifteen seconds of a local car dealership commercial featuring Bensonhurst Bobby and his basset hound, Tommy.

"So remember what Tommy says, if you're being hounded to make a deal, fuhgeddaboudit! Come see Bensonhurst Bobby and Tommy for a"— Bobby places his hands over the dog's ears—*"hound-free car-shopping experience."* (Tommy howls as the shot fades.)

But Tommy's howl is cut short. Bobby and Tommy are replaced by a shot of Earth from space. Superimposed across it, the words *Special Report*. A man with a deep set of pipes says, "We interrupt our regularly scheduled programming for a special report." Seated behind a green glass desk, a pretty Latina anchor in her midtwenties is caught off guard by the camera. She's fumbling with her earpiece and speaking to her producer. Beneath her, where the normal news crawl would be, are the flashing words *Breaking News*.

She looks up at the camera and says, "We are following two breaking stories this morning. One that may finally bring to an end speculation about the whereabouts of alleged pedophile and murderer Richard 'Ricky' Corliss. The other is a press conference to be held by controversial media personality, conspiracy theorist, and lightning-rod provocateur Roderick Ford. The press conference is rumored to have something to do with the tragic deaths of Patrol Officer Joon Jae-In, Ka'deem Washburn, and Marissa Leone, each shot at the Scarborough Houses two nights ago. But first, to Ronnie Chow in Rahway, New Jersey."

Chow, also a twentysomething, is standing in front of a line of police crime scene tape. Behind him is a flurry of police activity—troopers and local cops.

"I'm at Sergei's Salvage here in Rahway, where early this morning, acting on an anonymous tip, the police discovered the decomposed body of a man they believe to be Ricky Corliss. Corliss, as you know, disappeared several weeks ago after he was allegedly snatched off a Brooklyn street by an unknown assailant. Unnamed police sources and the press had speculated that the abduction was actually a carefully staged ruse for Corliss to escape scrutiny after a second mistrial was declared following the planting of evidence by disgraced NYPD detective Peter Moretti. It seems that the abduction was in fact carefully staged, but not as a ruse." He half turns, pointing at the salvage yard's sign. "Sources tell me Sergei Malankov, owner of the salvage yard, has ties to the Russian mob and is currently under investigation for money laundering and racketeering. He—"

The sound is cut off, and the Latina reappears. "Thanks for that report, Ronnie. Now, to the press conference by Roderick Ford.

"Good morning, ladies and gentlemen. I'm Ellen Bayles, Mr. Ford's media relations manager." Bayles is a petite woman with a prominent chin and neatly cut shoulder-length brown hair. She has a friendly but professional demeanor and is dressed in a black business suit. "Mr. Ford will come to the podium in a moment. He will make a statement and will direct you, at some point, to turn your attention to the large screen over my right shoulder. He will take a few questions when he's done, but only pertaining to the issue at hand." She turns to her right. "Mr. Ford."

"Four days ago this email appeared in my in-box. Please look at the screen." Ford waited a few beats. "Unfortunately, I ignored it. As you can see at the top, it was sent from a Bulgarian email address by someone calling himself Karl. In the email, Karl describes how he is fed up with the 'niggers'—his word, never mine—and how they get everything in this country while he and his people are forgotten and, quote, 'shit upon.' He goes on to tell me that he will take actions within the next few days that will 'wake the fucking shithole melting pot up from its sleep and shake its foundations.' Karl does not describe what actions he will take or how he means to do the things he threatens to do.

"I hope you understand that a man in my position, who stands for the truth in the face of constant and withering attacks from all sides, receives many such emails, texts, tweets, phone calls—some, I might add, that have been traced back to my enemies and are clearly attempts to entrap or frighten me. I digress. Until two days ago at the Scarborough Houses in Brooklyn, no one who had ever threatened to do violence in support of my causes or my name—or to do violence to me—had ever followed through. I want to emphasize that I have never advocated for violence, though my radical leftist enemies have, in the name of their diabolical agendas, accused me of such deeds. I have never called for violence against the police, though I have railed against their use as a political tool of the fascist left. They cannot disobey their orders.

"But the sad reason I stand before you today is that yesterday I received another email from Karl, this time from an address in Oman. Please look again at the screen. In this email, Karl describes in graphic detail—that which only the killer himself could have known—how he perpetrated the senseless acts of violence. See for yourselves how he describes making Officer Joon kill himself to save the two innocent people he held at gunpoint. Officer Joon was a hero. How many of us would have done what he did? Still, as Karl describes, he took Officer Joon's gun and shot the other two victims in cold blood. And I quote, 'I wiped the gun afterward and put the gook's prints back on it, dropping it near where he'd done himself. I put on some gloves, dipped my finger in the mongrel's blood, and wrote *NPLF* on the wall over his body. Yeah, the New Panthers Liberation Front. Fucking brilliant, right?'

"But the saddest and most damning proof was the video attachments Karl provided with the second email. One was an amateurish recording of audio and video clips cobbled together using first-generation syncing software. It purports to show an African American spokesman for the nonexistent NPLF describing how they had murdered Officer Joon and the other victims. My experts immediately saw it for what it was: a poorly conceived and executed scam. Sadly, the second video was all too authentic. It's from Officer Joon's body cam, and if you study it carefully, you catch sight of a Caucasian face flashing in front of the camera.

"I immediately turned all the evidence over to the NYPD, who will, I believe, be holding a press conference of their own at One Police Plaza after they have more carefully studied what I have provided them." Ford looked up from the written statement on the podium and stared directly into the camera. "Karl, if you're listening, please give yourself up immediately. Do the right thing and turn yourself in. You failed, and you senselessly ended the lives of three people. I stand for justice, if nothing else. And if you believe in my causes as you say you do, do as I ask. Remember, the truth will out."

The reporters started shouting questions at Ford, but he turned and walked away. That was Ford to a tee.

Nick clicked off the TV. Things had played out exactly as he had hoped. Ford acted in his own best interests by following the dance steps Nick and Lenny had laid out before him. Nick had seen tapes of New York City burning before. He was one of two men, working to near exhaustion in a synagogue basement, who had stopped it from happening again. He knew he should have been enormously proud of what he had done to prevent the loss of life and untold property damage. Then why, he wondered, did he feel like shit?

TWENTY-FOUR

Calista Barrows was forced to stand at the very back of the conference room at 1PP. Reporters from tiny outer-borough papers were treated like three-legged strays at a kill shelter. The only reason a reporter from the *Kings County Crier* got press credentials was Murray Kleinman's rep. Everybody seemed to respect him—just not enough that it mattered. Murray's rep got Calista inside the room, but never *in* the room. You sometimes heard her voice shouting questions. You never heard her questions answered. She once had a deputy mayor point at a fly banging into a closed window. "Flies get inside the room too. We don't pay attention to them either."

It was no different as she strained to hear Police Commissioner McAndrew praise Roderick Ford for his cooperation.

"We have not always appreciated Mr. Ford's opinions when it comes to the NYPD and other law enforcement agencies. We make no secret of that, but in this instance, Mr. Ford exercised proper judgment in turning over the emails and videos to our department as soon as it became clear to him what the perpetrator of this brutal and cynical plot intended. We in no way hold Mr. Ford responsible. The only person responsible for this is the man behind the calculated and cold-blooded murder of three innocent people in an attempt to exacerbate the tensions that already exist in this city.

"While we maintain that the two recent shootings involving NYPD officers were justified given the circumstances, we are neither blind nor deaf to the stresses between the department and the minority communities of this great city. To address these issues, we have established a task force on community policing that has already made significant strides in lessening the friction between the NYPD and the communities we serve. Now I'll take a few questions."

Calista didn't even bother. She was so far behind the rest of the press corps that she would have needed a bullhorn to be heard. Instead, she watched the carefully choreographed scramble. She knew that it looked and sounded like utter chaos on the screen: cameras flashing, questions shouted, microphones and voice recorders waved in the air. She could have predicted whose questions would get answered. It was always about the big outlets, followed by the correspondents and columnists who tended to be sympathetic to the police.

Predictable questions came with predictable answers.

We're working on some very strong leads. No, unfortunately, no arrests have been made. We can't reveal that at this time. Yes, we would appreciate the public's help in identifying the man seen flashing across the screen in the brief footage from Officer Joon's body camera. Blah, blah, blah . . . But she could not get the fake firefighters out of her head. There had to be some connection between the gas leak, the murders, and those men dressed in bunker coats, pants, and helmets. There just had to be! It was the only thing that made sense to her.

Calista Barrows was so lost in thought, she barely noticed that the wave of press had changed direction and was now moving past her like water around a boulder in a stream. She was in no rush. The *Crier* was published twice weekly, so she had no deadline. No twenty-four-hour news cycle for her. Odd thing was, Murray and she often did better work than the big outlets, because they could actually investigate stories without rushing to judgment. They had time to gain perspective. There was another reason for her lack of speed. Calista waited for the room to clear out before going upstairs to see Mercy Willis.

———

Lt. Mercy Willis did something or other for Chief of Patrol John Timmons. She wasn't quite sure what purpose she served at 1PP except as a Black female with rank and a pretty face to run out in front of the cameras whenever the department had a spate of discrimination suits to deal with. She didn't mind. It was an unspoken bargain with the powers that be. They could use her as long as she had a smooth path up the ladder. Passing the tests was not a problem, nor was her unbridled ambition. Her ambition was no secret. Her sexuality was.

While things on the job were easier for lesbians than they used to be, they still weren't easy. And Mercy had no intention of letting anything stand in her way, not even a little bit. She knew how to play the game, wisely letting slip some drunken details of the men she'd fucked. Everybody on the job bought it. Problem for her was that not everyone was as gullible as her colleagues. Calista Barrows wasn't gullible at all and had stumbled into Mercy's closet while doing a story on after-hours clubs in the outer boroughs.

Mercy had been an occasional unnamed police source for Calista, both because she feared that the reporter could out her and because she was incredibly attracted to Calista. For her part, Calista didn't enjoy playing on Mercy's fears and desires, but as Murray had schooled her, "A journalist uses whatever she must to get at the truth. It's a dirty business sometimes, but if you look carefully enough, every business has dirty hands."

Mercy Willis looked up from her computer screen and smiled at the sight of Calista Barrows standing in front of her desk.

"What can I help you with, Ms. Barrows?" she said loud enough for the other uniforms in the room to hear.

"I have one simple question."

"That is . . ."

"I have a New York tag number, but it doesn't show up in any of the databases I have access to. What does that mean?"

"The obvious answer is that you either misread the tag or transposed the numbers."

"Nope. I have an image of it."

"Then the next likely answer is that it was a counterfeit plate. It happens."

Calista opened her mouth to pursue it further, but Mercy gave her a slight shake of her head. "I'm sorry, Ms. Barrows, but for anything more than that, you'll have to go through channels."

"Through channels" was a code they had worked out. It meant that Mercy would be calling her within ten minutes. Calista knew she could have just called Mercy in the first place, but she was already in the building for the press conference. It was also a subtle way to pique Mercy's interest. Although she had slept with a woman only once, back in college—and had been kind of freaked out by the experience—Calista had to admit she was excited by Mercy's attraction. That's when another bit of Murray's advice came into her head. "Don't sleep with a source. It compromises both of you."

Calista was nearly to Pearl Street when her phone buzzed in her pocket. She recognized the number.

"Why did you really come see me?" Mercy asked, a hint of anger in her voice. "I don't know anything more about that shit at the Scarborough Houses than what you heard."

"It really was about a tag number." Calista told half the truth. "I swear."

"You looked hot."

"Thank you. Not too shabby yourself. You gave me the obvious reasons the tag didn't show in the databases. Explanations I already figured out. Give me some less obvious ones, ones that might involve . . . I don't know, city officials maybe."

There was a long silence on Mercy's side of the phone. Calista could almost hear the gears and sprockets turning. "Sometimes, for reasons easy enough to figure out, law enforcement agents' tags are kept out of databases to protect their identities. Other times, they get fake identities attached to their tag numbers."

"Can you do some checking around for me?" She read the tag number to Mercy. "I did some research and found out the car is a black 1969 Pontiac GTO. I'll send you the image I have."

"Have a drink with me."

"Just a drink?"

"It's a start."

"You get me the info and I'll buy the drinks."

She could feel Mercy's smile through the phone. "I like good vodka."

Calista noticed she was smiling too.

TWENTY-FIVE

The sky was a mournful autumn blue. Northern Boulevard was blocked off and the street in front of the Korean Methodist Church of Flushing was a sea of blue uniforms darker than the sky. Scattered in the blue sea were grays, khakis, blacks, and greens. Cops had come from as far away as Sitka, Mexico City, and Seoul. There was even a contingent of Mounties from Canada in their red tunics, gold-striped black jodhpurs, tall boots, and flat-brimmed tan trooper hats. The chiefs were there, the commissioner, the mayor, and other political A-listers. Quite a showing for a scared kid who had killed two innocent people and then shot himself in shame. It was a bona fide hero's send-off—flag-draped coffin, dignitaries, pipers, the whole megillah. Everything Pete Moretti's send-off was not.

It was difficult for Nick not to think back to that day in the driving rain, standing over Pete's grave. Just himself, Pete's wives, their kids, and Father Charlie Hannigan. Father Charlie wasn't actually a Catholic priest, not anymore. He was strictly pay-for-play, having left the priesthood to join one of those online sham churches like the Holy Order of Schrödinger's Cat, a church that allowed him to pursue his two great passions: women and Dewar's. Nick knew him from the job and had arranged for him to do the graveside service. Dressed in his old priestly garb, Hannigan put on a good show for the meager crowd.

As he shuffled into the church, past framed scriptural passages in English and Korean, it wasn't lost on Nick that without Pete's funeral, he wouldn't have been at this one. There was a bloody symmetry to it all, but sometime between graduation from the academy and Kandahar, he had come to the conclusion that there were things the universe made impossible to reconcile.

Until he woke up this morning, Nick hadn't intended to be anywhere near the funeral, but by the time he brushed his teeth, he knew he could be nowhere else. With help from Lenny Feld, he was responsible for this charade. Yeah, there was the part about preventing the city from exploding, but he wasn't about to hide from this aspect of it. He didn't know whether the Joon kid was a coward or just a fuckup. Either way, Nick had made him a hero and he had to face that head-on. "Own what you do, boy," his dad used to say. "Guilt is for people who turn away." So Nick donned his dress blues and drove to the staging area in the right field parking lot at Citi Field. When he got out of his GTO and took a few steps toward the buses waiting to haul the rank and file over to the church, he felt a powerful hand squeezing the back of his neck.

"Where you think you're going, Ryan?"

The man attached to the hand was Kenyon Cook. Cook was a larger, more imposing version of Clint Eastwood. He liked hearing the Eastwood comparison and fancied himself a kind of Dirty Harry. He was certainly dirty and was no friend to the Ryans. He wore the three gold bars of a bureau chief on his Department of Corrections dress uniform. It was one of those great New York City ironies that Cook, a sergeant in Nick Ryan Sr.'s precinct and a subject of the elder Ryan's testimony, had actually come out the other side of the Argent Commission hearings better off than before they began. While some of the cops Nick's father had testified against got sent away, none of the accusations against Cook stuck. Following a brief suspension, a cursory investigation, and some political horse-trading, Cook landed on his feet at the NYCDOC. He even got a step-up in rank and more power than he ever had as a sergeant in the NYPD. He'd since moved all the way up.

Cook made cartoon sniffing noises. "That cheese I smell? Sure is. You smell just like your daddy, the rat motherfucker. Your old man drink himself to death yet? You let me know when he does, 'cause I'll come to his funeral in a white tux and piss on his grave to send him on his way to ratfuck heaven."

Nick spun, right armed extended, chopping down on Cook's arm. He stared directly into Cook's eyes. "Keep your fucking hands off me."

"What did you say to me, you bottom-feeding piece of shit?"

Before the two came to blows, Deputy Police Commissioner Anthony Ricco stepped between them. "Chief Cook, I'm glad to see you're congratulating Detective Ryan on getting the bump to detective first. Always makes me happy to see good interdepartmental relations."

Ricco, dressed in a black suit that had fit him ten years and fifteen pounds ago, was smaller than both Nick and Cook. Smaller, maybe, but a match for either. Ricco was a legendary street cop who got where he got through hard work. He was allergic to ambition. Like Martellus Sharp, all Ricco ever wanted to be was in uniform. After thirty-plus years on the street, and at the urging of his wife, he had put in his papers. Neither retired life nor South Carolina took, so when they offered him the deputy commissioner's job, Ricco jumped at it, leaving Myrtle Beach in his rearview mirror.

"Excuse us, Kenyon, I've got to get my guy to the church," Ricco said, urging Nick away with a strong hand in the small of his back. The I'm-gonna-fuck-you-up expression on Cook's face did not go unnoticed.

"Thanks," Nick said when they got clear. "If he kept that up, it was going to get ugly."

"Some people can't let shit go, no matter how lucky they are or how high they rise."

This *my guy* treatment by the DC was new territory for Nick, as was almost everything since his trip to the Bronx. He had no way of knowing who was in on his deal with Joe and couldn't risk letting on, not to anyone. He would have to learn his way in these shark-filthy waters.

The trick was divining which sharks fed on the little fishes and which ones fed on the other sharks.

"Cook's got a real hard-on for you."

Nick shrugged. "Sins of the father. You know how that goes."

Ricco laughed. "Nick Ryan Jr., cool as mid-December."

If he was being tested, the right answer was to give nothing away. So he kept his mouth shut.

"You'll never hear this from the brass, but there are plenty of us who admire your old man. Took a lot of guts for him to stand up tall. All the other witnesses—what choice did they have? The commission lawyers had them by the cojones. For them, it was testify or do a longer bid of cop time upstate. Your old man—he did right because it was right. Runs in the family, doing the right thing. You got tarred because of what your dad did, but you didn't whine about it, didn't file suit. These days . . ." Ricco got a faraway look in his eyes. "These days, we got cops filing suit because other cops fart too loud in the locker room."

"Not my style."

As Nick turned to the bus, Ricco stopped him. He waited for the howl of a passing Delta 737 to fade away. The jet left a trail of burnt-jet-fuel stink in its wake as it glided down to the LaGuardia tarmac.

"Look at that blue sky. Since 9/11, I can't look at a blue sky without thinking of that day."

"Thanks again, DC."

"C'mon, Ryan," Ricco said, thumbing his own chest. "Forget the bus. You're riding with me. There's some people you should meet."

TWENTY-SIX

Nick had been to these services before—too many of them—though he'd never actually made it inside the church. He had always been stuck outside on the street in bone-numbing cold or steam-bath heat, listening to the services through temporary speakers. He was inside today, on a pew up front, next to Ricco. His life with Shana had schooled him that mingling with the rich and fabulous and the fabulously rich didn't mean you were in the club. Nick had been a freak show curiosity for that crowd. He never fooled himself that he was anything else. He didn't need to learn the lesson twice. Political power was just wealth in a different dress.

While Nick understood that it would take him some time to find his sweet spot in his new world, he didn't for a second believe he would be anything more than a handyman, the guy who showed up at midnight to fix the leaks and the broken furnace. Although he hadn't read it since high school, he remembered that part in *The Great Gatsby* about how Tom and Daisy were careless people who smashed things up and moved on, only to let other people clean up their messes. He didn't care. He was ready with the broom and dustpan to sweep up the broken glass. The rich and powerful weren't his concern. They always had ways to insulate themselves. He had taken the job because it was the people on the street and in the projects he cared about—the poor, the shopkeepers, and the cabbies. Those people mattered to him, not the folks who could hide above the trouble in their terraced Park Avenue apartments or fly to Saint-Tropez when shit got ugly. Then he thought about Becky. She was in a category of her own, and he would do anything to protect her.

Once the service was finished, Ricco took Nick by the elbow and marched him over to where the dignitaries were giving their condolences to the family.

"Sorry for your loss," Ricco said, patting Chief Joon on the shoulder.

Joon was a stoic man who seemed to wear the hardships of Korean history on his broad, flat face. His wife and daughter were inconsolable, holding each other upright. To Nick's surprise, Chief Joon asked Ricco to give him a moment with Nick alone. Ricco obliged.

When the deputy chief was out of earshot, Joon grasped Nick's right hand in both his white-gloved hands and gave him a bow from the waist. "Honor is preserved," was all Joon said, staring directly into Nick's eyes for several uncomfortable seconds.

Nick wasn't prepared for this. He didn't flinch. Whoever his new bosses were, they had let Joon know at least a portion of the truth about what happened at the Scarborough Houses, Building Six. Joon was now indebted to them. Chief Joon wasn't sure to what extent Nick had been involved, but the man clearly understood the deal. Nick's employers were shrewd. Any advantage, any favor, no matter how small, was worth having. One never knew when leverage would come in handy.

"Let's go, Detective Ryan." Ricco tugged him by the arm. "Chief Joon and his family have to leave. There's someone else you should meet."

Ricco walked Nick a few steps over to his right. They stopped behind a woman whose silhouette and voice were vaguely familiar. She wore a simple but expensive black dress. The tasteful design highlighted the shape of the woman inside it. She had lustrous black hair, cut as elegantly as the dress and falling in a trim line just short of her square shoulders. When she pivoted as gracefully as a swan, Nick recognized her immediately.

Ricco made a small gesture with his arm. "Detective Nick Ryan Jr., I'd like to introduce you to Senator Renata Maduro."

Her white smile was as measured as her attire. "Detective."

"Senator."

They shook hands. For her, it was all as reflexive and meaningless as a blink of an eye. Nick couldn't imagine what it would be like spending his life, day after day, having to be "on" this way, politely shaking the hands of strangers. This close to her, it was impossible not to see beyond her efforts to tamp down her beauty. She was probably ten years his senior but spent a lot of time in the gym. Her skin was a rich light brown with the inevitable lines that came with age. On her, they added something he couldn't quite put a finger on.

"A sad occasion on which to meet," she said, her Dominican-inflected Washington Heights accent all but gone. "A parent should never have to bury a child."

"Never."

"Deputy Commissioner Ricco tells me you served two tours in Afghanistan. Thank you for your service."

Nick said nothing. He never knew what to say to that. No one he had served with wanted thanks. Paradoxically, "Thank you" always seemed woefully inadequate.

Whether it was Nick's silence or her internal alarm clock, it was time for the senator to move on.

"It was a pleasure, Detective Ryan."

"It was." He bowed his head.

She was gone, and so, too, was Ricco. Nick wasn't sure what any of that was about with Senator Maduro—hidden messages or no message at all. Ricco had been a family friend, so it all might have been perfectly innocent. Or not. It didn't matter.

Nick walked out the front of the church and down the steps. With Ricco nowhere in sight, he headed to the bus for the ride back to Citi Field.

TWENTY-SEVEN

The pipers, the flag-draped casket, the endless rows of cops were gone. Calista Barrows was busy beating herself up when she spotted a lone cop in dress uniform ambling down the front steps of the church. He was a handsome man. Handsome in the way that made her palms sweat and her ears buzz. The initial, undeniable spark of attraction was a jolt. Her heart raced too, but not out of desire. She fumbled for her phone. When she had it, she scrolled to the photos from that night at the Scarborough Houses.

"Fuck me," she whispered. "It's him! The fake firefighter."

She had lied to Murray about where she had gone, despite his admonitions to let go of her hunches.

"You got bubkes, kid. A few blurry photos and intuition do not a story make. Wanting it to be a story doesn't make it so. You trust your nose too much and the stories you think you smell turn out to be dog shit. My people say rain on a wedding day is good luck, that stepping in poop on the street is good luck. Of course we do. Our whole history is wedding-day rain and dog shit. Don't make something out of nothing. It will ruin you."

Murray was usually right, but not this time. She felt it in her marrow, the way she knew she was close to the finish line without having to see the tape. She knew when to press, when to go to her final kick. That was why she had stood behind the barricades across the street from the Korean Methodist Church of Flushing instead of attending another meeting of some useless committee at Borough Hall. She hadn't been sure what she was looking for or what she might find. She just knew she had to be at Joon Jae-In's funeral.

Until the moment she saw the cop come down the steps, her time was wasted in terms of the story. Not in terms of her humanity. The ceremony, the solemnity of it, was all quite moving. She found herself welling up at several points during the long hours in the sun as she listened to the funeral service piped out to the street via portable speakers. But now, that was gone. She had to catch up to the cop. She pocketed her phone, pushed her way past the other reporters, and ran.

———

The production meeting in his office was getting Roderick Ford's juices flowing. He knew a winner when he saw one, and tonight's broadcast was going to be a big fat ratings winner.

"So," his producer said, "we've got video of the guy who killed the seven people in that Sikh temple in Tucson in a full beard, and we have his net search records showing he spent days checking out jihadist websites. His name was Martin Anselm, and he's perfect. They even found a dog-eared Qur'an in his apartment. Best part: we have Anselm's own video of himself shaving off the beard before he left for the temple with his modified AR-15."

Both the producer and Ford knew that Anselm was a bipolar white-supremacist loner, but neither man ever passed up an opportunity to attack Islam or give credence to white nationalism. Ford's cynicism and corruption were legion. He knew that Anselm visited those jihadi websites to fuel his own manic paranoia and rage, that he couldn't have cared less whether he killed Sikhs, Muslims, or Jews. He was an equal opportunity hater. That along with the Qur'an, the cops had also found copies of the Bible, *The Turner Diaries, Mein Kampf,* and the Unabomber's manifesto.

"We aren't going to have to deal with lawsuits from his family, are we?" Ford asked. "Are there going to be neighbors and friends protesting that Anselm wasn't actually a newly radicalized Muslim?"

The producer grinned. "He didn't have any family. His neighbors hated him, and he had no friends."

"Perfect." Ford clapped his hands. "Let's move on to the next—" He stopped in midsentence, hearing a muted ring from the lower right drawer of his desk. "Everybody out! Now!"

No one questioned Ford when he barked at them. He was a vindictive bully whose bite was far worse than his bark. He waited for the office door to close before punching in the key code and grabbing the phone.

"I have a name for you," said the distorted voice on the other end of the line.

"What is it?"

"No."

"What do you mean, *no*?"

"I was forced to break the legs of the video collection manager at Adamant Security."

"What do broken legs matter to me?"

"It matters. To obtain the CCTV footage I required to find our person of interest, I needed to persuade him to cooperate."

"Boo-hoo. That doesn't explain your refusal."

"There are additional reasons."

"Such as . . ."

"Money."

"I already transferred the agreed-upon sum into the account."

"Insufficient. The men and women whose legs did not require casts *did* require substantial monetary recompense to deliver their footage to me."

Ford was fuming. "Bullshit! Expenses are not part of the deal."

"Until now. What I will tell you is that your pizza deliveryman is an active NYPD detective. If I divulge his identity, how can I be assured you will not send any of those incompetents you surround yourself with to complete my task?"

"What concern is that of yours? You've already been paid."

"Let us say it is a matter of personal and professional pride and reputation. My assignment is exclusively mine. No one else is to be involved. Those are the terms under which we operate. Any alteration in the terms of our arrangement not mutually agreed upon would be most unfortunate for you."

"Are you threatening me?"

"Promising. Your life span would diminish considerably."

He laughed. "Says you."

The darkly tinted window at Ford's back broke with an almost imperceptible tinkle. A bullet whizzed past Ford's right ear so closely that it singed his earlobe. The bullet slammed into a stuffed effigy of the president. White fibers were suddenly everywhere.

"Says me. With all due respect to the commander in chief, that could just as easily have been your skull. Another hundred thousand in the account by the end of the banking day today. Understood?"

"Understood."

"Shall I eliminate the problem?"

"No! No! For chrissakes!" Ford was apoplectic. "That's the last thing I want. That detective possesses technical skills and software I need to access. Still . . ." He rubbed his earlobe as he thought. "I don't like being fucked with. Makes me look weak and this sort of provocation can't go unpunished. A lesson needs to be taught. A price must be paid. This detective—rattle his cage. Bloody his nose and make it splashy."

"Any other parameters?"

"I want him to have a sense it was me giving him the lesson, but do it subtly. I need deniability. I do pay you for your creativity and that additional hundred grand should inspire you." Ford felt a jolt of electricity surging through him. "Fuck with him. Make it hurt."

The line went dead.

Calista realized how far away she was from race ready. Her churning legs felt like wet ropes beneath her. She stumbled in front of a local CBS reporter doing her remote with the church at her back.

"Sorry," she said without looking back.

She bobbed and weaved through and around people walking in both directions along the sidewalk. The cop had half a block on her, and as she got her legs under her, she began making up ground in chunks. Her press credentials swung madly as she ran. She had made up almost all the distance and was nearing the bus taking cops back to Citi Field, when a big cop stepped in front of her.

"Whoa! Whoa! Where you think you're goin'? Don't you people in the press got any respect? We aren't gonna talk to you after we bury one of our own."

"Look, Officer . . . Mandel," she read off his nameplate. His badge number was covered by a black ribbon.

"*Lieutenant* Mandel."

"Excuse me, Lieutenant Mandel. My bad. This isn't about an interview. I promise. I just need to talk briefly with the officer who just got on the bus."

Mandel looked over his shoulder and recognized Nick Ryan. He turned back to Calista, a sneer on his face. "That prick? Nah, I don't think so."

"Why not?"

Mandel leaned in uncomfortably close and whispered, "Off the record?"

"Sure."

"Fuck him and fuck you!"

The bus pulled away. When Mandel and the bus were out of sight, Calista reached for her phone. "Hey, Mercy, you free for drinks tonight?"

TWENTY-EIGHT

Getting off the bus, Nick saw Ace leaning against his GTO.

"Get off the car."

"C'mon. He's waiting for you in there." Ace pointed at the stadium.

Nick took his car keys out of his pocket. "Give me a minute."

"Now!" Ace stepped in front of the GTO's door handle.

Nick's punch was a short, chopping left to the chest, but Ace slipped it, sliding effortlessly to his left. Nick's knuckles brushed Ace's jacket sleeve.

"My face didn't get scarred like this by accident, Ryan. Try that again, and I'll hit you twice before you can exhale."

"I still have to get some things from my car. So either we can make a scene of this or you can let me get them."

"Hurry up."

Nick grabbed a plastic grocery bag off the passenger bucket seat. "Okay."

———

They walked through the empty players' parking lot and entered the stadium via the players' entrance. Ace guided Nick over to an elevator.

On either side of the open doors were two men whose faces Nick recognized. One was the guy who had driven him to the Bronx. The other was the guy who had patted him down inside the tire-repair shop. Both nodded to him as he stepped inside the elevator car. Ace turned a key at the base of the control panel. The doors slid shut.

Outside the elevator, veering right, they emerged into the sunlight. They were high up in the right-field corner at Citi Field, a huge Coca-Cola sign behind them. *The Coca-Cola Corner.* Nick recognized it from TV. Ace's unbuttoned jacket was making loud snapping noises in the wind.

Ace nodded. "First row."

Nick walked down the aisle, the perfectly manicured green-and-brown diamond spreading out before him. The smell of fresh-cut grass filled his nose as a forgotten hot dog wrapper swirled in the wind above the pitcher's mound. Joe was seated at the rail, scanning the field below.

"Good thing the wind shifted and the jets aren't flying overhead like before. Makes conversation problematical."

"Maybe they should move LaGuardia."

Joe ignored that. "I grew up a Yankees fan, but this is a much more welcoming venue than the new Yankee Stadium. That place features the worst aspects of a mausoleum and a museum. The Yankees are prisoners of their own legacy."

"There a hidden message in there for me?"

Joe looked up at Nick. "Why do you ask?"

"Seems to be the theme of the day. Does DC Ricco know about me?"

"Very few people know. I can assure you Ricco is not one of them."

"Chief Joon knows."

"He knows only what he needed to know, which is very limited. He was told his son was a fuckup and that you helped wash the shame away. He has no idea how." Joe pointed to the bag in Nick's hand. "A gift?"

Nick took out the transponder that had been planted on his car and placed it on the green plastic seat next to Joe. "I disabled it."

"What else?"

Nick handed Joe a burner phone with a piece of white adhesive tape on the back. "There's a number written on the tape. You need me, you call that number. You may have a taste for this kind of dramatic bull-shit, but I'm not impressed with it."

Joe took the phone, sliding it into his jacket pocket. "You're right, I do have a taste for this sort of thing. Like you, Nick, I didn't grow up with much. I spent a lot of my early life looking up at people with money and power. I have money now and I don't really want power. Well, just enough to make doing things like this possible. I am curious, though. How did you manage it, getting a demagogue like Roderick Ford to cooperate?"

Nick shook his head. "Part of the deal is you don't ask those questions. You needed me to fix things. I fixed them."

"You did, yet it was awfully risky . . . that whole thing about the New Panthers Liberation Front. You could have made things much worse. Might have blown up in your face and taken the entire city with it."

"What if I did nothing or if I tried to rig it to look like a justifiable shooting? You want to send me back to making buy-and-busts, go ahead."

"Relax. No one's sending you anywhere. The deal is the deal. Did you think up that entire scenario on the spot?" Joe turned away from the field, staring Nick in the eye. "The fake radical group, calling the *Times*—all that off the top of your head?"

"I did."

"To think it up is one thing. To follow through and make it work . . ."

"Half measures are for frightened men."

"And you're not a frightened man?"

"Sometimes. Fear has value. The trick is in not letting it paralyze you."

"They were right to pick you. That philosophy will serve you well."

"You dragged me here to tell me that?"

"No."

Nick frowned. "Then why?"

"Because I could and to look you in the eye." Joe stood, putting the transponder back in the plastic bag. "Thanks for the phone. I'll call you within the next few weeks."

Nick didn't move.

Joe stopped after a few steps up toward the walkway, the wind blowing out his neatly coifed white hair. With his tanned bald pate and hair wings, he looked like a mad scientist in a fancy suit. He fought hard to push his hair back into place. He turned to Nick. "Why don't you go down to the field and run the bases before you leave? Haven't you always wanted to do that—run the bases in a major league ballpark?"

"I played championship basketball games in Madison Square Garden. I don't need to pretend."

"Good point."

"Why not run the bases yourself? Seems to me it's something you've always wanted to do."

"You really are a perceptive bastard, Ryan. But I already look ridiculous enough."

"Who cares? The only one watching would be me."

"You think so?"

Another message? Nick kept the question to himself.

"One more thing," Joe said.

"I figured there would be."

"Take some time off. You'll be notified when to report to the Intelligence Bureau."

Nick waited until he was the only person in the stands. After watching the grounds crew roll out the tarp to cover the infield for the night, he left too.

TWENTY-NINE

McCann's was fairly empty when Calista Barrows got there around nine. A few men had circled her. None of them had hit on her . . . yet. They would. They always did. Depending upon the venue, it usually took a few beers or Rémys for them to work up the nerve. Dressed in worn jeans, low heels, and a beat-up brown leather jacket, she suspected she didn't quite fit the usual McCann's profile. With her green eyes, short-cropped tightly curled hair, and subtly freckled skin, Calista surely didn't fit in, nor was she putting out the come-and-get-it vibe. She definitely wasn't a cop. With a white mother and a Black father, not fitting in was second nature. As she had told Mercy Willis last night over drinks, "To the Black girls, any white was too white, and to the white girls I was a . . . you know. With the boys, it was different . . . I was a trophy for them, white or Black."

Mercy, fuck! Lying to Murray was one thing, but by sleeping with Mercy, she had compromised just about everything she believed in. It hadn't been awful. She'd had more unpleasant experiences sleeping with men, but somehow that rationale didn't hold. She was never any good at faking it. As awful as some of those experiences with men had been, they weren't transactional. Her falling into bed with Mercy was just that—purely transactional. What made it even harder to bear was that Mercy knew it and still let it happen; that they used each other didn't make it any better.

"Here's his name and address," Mercy had said, pulling a slip of paper out of her nightstand drawer. "You sure can pick 'em. Good-looking man. He's a detective and a war hero. I'm going to shower. You want to out me, that's one thing. Nothing I can do about that now, but I never thought you'd just do me like this."

Calista grabbed Mercy's hand. "Come on, Mercy, this wasn't a one-way thing. You know that. And I would never out you. With my job, maybe it was better for you to believe I would. But I would never."

Mercy turned to her. "Yeah, okay, I was always curious about you. Now that itch has been scratched and the vodka's all worn off. Do me a favor: Lose my number and forget where my office is at. When I get out of the shower, don't be here."

Less than a day had passed, the sting of it still fresh. Callie never had a lot of friends. Losing one hurt. Losing a good source hurt almost as much. Yet having seen Nick Ryan in the flesh and having had a day to research him softened the blow. She couldn't stop thinking about him, wondering what he would be like in person. She knew it was foolish to have this kind of schoolgirl crush on the man, but she couldn't help herself. For the first time since she became a reporter, the story was losing out to her desire.

She checked her phone as she sipped her second glass of wine. Her first had been a house red, a liquid that barely qualified as wine.

"Are you certain you want red?" the barman with the faint Irish lilt had asked. "The shite's just awful."

She should have taken his advice. The red bit harder than a pit bull. She had switched to Pinot Grigio, which was at least recognizable as wine.

Nearing ten, there was still no sign of Nick Ryan. By even being at McCann's, she was risking an encounter with some cops she may have previously interviewed for a story, but the possibility of meeting Ryan was a chance worth taking. She considered trying to catch him coming out of his apartment. Mercy had disabused her of that idea.

"If you're thinking of staking out his building, don't. He'll spot your ass in a second. Try McCann's on Fourth Avenue." Those were Mercy's final words on the subject and probably her final words to Calista, period.

Feeling increasingly embarrassed by it all, she threw thirty bucks on the bar and left. Head down, she pushed her way through the thickening crowd. Coming out the door, she banged shoulders hard with someone coming in. They each grabbed for the other.

"Sorry," he said, gripping her jacket sleeves. "You all right?"

"No broken bones. You?"

He laughed. "Intact."

"Glad to hear it."

When her eyes focused, she saw that it was Nick Ryan. It was all she could do not to say his name aloud.

"I'm Nick." He let go of her and offered his right hand.

She took it. "Callie."

"Can I buy you a drink?"

"As long as it's not the house red."

"McCann's house red is an act of war. Mack let you order it?"

"He tried warning me off."

"Bourbon?"

"Well, if that toxic red shit didn't kill me, what harm could bourbon do?"

"None at all. I promise."

"For some reason, I trust you."

"Give me my hand back and I'll prove worthy of your trust."

She flushed, realizing she was still holding his hand, and let go. He held the door open for her and she stepped back inside.

"Follow me, Callie."

THIRTY

Nick's usual seat was taken, but there was always a nook at the corner of the bar, which most of the patrons ignored because of its obstructed view. If you were there to hook up, obstructed views wouldn't do.

Mack noticed Nick and Calista settling into the nook. He held up two fingers and mouthed, "Your bottle?"

Nick nodded.

Less than a minute later, Mack was pouring two fingers of Pappy's in each glass. He looked at Callie. "I'm surprised you'd come back in after drinking the house wines."

"I'm surprised too," she lied, sitting next to Nick and nervous as a teenager. But there was something about that jangly sensation she liked. "Next time, I'll take your advice."

"Well, watch out for this'n," Mack said, tilting his head at Nick.

"Thanks for the endorsement, you prick."

Mack bowed. "At your service, boyo."

They all laughed.

"You're staying even after Mack warned you about me?" Nick asked.

"He told me to watch out, not to leave."

"There's hope for me then."

"We'll see." She picked up her glass. "Pappy Van Winkle. I'm impressed."

"You know it?"

"I ran track at Kentucky."

"Horses, bourbon, and Wildcat basketball."

"An apt summary of the Bluegrass State. Cheers."

They clinked glasses and sipped. There was a silent moment while they both enjoyed the full experience—the beauty of the amber elixir, the hot tingle at the back of the throat, and the warmth spreading through their bodies.

"Long way from Kentucky to Bay Ridge," he said.

"You have no idea."

"That's not a Kentucky accent. Southern Wisconsin? Northern Illinois?"

She felt exposed. "Glencoe, outside Chicago."

"Money, huh?"

"How did you know?"

"About the accent or the money?"

"Both."

He took another sip. "Your accent? Two tours in Afghanistan. I spent a lot of time with men and women from all over. How did I know about Glencoe being a wealthy suburb? Cops aren't all cavemen. I read books, even graduated from college."

"That's not what I meant," she said, feeling herself flush again.

"C'mon, Callie, maybe a little bit?" Nick held his left forefinger and thumb close together.

"Okay, maybe a little."

"Then what are you doing in McCann's?" He didn't wait for her to answer. "Look around the room, as well as you can from here. There's only two types of people in here: cops and people who want to be with them. You don't strike me as either. You sure don't dress the part, and your affect is all wrong for this joint."

"And because I'm a little too Black to suit the setting."

"Possibly. After this summer, things between the Black community and the police aren't exactly wonderful. I'm sure the guys in here were a little wary of you."

"An honest man! I haven't spoken to one of those in a while."

"Honest to a point. Everybody lies." Nick shook his head at her. "But you're trying very hard to hide something. I can tell, so we can have another glass and wave so long, or you can just tell me what's up. I'm a good listener."

Calista considered herself adept at reading people, but Nick Ryan's ability caught her off guard. She recalled Mercy's warning about Nick's street smarts. *He'll spot your ass in a second.*

"I'm lonely," she said, surprising herself.

"McCann's specializes in loneliness." He waved to Mack. "That's what bars like this are about."

"You sound like a Billy Joel song."

He laughed at himself. "I do, don't I? Pop song psychology. I'll copyright the phrase and put it on T-shirts."

"Better give me credit as your muse."

"Deal."

Mack returned with Nick's bottle and poured another round.

"It's easy to be lonely in this city," Nick said. "People think that's impossible because it's so crowded, but the opposite is true."

That gave her an opportunity to deflect Nick's curiosity with the truth. "I was offered a coaching internship back at UK. I'd be lying to you if I said the loneliness hadn't gotten so bad at times that I considered taking it. But I can't imagine you ever being lonely, Nick."

"I could say the same for you. I've seen a million faces in my life. Few as exotic as yours. So why *are* you here?"

"A friend recommended this place."

"You were heading out of here like you were running the hundred."

"I ran the two hundred and four hundred, but you're right. I think it's me. I've never been comfortable just putting myself out there."

Nick was about to ask Callie another question when he felt arms encircling him. *Angeline.* He recognized her scent and the feel of her hands.

"Who's your new friend, Nick?"

"Callie, meet Angeline."

Calista held out her right hand. Angeline ignored it.

"If he starts discussing Kabuki with you and lets you drink his bourbon, you're in, girlfriend."

Nick broke free of Angeline's grip, took Callie by the hand. "Come on. You want to get out of here?"

Callie didn't need to be asked twice.

———

Outside it was chilly enough that they could see their breath.

"Is it all right if we walk a little?" Callie said, turning right toward the lights of the Verrazzano. The bridge dominated the night over Bay Ridge.

"I look at that bridge out my front window. Impresses me every time I see it."

"There are things and people I don't think we ever stop being impressed by." Callie crossed her arms and rubbed her hands over her biceps. "God, it's cold out here."

Nick took off his peacoat and laid it over the shoulders of her thin leather jacket. "Don't worry about me. I made an ally of the cold a long time ago."

"Thanks. Is Angeline your girlfriend?"

"Sorry about that in there. I think maybe she was a little drunk."

"No need to apologize, Nick. You didn't answer my question, though."

"We were together once. Been awkward since."

"Watch it, your honesty's showing again."

"I'll do better next time," he said, half smiling.

"Next time. There hasn't been a first time."

"I better not say anything else or my honesty might show again."

"We wouldn't want that," she said, laughing at herself. "Kabuki—what was that about?"

"McCann's is a steak restaurant, not a diner. People who go to that place know what they're there for, but like you, when they're new to the bar they don't know how to go about things. After a while, you see it's all very ritualized, like the dance of bees or Kabuki."

"You're pretty eloquent."

"For a cop, you mean."

"For anyone." About forty feet past McCann's front door, Callie turned her head to the left and stopped. She was admiring a hot rod with a glossy candy-apple-red paint job, shiny aluminum wheels, and wide rear tires. "Do you know cars?"

"That, Callie, is a '32 Ford three-window coupe that someone's put a lot of money into. The paint job alone probably cost ten grand. Thirties Fords are popular for hot rod enthusiasts, and this one's a beauty. Wish I could see under the hood to get a look at the power plant."

"How do you know so much about this stuff?"

He was about to answer when the world stopped turning. He felt the blast wave before the sound reached him.

THIRTY-ONE

When Nick opened his eyes, he was no longer vertical and his ears were ringing with a constant high-pitched whine. A few octaves below the ringing, a discordant chorus of car alarms wailed out of rhythm and off-key. He was atop Callie, who was facedown on the sidewalk. He got off her, turned her over. Felt her neck for a pulse. It was strong.

"Are you okay?" He shouted at her, though he barely heard his own voice. "Are you okay?"

Her eyes fluttered open, shock on her face. She shouted, "What happened? What was that?"

"A bomb." He got up and pulled her to her feet. "You okay?"

"Shaky, but yes."

He looked back to see that the front of McCann's had been blown out into the street, bodies and body parts mixed in amid the glass, brick, and concrete. One of the bodies was Angeline's. The force of the blast had blown off her clothes. Nick knew death when he saw it and he saw it in Angeline. He turned back to Callie.

"Run toward the bridge. There might be a second and third bomb set to go off when first responders show up."

"What about you?"

"Forget about me. I probably should be dead five times over. This is my job. Go!" He pushed her away and ran back to the bar.

———

Callie ran in spite of herself, Nick's coat still draped over her shoulders. She was digging her phone out of her front pocket as she went.

"Murray, pick up. Pick up!" she mumbled to herself.

"What?"

"Do you know McCann's on Fourth Avenue?"

"The cop hangout?"

"Someone just blew it up."

"How do you know?" There was that old reporter's excitement in his voice.

"I missed being killed by ten or twenty yards, that's how."

"Are you all right?"

"I'm talking to you."

"Come in and write it up."

"No. Can't have my name on it. I'll dictate; you write."

———

Nick stepped close to Angeline's naked body. The power of the blast had destroyed her internal organs and broken her bones, the jagged edges of her femurs jutting through the bare skin of her legs. When he looked up from her body, it was chaos: sirens in the distance, the recycling car alarms, the all-too-familiar screams of the wounded and dying, dazed men and women staggering around, the healthy pulling bodies—living and dead—out of McCann's. As always, he was the calm in the storm.

"Help the wounded out and take them as far down the block as you can. Leave the dead for now!" Nick screamed as loud as he could. "There might be more bombs. Leave the dead!"

As he ran inside, he saw Mack coming past him, a woman slung over his right shoulder. A man's brown alligator belt was tied tight around the ragged stump of her left forearm.

"Find my arm," she said over and over again. "Find my arm."

"She's in shock. Get her far away from here, fast," Nick said.

"Sadly, I know too well how this goes. There might be other devices."

Mack's demeanor and phrasing struck Nick as odd. He didn't have time to think about it.

When he was done helping drag and carry more wounded out of the bar, he grabbed one of the cops he knew, Tom Straw, a sergeant at the Six-One. "Tommy, get some of the troops and start making a sweep of the storefronts and cars parked on either side of the street."

Straw asked, "You think the bomber is watching?"

"Possibly. I saw the aftermath of some suicide bombers in Afghanistan, and I don't see the telltale signs of one in here. Doesn't mean this wasn't terrorism. There may be more bombs meant for the first responders," Nick said as brakes screeched and whirling colored lights strobed across both their faces. "Go. We don't have much time."

Nick stepped out of the bar. The entire facade was obliterated. He looked one final time at Angeline's wrecked body. She was beyond the reach of pity or apologies. Scanning the opposite side of the street, he sensed eyes on him. His instincts seldom failed him. Never when he felt he was being watched. A lean figure about five foot eight, sheathed from head to toe in matte black, emerged from the shadows. The figure in black hesitated, seeming to look directly at Nick before crossing Fourth Avenue at an angle. Moving with pantherine grace, the figure seemed to glide. Nick was transfixed. When he went to intercept the specter, there was another flash, followed by loud, rumbling thunder. As he anticipated, a second device. Nick dived for cover. To his left, the gas tank of a parked car exploded into a fireball. The car's trunk lid shot into the air, landing in the middle of the street, a twisted lump of metal.

Back on his feet, he looked all around. The specter had vanished. Pulling his off-duty piece from its ankle holster, Nick ran to the point at his right where he calculated that the figure in black had been headed. He put the Glock down at his side. The '32 Ford sped down Fourth

Avenue toward the bridge and the Belt Parkway. Left in its wake was a dissipating cloud of smoke from the coupe's rear slicks and the stench of burned rubber. If the Ford coupe's driver were the bomber, a switch car would be parked nearby.

It was wrong, all of it a contradiction. No one with half a brain—certainly not anyone this skilled with explosives and the art of distraction—would use such a ridiculously conspicuous vehicle as a candy-apple-red '32 Ford coupe to escape in. The whole point of dressing in matte black and a balaclava was to move under cover of the shadows until you could slip away without anyone noticing that you were there in the first place. Yet the bomber seemed to crave Nick's attention. The timing of the second explosion was too perfect to be coincidental. It gave the bomber just enough time to keep one step ahead of Nick. *But why?*

The answer hit him like the shock wave. It was horrifying and horrifyingly simple. Nick Ryan Jr. himself was the reason. The bomber's car, a hot rod Ford, was a subtle message written in other people's blood. *Hot = Angry. Rod = Roderick. Ford = Ford. Roderick fucking Ford!* That was why the bomb blew when Nick had gotten just far enough away from the blast zone. Ford didn't want to kill Nick. He wanted to *punish* him. Nick would never be able to prove it. Even to try, he would have to reveal what he and Lenny had gotten up to. What Ford couldn't have considered was who and what Nick had become.

There was something else, someone else—Callie. Had their meeting outside McCann's door really been coincidental, or was she part of it? She had been the one to stop at the Ford coupe and bring it to Nick's attention. Now she was gone, his coat over her shoulders. He needed to find her and it had nothing to do with retrieving his coat.

THIRTY-TWO

Nick faced Detectives Bill Dokes and Phil Baum just beyond the perimeter set up by the Bomb Disposal Unit. The scene had gone from chaos to something very different in less than an hour. The FBI and ATF were already on scene and waiting for the NYPD bomb-disposal teams, in their blast protection suits, to search the cars and stores adjoining McCann's for tertiary devices. At the center of it all was the bright white blast containment vessel in the middle of Fourth Avenue.

"All clear," a voice crackled on Dokes's handheld.

Everyone breathed a little easier, and there was a sudden burst of activity. Men and women in windbreakers emblazoned with an alphabet soup of initials and insignias swarmed over the scene.

Baum and Dokes were from the Counterterrorism Bureau. They had been over Nick's statement twice. Despite their best efforts to look unfazed, it was clear to Nick that the detectives were unnerved by the bombing. Everybody was. It was obvious this hadn't been the handiwork of some inept loner who cobbled together two pressure-cooker bombs. Nick was careful to omit mention of Roderick Ford and Callie. He had been otherwise transparent, giving full descriptions of the candy-apple-red Ford coupe and the alleged bomber. He was going over some final details when a uniform from the Six-Eight interrupted.

"Excuse me, Detectives, but they located the subject vehicle. CSU is headed over there now."

"Where?" Baum asked.

"A few blocks from here, on Shore Road between Ninety-Sixth and Ninety-Seventh Streets."

If Nick had any doubts about the bombing being tied to the tango between himself and Roderick Ford, they had just melted away. Nick's building was on Shore Road between Ninety-Sixth and Ninety-Seventh.

"Okay, thanks," Dokes said, dismissing the cop. "Phil, you finish up with Ryan here. I'll go see if we got any street cameras in the area or if any of the buildings on that block got outward-facing cameras."

Phil Baum looked at Nick sideways. "You okay, Ryan? Want me to get an EMT over here? You got some cuts on your face."

"I'm good."

"I think we got everything. I'll be in touch if we have any other questions." He shook Nick's hand. "Thanks."

The handshake was a rarity. It wasn't SOP and very few cops shook the hand of Nick Ryan Sr.'s eldest son. Nick didn't get five feet before he was stopped by Deputy Commissioner Ricco.

Ricco cupped his hand behind Nick's neck in a gesture that men understood as a kind of hug when hugging wasn't quite appropriate. He let go of Nick with a pat on his cheek. "Glad you're okay. Where were you when it happened?"

Nick pointed to a vacant parking spot. "Would you believe I was admiring the car the bomber used to escape?"

"No shit?"

"No shit. What are the casualty figures?"

Ricco bowed his head. "Five dead—three of our own and two civilians. One of them a woman. Twenty injured, three of them in critical condition. Last I heard, two were getting last rites on the bus to the hospital."

"I knew the dead woman."

"Oh, for fuck's sake. Did you know her well?"

"What does it matter?" Nick was angry but mostly at himself. "I knew her and now she's dead."

"You're right, Ryan. That was stupid of me. Sorry." Ricco shook his head. "This thing's got me, you know. We've had bombings since 9/11, but this was aimed at us, and I've seen too many dead in my time."

"I know, DC."

"I saw cell camera footage of you taking charge of the scene."

"I wouldn't put it like that."

"Doesn't matter how you would put it. I've listened to a lot of our people give their statements and to a person, they credit you with handling things. It was a terrible incident, this, but we owe you a debt for preventing it from being worse."

"For the dead, it doesn't get worse."

"Get yourself looked at—your face is cut up. How's your hearing?"

"Low hum now. I'll be fine."

"One more thing, Ryan," Ricco said, grabbing him by the forearm and quickly letting go. "You're a regular here, right?"

"You could say that."

"I hear the bartender also did good work in the aftermath of the explosion."

"Mack, yeah. Last time I saw him, he was carrying a woman out. Why?"

"We can't find him. We need his statement. The device got inside the bar somehow. Maybe he saw something."

"Shit, DC, he was inside when it blew," Nick said even as Mack's words went around in his head. *Sadly, Nick, I know too well how this goes. There might be other devices.* Mack's calmness and his mention of "devices" had gotten Nick's attention. Mack's vanishing from the scene only heightened his curiosity.

"C'mon, Ryan, you know better than that. Maybe he had a hero complex and wanted an excuse to look like a savior. You know, like those volunteer firemen who torch a place so they can rescue people from the burning building. People are willing to sacrifice themselves for all sorts of reasons. Even if we establish he's not a person of interest, he saw the comings and goings. If the bomb was planted during his shift, this Mack character might've seen the bomber's face. All we got now as a description from you and the others is that there was a slender guy between five eight and six feet tall, dressed in black."

"I only know the guy as Mack, DC. Don't have a last name or an address. He's definitely old-country Irish, but that's all I got. You need a physical description?"

He patted Nick on the shoulder. "Nah, we got some cell phone footage of him. Go ahead, get some sleep. Thanks again for taking charge. Somebody had to do it."

Nick watched Ricco dip under the tape. He turned away and walked down Fourth Avenue toward Shore Road. He had heard it said a thousand times that the only person responsible for a murder is the murderer. This was the second time in his life he was forced to reject the notion.

Lenny Feld used to joke about the differences between Catholic guilt and Jewish guilt.

"Jewish guilt is personal. Catholic guilt is institutional. It's the difference between Mom and Mother Mary."

This was no joke. There was blood on his hands, and it didn't get more personal than that.

THIRTY-THREE

CSU had cordoned off his entire block while examining the '32 Ford coupe. Nick didn't want to show up on a crime scene logbook, so he got into his building through the garage. Sooner or later, some eager detective or bored uniform would figure out that Nick Ryan lived across from where the Ford coupe had been found. Maybe not. If and when the questions got asked, he'd figure it out. Until then, he had more important things to do.

His underground garage was tomb-like. Even in daylight, it was a place of shadows and echoes. Above the constant buzz of traffic from the Belt Parkway, each step he took made a scratchy, sandpapery sound against the concrete floor. He was conscious of his own footfalls when he felt it again: eyes on him. *The bomber?* He didn't want to provoke a response by going directly to his ankle holster. Instead, Nick feigned tripping over a crack in the floor, giving him an excuse to kneel.

"No need for the pantomime, Ryan," Mack's voice resounded in the garage. "For fook's sake, boyo, I've been pouring drinks for the likes of you and your kind for years. I know where off-duty pieces are kept. You lot are as transparent as cling film."

"Cling film?"

"Plastic wrap."

Nick nodded. "Do me a favor, Mack. Tone down the they're-always-after-me-Lucky-Charms routine for me. No need for the 'boyo' or 'lad.'"

Mack stepped out from behind a pillar. "Fair play to you."

"The best bartenders often have a touch of the performer in them, but I always sensed it was more than a show with you." Nick's voice took a turn. "Time for a different kind of show. Show me your hands."

"You've nothing to fear from me, Nick Ryan," Mack said, waving his empty hands. "You were the bright one of the lot, the one in the crowd I worried about. Maybe I did put it on a touch too thick."

"I figured you had your reasons."

"That I do. A feckin' legion of 'em."

"They're looking for you, Mack, but you already figured that out or you wouldn't be here."

Mack twisted up his face in confusion. "You were one of them, last I checked."

Nick ignored that. "How do you know where I live?"

Mack smiled his glad-handing-lovable-son-of-the-old-sod smile. "Come, now, Ryan. Think about the number of women you've had up to your flat who've cried in their beer to me over you."

"You're a good listener."

"The best—trained to be. But that's not how I knew. Do you not remember the night when you returned home from Afghanistan and got legless drunk in the bar? Your little brother and me had to carry your arse up to your flat?"

"My memory of that night is a little vague."

"No surprise there."

"You're not here to reminisce."

"I'm here to ask your help."

"First, assume the position." Nick was all business, pulling his Glock. "Then, we'll talk."

"I don't suppose me swearing on me dead relatives that I had nothing to do with the bombing will speed the process along."

"On your knees facing the other way, hands behind your head."

Mack did as he was told. But as Nick patted him down, Mack said, "You should have cuffed me. Never get in this close without backup."

"Why's that?"

Mack sprang to his feet, swiped at the gun, barely missing it, and had Nick's free hand in a thumb lock. Nick pressed the gun muzzle hard into the flesh of Mack's neck.

"Break my thumb, go ahead, but it's the last thing you'll ever do."

Mack released the thumb lock and dropped back to his knees, hands above his head. "You asked why, Ryan. That's why. Five years ago, had you tried that, I'd be holding the Glock and you'd already be stone dead."

"Five years ago, I didn't know you."

"You don't know me now."

"Guess not. And for the record, five years ago, I would have been five years faster too."

"Can't argue that. Now, can we go to your flat and talk? I like chatting in a car park as much as the next fella, but this is no place for me to say what I have to say."

———

Before opening his apartment door, Nick put his forefinger across his lips. Mack nodded. Inside Nick went directly to an innocuous piece of electronic equipment that looked like a modem. He clicked it on and waited for a panel of lights to go from solid red to flickering green. With the green lights flickering, he waved Mack in.

"A frequency jammer. Very cute indeed. But why would an NYPD detective have need of such a thing?"

"And how would a big-bellied Irish barman even know what it is?"

"I was never much for dancing, Ryan, so can you give me a drink and let's stop the pas de deux? Neither of us, it would seem, is what the world thinks we are."

"Scotch okay?" Nick asked, walking over to the shelf where he kept his liquor. He held up the bottle he had served Shana from.

"Laphroaig, yeah, that'll do me nicely. What's that shite you're pouring for yourself?"

"Weller. Not Pappy's, but good stuff."

Nick waited for Mack to drink. "Okay, talk."

"You could say I'm a wanted man."

"I guessed as much," Nick said. "I saw your face back there when you were carrying the woman out. I know resignation when I see it. I heard the words you spoke and the ones that went unspoken. This wasn't your first experience with bombings."

"Far from it." Mack finished his scotch and held his glass out for a refill. "I'm not proud of it, but I've planted a few me own self, nor was it lost on me that the device went off only seconds after you left."

"Coincidence." Nick shrugged.

"Ya think so? I, for one, don't."

Nick took a sip of his bourbon and poured Mack another single malt. He changed subjects. "What are you, sixty?"

"Sixty-three."

"Given your age, your skill level, and your accent . . . are you IRA?"

Mack shook his head. "Try again."

"UDA?"

"You know the Ulster Defence Association? I'm impressed. Most Americans only know the Catholic side of the Troubles."

"Thanks for the compliment, but you didn't answer the question."

"Not the UDA, no."

"At least tell me I'm in the right theater of war, because if you're a mercenary and worked for al-Qaeda, ISIS, or—"

"I'd never work for them murderous fookers, Ryan. You had it right. Just had the wrong team, is all."

"The Brits!"

"Took you a while, but you got there."

"Military?"

"Intelligence."

"MI5, MI6?"

"Neither." Mack took his second scotch in a gulp. "One of those departments that has neither a name nor a number. Our cover was so deep, not even the other services had any notion we existed. The kind of operation that gave Her Majesty's government plausible deniability. We did some dirty things, Ryan. Nasty shite to both sides—keeps a man up at night, no matter how hard he tries to drink himself to bed."

"But someone knows or you wouldn't be here."

"After the Good Friday Agreement had held for several years, people from my team began dying at an alarming rate. Oh, you know, nothing suspicious on its face. A motorway crash outside London. A helicopter going down in the Scottish Highlands." Mack put down his glass and took the bottle of Laphroaig off the shelf. Took a swig. "Two suicides. A jewelry store robbery during which only a patron was killed. They didn't train me to be a fool."

"You got out."

"That I'm standing here before you drinking your single malt out of the bottle is proof of that."

"It can't be that simple." Nick rubbed his chin. "In the States, New York or Boston would be the first places they would come looking."

"True, but they don't generally search for dead men."

"Faked your own death before they could arrange for the real thing."

"In Morocco, a single-engine plane crash outside Marrakesh. Pilot lived, but his passenger didn't make it." Mack couldn't help but smile at his handiwork. The smile vanished as quickly as it came.

"Can't fake a death without a body," Nick said. "No body, and they wouldn't be convinced."

"Bit of a tough go."

"Tough go?"

"Wet job. Didn't overdo it with the proof. Sure sign of fakery, giving too much evidence." Mack slipped out of his right shoe and took off his sock. The outside third of his foot was completely gone, and the healed wound wasn't a pretty thing to look at. "Hacked it off me own self. Hurt like a bastard. Left them a little charred flesh and bone, but forensically testable. Half-burned passports, real and forged, the pilot's eyewitness testimony. I also had someone on the inside who was apt to back the story. In the end, they bought it."

"Who did you kill to take your place?"

"A drug-smuggling shite, but I'm not sure he deserved it. Last bit of the dirty work I'd done. It was buttoned up tight until tonight. Tell me, Ryan, is my face on mobile phone video?"

"You know it is."

"I'm fucked."

"And what makes you think I can help you—or that I would?"

"Truth?"

"Might as well."

"I possess an instinct for survival and I've a sense about you. Let's say that your frequency jammer, among other things, confirms it."

"Other things?"

"There isn't another man or woman comes into McCann's could have stopped me from relieving them of their weapon. You're a different sort of beast, Ryan. If I didn't know better, I'd say you were one of us."

"No need to insult me."

Mack laughed. "You might take it that way or you might take it as a compliment."

"Here we are again with an unanswered question."

"I don't know that you *can* help me, but if there's anyone I've met who might, it's you."

"*Why* should I help you is the big question."

Mack sat down on Nick's couch, put the Laphroaig on the coffee table, and stared out the window at the bridge. "Maybe you shouldn't. Fact is, I've blood on me hands, innocent blood. I'm not talking about the shite I killed in Morocco. I'm talking men and women who, like this evening, were down at the boozer for a jar of the black stuff. Men and women who were no more political than this bottle here." Mack spun the green bottle on the glass tabletop. "People out for a moment of relief in their sad lives, who were in the wrong place at precisely the wrong time. People who became statistics to be broadcast on the telly.

"There were times it was me who planted the device, but more times,

I was the observer. The man on hand to assess the damage. Many were the instances I sat in a motor across the way, waiting, watching folks coming in and out of the pub or café. Some laughing. Some legless drunk. At first, I would play a game with meself, betting on who would be the fortunate ones and who would be the poor unlucky bastards. That game got old fast, Ryan. Very old, very fast."

Nick came and stood in front of Mack. "I'm not hearing an answer."

"I thought getting out, saving my own skin, was enough. That I could shut it away and forget as easily as I could push aside an errant pass on the football pitch when I was a wee lad. There were times here when I was tending bar I almost made myself believe it. But the bad dreams never left me, Ryan. There is no turning my back on the things I've done and witnessed. Tonight sealed it for me."

"Sealed what?"

"I need a chance at . . . well, if not redemption, something akin to adding back to the world and evening the account a bit. I have the skills."

Nick thought about it. Mack's tale sounded reasonable enough, but the man was a clever liar, a killer by training and trade. One of Nick's talents was recognizing the skills he himself possessed and those he did not. And with his new job, a man of Mack's experience could be of tremendous use. Nick didn't say another word. He left the room and returned with a yellow legal pad and pen.

"Full statement about tonight from the start of your shift until you showed up in my garage, Mack—that isn't actually your name, is it?"

"No, but it fit the image." He didn't offer his real name.

"When I get out of the shower, we'll go over it. I might be able to help you, but it won't be a one-way street."

"Never is, boyo. Never is." Mack held up his palms. "Sorry for the 'boyo' crap, Ryan. I've been Mack for so long, I'm not sure where I stop and he begins."

Nick put the pad and pen on the coffee table. "Everything. I know you're a skilled liar, but lie to me and we're done. Understood?"

"Understood."

"Get to work. The page is still empty."

THIRTY-FOUR

Calista Barrows was freaked. She had covered many horrible events, some far deadlier than the bombing at McCann's. Conspiracies of carelessly placed candles and cheap drapes, or faulty kerosene heaters. Midwinter fires in subzero temperatures that erased entire families, their burned bodies laid out on sidewalks, encased in thin ice cocoons from fire hose nozzle mist. She reported on tragedies but had never been part of one. She had a new appreciation for the cruelty of becoming a statistic. For every dead or wounded, there was a story and a life that readers would never know.

She had gotten into the shower, letting the hot water pour over her until it turned cold. The chill would not leave her. The smells of burning gas and flesh and hair, the taste of hot metal in the back of her throat, the bruises from the blast, the ringing in her ears, the searing heat . . . There wasn't enough soap in the world to wash all that away. Worst were the things she could not unsee. Mangled body parts in the street, like the arms and legs off broken dolls; the panic on the faces of the living; and the neutrality on the faces of the dead. She rubbed her eyes hard, trying to erase the memory of Angeline's face.

She tried organizing her thoughts. She was a good journalist and had done a professional job dictating the story of the blast and its aftermath to Murray. Done it without losing her composure. She had taken the first photos to hit the newswires. Murray assured her there would be money in that for her. She demanded he take the photo credit. What she was sorting through at the moment was new to her. She was reversing the familiar process of stepping outside the incident she was covering and placing herself back inside the story as a human being. Walls were crucial for a journalist—the only way to maintain objectivity. Callie had met several journalists, as well as camera operators, who had been frontline war correspondents. Until last night's bombing, she hadn't ever appreciated their paradoxical detachment and exhilaration. It was one thing to credit oneself with surviving the grind of daily living. It was something else to survive an attempt on one's life. She went to bed still feeling cold inside, a little guilty too, yet flush with excitement.

———

An hour before sunrise the next morning, cup of coffee in hand, she went over things in her head. She could not get past the timing of the events at McCann's. She had woken up thinking about it—how close she had come to dying. Had the bomb gone off thirty seconds earlier, Nick and she would likely have been killed, their limbs scattered about Fourth Avenue amid the debris.

She put the coffee down, went to her desktop, and opened the photos she'd taken of the scene. Callie noticed details that had been too small to see on her phone screen. Things she was blind to as she held herself together, fighting off the aftereffects of the bomb. With the photos enlarged, she saw the roughly triangular pattern of the blast. How she and Nick had been just at the edge of the blast-zone debris. It dawned on her that in a post-9/11 world, no one was completely naive about suicide vests, IEDs, backpack bombs, shoe bombs, underwear bombs. It was a sad commentary on modern life. She wondered if her survival was a simple matter of good fortune.

She scrolled through photos over and over, sensing she was missing something obvious. But how can you know what you're *not* seeing? That was her rational brain speaking to her. Her experience as an athlete had schooled her to trust the things that existed at the outer limits of her senses. She knew that the universe was a trickster, operating by its own rules independent of us.

Callie was distracted, barely conscious of the photos on the monitor, thinking about Murray's constant lecturing, when she saw it: a figure in black. She watched it move, frame by frame, across Fourth Avenue. Then, the fireball from the second explosion obscured almost everything else in the photos. There was something else she'd missed—someone else: Nick Ryan. She went back and clicked through the photos one shot at a time. As the figure in black moved from one side of Fourth Avenue, Nick moved from the other.

Though she didn't understand it, she felt it in her bones that Nick Ryan was, in one way or another, at the center of it all. As a journalist, Calista Barrows was more skeptical than most about coincidence. It was an occupational hazard she guarded against, making sure not to dismiss coincidence out of hand. Still, she could not make herself accept that Nick Ryan's presence at the Scarborough Houses on the night of the stairwell murders, *and* at McCann's on the night of the bombing, were matters of sad serendipity. Nick Ryan was the common piece of both puzzles.

She was determined to find answers to the growing list of questions in her head. Before she left, Callie grabbed Nick's coat, held it up close to her face. She smelled the faint ghost of his cologne on it and confessed to herself that there was more to her mission than journalistic curiosity. She had fallen down rabbit holes before, but this time she was eagerly jumping in of her own accord.

THIRTY-FIVE

They met on the Coney Island pier. Rebuilt of concrete and steel after Superstorm Sandy, it jutted out at right angles from the boardwalk into the Atlantic, like a middle finger. The Parachute Jump stood a few hundred yards behind them, the top of its orange metal skeleton amputated by roiling black clouds. The chilly and damp promise of the previous evening had been fulfilled, the wind whipping needles of cold ocean mist into their faces.

Joe wore a beige trench coat and an Irish shepherd's cap of gray wool. He kept grabbing the cap with his right hand to prevent its abduction by the wind. He held a thick vinyl binder pressed tight between his left arm and his ribs. Eyes red and puffy, his white side hair disheveled, he looked as though he hadn't gotten much sleep. Even his tan seemed to have faded. The lack of sleep made them equals, since Nick had been up all night debriefing Mack about the explosion at McCann's and going over every detail of his written statement.

Nick shook Joe's hand. "Bombing keep you up all night?"

"It did," Joe said. "I heard you probably saved some lives. Pretty heroic stuff."

This was razor's-edge territory for Nick. He had summoned the man here to talk about a matter related to the bombing. He had no intention of discussing his theory about who was behind the bombing or why. Like Mack, Nick had a knack for self-preservation. He realized that if he proved to be more trouble than he was worth to his new employers, he was as expendable as Ricky Corliss. As Joe had repeated several times during their meeting in the tire shop, they had plenty of killers at their disposal.

"Heroes are just men and women doing their jobs, is all. Calling people 'heroes' makes survivors feel less like cowards. They shouldn't feel like that, but I can't change human nature."

"There's something you *can't* do?"

"Funny man, Joe."

"Unfortunately, there will be a medal and citation for your actions last night."

"No, thanks. You guys don't want the spotlight on me. *I* want it on me even less."

Joe smiled. "God, you are a smart motherfucker, Ryan. You really are. Why did you choose to be a cop?"

"All I ever wanted to be."

"A shame."

"Not for me."

"We'll see about that after your next assignment. But discussing the human need for heroes isn't why you got me here."

Nick took an envelope out of his coat pocket and handed it to Joe. "Last night Mack, the bartender from McCann's, disappeared. That's his full statement. You have my word he wasn't involved in the bombing."

Joe slipped the envelope into his trench coat pocket. "Your word."

"My word."

"Why didn't this Mack fellow give it to the detectives on the scene?"

"You're too clever to play dumb."

"He's wanted."

"Not by us and not for a crime. I won't say more than that."

"What's your interest in him? Never mind that." Joe waved his hand dismissively. "More importantly, what's *my* interest?"

"He'll be an asset."

"For . . ."

"Us. I need someone to watch my back. No offense, but I don't trust you or our employers. I don't want Ace or anyone from your private goon squad anywhere near me when I'm working. You may think they're anonymous, but they're not."

"I'll see what I can do."

"Not good enough, Joe. You promised me I could have whatever I needed and I need this guy. He's got the training, the skills, and the judgment."

Joe asked the inevitable. "Where is this mystery man?"

"No clue," Nick lied. "He said he'd be in touch soon."

Joe accepted that answer. "Okay, Nick, give me the particulars."

He detailed them and each one of Nick's demands about Mack etched the frown on Joe's face that much deeper. As unhappy as he seemed, Joe didn't raise any objections to Nick's terms. "But there are some limitations to what I can do. You realize the FBI and ATF will want to debrief him. There's nothing I can do about that."

"Tell the feds he's a crucial CI on a local terrorism investigation and that exposing his face to the public will be a blow not only to the city's security interests but to the national interest as well. You tell them that and I can probably arrange some sort of phone meeting, but the cell phone footage of him cannot see the light of day."

"As far as the NYPD is concerned, I can make that happen. I'll let you know about the feds as soon as I can."

But instead of turning and walking into the mist, Joe lingered.

"I didn't figure you came just because I called." Nick pointed at the binder under Joe's arm. "That for me?"

"Who else?"

"It wasn't lost on me that you were surreptitious when we met at Citi Field," Nick said. "Full of implications and hidden messages."

"It was a little bit of grandstanding on my part. No pun intended. I wanted to see if I could impress you."

"I was more impressed by Totonno's pizza."

Joe held out the binder to Nick but didn't hand it to him. "Do you recall, when we met in the Bronx, my mentioning that we knew things about you—some you yourself weren't even aware of?"

"You know I do."

"Keep in mind as you read through it, your brother's future is tied to the outcome."

"What's Sean got to do with this?"

Joe gave the binder to Nick without answering his question.

Nick undid the clasp and removed the file inside. He got a sick feeling at the name on the tab. *Aaron Lister.* "I remember this file too. You guys and the feds have had Lister for months and haven't gotten word one from him. What do you expect me to do? You're kidding me, right?"

Joe smiled that icy smile of his. "Do I strike you as a kidding sort of fellow?"

"I don't know. Give you a violin, teach you a few one-liners, and you could do a Henny Youngman tribute act."

"Take Aaron Lister . . . please."

"Your comedic timing is shit."

"Unlike you, Nick, I possess few talents. As a partial answer to your earlier question, our employers have always found that people in your position try just a little bit harder when something personal is at stake."

"Something personal?"

"Your brother is broke, drinking again, and his wife has already consulted a divorce lawyer. Sean is one false step away from losing his career. Now, I could have reminded you about all the folks in the local police unions who have lost their shirts to Lister," Joe said, looking out at the Atlantic. "But I get the sense that saving your brother's ass matters more to you. Find out where Lister hid those funds and Sean's financial difficulties will disappear. We'll send him to a top-notch rehab facility on our dime and make sure his next few disciplinary hearings go away. As for the divorce . . ." He shrugged. "He's on his own."

"Always the carrot and stick with you, Joe. Maybe 'Satan' was the better name for you."

"Maybe."

"Don't call me smart one minute and treat me like a schmuck the next." Nick snapped the binder shut. "You don't care about my brother or all the cops' broken dreams. Someone wants to claim an election-year victory. Someone who can say, 'Look what I did for you. I'm really on your side.'"

"I'm an errand boy. Like you, I don't get to choose the assignments. That's the deal we've both made. And, Nick, a word of advice because, believe it or not, I like and admire you. Don't be *too* smart. Be just smart enough. Remember, you get the money out of Lister any way you want. You'll get whatever resources you need to facilitate that result, but get it. I'll be in touch soon."

"How soon?"

Joe smiled at Nick. "Don't make any plans for after the weekend."

THIRTY-SIX

Mack was on the floor of the GTO's backseat, under a blanket. Nick sat behind the wheel, pretending to talk on his cell phone. He used this charade many times during his undercover work. Having Mack along was a test for them both. Nick knew that Mack possessed the martial arts skills. This was something else—a chance to see how they worked as a team.

"Was I clean?" Nick asked, eyes straight ahead.

"Not at all. Two minders. One African American man with a face that's failed to duck too many left hooks."

"Ace."

"Well, Ace was watching you through Steiner M2080s from a bench on the boardwalk."

"Was he listening to my conversation?"

"He wasn't privy to the conversation, no. Can we move this along or get back to your flat? This hump in the floor is wrecking all the fine efforts of me chiropractor."

Nick wasn't reassured. "How do you know he wasn't listening?"

"You mean other than his having no earpiece with which to listen?"

"Other than that, yeah."

"Body language. He was watching, not listening."

"Like how someone watching me now would be sure I wasn't talking to someone on the floor of my backseat?"

"Point taken, Ryan," Mack admitted. "My professional assessment is, he wasn't listening."

"And the other?"

"A larger man. White, about six foot three. On a rock jetty east of you, also with Steiners. No earpiece."

"Get used to these guys. The man I met with travels with an interchangeable group of them. Ace is the special one, the dangerous one. As a heads-up, he carries a Colt Python."

"A Python, eh? Silly weapon, that, but it does make an impression. Now, can we get moving along and get some heat blasting?"

Nick stopped pretending to talk on the phone and dropped the cell on top of the vinyl binder, turned the ignition key, and put the GTO into first.

"You want to share a bit more about this mysterious fella you met with and his coterie?" Mack shouted over the engine rumble.

"All you have to know is that he might be able to save your ass and let me give you a job."

"And what's your professional assessment on that front, Ryan?"

"You may have to do a debriefing from the feds about last night, but the footage of your pretty face is likely to vanish."

Mack's silence indicated he wasn't pleased about the debriefing but knew better than to argue with the man who held the key to his fate.

Nick got back to the subject. "Was there anyone else? Anyone suspicious on the boardwalk? Anyone taking a keen interest in my meeting?"

"I saw a runner, a woman. Runners are maniacs. No matter the weather, they're out there. She was the only one."

"Describe her."

"Tall, maybe five foot eight to six foot, lithe and athletic, leg muscles rippling through the polyspandex."

"Her face?"

"What about it?"

"Was it the woman I was with at McCann's last night?" Nick fought the urge to look behind him.

"The exotic looker, Callie? Couldn't tell. The runner had a hood covering her head and a neoprene face mask against the chill. Why do you ask?"

Now it was Nick who fell momentarily silent. Suddenly, there was a new factor to be considered: Callie. He didn't think she was involved in the bombing, but a good detective didn't ignore possibilities. She didn't fit in at McCann's. It was Callie who had broached the subject of race. *Shit!* Even if she had nothing to do with the bombing, something about her being there wasn't coincidental. He needed to find out who she really was.

In the far left lane, only a few hundred feet from the Fourteenth Avenue/Bay Eighth Street exit on the Belt Parkway, Nick said, "Change of plans, Mack. You'll be down there a little longer than anticipated. Hold on tight."

"What the fuck are you—"

Mack couldn't finish his sentence. Nick downshifted, taking the GTO from seventy to thirty, swerving in front of an oncoming black Escalade in the center lane that came within millimeters of swiping the Pontiac's ass end. He cut off a silver Hyundai Tucson in the right lane that was aimed squarely at the GTO's passenger door. The Hyundai missed him by less room than the Escalade. The old Pontiac thumped across the broad white lines of the exit triangle, fishtailing as Nick revved the engine and shifted up through the gears. He quickly got the car up to a hundred along Shore Parkway, nearly losing control as he turned hard right onto Bay Eighth.

He didn't think he was being followed, but even if he had been, no one could have kept up with him after that maneuver. Running on fumes from lack of sleep, he was now pumped with adrenaline and questions about Callie. He didn't have a lot of time to figure things out, so he was headed to see the one person he was sure could help.

"Mack, when I park, I'll leave the keys in the ignition. Go back to my apartment and keep your head down. I'll find my way home later."

THIRTY-SEVEN

Lenny Feld was no happier to see Nick than he had been the last time. Joy was no longer a piece of his emotional vocabulary. His disfigured face was expressive in a way that unscarred faces could never be. Somehow, Nick didn't think Lenny saw that as a gift.

"Come in," Lenny said in a voice devoid of emotion.

Nick made sure the synagogue basement door slammed shut behind him. They did the long walk as they always did, Nick following Lenny down the dark hallway to his pitiable room.

"So . . ." Lenny gestured for Nick to enter first. "You shook the wasps' nest with those videos and someone else got stung. I warned you what might happen."

"The bombing?"

"What else? A man like Roderick Ford, a coward beneath the bravado—he can never stand to be seen as losing. He worries that the people who surround him will see him for the weakling he is." Lenny waved a finger stump. "But what he is actually afraid of is seeing it in himself, admitting to *himself* what he is."

"How can you know it was him?"

Lenny shrugged. "Knowing it and proving it—not synonymous,

are they? Maybe he had one of his proxies do it. Maybe it wasn't him at all and I just need a boogie man to sleep under my bed at night to keep me alive. What I know is that in the magazine, I tweaked Ford's nose about some of his crazy conspiracies, and I lost my family. Tea?"

"Sure. The woman who was killed in the bombing . . ." The words stuck in Nick's throat. "Angeline Norton. I knew her."

"I'm sorry, Nick." Lenny fussed with the water. "I didn't mean to scold."

"Yes, you did. It's okay. I slept with her once."

"No crime in that."

"I feel like I used her."

"Did you?" Lenny turned to look at Nick. "How so?"

"I was on the verge of doing something that might've forced me to sacrifice most of my life as I know it. I wanted the comfort of a woman. If it hadn't been Angeline, it might've been anyone."

"Should I ask what you were meaning to do?"

Nick shook his head.

"People use each other to salve their wounds all the time. Did you ask Angeline why she went home with you that night? Did she seem unhappy or displeased? Did you profess love for her?"

"No. No. And no."

"There you are."

"Leaves me kind of empty feeling, though."

"I am well acquainted with emptiness, Nick. I am sorry for her loss, but you didn't kill her."

"She was mad at me when she died. Jealous. I don't like that she died feeling that way."

Lenny went back to making the tea. "Jealous? Why jealous?"

"I was with someone else last night at the bar. The other woman— she's one of the reasons I came to see you."

"I am the last person on earth you should speak to about such things." Lenny poured steaming water out of the kettle into two mugs. "I only ever loved one woman. She was the one woman I ever slept with. I will die with those two things being true."

"I wish I had known your wife."

"Known? How can you know someone else? That was one of the mysteries of my love for her. It wasn't so much knowing her as every day getting more hints at who she was beneath the mask she showed the world."

"Mask?"

"Come now, Nick, you more than anyone understand the difference between who we are inside and what we show the world we are. With Esther, I loved the mask and loved each bit of the woman she revealed beneath it."

"That's not why I came to you."

Lenny handed Nick his mug. "Careful, it's hot."

"Thanks, Mom." Nick sipped the Earl Grey. Only then did he realize how the chill of the pier hadn't quite left him. "I needed this."

"What else do you need?"

"The other woman from last night. Not Angeline."

"Yes."

"Callie."

"Spelled?"

"Good question. C-a-l-l-i-e, but that's a guess, and I have no clue if that's short for something or it's the whole ticket."

Lenny didn't need to scribble things down. His retention was remarkable. "What about her?"

"Anything at all. I don't think she was connected to the bombing, but something about her being there doesn't seem kosher."

Nick spent the next ten minutes describing his meeting with Callie, detailing how they bumped into each other, her physical description, the biographical details—true or not—that she revealed about herself.

Lenny asked, "Are you finished?"

"That's all there is to tell."

"Did you believe she was sincere when she told you these things?"

"She was hiding something."

"And this Callie—she was the one who brought the Ford coupe to your attention?"

"Yep."

"I understand both your suspicions and your doubts about her involvement."

Nick said, "I need you to do a deep dive on her."

Most people would have moaned about having so little to work with, but Lenny thrived on the challenges Nick presented to him, even though he acted as if they were burdens. He lived for them because he had little else to live for but the day of reckoning.

"Easy enough to research University of Kentucky track team history to begin with and go from there."

Nick said, "There's one other thing."

"Always is. What?"

Nick placed the binder on Lenny's workbench.

"Aaron Lister!"

"I'm sure that file is pretty extensive. I'll wait while you scan it."

Lenny gave Nick a skeptical look. "If it's extensive, what do you want from me?"

"I want you to find what isn't there. The way you do. The things others ignore or dismiss."

"Anything else while I'm at it? Shall I prove a negative or build you a small nuclear device?"

"The stuff on Lister is more urgent."

Lenny smiled in spite of himself. "Okay, let me start scanning."

"Once I get the stuff from you on Lister, I'll be out of touch for a few weeks," Nick said, placing his empty mug on the bare floor.

"Undercover work again?"

"Something like that."

"Mysterious."

"Why women love me."

"They love you because you're a handsome bastard, smart, and dangerous. I have never quite understood the attraction of danger."

"It's only attractive until you've experienced it."

"And this information about the woman—what do I do with it until you reappear from your assignment?"

"I'll be in touch when I need it."

"More mystery?"

"Thanks for the tea and the help, Lenny."

Lenny held Nick in his gaze, seeming to freeze him in place.

"What?"

"Something is different, Nick. You have changed."

"It's the bombing."

"It's more than that. I felt it the last time you were here too. Before, when you came for my help, it was as if the stakes were smaller. You were fighting skirmishes."

"And now, what?"

"You are back at war."

"Maybe."

Lenny stepped close and hugged him. "Remember, Nick, the casualties of war are different. I don't need to tell you."

"But you're telling me anyway."

"You're my only friend. I can't afford to lose you."

"I'm not going anywhere."

"Says the man who was nearly bombed to death less than twenty-four hours ago."

Nick gently pushed Lenny back to arm's length, then patted his scarred face. "That's right, Lenny. Says he."

———

Calista Barrows sat across from Murray Kleinman in the paper's laughable offices. It was in the wake of events like the McCann's bombing that his heart broke over the plight of newspapers. At the moment, he was more concerned about Callie. He could see she was shaken. He understood in his marrow the difference between covering the aftermath of violence and being a victim of the violence.

The kettle whistled. Murray stood up, fixed two instant coffees, and brought them over to where Calista sat motionless. She was in it now, deep inside her own head and a thousand miles away.

"Here, kid, drink this."

She took the cup without looking at it, put it to her lips, and sipped. The coffee did the trick. "God, Murray, this stuff is horrible. How did you ever drink this crap?"

He smiled and patted her cheek as if she were his daughter. "You think this is bad, you should have tasted coffee when we used to percolate the hell out of it. Came out of the pot black as ink and thick as molasses. Gives me the chills just thinking about it."

She laughed but didn't know why. "I have to tell you something, Murray."

"No, you don't. I understand."

She sipped more coffee. "I have to."

"I'm listening."

"I was in the bar last night because the detective I saw the night of the murders at the Scarborough Houses was at the funeral of Chief Joon's kid."

"Okay, you were following up. I get it. You smelled a story and you went for it even though I warned you off. If I hadn't done that kind of thing, that Pulitzer wouldn't have been mine."

"I didn't go as a journalist."

That got Murray's attention. "Now, I think you better explain that to me."

"I didn't tell him I was a reporter."

He shrugged. "If we announced who we are all the time, we'd never get a story. Journalists have to do a little undercover work sometimes too."

"No, Murray, it's not that. I kind of let him hit on me at the bar. I wanted him to. I would have slept with him. I wanted to."

He threw her a lifeline. "But you didn't."

"The bomb saw to that. Here's the really screwed up part of it. The woman killed in the bombing, Angeline Norton . . ." Calista fell apart. She put her head in her hands and sobbed. Gathering herself, she said, "The detective, Nick Ryan, knew her and had been intimate with her."

"And . . ."

"Instead of feeling sympathy for the dead woman, I was jealous."

She shrank back, bracing for Murray's reaction. "I'm a horrible journalist and an even worse person."

"Listen, kiddo, lying to Ryan about who you were and what you wanted—we need to talk about that sometime soon. But this other thing, the thing about the dead woman—that's different. Being a journalist doesn't mean you don't get to have human feelings. A journalist without them is worthless. What it means is, you have to ignore them if they get in the way of the story that needs exposing."

"Thank you for saying that."

"Don't thank me, because you're suspended. I can't have you working for this paper in the state you're in. Even this pathetic, unimportant little paper has to stand for something."

She put the coffee down. "I understand. Will you be all right? Can you handle stuff on your own?"

"You should have thought about that before you walked into McCann's. Last piece of advice?"

"I'm listening."

"Go chase it down—the cop or the story, but not both. Get past this or you'll be worthless to me and to yourself."

She left without another word, still convinced that Nick Ryan was somehow at the center of it all.

THIRTY-EIGHT

Nick knew the secret. That people liked to think life was classical music, carefully orchestrated with God waving the baton from the podium. It was how they made themselves get out of bed in the morning. Nick knew better. Life was jazz, an improvisation. He had to be ready to play along with, or in counterpoint to, whatever was thrown his way in the moment. Nick lived jazz but never listened to it. He mostly hated it. He had a weakness for punk rock's three-chords-played-badly attitude. *Attitude was everything.*

By the time he walked through the lobby door of the beige brick high-rise at the ass end of Coney Island, Nick was 90 percent attitude. He didn't get three strides toward the elevator before he was scoped out by a shorty working lookout. Ten years old, his brown face mottled with patches of white, the kid's eyes were already old, wary, and disappointed. The vitiligo lent the kid an otherworldly quality, but it was those eyes that gave Nick pause. The shorty disappeared around a corner and was no doubt signaling upstairs that Twelve was on site. *Twelve. One-Eight-Seven. Coast Guard. Jake. Blue Mafia.* There were a hundred names that all meant "cop." Since he had now lost the element of surprise, Nick hung his shield around his neck to keep civilians away.

Waiting for the elevator, he scanned the lobby. Unlike at the Scarborough Houses, the doors and walls were tag free. There was a reason for that. This building was a wholly owned subsidiary of the Surf Avenue Posse. No one who valued his life would be stupid enough to tag it with a rival gang's signature. When the elevator doors opened, Nick had his hands at chest level, palms facing out. The elevator car was empty, but he was being watched. While he had no doubt the housing authority and/ or NYPD Viper Room camera was disabled, he was sure the SAP had set up their own camera, which no one would be willing to fuck with.

Once the doors closed and he pressed the button to the top floor, Nick laid his nine and his backup piece on the elevator floor. He placed his hawkbill folding knife and phone on the floor next to his guns. Where he was headed, he needed protection and allies that didn't look, smell, or act like cops. Aaron Lister hadn't stolen a billion dollars by being a fool. For this plan to work, Nick needed Lister off his guard. Nick didn't flatter himself that he was magic. Nick understood that he was the means of last resort, the guy they came to when the begging, cajoling, plea bargains, and threats had failed. Nick wasn't surprised that Lister had refused to budge. Lister had grown up with nothing. For him, it wasn't about the money per se, but about what the money represented. Revenge.

The elevator shuddered and squealed to a stop. The first thing Nick saw when the doors parted was the center black hole on the sound suppressor attached to the barrel of an MP7. The submachine gun looked like a Christmas toy in the huge hands of the man pointing it at him. The man stood six foot seven and weighed around three hundred pounds, only a tiny percentage of it fat. His head was razored clean and covered in an array of tattoos. The four five-pointed stars cascading like tears down from his left eye indicated he had killed four times. His eyes lacked any hint of humanity. They might as well have been transplanted from a shark.

Shark Eyes used his foot to sweep Nick's guns, knife, and phone into the hallway. He stared at the blue-enamel-and-gold shield and spat on the floor.

Shark Eyes said, "Press *L*, motherfucka, and step out."

Nick did as he was told. As he stepped out of the elevator, the big man grabbed him, pinning him to the wall. Nick felt the suppressor muzzle digging into his ribs as the elevator doors shut beside him. There would be no turning back.

Another man, smaller and more agile but no less menacing, appeared out of an apartment door to their left. Shark Eyes backed far enough off to let the new guy pat Nick down. When he was satisfied Nick was clean and wasn't wearing a wire, he stepped back.

"You ain't got no business here."

He was a light-skinned Black man dressed in a loose-fitting black tank top, baggy jeans, and a two-hundred-dollar pair of retro Nikes. He wore a tightly wound red bandanna across his forehead. He had a sinewy upper body that was something out of *Gray's Anatomy.* He was a killer too, according to the red stars inked into his cheek. His tats also marked him as a member of the Surf Avenue Posse. The SAP was with the United Blood Nation, East Coast affiliates of the Bloods. They made most of their money with drugs and extortion. They used the top floor of this building as their headquarters. They did their processing and packaging off campus.

Nick didn't react. All he said was, "I'm here to see Skinny Mo."

Gray's Anatomy tugged hard on the chain holding Nick's shield, snapping it. "You think this shit here get you a pass?" He handed the shield to Nick. "Get the fuck out!"

Nick pocketed his shield. "Just tell Skinny Mo Nick Ryan is here to see him about Ahmed."

Both Shark Eyes and Gray's Anatomy tried to look unfazed, but it was obvious they had to force themselves not to react.

Gray's Anatomy said, "Keep this motherfucka company." He turned on his heel and glided down the hall, disappearing behind a heavily reinforced steel door.

A long two minutes later, he reemerged, curling his finger at Nick. "C'mon, now."

Nick walked to the door, stepped inside. Gray's Anatomy stepped out and slammed the door shut at Nick's back. Nick stood inside what had once been somebody's living room but was now empty of anything except a huge wall-mounted flat-screen, several gaming consoles and controllers, and a cream-colored leather couch. Two other members of the crew stood guard where the living room fed into the hallway. One held an AR-15 with a bump stock, the other a Benelli M4 shotgun. The one with the Benelli nodded for Nick to go down the hallway.

"Door on the right."

Nick didn't hesitate, walking past the two men. If he had waited for Skinny Mo's permission, he would have looked weak. Gangs were always taking the measure of their enemies and of each other. There was a blurry, moveable line between respect and weakness, and Nick had been surfing it since he stepped into the lobby. That was why he had come armed the way he had. He knew there was no way he would get to see Skinny Mo with anything more dangerous than a toothpick in his pocket, but the two guns and knife were a show of respect for the power of the Posse. Had he come in unarmed, it would have been seen as condescending.

Skinny Mo, boss of the Surf Avenue Posse, was seated behind a Costco foldout table. He was framed by two monitors. Nick smiled because Skinny Mo was anything but skinny. He was doughy around the middle and had fleshy cheeks that sagged below his jawline. Nick didn't mistake fat for harmless. There was an open bottle of Courvoisier in front of Skinny Mo and his pudgy fingers were curled around the short stem of a snifter. Smoke drifted up to the ceiling from the lit tip of a thick cigar hanging off the table's edge. The burning tobacco smelled sweet and earthy.

"Whatchu smilin' at, dog?"

"Was I smiling?" Nick pointed at the cigar. "Cuban?"

"Man, I ain't got time for your bullshit." Skinny Mo's voice was a whispery rasp, the result of a razor slice across his throat from a Latin King when he was just a shorty.

"You looking tired, Mo. You put quite a dent in that cognac. Heavy is the head that wears the crown."

"You got that shit right. But fuck y'all. You ain't come to hold my hand. You here to sell me some shit I ain't about to buy."

"I got no bullshit to peddle."

"Y'all got a message to deliver 'bout my brother. Deliver it. You lucky I let you walk outta here at all."

"Not a message, Mo. A deal. One-time nonnegotiable offer."

Because of the old razor cut, Skinny Mo's laugh sounded like a wheezing cartoon sneeze. "Whatchu offerin', Ryan? Gettin' Ahmed kitchen duty or some shit?"

"If that were all I had, I wouldn't be here. I wouldn't do you like that. We've had business before and I've never come to you with empty hands."

"What Ahmed got to do, rat out some bruthas? Other Bloods? Nah, dog, it don't go like that. You know better."

Ahmed was Skinny Mo's brother. More importantly, he was his most trusted captain. That was right up until a year ago, when he got sent to Attica for manslaughter. Nick knew that it was a trumped-up charge and that Ahmed wasn't directly involved in the crime. The only thing he was guilty of that night was being at a bar where the bouncer got beaten to death for kicking out a member of an affiliated gang. But the state gang task force had been hungry for a pelt to hang on its belt and the pelt they got was Ahmed's. They tried to get him to roll over on his big brother, but Ahmed told the DA to go fuck his mother and took the max.

"This is what I know. The deal is a move out of Attica to Altona or Cape Vincent. You help me out and I'm successful, Ahmed does a nickel and comes back home to CI and his big bro. Whether my thing works out or not, first part of the deal is written in stone. He gets moved to a medium facility no matter what."

Skinny Mo tried hard not to react. But Nick knew that the deal would get his attention. He could see how Mo was suffering without his little brother around. Because of his UC work, Nick had dealt with gangs for years and understood their workings. Gangs were no different from any other organization. There was always some dissatisfied element in the ranks, always someone after your job. Difference with gangs was, they didn't send you on your way with a golden parachute. The way someone else got the crown was by taking it. Without Ahmed to insulate him, Mo was getting paranoid.

"You still didn't answer my question. What Ahmed got to do?"

"Nothing. It's what *you've* got to do."

"That is what, exactly?"

"I got some names written on a piece of paper in my wallet," Nick said. "I'm only reaching for my wallet. That okay?"

Skinny Mo nodded but moved his left hand. Nick heard Mo's piece scrape against the table. Nick slowly lifted his wallet from his back pocket. Opening it, he took out a piece of paper and put it on the table in front of Skinny Mo.

"If my intel is right, those five guys belong to you."

"Only white man owns other human beings. I don't own nobody."

"Bad choice of words. My intel says they're SAP and they're out in Riverhead in the Suffolk County Jail."

"And so what that got to do with anything?"

"I need two of them to do what I say, no questions asked."

Skinny Mo made an unmistakably skeptical face. "You want them to smoke somebody fa you out in Riverhead?"

"I'm going to be inside."

Skinny Mo was confused. "Inside where?"

"Riverhead."

Skinny Mo smiled. "You goin' in on the down low fa some UC kinda shit."

"I am. I may need some of your people to have my back or to kick my ass. See, nobody is going to know I'm there—not the COs, not the SCPD, not the other inmates. Fact is, I'm risking my nuts just telling you about it."

"True dat." Skinny Mo's smile got nearly as big as his belly.

"Don't gloat, Skinny Mo. For one thing, it's not polite."

"And for another?"

"Anything bad happens to me in there that doesn't go down the way I want it, Ahmed's going to get it twice as bad in Attica. You do want him back in one piece, right? I don't come back, he ain't coming back either. We understand one another?"

Skinny Mo wasn't smiling anymore. "How this shit gonna work?"

"You circle the names of the two guys on the list you trust most. I'll make sure they get housed where they can be of use."

"You ain't got the juice for this here shit, Ryan. Gettin' Ahmed a nickel and a transfer, movin' inmates around a jail—ain't even in your jurisdiction. Your own people don't even like you 'cause your daddy's a rat."

"Can't argue that last part, but don't worry about what juice I got. Someone always has the juice. You know that. Ahmed only gets a nickel if everything works out. He gets the transfer no matter what. You agree, you'll hear from your brother Monday morning. But I need your *yes* or *no* right now or I move on to the Latin Kings. They're pains in the ass, but they'll make the deal." Nick knew mention of the Latin Kings would do the trick.

"Yeah, uh-huh, I'll do it." Skinny Mo circled two names on the list. "These two will do whatever they get told to do."

"You sure? I may ask them to do some shit that won't make sense to them."

"They ain't the askin'-questions type. They do as they do. That's why they got jammed up out there in Whiteville fuckin' County in the first place. But how we gonna work this shit?"

"I'll get word to you and you pass it on to them. I'll make sure they get twice-a-day phone privileges."

"How I know if Ahmed gets the nickel or has to do the whole bid?"

Nick stood. "Because I'll be back to tell you one way or the other."

He didn't offer his hand, in case someone was watching or listening. It wouldn't serve Skinny Mo's interests to be seen shaking Nick's hand. He could already see Skinny Mo's gears churning, trying to figure out how he would explain Nick's visit if he had to. That was why Nick anticipated the inevitable bit of street theater to follow. When he opened the door and moved down the hall, Skinny Mo was close behind him. Skinny Mo shoved Nick hard so that he barely kept his footing.

"Get the fuck out my office with your bullshit. I ain't got no time for your lies."

Nick raised his hands. "I had to try. I take orders too."

"I don't take no orders from nobody, so get gone. See the man get his shit and show his ass out," Skinny Mo barked at the two armed men by the elevator. "Yo, Happy Meal," he said, pointing at Shark Eyes, "escort this motherfucka out the building."

Happy Meal handed his MP7 to his partner. "C'mon, Mr. Police, you heard the man."

Happy Meal collected Nick's guns, knife, and phone before riding the elevator down to the lobby. He handed Nick his things only after they had stepped through the exit door. When Nick looked back, Happy Meal was gone. The shorty with the mottled skin was staring at him as Nick walked to his car.

THIRTY-NINE

Nick was one of nine men being shipped from New York City to the Suffolk County Jail. He had been on Department of Corrections buses before, but never on the wrong side of the cage door. He didn't bleed for people who did wrong. If you did wrong, you deserved to pay a price. He believed that to his core, and people who didn't believe that had no business wearing a badge. That price criminals paid was loss of time and loss of freedom. Nick wasn't sure the price for doing wrong should include taking away someone's dignity.

His hands were shackled for the ride. It's easy to believe that shackles and cages are for safety and security. They were, but they were also there to rob you of your pride. Nick studied the other eight men on the bus to Riverhead—with few exceptions, they were barely more than kids. Kids or not, they all had the long-distance stare. Jail was largely for people awaiting trial. Most would be convicted. The others, though, would walk away changed. The system chewed you up, and when it spat you out, even if it was early in the process, you were never better for it. The system always took its share, a percentage of your dignity.

He was thinking of the roads not taken as the bus slowed to a crawl between Exits 57 and 58 on the Long Island Expressway. Out the caged windows, there wasn't much to see but an ugly glass casino on his left. Nick never spent much time on Long Island, a vast middle-class wasteland of split ranches and strip malls wedged between the Queens County line and the Hamptons. A huge number of the NYPD, like Sean, lived out here, insulated from the world in which they spent their working lives. Nick had never wanted any part of it. New York City was in his genome.

He was thinking of Shana's visit, of Becky, and of what his life might have been with them both. The road not taken, indeed. Shana had tried many times to persuade him to go to work for her father, as his uncle had done. Nick never questioned his uncle's chosen career, but he couldn't have lived a life where money and toys were the only ways to measure himself. Making the rich richer while enriching himself seemed an empty sort of life. As much as he resented his father for testifying, he admired him for having the willingness to do the right thing. Problem was, his dad wasn't the only one paying the price for his ethics. When the bus started moving again, Nick focused on what lay ahead of him.

———

The Suffolk County Sheriff's Office Riverhead Correctional Facility was a mouthful. It wasn't Riker's, not by a long shot. It was surrounded by woods and a lake and was a stone's throw from the Hamptons. It was also surrounded by razor-wire-topped fences. A jail was a jail was a jail. Pretty surroundings didn't make it better. Most of the men on the bus with him had already begun shutting down, walling themselves off. They were going back inside. Suffolk County was known on the street as Suffering County because the conviction rate out here was something like 90 percent plus. For Blacks and Latinos, Nick imagined it was 90 percent-plus-plus.

Intake was another exercise in pride depletion. Off the bus, Nick was connected to the other inmates in a dolly chain. They were marched into a big holding cell and were called out one by one. When Nick was called, a CO asked him a series of questions. The CO was as bored as an assembly-line robot. Nick wondered if his face even registered with the man. He had known a lot of COs who had succumbed to the corrosive effects of spending their lives in jail. Having the keys and getting to go home at the end of shift didn't mean you were somehow immune. Most of the COs he'd had dealings with were okay. A few were stone alcoholics. Others worked as much overtime as they could get, because they had gradually lost the ability to deal with the outside world of friends and families. They had become inmates too, of a sort.

The questions the processing CO read off the computer screen were what Nick expected—stuff about his religion, emergency contacts, lawyer, visitors, and physical health. There was an extensive list of questions about his state of mind. Did they really give a shit whether he killed himself inside? Probably not. Nick understood it from a cop's point of view. Paperwork was a bitch, and no one wanted to go through the investigation or be part of a lawsuit. The purpose of the questions was to determine where to house him. His accommodations were a forgone conclusion. The cover story was that Nick was an out-of-control cop who had nearly beaten a civilian to death during a road-rage incident. To keep the story quiet, the Manhattan DA had shipped him off to Suffolk County.

After the intake interview, they fingerprinted him and gave him his jail clothes: green pants, green shirt with the letters *SCSO* on the back, and ugly black sneakers with white rubber soles. He was patted down, given bags for his street clothes and property, and shipped on to medical. After medical, he got sent directly to what they called Obs Bay.

"Obs Bay?" Nick asked, his bedroll tucked under his left arm, and a net bag with his toiletries in his right hand.

"Observation Bay. Where we can keep eyes on all of our most special assholes. Normally, we'd stick you on the Reception Tier for a day until we figured out where to house you. But we never put cops in the general population."

"Too bad. I was looking forward to one of these skells giving me shit so I could put him in the hospital."

"Well, you're one of *them* now. You give us shit, you're gonna get shit back. Don't think that because you used to wear a uniform you'll get privileges. You're all green to us. We have to send you up to the fourth floor for being a dick, you won't like it."

Nick didn't ask. In jail, they gave you just enough—TV, reading material, etc.—that they could then take away from you if you fucked up. There was always a way to punish you.

"Here we are," said the CO, stopping in front of the second of five cells.

As he waited for the CO to open his cell, Nick stared into the first cell. Aaron Lister stared back at him, a malevolent smile on his face. Lister, like Roderick Ford, exuded a sense of superiority that grated on Nick. He wondered if Lister's smug malevolence was his natural state of being. Nick had studied all the available footage of Lister. He came off as a man who believed he had a secret no one else had access to. Maybe he did. No one had been able to locate one cent of the money he had stolen. Nick was determined to find the secret. Not because some politician needed campaign material. He wanted to save his little brother, and he wanted to shove that smile so far down Lister's throat that he would shit it out the next morning.

Nick nodded at Lister. Lister nodded back. His smile remained.

FORTY

Nick's new home was a barred concrete box with a metal bed stuck to the sidewall and a shelf above. The metal toilet and sink were on the back wall. The bars were there instead of doors, so the CO at the desk could keep a close eye on them. There was a trade-off for the lack of privacy because mounted on the wall to the left of the Obs Bay CO's desk was a TV that the inmates in all five cells could see. It wasn't much of a bargain if you didn't like what the CO was watching. Nick adapted quickly. He always did.

Three days in and he'd already gotten used to the fact that there were no pillows for the inmates. He had to make do with a hump on the metal bed. He'd gotten used to eating in his cell. He'd read and reread the inmate handbook, which explained everything and nothing about jail life. There were the written rules and the real rules. The job was the same way. You were guided by the unwritten rules as much as the ones put down on paper. Nick enjoyed that his new job afforded him a chance to make the rules up as he went. The man in the next cell was going to learn all about Nick's new rules.

For two days he avoided any contact with Lister. The only thing they had shared was the stink of their trips to the toilet. No greetings. No chatter. Nick figured the powers that be had already tried a jail-buddy snitch with Lister and failed. *C'mon, pal, you can trust me. We're in this shit together.* One look at Lister's face and Nick knew that such an approach was doomed. John Donne had it all wrong. Some men were islands. Nick did his first two days of yard time alone. Today would be different.

Nick heard Lister's cell door open and shut behind him. His opened shortly afterward.

"C'mon, let's go." The CO crooked his index finger at Nick.

Nick stepped out of the cell. He walked down the hall and out into the yard. The yard was divided into three different fenced-off sections: one with a basketball court, one with workout bars, and one that was a larger space for walking. Nick and Lister were alone in the big yard. The CO stood between the fences with a clear view of all three yards. He held an air horn in his right hand just in case he had to call for help.

The two other yards were empty except for two large African American men doing pull-ups and dips on the workout bars in the next yard over. Nick knew that word about him would filter back to Lister, about his being NYPD and a crazy motherfucker who had an ugly record written in reprimands and bruises. He wanted Lister to fear him. While the Suffolk County Sheriff's deputies hadn't been victims of Lister's scam, many of them had family or neighbors who were NYPD.

In the yard, Nick kept his back turned to Lister. He felt the man's eyes on him. Then, he heard him approach. Lister stopped a few feet behind Nick.

"What's it going to take?" Lister asked.

Nick kept his focus on the other yard. "Take for what?"

"For you not to beat the shit out of me. I heard about you. I need someone to have my back in here."

Lister didn't dance around the issue. That jibed with what Nick had read about the man. He could be charming if he had to be, but preferred the direct approach. He took full advantage of people's greed. Unlike Madoff, he didn't wait for people to come to him. He'd simply bribed the investment brokers who advised all the uniformed New York

City unions on discretionary investments. Lister knew that cops were mistrustful on the job, yet foolishly trusting of authority figures with titles and degrees.

Nick turned to face Lister and said, "Get the fuck away from me, asshole. You're lucky I threw away any extra investment money I had on football, ponies, and child support."

"That's not an answer."

"It's an answer, just not the one you wanna hear."

"So, you're not interested in either smacking me around or working for me?"

"Not any more or less than anybody else. You don't stop botherin' me though, that could change quick. I don't give two shits about the pricks I worked with. Not one of them ever stuck his neck out for me when I needed them to have my back with IA. So fuck them and their money. One of them wants to come in here and slit your throat, that's his business. I'm not gonna do it for them. Let me ask you somethin', Lister. How'd you hear about what I done to that guy in the city?"

"My cell is right next to the hallway. I hear everything the deputies talk about on their way to the CO mess hall. I know who's fucking whose wife and which of them think the other COs are lazy shits. That's how I heard about you."

"Bullshit, Lister. Lying to me is not how to get off on a good footing. I'm not stupid. There's always somebody who needs money bad enough to slip you a cell phone or feed you information. You got at least one of these guys on your pad."

Lister said, "Very good. No, you're not stupid at all."

"Another thing I know: on your payroll or not, he can't protect you in here."

Nick turned back around. Using his body to block Lister's view, he signaled for the two men in the other yard to come his way.

"Look at these two motherfuckers." Nick pointed through the fence at the men from the Surf Avenue Posse. "You think they're coming for me or for you?"

Lister's laugh was almost as malevolent as the smile Nick had seen on the man's face. "I'd say you were on their menu. I didn't target Black people."

"No, you were an equal opportunity scumbag. Me too. I can't help it if the guy who hit my car was Black."

"Nice turn of phrase. You sure you don't want to watch my back? Could be profitable."

Nick kept his back to Lister. "We're both headed to prison," he said. "Inside, money only buys you so much. Cop time in prison is a bitch. Money won't do me much good."

"That's where you're mistaken. It's impossible to overestimate people's greed. Believe me, I've got a billion dollars' worth of proof. Like lead to feathers, money always outweighs conscience. Can't buy Porsches or pay down your mortgage from the moral high ground."

The Surf Avenue Posse duo were about halfway to the fence of their yard. Skinny Mo had chosen wisely. These guys were twice as menacing as Happy Meal. They had dead eyes and rippling biceps as thick as anacondas.

"Yeah, yeah, yeah, everybody's got a price," Nick said. "Now, get the fuck away from me like I said."

"You change your mind, the offer stands." Lister hesitated a beat and then said, "And just to be clear, it's where you're going. I'll never see one second inside a prison. It's all about lead and feathers. Greed is the most powerful force in nature."

Nick listened to him take a few steps back. The man was a manipulative SOB. Nick pondered what Lister had meant by saying he was never going to see the inside of a prison. Did he already have an out? Was he planning on jury tampering? One thing was for sure: Lister wasn't implying he would commit suicide. He wasn't the type. But whatever he meant was moot—no matter what Lister had planned, this was Nick's game and he was going to play by Nick's rules, like it or not.

The two SAP gangstas reached the fence, giving Nick a withering stare.

"You got the word from Skinny Mo?" Nick asked.

They nodded in unison.

"A few more days and then we're a go."

The guy on the left lifted one corner of his lips at the happy prospect of Nick's plan.

"For now, just yell some shit at me and him," Nick said. "Threaten me loud enough for him to hear."

Almost before Nick finished, they were shouldering the fence inward, pointing, screaming at Nick. "You gonna die in here, you pig motherfucka," was the most pleasant thing they said. "Whatchu lookin' at, Lister? We'll fuck you up too, motherfucka."

The CO came running over, blowing the air horn. He pointed at the Surf Avenue Posse inmates. "Get the fuck away from the fence now or it's the fourth floor for you. Now!"

They walked backward to the other side of the yard, facing Nick and Lister the whole time. Both made throat-slashing gestures as they went.

Taking them back to Obs Bay, the CO asked Nick, "What did you say to the brothers that pissed them off?"

"I didn't have to say nothing."

"Didn't help that you beat a brother half to death."

That gave Nick the opening he was hoping for.

"Let those assholes in the yard with me and I'll make them sorry they disrespected me."

"That can be arranged, asshole," the CO said, smiling. "I'd bet on them."

"Okay, make it happen and I'll put on a show for you and the other deputies."

The CO didn't say another word, but the seed had been planted.

FORTY-ONE

Two days later they were outside again. This time, they were in the yard with the Surf Avenue Posse inmates. Every few minutes, the gangstas would stop their workout to look over at Lister and Nick. Nick paid them little mind. Lister was focused on them like a laser. He'd heard their threats. His scams may not have targeted African Americans, but he was rich and vulnerable—neither a good thing to be. Maybe they wanted a piece of the pie. Maybe they just wanted a piece of him because . . . well, just because. As Lister watched them, Nick watched Lister watching.

Forty-five years old, Lister exhibited all the physical attributes of a wealthy sociopath: perfectly veneered white teeth, a flawless hair transplant, a permanent authentic-looking tan. He was in good shape for his age. His dossier said he possessed some martial arts skills. His Krav Maga lessons and personal MMA training notwithstanding, he would be no match for the men across the way. Nick knew it. Lister knew it. Nervous, he paced like a caged jaguar. Any cage was probably too small for Lister. And Nick was about to shrink the cage.

Nick gave the signal. The two Black men stopped what they were doing on the bars. They didn't rush across the yard, but walked the fence perimeter as Nick had instructed Skinny Mo and as Skinny Mo had instructed them. Nick turned back to look at Lister, who was already on the move, cutting across the yard toward the CO. Nick intercepted him. Lister tried to step around him. Nick stepped in front of him.

"Where you goin'? You don't wanna be my friend no more? You don't want me to have your back?"

"Get outta my way." Lister's calm voice was betrayed by his darting eyes and the sheen of sweat covering his face.

Nick nodded over his right shoulder. "What? You worried about them?" The Posse gangstas were halfway to them.

"Move." Lister tried once again to step around Nick.

"I don't think so."

Lister's eyes were widening as he saw the men closing in. There was something else besides fear in his eyes—indecision. By the time Lister decided to call to the CO for help, it was too late. The afternoon shadows of the other two inmates fell on Lister and Nick. Close up, they towered over both men.

"Take it easy." Nick patted Lister's right biceps and smiled reassuringly. "Nobody's getting physical with us—not yet, anyway." Nick turned his gaze away from Lister. "Gentlemen, give us a few minutes."

The Posse inmates backed off a few yards. The CO ignored them all, interested in everything but what was going on in the yard.

When they were out of earshot, Nick said, "I'm not who you think I am. I'm NYPD Detective Nick Ryan. I'm an undercover specialist. Have the CO in your pocket Google me. You'll see I'm legit."

Lister opened his mouth.

Nick raised his palm. "Don't even bother denying it. You've got someone on the inside on your payroll. Remember the lesson you gave me the other day. Money outweighs conscience. I'm a quick learner that way."

"I'm listening."

"They've already tried a jailhouse snitch on you. He was gonna be your best friend. You and him against the world, right?"

Lister nodded.

"You sussed that move out in what, five minutes?"

"Less."

"They stick a gun in your mouth yet?"

"Twice."

"Stupid." Nick shook his head. "See, it's binary. They pull the trigger, they have the satisfaction of killing the fuck that stole their money, but they don't have the money."

"Shrewd analysis. You should come work for me."

"That's what I have in mind . . . sort of."

There was that malevolent smile on Lister's face. "I see your play now."

"You only think you do. When you find out my history, you'll understand. I'm a fucking war hero, a superstar cop, but I'm fucked, truly and royally. My career is done. I like money. I'm used to money. I inherited a lot of it. You'll see that too. Thing is, I'm almost out of it, and I'm stuck in a place where I'll be a doormat until I put in my papers. Do I strike you as a doormat kinda guy?"

"I don't see WELCOME tattooed on your forehead. I'm still listening."

"They didn't pull the trigger when they had the chance. Why? Simple. They couldn't convince themselves you wouldn't trade back the money to save your life. They assumed you would because they would have. They offered you plea deals?"

"More than you can count."

Nick smiled. "But they all came with prison time attached. No matter how bad they wanted the missing money, they couldn't justify no prison time to the public. What'd they offer—ten years and a percentage-reduced sentence for good behavior?"

"Eight years, but you got the basics."

Nick shook his head. "Eight years is seven years and three hundred sixty-four days too long for a man like you."

"All right, Ryan, I'm impressed. Get to the point. What was the play?"

Nick pointed to the Posse. "Those guys—they're contracted to me. Original play was to have me be your savior. They'd rough you up and I'd step in and save your worthless ass. I'd gain your trust, offer to get you out in exchange for telling me where the money is, so we could split it, and—"

"Whose brilliant plan was that?"

"Not mine."

"I didn't figure it was. It had about as much chance to succeed as—"

Nick cut him off. "Let me finish, Aaron. You see, this was their last try. They've run fresh outta hope. If you didn't come through for me, they were going torture you to death in a safe house somewhere. So no matter what cute deal you think you have to get out, forget it. They figure they've tried everything on you and they're finally convinced you won't give up the money. You win, but talk about your Pyrrhic victories . . . They're going to get some satisfaction. No money, then a pound of flesh—yours. You need to understand this: you're a fucking dead man without me."

Lister tried to keep his composure. He was too smart to dismiss what Nick was saying out of hand. It made a fatal kind of sense. Although Nick was improvising, he wasn't sure the powers that be wouldn't kill Lister. The man had made a lot of powerful people look impotent. During his years with Shana, Nick had learned that power was partially a function of image and fear.

Lister had done the calculus in his head. "What's your play, and what's your price?"

"I don't want half the money. I don't wanna be your partner. I don't wanna know where you go from here."

"You're just a good Samaritan, huh?" There was that smile again.

"I said I didn't want *half.* I didn't say I didn't want any. I want fifteen million transferred into an offshore account I've got set up. The second we're clear, I want the transaction taken care of. I don't wanna know where the money is or where it comes from. I just want the money. I'll take care of the brothers out of my end."

Lister clapped his hands together and laughed. "Fifteen million? Why so little? Why not a hundred million?"

"Don't be a prick. That's my price, take it or leave it."

"And how are you going to pull this off?"

"We, not me. You, me, and them." Nick pointed at the Posse. "We're going to do exactly what the police expect us to do."

"Which is what?"

Nick laughed. "Take a beating from the brothers. One that Medical here can't handle. One bad enough to get us into an ambulance off campus."

"You volunteered for this, not me."

"Easy choice. Take a beating and get free, or get tortured to death. You say no, I walk out of here and go back to the street. You go straight from here to getting dead and dumped in the Atlantic."

"You made your point."

"Don't worry, you'll heal. What I got planned once we're through the gates is what they don't expect. The cops think I'm their dog, but I'm a cat. They think I'll be happy with a pat on the head and a tummy rub. Fuck that. Fuck them. I have all the medals I need. First, have your boy check me out to see if I'm full of shit." Lister began walking away. Nick grabbed his arm. "Remember them." He pointed at the Posse. "You try to play me or roll on me, you're theirs. They won't be cruel to be kind. They'll just be cruel."

Lister's facade was finally showing hairline fractures. He shook off Nick's grasp. Nick had gotten to him, but he wasn't overconfident. Experience had schooled him that the universe paid little heed to human plans.

FORTY-TWO

Skinny Mo came out the maintenance entrance of the building. An inch of dirty snow blanketed the ground, a few flakes still drifting down. He was with Gray's Anatomy and Happy Meal. They walked to the car under cover of darkness, secure in the knowledge that no one would fuck with the leader of the Surf Avenue Posse on their own turf. Besides, the Posse spread the cash around their building and the surrounding buildings. Whoever said you couldn't buy loyalty didn't know shit about being poor. Hard to bite the hand that fed you when you didn't know whose hand would replace it.

Skinny Mo was feeling better than he had in months. He hated snow when it came so early, but not even that could dampen his buzz. The Mexican product they were getting was pure enough that they could stomp on it like a marching band. After kicking up and paying off those who needed paying off, the Posse was clearing more money than they had ever seen. Nick Ryan was true to his word. Ahmed had been moved to Altona, and if shit went down right in Riverhead, Ahmed would be doing less than four more years of his nickel. Until Ahmed got sent away, Skinny Mo had never understood that shit about carrying the weight of the world on one's shoulders. Without his brother to watch his back, he had spent the past year distrustful of men he had known since he could remember.

"Where y'all wanna eat?" Skinny Mo asked, turning up his collar to the cold. He slapped Happy Meal on the shoulder. "Everything on me tonight. How 'bout some steak? Wanna try that steakhouse on Fifth Avenue over by the bridge?"

"Nah, man, that place too fuckin' white. I can do Red Lobster?"

Gray's Anatomy didn't like that. "Dat's all the fuck the way over in East New York. I don't like drivin' in snow."

Skinny Mo was already regretting his largesse. "All right, okay," he said. "Y'all can decide when we get in the car, but I don't wanna hear no cryin' after 'bout where we shoulda gone to."

Happy Meal opened the back door of Skinny Mo's tricked-out black-cherry Chrysler 300M. As he bent down to get in, Skinny Mo got a bad feeling. Then, under the dome light, he saw the unwelcome face of a man already seated in the back of the Chrysler. Skinny Mo braced his left hand against the snow-draped roof and planted his right foot against the curb. Reflexively, he reached his right hand under his black leather jacket for his piece. He wasn't quick enough. Happy Meal yanked the Smith and Wesson away from him in a single graceful motion and shot Gray's Anatomy once in the chest. Gray's Anatomy stood stone still for one long second. He stumbled sideways, coughing up red foam, fell to his knees, then kissed the pavement with unfeeling lips.

For insurance, Happy Meal put a second bullet through the back of the fallen man's head. The blood spatter turned the snow-covered Coney Island sidewalk crimson. Skinny Mo's hand slid off the wet roof and his foot slipped. He fell awkwardly to the ground, the air coming out of him as he hit. The dead man's wrecked face was turned toward him, a hole where his right eye used to be. Skinny Mo saw his future in that empty hole.

Skinny Mo looked up at Happy Meal. "So this the way it's gonna play."

Happy Meal was silent, unsmiling. Grabbing a handful of black leather, he pulled Skinny Mo up toward him and slammed his fist hard into his jaw. Skinny Mo was in that brain space where he was aware of what was happening to him, but unable to do a thing about it. Happy Meal shoved him in the back of the Chrysler, closed the door, and got behind the wheel. There wasn't going to be any steak or Red Lobster on the menu tonight—at least, not for Skinny Mo.

————

Kenyon Cook heard his phone buzzing in his pants pocket on the other side of the motel room. He was in no mood to do anything about it, but the woman on her knees in front of him hesitated. She looked up at him, asked, "Should you get that?"

He grabbed her by the hair and slapped her across the face. "You're not here to be my receptionist, bitch. You wanna keep your job in my office and not go back to working Riker's, you'd be wise to know when to open your mouth."

Kenyon Cook was a violent man. His sadism, in its varied expressions, was why Nick Ryan Sr. had so willingly testified against him at the Argent Commission hearings. But few of Cook's victims—prostitutes, corner dealers, street kids, bodega owners—had come in to back up the elder Ryan's testimony. Given Cook's current position at the Department of Corrections, theirs had been the wiser choice. The handful who appeared under subpoena lived to regret it. Cook had their names on a "hot list," and when one of them showed up back in the system, he made sure they suffered for every syllable spoken against him.

The slap he had given the woman got his blood up. He didn't let go of her hair, clenching it tighter and tighter until some of it pulled out of her scalp. She clawed at his thighs, but Cook didn't let go until he was fully satisfied. She collapsed onto the carpeting, crying.

He couldn't have cared less. "Go clean yourself up and bring me out a soapy washcloth and a towel. And don't use that cheap hotel soap that smells like your grandma's closet. Use the soap I left on the sink and run the water until it's hot."

She crawled a bit before standing. She closed the bathroom door behind her.

Cook retrieved his phone and sat at the edge of the bed, looking at the unfamiliar number from the call he missed. It was from the 631 area code, Suffolk County. There was a message. He put it on speaker and read the transcript as he listened.

Cook, Luis Paradiso here. My dad used to work with you at the Seven-Seven. Remember him? He got fucked when that Argent shit came down. I work for the Suffolk County Sheriff's Office at Riverhead. My dad says you're a man who knows how to take care of his friends. I think we are going to be amigos, you and me. Guess who I saw on the yard today? A real two-for-one mother-fucker of a deal. You want to talk, call me back. If not, there'll be other takers. Giving you the first shot because you got what I want most, but I want lots of things.

Cook remembered Paradiso's father, a real piece of shit. Always had his hand in other people's pockets. Like father, like son. He thought about deleting the message, but it intrigued him.

"Paradiso, this is Kenyon Cook. I'm listening."

"I want to get back into the city system and retire as a deputy warden."

"We all have things we want, Paradiso. Show me yours and I'll show you mine. You got two names. Give me one."

"Aaron Lister."

"Holy shit!" Cook's reaction surprised even himself. "I was wondering where that bastard was. Thought he was in federal lockup."

"That's what everybody was supposed to think, but his ass is in our Observation Bay here in Riverhead."

"Okay, that gets you a shot at captain's bars if you can get access to Lister and help me. Otherwise, thank you and go fuck yourself. Your old man was a thieving prick. You sound like you didn't fall too far from the tree."

Paradiso let that go. He had his eye on the prize. "Access . . . not a problem. But what you gonna do with it?"

"Lister screwed a lotta my people, but he fucked me too. I'm never seeing that money again, but I'm not gonna let that weasel spend the rest of his days in a country club without paying a price."

"What price?" Paradiso's voice cracked.

"Not your concern. Just get access to him when I say so, and you got your captain's bars."

"You didn't hear the other name. I think you'll have a new deputy warden when you hear it."

"I doubt it."

"Nick Ryan Jr."

There was a second of dead silence, then "Nick Ryan Jr.! Well, fuck me. You weren't kidding. With a batting average like this, they'd build you a separate wing in Cooperstown."

Paradiso had him hooked. "I think it's more like fuck *him,* no?"

Cook was confused. "What's he doing there?"

"Remember that story last week about the cop who beat the shit out of the Black guy after a fender bender?"

"Uh-huh, but that wasn't Ryan."

"It wasn't nobody. It was a bullshit cover story to get Ryan close to Lister. They got put next to each other on Obs Bay and been in the yard together a few times, says my man on that post."

"I may not be able to get you a DW title, Paradiso, but I'll put you in a tit job with captain's bars and three years of overtime you won't have to work before retirement. Might be the best I can do."

"Sold."

"I'll be in touch."

When the woman came out of the bathroom holding the washcloth and towel, her cheek was cut and swollen. Her left upper lip was fat and bruised. She got down on her hands and knees and began washing Cook.

"Look at your face, Christ!" He yanked her up by the hair and bent her over. She screamed in pain. "Scream all you want," he whispered in her ear. "I enjoy it."

———

Roderick Ford locked the office door and collected the special phone out of the desk drawer. He was already beyond angry before saying or hearing a word. He could go from dead calm to nuclear without any interim steps. His ladder had one rung.

"You haven't called me. Part of our agreement is a daily report!" he screamed into the phone.

There was momentary silence at the other end of the phone. Then, "Don't ever think I am one of your employees, Mr. Ford." The voice was distorted but calm, as always. "Did you forget the bullet through your window?"

"Are you threatening me now?"

"A friendly suggestion."

Ford moved on. "Where is he?"

"Disappeared, just as I told you the last time I reported."

"How did he disappear?"

"I will try to explain this to you one last time and I will not repeat myself. Ryan went to Riker's to question a suspect in a drug case. I've come to believe it was a cover story. I got onto the island under the guise of a defense attorney visiting a client. I could not get too close to Ryan, because of limited access for visitors. There are obviously restricted areas that are available only to law enforcement. I could not employ drones to keep an overview, because of the proximity to LaGuardia Airport. I waited several hours for Ryan to leave, but the police vehicle he was using remained in its spot. I was forced to depart before drawing unwanted attention to myself."

Ford was unsatisfied. "Did he simply vanish?"

"Riker's only land access is over the bridge from Queens, so there are but three other routes of egress: helicopter, boat, or a vehicle other than the one he arrived in. I cannot say which one is more likely than the others."

"There is one other possibility. He stayed."

"I suppose."

"Supposition isn't satisfactory. I cannot afford to lose Ryan."

"He will reappear."

"Excuse me if I'm less than confident in your assessment. You're the same person who assured me you wouldn't lose him."

"Feel free to find someone else. I can always find you."

"More threats?"

"Not at all. As a parting gesture to the dissolution of our working agreement, I'll tell you a secret."

"Parting gesture?" Ford snarled. "I didn't fire you. I'll tell you when I'm—"

The voice cut him off. "Nick Ryan has someone else watching him—a journalist. She's small-time but determined. If she exposes him, she may ruin whatever you have in mind."

"A reporter!"

"Goodbye, Mr. Ford."

The line went dead. Ford swept everything off his desk, kicked his wastebasket across the room, and raged to no one. He turned off the rage as quickly as it came on and got on the intercom. "Get security in here. Now!"

———

Skinny Mo's face was barely recognizable as human. Until the last several punches, his eyes were two dark lines on a fleshy, blood-swollen balloon. No more. Those last blows opened him up and turned his face into a grotesque, bloody mess.

A voice came out of the darkness. "He awake?"

Happy Meal shrugged his broad shoulders. "He's mumblin' somethin'."

"What's he sayin'?"

Happy Meal leaned in close.

"Why you do me like this, Meal? We're brothers. I been good to you."

Happy Meal got a knot in his belly.

The Mexican, a diminutive and lean man, stepped out of the shadows. "I will take it from here. Go wash off. He's your friend, no? You don't want to see this."

Happy Meal didn't hesitate. "I'll be outside, you need me."

The Mexican took out an old-fashioned straight razor.

"Listen to me, Skinny Mo," the Mexican whispered in his ear. "Not like your friend here, I enjoy hurting people very much. I have peeled the skin off women's faces in front of their children and killed children in front of their mothers, so you are nothing to me. Move your finger if you understand."

Skinny Mo moved his left thumb, the only finger Happy Meal hadn't snapped.

"Good." The Mexican patted the top of Skinny Mo's head. "One last time before I start cutting parts of you away. Answer my questions and the pain will end quickly and forever. Who did you give up to get Ahmed the pass?"

A voice came out of the darkness. "And don't think Ahmed gonna get no revenge for yo, neither. He's a dead man walkin'. He just don't know it."

Skinny Mo's body shook as he laughed. The laughs turned quickly into sobs. "I tol' you. Nobody. Nobody. Nobody. Nobody . . ."

"Wish I could believe dat shit, Mo," the disembodied voice said. "But we checked out your cop friend. He ain't nobody. Ain't got no juice. His own people hate him 'cause his daddy's a rat like you. You was goin' down anyways, Mo. Your own people sayin' you been crazy lately."

"Last chance," said the Mexican.

But Skinny Mo was beyond hearing and kept whispering, "Nobody," over and over again. He kept repeating it until the Mexican cut off his belt, pulled off his pants and boxers, and went to work. The mumbles and whispers turned into screams.

——

She peeked out the curtain of the motel room window, watching Kenyon Cook's car pull away. She waited ten more minutes until she was sure he wasn't coming back. Even then, her hands shook as she made the call. As she listened to the ringing, she tried remembering exactly what she had overheard through the bathroom door.

"Take the next two days off," he'd said, pinching her left nipple so hard she gasped in pain. Her throat was already raw from screaming. He laughed at her.

Two days off! As if that were somehow a fair trade-off for how he had brutalized her. She was almost madder at herself than at him. She'd been warned about Cook by other women in the office and by two female COs who had transferred back to jail duty rather than work for him.

"He has a jones for us dark-skinned girls. Get gone, fast. He's gonna be all over you."

But she wanted no part of being back inside. Three months away from working Riker's and she still couldn't get the stink of the place off her clothes.

When the ringing stopped and the recording began listing menu options, she dialed the extension.

"Lieutenant Winslow, how can I help you?"

"It's Keisha. I need a favor."

"You all right? You don't sound good."

She lied. "I'm just tired is all."

"What's up?"

"I need a phone number. He's a detective."

"Shoot."

"Nick Ryan Jr."

Keisha Williams listened to her friend tap out the name on his keyboard.

"It's restricted, Keisha."

"But you have access."

"You know I do. What's this about? If any bad shit goes down . . ."

"He'll thank you for it. I promise."

"You sure?"

"Hundred percent."

He gave it to her. After goodbye, she couldn't punch in Ryan's number fast enough.

FORTY-THREE

When his call went to Skinny Mo's voice mail, Nick's radar kicked on. It was the first time the guy didn't pick right up. He understood that Skinny Mo couldn't take his call if he were with his men. As it was, they had to be careful on both ends of the conversation because Nick's jail calls were recorded. They had worked out a code involving expectant mothers, twin boys, and due dates. No texts and no voice mails, no traceable footprint. They were well aware of the risks they were taking by dealing with each other the way they had.

When his second call went to voice mail, Nick gave up the phone to the inmate behind him. While he waited for his turn to come up again, he wondered what made men like Lister and Madoff tick. What kind of narratives did they tell themselves to justify making sacrificial lambs of their families and hurting so many people? How empty did a person have to be to think he could fill the void with the ruination of people's dreams? When he was on the yard with Lister, Nick compartmentalized. He never thought about Sean or the other victims. Never asked himself the big questions. All he thought about was getting the job done.

When the phone came back to him at the end of rec time, Nick tried Skinny Mo's number again with the same result. Now he was concerned, but it was too late to stop. Lister knew the basics. Tomorrow Nick would fill him in on the final details. The following day they would make their move. He began to punch in his home number to get Mack on the phone. He wanted to give Mack a final confirmation that it was a go.

"Phone down," the CO yelled. "Back inside, now!"

Nick held the phone up to the CO. "C'mon, man, please?"

This was one of those unwritten rules. Rec time was a half hour. A lot of things inside were at the CO's discretion. He could have extended phone time a few minutes. Nick had seen it done. But for whatever reason, the CO wasn't in a doing-small-favors kind of mood.

"Fuck you. Inside. Now!"

Nick did as he was told. At this point, causing trouble with the COs wasn't an option.

———

Calista Barrows had lived out of her car for a few days. Last night was worst of all, with the snow and the low temperatures. She had parked in various spots close to Nick Ryan's building, making certain she could see both the main and garage entrances. Whenever she returned from a food run or bathroom break, she would check the building's garage to make sure Nick's vehicles—the GTO and Norton parked behind it—were still in place. That their engines were cold to the touch.

She was chasing it down as Murray advised her to do. Problem was, Nick Ryan seemed to have vanished. So much time alone to think darkened her mood. Her foolish jealousy over Angeline was eating away at her. She hadn't wanted to see Glencoe again for anything more than a Christmas visit, but the idea of moving home was becoming more appealing with each passing minute. Worse, as she had told Nick at McCann's, her old coach at UK had been in touch and had offered her an assistant-coaching internship that would almost certainly lead to a job offer.

"One more day," she told herself. "One more day."

———

Mack looked at the clock, grabbed the keys to the GTO, and rode the elevator down to the parking garage.

Regardless of his promises and Nick's assurances, he had decided to slip out of the false life he had created for himself and into another. Creating new identities was much like killing—it got easier with repetition. He meant to run because it was the smart thing to do despite having grown accustomed to being Mack. The life fit him.

His life in Brooklyn gave him respite from the ghosts he'd left behind him in Derry, Belfast, London, and Dublin. He wasn't haunted by the bodies so much as by the betrayals. Unlike the killing, the betrayals got more difficult with time. How many men had he called *comrade*? How many women had he called *lover*? How many jars of the black stuff and Jameson had he shared with men and women, only to speed them to their deaths?

He supposed he trusted Nick as much as the capacity to trust still lived within him. The man had kept his promises. Ryan had been as good as his word, but trust was a motherfucker. Mack had wielded it like an ax. He didn't know all the intricacies of what Ryan was involved in. He didn't need to know to understand that Ryan was falling into a life not much different from the one he had tried so hard to leave behind. He had no clue who Kenyon Cook was or why the man despised Nick Ryan, but given what the Keisha woman had said to him when she called, Mack knew that Ryan was now arse-deep in the shite.

He got to the GTO and was glad to be in the driver's seat instead of bending his spine over the transmission hump. The car rumbled to life with the twist of the key. His plan to save himself was a simple one. He'd make a quick stop at his flat to pick up his go bag. Somewhere far outside the city, he would ditch Ryan's Pontiac. Jesus wept at the thought of abandoning such a beautiful machine. But Nick Ryan and his car be damned. One last betrayal, and he'd be free—at least until the next time. That was the story he told himself as he pulled out of the garage.

———

Callie, half-dozing, heard the GTO before she saw it. She started her Civic, but it took her two moves to get it out of the spot it was boxed into. The GTO was a block and a half ahead of her, heading toward the Verrazzano. She had to close the distance between them to less than a block or lose him. The trick was not to get caught at a red when he had green. She flew through a yellow and hoped she was now close enough to be on the same traffic-light sequence.

At the next red light, she realized two things: she didn't really have a plan, and she looked like shit. When the horn blasted behind her, she stopped looking at herself in her visor mirror and hit the gas.

———

Mack noticed the Honda blowing through the yellow light, but he didn't think much of it until he saw it still in his rearview on Ocean Parkway. If he was being followed, it wasn't by anyone with training. The Honda driver was practically screaming, "Hey, I'm back here! Look at me!"

At this point, Mack couldn't afford to let any random elements fuck up his disappearance. Was the Honda a distraction meant to keep his eye off what was really going on? It was a technique he had been taught— one his team had used to capture a rogue member of the UDA. Keep the target subject's attention over here while you come at him from his blind spot. Maybe Nick hadn't been as successful as he claimed. Mack worried that someone might have spotted him in the aftermath of the bombing. He needed to know, and to do that, he let the Honda keep up. He turned off Ocean Parkway onto Avenue P, and just before turning left onto West Fourth, he sped up just enough to set the trap.

———

Callie was proud of herself until she turned left onto West Fourth Street off Avenue P, and the GTO was gone. She slowed down to a crawl, searching for it. She ignored the orange construction signs hung on all the lampposts. She ignored them until the large wooden barriers that dead-ended the street, blocking her way. Three large signs hung off the barrier: Utility Work. Detour to Quentin Road via Ocean Parkway. No Thru Traffic.

"Fuck!" She slammed her fist into the steering wheel.

She put the car in reverse and backed up slowly, but before she'd gotten fifty feet, a car pulled out of a driveway to box her in. In the glow of the Honda's backup lights, Callie saw that it was Nick Ryan's GTO. Embarrassed, red-faced, she put the car in park and waited.

——

Mack got out of the GTO, holding Nick's off-duty piece at his right thigh, and circled around to the passenger side of the Honda. His knuckles rapped against the window. When the window came down, there was an awkward moment of silence as neither Mack nor Callie saw the person they were expecting to see.

"You're Mack . . . from McCann's."

It took him a beat longer to shuffle through the thousands of faces he had served.

He pointed his left index finger at her and smiled his happy-Irishman smile. "Callie? You're the woman with Nick the night of the bombing, are ya not?" He was smiling but kept his finger loose on the trigger guard.

"That was me. Isn't that Nick's car?"

"How would you know that?"

"He told me about it."

"Is that why you were following me? You supposed it was Nick driving?"

"The night of the bombing, Nick loaned me this . . ." Callie reached into the back seat. Mack moved his finger from the trigger guard onto the trigger itself and raised the Glock up to just beneath the Honda's windowsill. She showed Mack Nick's peacoat.

"Here," he said, "let me take that."

"I'm so embarrassed. Will you please give it to Nick and thank him for me?"

He recognized the coat as Nick's but was skeptical of her all the same. "Ya troubled yourself terrible just to return his coat. Surely there were easier means of doin' it. If ya knew where he lived, why not ring his flat number and bring it up?"

She ignored the question and asked one of her own. "How is it you're driving Nick's car?"

Mack was a more practiced liar. "There was a wrecked pipe in the flat above mine. The leak banjaxed me walls and ceiling. I needed a place to lay my head while me gaff was being made right. Nick offered me his flat while he's on vacation." He thought about pushing her harder, until he caught sight of her press credentials sitting in the cup holder. "I'll be happy to pass on your thanks, Callie," he said, wrapping Nick's coat around his gun hand. "Glad to do it. How are you—since the bombing, I mean?"

———

His story made sense and he seemed sincere, but she didn't quite believe him. She wanted to keep him talking until she could nail down what was really going on. "Still a little freaked out, I guess. And you?"

"Me as well. If not for being behind that great, thick bar . . . I don't even like to consider what might have been. As I say, I will pass on your thanks. It won't take a moment for me to move the car and let you pass."

Callie called after him, but he had stepped away. "Shit!" She bowed her head against the steering wheel, chiding herself for getting exposed the way she had and getting caught completely off guard. Mack suddenly reappeared at the still-open window. Callie startled.

"Sorry, lass, didn't mean to give ya a fright. I think you should have a look at your rear passenger-side tire. It's low to the pavement and sounds as if she's hissing air."

"Thanks."

She watched him in her sideview mirror as he hurried back to the GTO. By the time she was out of her car, the GTO was backing onto Avenue P. Mack was right. She heard the hiss of escaping air even before shined her phone flashlight on the tire. She kicked the tire when she saw the gash in the sidewall.

"That son of a bitch!"

———

Mack threw the weathered Gladstone bag on the front floor. In it were his five passports—Irish, Canadian, US, South African, and Moroccan—each in a different name, and five thousand dollars in cash. He'd left behind nearly his entire wardrobe. A new life required new attire, after all. But there on the passenger bucket seat was Nick Ryan's peacoat. He had looked at it on and off for the entire mile drive from where he had stranded Callie. The damned coat spoke to him in the voice of his own shame.

"Ah, for fuck's sake!"

Instead of heading west on the Belt Parkway to Staten Island, New Jersey, then beyond to that new life, Mack went east toward Long Island. He'd been wrong. He didn't have one last betrayal in him.

FORTY-FOUR

Nick's concern over his inability to reach Mack and Skinny Mo was heightened by the change in routine. The CO in charge of Obs Bay was not the guy who had been on the seven to three shift since he arrived. He was a CO Nick didn't recognize at all, a guy with a disquieting smile who kept staring into Nick's cell. The hour for yard had come and gone. That was the real trouble because the plan was time-dependent. They had to have yard at the same time as the guys from Skinny Mo's posse, or it would all go to shit. And Mack had a slim window in which to divert the ambulance and then lay the spike strips across the secondary road. The only things that had gone to schedule were breakfast and lunch.

An hour past the normal time, a CO called out, "Yard. Back away from the door."

This was it. Nick had known that it would be a hard sell, convincing Lister he could get him out of jail and free to make his way out of the country. That so far, Lister was playing along until he could figure out Nick's real angle. The man hadn't bilked people out of all that money by being a fool. Easy to agree to give a man millions of dollars if you didn't think it was ever going to happen. Nick worried that the change in timing might shake Lister's already weakened confidence in the plan.

The minute the door clanked opened, any sense of normality disappeared with the rattle of shackles and chains. Another unfamiliar CO stood outside Nick's cell, shaking the restraints. He was a huge nasty-looking white man who filled the open cell door. He had severely chapped lips that made his mouth look like a seam of bad sutures. Nick peeked over the nasty bastard's shoulder and noticed that the CO at the Obs Bay desk was gone. Refocusing on Franken-Face, he saw that the big CO's shirt was wet with sweat and splashed with blood. There was spatter on his pant leg and shoes as well, and a light spray of it on his left cheek.

"What the fuck?" Nick said, refusing to step forward.

Franken-Face stepped closer. He reeked of sweat. "You gonna make this even more fun for me, shithead? I'm already loosened up. Your choice."

Nick shook his head. "I want to see my lawyer."

"And I wanna fuck Beyoncé. I like my chances better."

"What's your name?"

"Kelly, Mike Kelly. But it ain't gonna do you no good where you're going."

Nick heard some sharp slaps coming from Lister's cell. Hearing Lister cry out, he relented. He stepped forward with his hands in front of him and ankles close together. No matter what was going on, he had to keep Lister alive. He had to keep himself alive. Kelly seemed almost disappointed that Nick had acquiesced. He snapped the shackles tight around Nick's ankles.

"You're just a pussy, huh?" he goaded. "From what I heard about you, I thought I'd have to tune you up to motivate you a little. I'll let you have one free shot."

Nick ignored the offer. "'Motivate.' That's a big vocabulary word for a second grader."

Kelly didn't say a word. Instead, he stepped back and yanked on the chain connecting the handcuffs around Nick's wrists to the braces around his ankles. Nick struggled to keep upright—an impossibility given his inability to use his arms and legs for balance. He toppled forward out of the cell, bouncing his right shoulder hard off the floor. He saw another big CO standing next to Lister. Lister's lips were split, blood dribbling down his chin. Yet he maintained the same malevolent smile that was his default expression. Nick was just glad Lister wasn't falling to pieces.

Using only his right hand, Kelly lifted Nick to his feet. "Okay, Tommy, let's move 'em. To the yard, assholes. Now!"

Nick followed Lister, both shuffling along, eyes forward, concentrating on keeping upright. Still, it was impossible for Nick to miss the blood on Tommy's sweat-soaked uniform. Nick knew men like Kelly and Tommy, people who enjoyed the dirty work. He got the sense that they had something more than a beatdown in store for Lister and him. Nearing the door ahead of them, Tommy slammed Lister against the wall.

Kelly said, "You're gonna get to see a part of the jail I hear inmates don't never get to see." Kelly turned them left, down a hall they'd never been in.

Nick smelled where they were headed before he could see it. Gyms had a telltale odor. It was the urethane on the floor and the dank sweaty air that lingered and seeped into the walls.

"Stop," Tommy said, taking a six-inch gray metal rod out of his pocket. Then, with a flick of his wrist, the metal rod telescoped to about a foot and a half in length, a ball bearing at its tip. "You two stand still. You move and you'll get this across your fucking thighs."

Nick had used a baton like it on Ricky Corliss. Even a light strike across any large muscle group hurt like a gunshot. Hit someone hard enough and it could break bones. They stood dead still, Nick hoping Lister wouldn't try to charm or buy his way out of the inevitable. Lister stayed quiet.

Tommy said, "Let's leave 'em in restraints. It'll make it easier."

"Nah." Kelly patted Nick's shoulder. "Can't have it look like hunting with the animals still in their cages. Orders are to take 'em off. We take 'em off."

"I don't know why we have to go through all this bullshit." Tommy bent down, opening the shackles around Lister's ankles. "They want to get rid of these two, they should just gate 'em and t'row 'em in the fucking ocean. Fish gotta eat too."

Gating, shit! When you talked gating, someone wasn't walking away. Nick realized this wasn't about a beating. These goons meant to kill both of them. The only positive in all this was that his and Lister's arms and legs were free. Whatever or whoever was waiting for them behind the gym door, at least freedom of movement gave them a chance.

Kelly said, "Tommy, go get the others. I'll handle this."

"I still say this is a lotta trouble for nothing."

"Get the fuck in there!" Kelly shoved Lister through the gym doors but held on to Nick. "Don't worry, Ryan, you'll be joining your boy in there soon enough. I just wanted to deliver a message to you from Chief Cook. He says you and your ratfuck father should go fuck yourselves."

"Eloquent prick, isn't he?"

Kelly seemed disappointed that Nick didn't flinch. He tried shoving Nick into the gym. Nick held his ground.

"What's your deal, Kelly?"

"Why the fuck's it matter to you?"

"Because when I get out of this, you better watch your back. You won't see me coming, but I'll be coming for you."

"You ain't coming back from this, Ryan. The inside of that gym is the last place you're gonna see with your skull in one piece. Just so you die knowing, I'm NYCDOC. Worked Riker's for twenty years."

"Yeah," Nick said, "I figured. I'm smart like that."

Kelly smiled with his mouth wide open. Behind those ugly lips were a set of teeth as white and straight as a movie star's. "Smart ain't gonna do you no good in there, pal. Say goodbye."

As soon as the doors slammed behind him, Nick heard chains being looped around the gym door handles. There would be no going out the way they came in. There was something in the air besides gym stink— odors all too familiar to Nick. The taste of copper on the tongue and the stench of feces and urine meant one thing: death.

Turning away from the doors, he saw Lister frozen still, face drained of color, that default smirk now gone from his face. The reason for Lister's change of expression was obvious. The two guys from the Posse were motionless on the gym floor. Their battered bodies were atop one another on a pair of gym mats. The mats were covered in blood.

Lister's expression may have changed, but he had maintained his jaundiced view of things. "I don't suppose this was part of the plan. Weren't they the men who were going to rough us up just enough to get us taken to the hospital?"

Nick didn't have time for Lister's sarcasm. Both of Skinny Mo's men had suffered multiple compound fractures to their arms, legs, and ribs. Their ragged white bones sticking through their dark skin like the quill ends of feathers through worn pillow fabric. One of the men lay faceup, with unseeing eyes. His broken teeth were scattered over his bloody green shirt and the mat below. Nick checked for a pulse. Feeling none, he pushed the dead man aside to get to the man beneath him. He was facedown, teeth fragments swimming in a puddle of blood. Nick reached for the man's neck and felt a wisp of breath on his fingertips. There was a faint, irregular pulse.

"Help me turn him over," Nick shouted to Lister. "He's alive."

"Fuck him. You better figure out how *we're* going to stay alive."

Nick rolled him over on his back by himself. The man was glassy-eyed and exhaled much more red foam than air. He spat blood as he struggled to speak. He whispered something. Nick put his ear close.

"Skinny Mo dead."

"How?" Nick whispered.

There was no answer, nor would one ever come. His body shuddered with a loud intake of air and then went lax.

Lister said, "We're fucked!"

"They think we are."

"Me too."

"They think we're going to panic, but we're not." He shook Lister. "They're going to outnumber us. One or more of them will have jail weapons, like toothbrush shivs or broken glass. They'll want this to look like we got caught in the middle of a fight between factions of the two rival gangs. When they're done, they'll move the bodies to a more convenient place in the jail."

"If you're trying to reassure me, you're doing a shitty job of it."

"I don't need your bullshit right now, Lister. I've got to keep us alive."

"This I gotta see."

"No, this you gotta *do*. We don't have much time. Now's the time to remember your martial arts training. You have some MMA training, right?"

"Enough to fight someone my age and skill level."

"Some Krav Maga too, right?"

"You do know a lot about me."

"Don't go to the ground," Nick said. "Keep your feet. You go to the floor, you're dead—*we're* dead." He grabbed two mats off the walls. "They're gonna come through that other door any minute. We're going to use the walls to stop them from flanking us. The longer we can keep this going, the better our chances of rescue become."

"I can't wait."

"You won't have to. If you give a shit about breathing, come over here and help me with these bodies and mats."

Lister jumped.

FORTY-FIVE

The doors burst open. Four men—two white, one Black, one Hispanic—in green jail shirts came into the gym. The sound of chains being wound around the door handles behind them echoed through the space. Four against two wasn't the worst odds, but Nick understood that these guys were here because they were nasty motherfuckers.

The four of them walked cautiously across the gym, barely acknowledging the battered bodies of the dead men. They moved toward the bloodied blue mats in the far corner of the gym. The mats were propped up like a lean-to. Fanning out in a semicircle as they approached, their progress slowed. Nick studied their body language like a lion watching a herd to spot the weak. Unfortunately, he and Lister were the prey. As anticipated, at least three of the four were armed. The two on either end rolled toothbrush shivs in their palms. One thumbed the edge of a knife-shaped glass shard with a duct-tape handle. A nasty weapon. Stick it in, break it off, and the victim can't pull it out. The other was empty-handed.

Nick kept motionless, holding his breath. He watched, waited. It was important to know whether these men had a leader. If they did, it increased their odds of success. The army had taught him the importance of command in battle. As the four of them got within six feet of the mats, they stopped, each looking at the others, hesitating, waiting for someone else to act. *Good*, Nick thought, *no leader*. Once the shit started flying, there would be no cohesion. Every man for himself meant four individuals, not a team.

"Okay, fuck you *putos*, I'll do it," the one with the glass knife said. He was short, squat. His body, neck, and face were covered in tattoos that marked him as a member of MS-13, Mara Salvatrucha, the most violent of all street gangs. Sneering at the others, he stepped forward and spat at their feet. He pointed at the barely visible tips of four black jail sneakers jutting out from beneath the edges of the mats. The others laughed nervously.

Nick tensed, hoping Lister was paying careful attention.

MS-13 ripped back the mats. He thrust the glass knife upward, but there was nothing behind the mats but two empty pairs of sneakers.

"What the fuck?"

The world changed speeds.

One of the dead bodies rolled forward, and Lister popped out from beneath it. He ran to the opposite end of the gym. Stunned, the gang of four turned and chased him. When the other body rolled onto its stomach, no one took notice. Nick, covered in blood, had the dead man's jail shirt wrapped around his left forearm for protection. He jumped on the inmate closest to him, a tall white man lagging behind the others. By the time the guy realized what was happening, it was too late.

Nick made a four-knuckle fist and punched the guy's throat, crushing his windpipe. The man dropped the shiv, both hands clutching his ruined throat. In one swift motion, Nick scooped up the shiv and stuck it into the suffocating man's exposed left armpit. The shiv wasn't long enough to reach his heart. He jabbed him again and again until the shiv hand was wet and slippery with blood. The man stayed upright, hanging on to life long enough for MS-13 to catch on and come at Nick.

Nick clutched the dying man to him as a shield. MS-13 was fast and experienced. He knew to move to Nick's left side, away from the shiv hand. Using the dying man for protection was a mixed bag. His weight burdened Nick. It was like slow dancing with a three-legged giraffe. Adding to Nick's burden was concern for Lister. He had lost sight of him. He heard lots of pounding, men cursing, primal grunts. He couldn't afford to lose focus. To do that was to die.

As MS-13 came around the dying man's right side, his hand thrusting the glass knife forward, Nick swung his dance partner around to block the thrust, but not quite fast enough. The burn spread quickly from the puncture wound in Nick's left side. The good news was that the lame giraffe's body had prevented the glass from penetrating deeply. The pain was even worse when MS-13 pulled the glass back out.

As the last bit of stubborn went out of his dance partner, Nick pushed the man's limp body onto MS-13. MS-13, slow to react, was knocked off balance, absorbing the momentum of the dead weight. Stumbling backward, he threw his hands out to keep his balance. Nick charged, launching himself, left leg outstretched. His foot slammed into MS-13's right knee with a nauseating crunch and snap. They both went down. Only one got up.

Nick didn't have time to fuck around. He needed to get to Lister, and fast. First, he scooted around to MS-13's head. MS-13 used his good leg and free hand to pivot, maneuvering to ward Nick off. He didn't manage to get fully around, though he spun far enough that Nick's first stab missed. MS-13 rolled away, his unhinged right leg thumping on the floor. Nick scrambled after him, lunging. This time, he stuck the shiv in MS-13's carotid artery. But as Nick landed, he fell on the glass knife in MS-13's hand. Warm blood sprayed from the dying man's neck into Nick's face. He ignored it. But he couldn't ignore the pain. The second wound, in his abdomen, was deeper than the first. Gritting his teeth, he carefully lifted himself off the glass blade and left MS-13 to bleed out.

Lister had managed to get one of his attackers down. The lanky Black man was on the floor, writhing in pain from what looked to be a dislocated shoulder or broken collarbone. Nick considered using the shiv to kill him, but he had no appetite for more blood, so he kicked the man in the jaw and put him to sleep.

Aaron Lister was being choked by a meaty forearm against his throat.

Unlike Nick, the burly white guy attached to that forearm seemed to be having a good time. Nick kneed him in the ribs, knocking him off Lister. The air went out of him. Nick kidney-punched the prone man, rolled him over, and kicked him hard in the crotch. The guy puked up his breakfast. He would be worthless for a few minutes.

"You okay?" he asked, helping Lister to his feet.

"Fuck, look at you!" Lister actually sounded concerned. "Is that your blood?"

Nick did a quick check of Lister. Before either said another word, screaming came from the other side of the doorway, and they could hear the chains being unwound from the door handle.

Nick asked, "Are you okay?"

"Pretty much."

Nick snorted. "That's too bad." He stuck the shiv into Lister's side and punched him in the face hard enough to knock him silly.

Nick fell to the floor beside the man he had just stabbed. Once again he was in that hazy state between consciousness and oblivion. The haze faded into black.

FORTY-SIX

As the darkness lifted, Nick was floating, drifting downstream with the current as if on an inner tube. The incessant wailing in his ears sounded nothing like the rush of river water. A blurry face blocked the cold white light of the sun.

"Stay with me, buddy. What's your name?"

Nick asked, "Where's my friend?"

"Friend!" Lister screamed. "That prick stabbed me."

"Take it easy, take it easy," the EMT said to Lister. "All that will be sorted out by someone else. Right now I need both of you to be calm." He turned back to Nick, a puzzled look on his face. "What's your name?"

Nick tried raising his left hand, but it was cuffed to the gurney. Slipping his right arm out from under the restraining straps, he pushed the oxygen mask off his face. "Name? Nick is my name. How long has it been since we left . . . the jail?"

"All right, Nick. You're in rough shape, but—"

"How long?" Nick grabbed the EMT's forearm. "How long?"

The EMT looked at his watch. "About three minutes. Why?"

Nick found himself drifting downstream again.

———

Mack checked his watch for the eighth time in the long last hour. Things were so far behind schedule, he wasn't sure any of it would come off. Slapping the steering wheel and cursing himself for his choices, Mack tilted the rearview toward him. "Ya feckin' eejit! Ya should be halfway to Chicago by now." He'd ignored his instinct to run for self-preservation. He also had to admit he felt his juices flowing again for the first time since coming to the States. Flowing juices or not, if that ambulance didn't show soon, he'd turn right around and head west.

———

"Nick! Nick! Stay with me here. Stay conscious. My name's Jimmy," the EMT said, gently replacing the oxygen mask.

Nick's eyes fluttered back open. "How long was I just out?"

"What's so important?" Jimmy asked, confused. "You've lost a lot of blood, but you should be okay. Try to stay awake, but don't exert yourself. Just lie there and take it easy. We should be at the hospital soon."

Nick hoped not. The timing of the plan was already off by over an hour. If they made it to the hospital, the trail of blood and bodies they had left behind them on the gym floor would be for nothing. The motion of the ambulance rocked Nick back into sleep. But there was a persistent voice that would not let him be.

"Nick!" Jimmy's face came back into focus. It was a young face, eager and unlined. A nice, reassuring face for people to look at as they headed to a place from which they might never return.

"Fuck him!" Lister shouted. "Let the prick drop dead."

"How long?" Nick repeated.

"Two minutes since you asked the last time."

About five minutes. Okay. There's still a chance. If it gets to nine minutes, we're fucked.

Jimmy looked away from Nick, to Lister, and then to someone else. "He's awake. You can talk to him, but don't stress him."

The face replacing the EMT's was a weathered, angry face with threatening eyes. "I'm Sheriff's Deputy Samuels." Samuels rattled the handcuffs that attached Nick's wrist to the gurney. "So you stabbed Lister, huh? Lotta people would want to do that."

Nick paid no mind to the deputy, noticing that handcuffs weren't the only thing attached to his left arm. His eyes followed the path of a thin clear plastic tube, leading from the middle of his arm up to a plastic bag of saline. For a brief second, the focus took his mind off the intense pain from the two hot spots where sharp things had been stuck inside him.

Jimmy stepped between the CO and Nick. He was pissed. "Stop it, now! Just sit there and do your job." The EMT may have been young, but he had balls. Nick liked that.

———

Mack checked the side-view mirror on the old Caddy parked at an angle on the shoulder of the county road. Traffic was sparser along this stretch of blacktop that led from the Suffolk County Jail to Peconic Bay Medical Center than he would have thought. Nick had explained that but for summer, weekday traffic on the east end of Long Island could be nearly nonexistent. What Mack spotted in the mirror brought all the unpleasantness of his old life back to him. It was a dark blue, yellow-striped Ford. The words "State Police" visible as it pulled up alongside the car Mack had stolen from the Long Island Railroad parking lot in Medford.

Mack wasn't much for religion, but the vestiges of Catholicism that remained prayed mightily for the trooper not to check the tag numbers on the old Caddy. He'd know soon enough as the trooper donned his flat-brimmed hat and rolled down his passenger side window. Mack's window was already rolled down. As he turned toward the trooper, he tucked his 9 mm beneath his right thigh. He then made sure to put both hands on the wheel. It reassured cops, seeing both hands on the wheel. It was exactly how he'd lulled the RUC man into a false sense of confidence on the road between Aghalee and Glenavy in '94. He'd done it just before shooting the cop in the gut and driving off. The stakes were higher then—a bomb hidden in the trunk meant to disrupt a meeting of the area's Sinn Féin leaders.

"What seems to be the problem, sir?" asked the trooper.

"Alternator belt," Mack said, affecting his near-perfect Brooklyn accent. "Triple A should be here in a few minutes. Thanks for asking."

The trooper nodded, seeming to buy the story. The faster he moved on, the better. Not only was Mack concerned about the trooper and the Cadillac. He didn't want the trooper to spot the rental car he had hidden in the scrub pines the previous evening.

"All right, then." The trooper rolled up his window, waved, and moved on.

Less than a minute later, the ambulance finally appeared, siren screeching, lights flashing. Mack turned the Caddy's key. He put the car in drive, keeping his right foot pressed down hard on the brake. *Three hundred yards . . . two hundred yards . . . one hundred yards . . . fifty yards . . . twenty-five yards . . .*

———

Without warning, the ambulance swerved hard to the left, and that easy, floating sensation vanished. The ambulance tipped to one side then the other, nearly flipping over. It righted itself just before dipping down. After the dip, the ambulance launched itself into the air and came crashing down with a thud. When it bottomed out and rebounded, Jimmy and Deputy Samuels went airborne. They landed on the floor of the ambulance. The cuffs and restraining belts held Lister and Nick to their gurneys. Then, just as it stopped bouncing, the driver floored it.

———

Mack backed the Caddy onto the shoulder where it had been, now that it had served its purpose. He ran to the bland white rental, started it up, and followed the ambulance's path across the center median and down the access road leading to the local sump. He had to catch up to it before the driver could regain full control and call for help.

———

There was a screech of brakes and tires, the ambulance fishtailing before coming to a full stop. As soon as it had come to rest, it was in motion again. The driver floored the accelerator. The ambulance's diesel engine clattered and whined, straining to gain speed. The cycle was repeated—brakes and tires screeching, the stink of burned rubber heavy in the air. This time, though, the nose of the ambulance veered hard to the right, tires *ba-dump, ba-dump, ba-dump*ing over the warning ridges cut into the asphalt. *Bang!* The ambulance crashed through a cyclone fence gate.

Just as Jimmy and Samuels had regained their balance, the ambulance hit a mound, once again launching the front end high up into the air. The rear end landed harder than before, sending everything that wasn't secured flying. Jimmy and Samuels went sprawling. By the sound of it, the back wheels had landed on grass. They spun hard, trying to gain purchase, but it was no good. They skidded sideways, the ass end of the ambulance trying to come around front. When the front end dipped forward into a drainage ditch, the ambulance tipped over on its side with a metal-twisting bang. It slid that way for what felt like a hundred feet. When it finally came to rest, everyone inside was a little dazed.

———

Mack gloved up; grabbed the Glock, the Taser, and the mask; then bolted.

———

The ambulance's alarm went silent. After about thirty seconds, there was a pounding on the rear doors.

"Good," Jimmy said, struggling forward to unlatch the rear. "Maybe it's the driver or someone who saw the accident. Everyone all right?"

Nick and Lister answered that they were. Deputy Samuels was stunned, blood pouring down his face from a gash over his right eye. Nick yanked the IV out of his arm and stretched his hand toward the key ring on Samuels's belt. Samuels was too dazed and preoccupied to notice. No matter. Nick's fingers were still a few inches short of their target.

When Jimmy unlatched the rear doors, gravity slammed the right one down on the grass. Instead of the driver, a man in purple gloves and a red-and-black hockey mask crawled inside. He carried a pistol in his right hand and a light-blue stun gun in his left. Without hesitation, he stepped over to Samuels, pressed the business end of the stun gun to the deputy's neck, and zapped him. Hockey Mask pocketed the stun gun and took Samuels's Glock from its holster. He dropped the magazine out of its handle and kicked it outside through the open door. He racked the slide to make certain there wasn't a round in the chamber. *Empty.* The gun locked out. He tossed it.

"You," Hockey Mask said to Jimmy, pointing the muzzle of the handgun at him. "Get the handcuff key off his belt and free them both."

Again Jimmy showed balls. "All these men are seriously injured."

"Do it now, son! I am unlikely to ask as politely a second time."

Jimmy did as he was told. Freed, Nick moved too quickly, nearly blacking out again from the pain. He pulled the IV out of Lister's arm. Lister moved much more easily.

Nick asked, "Jimmy, where are your syringes and EpiPens?"

He pointed to a storage container on what was now the ceiling of the ambulance. "What the hell do you need—"

"Let me worry about that," Nick said, cuffing the EMT's hand to the gurney and his other hand to Samuels. Finished with that, he grabbed a handful of packaged syringes. He located the storage drawer marked "Code Drugs" and lifted several ampules. He gathered up some other supplies and apologized. "Sorry about this. I appreciate the help. We'll call this in as soon as we're clear."

"How's the driver?" Jimmy wanted to know.

Hockey Mask, whom Jimmy would later describe as having a weird accent, gave the EMT a thumbs-up. "He'll be fine. I had to put him to sleep for a bit. We'll be leaving now."

Nick was out the ambulance door first. Lister followed. The gunman came last.

"Jee-sus, these feckin' masks are hot," Mack bitched, lifting it off his face. "We're parked over here." He nodded straight ahead at a white Chevy Impala.

As they walked, Lister barked at Nick. "Why did you stab me?"

"It's nothing; relax," Nick said, keeping a wary eye on him. "For you to get out and for me to get my money, I had to make sure you were injured bad enough to get loaded on the ambulance with me."

"You're sure the stab wound—"

"Stop whining. I made sure not to hit anything vital. I shoulda stabbed you in the heart since you don't seem to have one. Me, I'll probably bleed to death before I can spend my money."

Satisfied he would live and that Nick might not, Lister resumed his expression of baseline malevolence. Nick knew that smile, knew that it was only a matter of time now. Mack knew it too, so he ended any dream of escape before their man had a chance to bolt. Putting the stun gun to Lister's neck, he zapped him good and long until Lister was down and out. He didn't bother asking Nick for help—just tossed the dead weight over his shoulder.

"You're in bad shape, Ryan. Those are some nasty wounds. They're already bleeding through the dressings. You might want to think about getting back to that ambulance and letting them people fix you up. Me, I'll deal with this thievin' shite. I've been trained to work with the likes of him. He'll have no secrets from the world when I'm done with him."

"No doubt, but I'll come along if you don't mind."

"Your funeral, Nick Ryan."

"Where's my GTO?"

"Safely tucked away in the long-term car park at MacArthur Airport. I had to go there to rent the Impala. Your ride calls too much attention to itself. Bloody thing shines so bright, you can see it from low Earth orbit. Nor did I think you'd have been pleased had I been forced to nudge the ambulance off the road."

"Good points. What happened to the spike strips and the other diversion?"

"It's called improvisation, son. I felt it better to keep it simple."

As they got to the Chevy, Nick collapsed. Mack stopped to help.

"No, get him in the car." Nick waved Mack away. "I'll be fine."

Once Mack had loaded Lister into the back seat and zapped him again, he came and collected Nick. He strapped Nick in and tossed a blanket over him.

"Mack, call 911."

"In a minute, once we get moving. Christ, I'm shocked there's any blood left in you!"

"Drive," Nick said.

FORTY-SEVEN

There was a loaded syringe and an unopened can of Coke Zero on the chipped Formica nightstand. The nightstand abutted the king-size bed to which Aaron Lister was bound—arms splayed above him, legs splayed below. Nick was certain Lister wasn't the first person who'd been bound to the bed in room 132 at the Airport Drive Motor Inn. Nick's choice of motel was a matter of poetic justice. It was the same place where Pete Moretti had eaten his gun.

As they waited for Lister to come around, Mack finished taping up the new dressings on Nick's body.

"I've had some experience with stab wounds. The one is seriously deep, Ryan."

"Guy stuck a six-inch piece of glass most of the way into me."

"How's he faring?"

"Dead."

"Not the forgiving sort, are you?" Mack changed the subject as they waited for Lister to rouse. "You know the woman, Callie, you were chatting up the night of the blast?"

"What about her?"

"She was tailing me from your flat, thinking it was you."

"Why would she do that, and how did she know where I lived?"

"The very same questions I posed when I doubled back behind her and boxed her in on a dead-end street. She claimed she was only interested in returning your coat."

"Did you believe her?"

"Believe her?" Mack snorted. "Not even before I caught sight of her press credentials in the cup holder. Your coat is in the front seat of your motor, by the way."

"She gave it to you?"

"I wish to hell she hadn't."

That got Nick's attention. "Why?"

"Because . . ." Mack checked the wall clock. "Without that coat staring at me, I would have been to Chicago by now, on my way to another new life."

"Care to explain?"

"That I'm sitting beside you is the only explanation you'll get from me."

"Okay."

"And about Callie . . . Well, I'd say it's a fair wager she's onto you. What will you do about that?"

"One thing at a time, Mack. Look who's about to join us."

Lister shook his head, trying to clear the cobwebs. Once he woke, it took him about thirty seconds to assess the situation. Nick undid the gag.

"Scream and I'll have my friend zap you again. I wouldn't recommend it."

"Screaming's not my style. But I thought you would have caught on by now. I didn't tell the law when they shoved a gun in my mouth or when they offered me all sorts of deals. You know, they even offered to let me keep a percentage."

"Desperate people do stupid things."

"If I didn't tell them, I won't tell you."

"We'll see," Nick said, patting Lister's cheek. "You were about to run after we got you free. I should kill you just for that."

Lister shrugged his shoulders as best he could. "Given my current predicament, I was smart to try. You won't kill me. You're in the same spot as all the rest of them. No Aaron Lister, no payday. Whoever you really are, you need to learn how to negotiate. Simply because you've got me tied up here doesn't mean you're in the position of strength. I'm about to give you your first lesson."

Nick patted Lister's cheek again. "Whatever you say, Professor. Meanwhile, you want a drink? Your throat must be pretty dry."

"Sure."

"Let me get you a cup."

He grabbed the can of Coke Zero off the nightstand, making sure Lister turned his head and saw the syringe. Nick went into the bathroom and came back carrying a plastic cup full of Coke. He placed his hand under Lister's head, lifted it, and poured some down his throat. Lister made a face.

"Tastes funny."

Nick said nothing.

"What's with your trained donkey over there?" Lister nodded at Mack, standing silently in the corner. "Not very talkative out of his hockey mask. What, he out of work since the Westies were taken down?"

"Never mind about him."

About fifteen minutes later, Lister was making throat-clearing noises, his face flushed red. "What the . . . fuck?"

Nick sat down beside him on the bed, picking the syringe up off the nightstand.

"You know those little packets of peanut butter they gave us with breakfast in Riverhead?" Nick said, tapping the syringe, squirting a bit of it into the air. "I saved mine because I read all about you, Aaron. I know about the tibia you broke falling off your bike when you were ten. I know that in first grade you took a bite of your friend's PB&J even though your mom told you to never eat peanuts or to share anyone else's food."

"You fucking . . ."

"What's the matter, Aaron? You don't like the flavor of Coke Zero and peanut butter? Can't scream? Your tongue thickening up on you? Feeling dizzy because your blood pressure's dropping? Throat tightening up? A doctor told me choking to death is an uncomfortable way to die.

That's why, when they hang someone, they are actually trying to snap his neck, not suffocate him. Suffocation, strangulation—different but kind of the same. Ugly stuff. I see you're breaking out in hives. There's that too. A shame you can't move your hands to scratch." Nick ran the tip of the syringe along Lister's thigh. "See, this is different from those guys sticking a gun in your mouth. If they fired, you were dead. Can't shoot someone in the mouth a little bit. You want to save yourself a lot of trouble, tell me where the money is."

Lister said nothing even as he began wheezing and gasping for breath.

"No? Okay, I guess I was being optimistic. See, here, with this, the bullet is already in you, but I can back it out and put it back in and . . . like that. Don't worry. You're not going to die this time. I only put a tiny bit in your soda. Watch, I'll fix it." Nick jabbed the syringe full of epinephrine into Lister's thigh and pushed the plunger. "You'll feel better soon—not a hundred percent, but better.

"See, I've been told that with each exposure to the allergen, the clock speeds up. So the next time, when there'll be more peanut butter in your soda, your body will start reacting more quickly and potentially with more violence. I wonder what would happen if I just squeezed a whole packet down your throat." Nick pointed to the clock on the wall. "This round took your body about fifteen minutes to dump all those nasty chemicals into your bloodstream and send you on the path to shock and death. I have a friend, J. P., a trauma-room specialist. Great guy. He tells me there's a point of no return, when no matter what measures are taken, a person can't be resuscitated. He calls it *crumping*. We'll kind of be playing crumping roulette." Nick took a peanut butter packet out of his pocket and waved it at Lister. "Your life. My bullets. Tick tock. Tick tock."

Nick gave Lister an hour of recovery between doses to think about it, because it was the thinking about it that mattered most. The human brain was an amazing thing because it evolved to react to pain but not to remember it. Fear and panic, on the other hand, stuck with you. Anyone who had been in battle understood how fear eats at you. Nick had seen men in his unit crack, though not in battle. They would tough it out through the fight. It was always before the next op when they would freak. They were overwhelmed as the recollection of panic morphed into panic itself. Anyone who had come close to drowning or survived a plane crash understood it too. You could relive the experience decades later as if it were happening to you in the moment.

"You're frighteningly adept at this, Ryan," Mack said between the third and fourth go-rounds. "You would have been quite an asset in my unit."

"Am I supposed to take that as a compliment?"

"Take it as you like. I won't tell a man what to feel about the truth of things. I have to say, my colleagues and I had more of a fondness for battery chargers. Shortened the process considerably."

"Different situation. I don't want to kill him."

"If you've convinced yourself of the lie, I won't argue."

"I've got a job to do."

Mack laughed. "Me old mantra, that. I think everyone who's ever done wet work tells themselves they've got a job to do."

"Did it work for you?"

"I forget."

Nick shook his head. "I think it's time. Let's get back inside."

"Forget that guy, you're leaking blood your own self. I don't know how much more you could withstand before you beat that bastard to the grave."

The malevolence was gone, replaced by sweaty, fearful anticipation. Lister kept turning his head right, looking nervously at the opened packets of peanut butter Nick left on the nightstand next to the syringes. With each round, the packets were a little emptier. Nick grabbed an unopened packet off the nightstand and walked toward the bathroom. Stopped. About-faced.

"It's the whole packet this time, Aaron. Time to get right with the Lord."

In the bathroom Nick placed the same tiny amount he had put in each time. Any more would have killed Lister by now. Nick wasn't sure the guy could last much longer. Each time Mack forced the tainted soda down Lister's throat, his reaction was faster and more severe. And the recovery was a little less hardy with each successive exposure. Lister was just as keenly aware of these things as Nick. That was the point.

"Hold him while I pour," Nick said to Mack.

Lister was so weakened from the ordeal, he could barely struggle. His defiance took the form of pissing the bed. After pouring the soda down his throat, Nick took the clock off the wall and held it in front of Lister's face.

"Only five minutes the last time, Aaron. How long this time?"

Nick had barely gotten the question out of his mouth when Lister's face flushed. He was already wheezing and gasping for air. There was real panic in his eyes, as if he could feel that this was it. Lister was frantically nodding yes.

"I'll tell . . . I'll . . . tell you. Help . . . me."

But instead of going for the syringe, Nick tossed the clock and grabbed the Glock from the TV stand. "You've got one chance. You fucking lie to me and I swear I'll blow your nuts off and leave you here to bleed to death. So the next words you choke out better check out. Understand?"

Lister seemed almost to be laughing in the midst of dying.

"I say something funny? Tick. Tick. Tick."

"Under . . . their no—their noses. In . . . Man . . . hattan. Harlem. Foreign . . . trade zone ware—warehouse. Unit three two . . . nine. Van Gogh, Bas . . . quiat, Warhol. Dual citizen . . ." Lister's eyes got wide. "Idiots."

Although none of it made sense to Nick, he had no choice but to take Lister's word as the truth. He wouldn't last another round. Nick slammed the needle into Lister's thigh and waited. It was ten minutes before the subject was breathing regularly again. He was out of it. After writing down what Lister had said, Nick collapsed beside him on the bed.

"That phone," he said to Mack. "Did you bring it?"

"Left in your flat. I was splitting. New life, remember? Chicago?"

"Better get us to a hospital, then. Stony Brook Medical Center. Drop us by—"

"I'll figure it out, Ryan."

"Not a word about . . ." Nick was losing consciousness.

"For fook's sake, Ryan, no one'd believe a word of it anyway."

Mack's comment went unheard.

FORTY-EIGHT

Sometime between asking Mack to get him to a hospital and fading into unconsciousness, he had dreamed of waking up in Shana's arms. Dying men were allowed their dreams. He had to confess to himself at that moment that he and Shana would be tied together forever. Becky made the thought of anything else an impossibility. Though his dream went unfulfilled, Nick was glad to wake up at all. He realized he wasn't quite alone.

A shadowy, silent figure stood by the window. Nick sat up too quickly to see who the silhouette belonged to. He yelped in pain. The shadow turned to look.

"You're awake." *Joe!*

"Sherlock Holmes has nothing on you." Nick's voice was brittle.

"Your smart mouth is still intact, I see."

"I didn't get stabbed in the mouth."

Joe came away from the window and sat on a chair next to the bed. "Time to utter clichés about how lucky you are to be alive."

"More like *you're* lucky I lived long enough to do my job. Turn the light on. I want to see it's really you."

Joe used the controller hanging off the bed rail. The light snapped on. "Oh, it's really me, all right."

Joe was decked out in weekend-squire mode: camel-hair sport jacket, blue crewneck sweater, tan slacks, and brown leather boots.

Nick looked over the railing. "Italian?"

Joe was perplexed. "What?"

"The boots."

"Italian leather. Handmade in London. This is what you're thinking about—my boots?"

"Not really."

"What then?"

"Lister."

"He's in rough shape," Joe said, shaking his head at Nick. "He's a wreck, but he'll live . . . for now."

He didn't ask Joe to explain. Nick knew that they couldn't let Lister survive now that he was no longer of any use to them. "What day is it?"

"Your adventure in Riverhead ended two days ago. What a mess."

"It wasn't part of the plan."

"I didn't suspect it was."

"The ambulance—that *was* part of the plan. What about the crew?"

"They've been seen to. The driver got his wish and is now a member of the FDNY. The EMT has been accepted into the next physician's assistant class at Hofstra, tuition free. Deputy Samuels got his three-quarters medical pension. All have developed a severe and permanent case of Nick Ryan blindness. Now, can we move on?"

"You almost looked happy before, when you saw I was awake."

"Relief." Joe cleared his throat. "I looked relieved. I have a life beyond being an errand boy and a recruitment officer. We both know there aren't many people who could do what you can do. Speaking of that, how did you manage it?"

Nick answered indirectly. "So Lister was telling the truth? He was babbling about things I didn't understand. Warehouses and artists. I wrote it down just before I blacked out."

"The note was found in your pocket."

Nick had no idea of Mack's whereabouts. For all he knew, Mack might have taken off for that other new life he mentioned. Nick was okay with that. The man had come through for him when it counted. He hoped Mack had left the peacoat behind.

Nick asked, "You found the money?"

"In a manner of speaking."

"I'm not up for riddles."

"Lister converted the stolen funds into art and that art was stored in a special kind of warehouse in Manhattan."

"What the hell does that even mean—a 'special kind of warehouse'?"

"I think I should have said a *very* special kind of warehouse, called a free port. There are other names for such places: secrecy jurisdictions, gray or foreign trade zones, special economic zones. Like museums, they are climate-controlled storage areas and have a similar status to foreign embassies. Places within a given country that are considered the sovereign territory of a foreign nation. Territory beyond the reach of all law enforcement and—perhaps more importantly for most of the people who avail themselves of their use—beyond reach of the taxman."

"Sounds like something the Swiss would invent."

Joe laughed. "You do surprise me at every turn, Nick. It was indeed a creation of our cuckoo-clock-making friends."

"But the money . . . how—"

"You know, it wasn't that the money Lister stole simply vanished, although that's how it was portrayed in the tabloids. Law enforcement traced much of it through a series of bank transfers done via several dummy corporations over the course of years. The funds were split into smaller and smaller pieces, divvied up between numerous banks. Then, those pieces would vanish but not turn up in other banks or in real estate transactions. Real estate is the go-to investment for money launderers. The law couldn't find the money in the banks or as part of any other recorded transactions. Their first thought was that the money was washed via drug cartels, but all reliable sources in the cartels denied it.

"These free ports, it seems, are part of a gray-market economy specializing in art, gold, jewelry—any commodity that isn't quickly perishable. Turn money into art; then, when you need funds, you turn the art into money—all clean, usable, and beyond the reach of the law and the taxman. But the art itself never has to leave the warehouse. It's all anonymously brokered. The art, or whatever the commodity, is simply shifted from one storage unit to another, or not at all. Neat trick."

Nick didn't like it. "I've never heard of these places, but people like you must've known about them. Didn't you guys look at them?"

Joe put his palms up. "Not my organ. Not my monkey. But, yes, your point is well taken. It seems now that you've got Lister talking, he won't shut up. Apparently, he had bought himself citizenship of another 'friendly' nation and shielded his transactions through both that citizenship and proxies in that country."

"What's my cut for the recovery?" Nick laughed and immediately regretted it.

"Bad pun, given your condition."

"I know. That's a lot of money invested in art. I mean, how many paintings did he own?"

"Not as many as you'd think. The market is at an all-time high, driven in part by people's ability to shield their collections from the taxman. But just as an example, Jackson Pollack's painting *Number 17A* sold for two hundred million dollars. A De Kooning has sold for three hundred million. It took some pressure from the State Department, and a little arm twisting, but we gained access to Lister's unit. He had about twenty paintings, including a Pollack, a Basquiat, a minor Van Gogh, a Warhol, a Jasper Johns . . . In total, the estimate is that his collection accounts for about ninety percent of the missing money. The rest of the money is probably in the pockets of corrupt bankers and politicians—the price of doing dirty business. So what went wrong back there?"

"Kenyon Cook found out about Lister and me," Nick said. "He called in some big markers and nearly got us killed. I had set it up for two inmates who were members of the Surf Avenue Posse to tune us up just enough to get us rushed to the hospital. They were killed by two outside corrections officers Cook brought in from the city. Then, they locked us up with four other inmates."

"But you got out."

"Self-evidently. Lister did good for himself. What Cook didn't realize was that we were fighting for our lives; the inmates they sent in after us were probably fighting for better phone privileges. We knew they were coming. The element of surprise counts for a lot when you're outnumbered and outarmed. How are you going to handle all that blood?"

"Already done." Joe pointed at the TV on the wall. "You'll hear all about it."

"Can't wait."

Joe's expression turned quite grave. "You know, Nick, when I was given the task of handing you this assignment, I thought there would be no chance of you succeeding."

"Your confidence in me is overwhelming."

"Seriously, Ryan, I'm stunned. People with all the resources in the world have been at Lister for months."

"When it came down to it, he knew that the other threats were bluffs. I showed him I wasn't bluffing. It's one thing to threaten a man's life; it's another to show him a preview of his death."

"That's cryptic, but you did succeed. That was the deal: whatever it takes."

"I succeeded, but you don't look happy about it."

"Get out, Nick," Joe said, putting his hand on Nick's forearm. "Now, while you still can."

"I don't think I will, but I appreciate the advice."

"Okay." Joe stood up. "I understand you were born to this. You should be out of here in a week. Then, there's to be a ceremony about your heroics at McCann's after the bombing."

Nick wasn't pleased about it, but he understood the need for it. "All right. Any progress with that?"

"None." Joe turned to go.

"A favor."

Joe stopped. "If I can."

"Kenyon Cook. You leave him to me. I won't kill him, but he has to pay."

"You've earned it."

"So Cook is mine?"

Joe smiled. "Who?"

"Be seeing you."

"Unfortunately, it seems you will. Feel better."

Nick watched him retreat, then fell hopelessly back to sleep.

FORTY-NINE

Ace was waiting for him in the same blue Ford that had taken him to the Bronx. *The Bronx!* All that seemed a lifetime ago. Taking men like Ricky Corliss off the street was what Nick had believed he was meant to do. Yet here he was, torturing rich men out of stolen money and covering up the deadly mistakes of a cop who never wanted to be on the job in the first place. Despite Joe's advice to get out, he saw things for what they were. There was no getting out, nor was there getting in. Only the dead were out of it. For the living, there were only different rungs in the machinery, even if his new bosses didn't see it as such.

His employers would soon come to understand what Aaron Lister had come to understand about Nick. He knew all about negotiations and value. He had learned it at his uncle Kenny's knee and during all those years with Shana, among the wealthy and powerful. If you proved your worth, you could do as you pleased and worry about the consequences later. "It's easier to ask forgiveness than permission," Shana's dad was wont to say. Nick had proved his worth to the tune of nearly a billion dollars—dollars that would soon be flowing back into the bank accounts of firefighters, cops, corrections officers, sanitation men, and Sean Patrick Ryan. For the power elite, it always came down to money. Blood was just an added expense.

Nick had warned Joe about his distaste for Ace, but even six days after waking up in the hospital, he was still too weak to be bothered. He slid into the front seat.

"Pretty fancy work, Ryan."

"Getting stabbed and killing people. Yeah, real fancy."

"Don't be such an asshole. I know what you did."

"Sorry."

"I know I'm the last person you wanted to see, but—"

"Not the last person," Nick interrupted, "but pretty close."

Ace smiled in spite of himself. "You're gonna need me near you. I walked in your shoes for a short while, but I wasn't skilled at it. I couldn't have worked out what you did after the Joon kid fucked up. And this last thing—man, no one could get a word out of that prick but you. I couldn't navigate in some of the waters you swim in."

"Skin color?"

"That was part of it, definitely. Scar tissue too. The stuff around my eyes, but mostly the kind inside. Could never get past who I was and who came out smelling sweet for my sweat. The thing about it is, I get the sense you don't like the people on top any better than me."

"Money is a retreat, not a fortress. I read that in a book once. The rich can be assholes," Nick said, staring out the window at the passing traffic. "No one can testify to that like me. All the same, their pain is as real as yours or mine. I know. I've seen it."

"Maybe."

"So you said you had the job for a while, but you're still hanging on."

"I have my talents."

"For violence?"

"That too. Don't shut me out, Ryan. I know the landscape better than you think. You may be batting a thousand, but nobody bats a thousand forever."

Nick remembered Angeline's body, strewn like so much litter on the sidewalk outside McCann's. "You're right. Nobody does, not even for a week."

Nick hadn't thought about any of that, not about Angeline or

Roderick Ford, since he stepped on the bus at Riker's. He was glad to be free of it for a short time. He had seen the toll taken by looking behind and living in the past. Seen his father, Lenny Feld, his army buddies, crushed by it. He had taken his time in the hospital to heal and to clear his head.

"Ryan!"

"What?"

"You okay? You zoned out on me there. Need to go back to the hospital?"

"I'm fine."

"So you say."

"What's your story?" Nick asked, pivoting away from the past.

"I'm not going there."

"You want to stick, you need to tell me. Otherwise, how can I trust you're not just Joe's man? How do I know you're not there to watch Joe and me?"

Ace screwed up his face. "Joe? Who the hell is Joe?"

"Your boss. The guy you drive around. That's what I call him."

Ace laughed. "Joe, huh?"

"You know who he is for real?"

Ace nodded.

"Maybe I'll need to know someday, but not today. What's your deal?"

Ace's body language was more eloquent than a muzzle flash. "Remember a few years ago, there was a detective killed serving a warrant on a house in Washington Heights? Got all shot up."

"What I remember about a few years ago is the geography of Afghanistan."

"I guess that's right. Well, what the media said about how it went down, how the detective was killed . . . it wasn't like that."

"He was dirty?"

"She."

Nick could see where this was going. He thought about leaving it alone, then decided to let Ace get it off his chest.

"She was protecting a Dominican crew who were distributing for the Sinaloa Cartel. Them boys don't fuck around, but they pay big money."

"But even a clued-in Narcotics detective can't know all the moves inside the department."

"She can if she's sleeping with the right person on the task force."

"You?"

"She was an old girlfriend. I loved her once, but I wasn't on the task force, no."

"You killed her."

"My first assignment."

"Do you think they knew . . . about you and her, I mean?"

Ace's laugh was as dark and empty as outer space. "What do you think?"

"I think I better keep you around. You know Kenyon Cook?"

"That piece of shit? Yeah. Why?"

"He didn't stab me, but he might just as well have."

"He's got some big people behind him. You go after him, you best be careful. You know what they say. You take a shot at the king, you better not miss."

It was Nick's turn to laugh. "Someone should have reminded him of that before he went after me."

"What you need?"

"In a few days, you and me, we need to borrow some shit from evidence lockers."

"Shit like what?"

"You'll see." Nick patted Ace's arm. "I also need the names, addresses, and phone numbers of the women who work directly for him in his office."

Ace didn't say a word as the car slowed in traffic. He seemed to know that he was being tested and that if he objected or said no, he would be on the outside with no way to get back in.

FIFTY

The medal ceremony was a muted affair, overshadowed by the news of Aaron Lister's death and the recovery of the retirement funds. Elite auction houses were already clawing over each other to win the chance to host the bidding. Nothing like a little infamy to add value to already invaluable art. Neither news item came as a shock to Nick. And he now knew who was to be the direct beneficiary of his hard work. Senator Renata Maduro's face had been all over the media as she claimed credit for uncovering the whereabouts of Lister's art stash. Nick had lost count of how many photos he'd seen over the past few days, featuring Maduro posing with the recovered paintings. If someone had to take credit for it, he was good with it being her.

Lister's death had been conveniently attributed to stab wounds he received in a jail-yard fight between three rival gangs. Nick didn't ask and didn't want to know the actual cause of death. All the other bodies had been moved from the COs' gym to the basketball yard at River-head. Nick had a pretty good sense of how it would play out. A few COs close to retirement would get shown the door with a slap on the wrist, full pensions, and sizable tax-free bonuses for falling on their swords and taking the blame. The families of the dead inmates would get nice settlements, and that would be that. Nick kept Mike Kelly's name to himself. He would see to him on his own terms, on his own schedule. For now, Nick wanted him to sweat. Lister's death, the gang fight in Riverhead—it would all fade away, just as the story of the bombing at McCann's would, after the medal ceremony at One Police Plaza was concluded.

Nick, Tom Straw, and two patrol officers, Chris Gaines and Toya Claxton, got to shake white-gloved hands with the commissioner and the chief. The two uniforms got medals and the bump to detective for their decisive actions following the bombing. Nick and Straw got medals and the respect of a grateful city, or so said the commissioner. After the ceremonies ended, Straw, Gaines, and Claxton posed for family photos. The only party there for Nick was Deputy Commissioner Ricco.

After Ricco and Nick hugged and patted each other's shoulders, Ricco offered to take him out for a drink.

"Sorry, another time maybe," Nick said. "There's something I need to take care of."

Ricco seemed to understand, wishing Nick well. He went back to the podium to confer with the chief and the commissioner.

Nick walked straight into the small crowd of media gathered in the rear of the auditorium. A few of the reporters asked Nick questions as he waded into their midst, but he had only one media member in his sights.

"Hi, Callie," he said, tugging at the press card slung around her neck. "Calista Barrows. That much was true."

"Detective Ryan." She nodded. "Congratulations."

In a voice loud enough for the other media to hear, he said, "I believe we have to arrange that exclusive interview I promised."

She was momentarily flustered but quickly regained her footing. "Would you like to do it now over a cup of coffee?"

"Absolutely."

They waited until the others had cleared out. Heading toward the exit, Mercy Willis walked past them, glaring at Callie.

"What's the deal between you two?" Nick asked as they stepped out of the ugly reddish-brown cube that served as NYPD headquarters.

"Who?"

"Callie, if you're going to keep lying to me, what's the point?"

"Mercy and me? We were once close friends. Not anymore."

"No shit!" Nick laughed. "She gave you the most vicious stink eye I've ever seen. C'mon, what's the deal?"

"She thinks I used her."

"Did you?"

"I'm the journalist," she deflected. "I'm the one who's supposed to ask the questions."

"So you did use her."

"I suppose I did."

"Was it worth it?"

"We're here together, aren't we?"

Nick smiled. "Mack told me you followed my car from my condo. I was curious how you got my address. No wonder she's pissed. She risked her career to sleep with you."

"How can you—"

"I'm good at what I do, at reading people," he said.

As they walked toward Tribeca, nearing where he had saved D'Anton Waller, Nick stopped and threw the case containing his new medal down a sewer.

"What did you do that for?" Callie was stunned.

"Medals . . . I don't think you'd understand."

"Try me."

"They don't mean anything," Nick said. "I had to accept it because I didn't want to embarrass Deputy Commissioner Ricco, but no one says I had to keep it. You were there. I was just doing my job. Most of the time, men and women who get medals are just doing their jobs. Medals are for the people in the audience, not for the people who get them."

They didn't speak again until they got to Le Pain Quotidien at the corner of West Broadway and Warren Street.

He sat. She got the coffees. It gave her time to recover.

"I didn't know how you liked it," Callie said, placing the cups on the table.

"Something you don't know about me?" He sipped. "Black is fine. Thank you."

"Please don't get Mercy in trouble. I would deny it was her anyway."

"And I would have a keystroke search done and she'd be fucked. All inquiries are recorded. Look, I'm not interested in hurting anyone—not you, not her—but I suggest you start telling me the truth, or my interests could change. I'm a nice guy, up to a point."

Callie pulled her laptop out of her backpack and placed it on the table. "Give me a second." She punched a few keys and spun the laptop around so that they both could see the screen. "That's you, isn't it, in the firefighter's outfit?"

"On the record or off?"

"For now, off the record."

"Okay. If that is me, so what?"

"That's your car. Not many of those on the road these days."

"And . . ."

"And I'm not a big believer in coincidences," she said. "Pretty amazing that you should be at the scene of both the Scarborough House murders and the McCann's bombing. The second coincidence is that the bomb should go off just when you got to the edge of the blast zone."

"When *we* got to the edge of the blast zone. You were standing next to me. I could say the same things about you since you were apparently at both scenes as well."

She grinned, shaking her head. "Nice try, Detective Ryan. You sound like a lawyer. I can explain my presence at both places."

"As can I. There's nothing amazing about any of it." Nick was making it up as he went along. "We had CI—do you know what that is?"

"Confidential informant."

"Very good. We had CI intel that there was a new heroin gang dealing out of Building Six of the Scarborough Houses. The firefighter getup let us gain access to the building unhindered and without being seen as cops during a gas-leak evacuation. That's all."

"You know, Nick, I did some checking. There was never any gas leak."

"You'd have to talk to someone else about that. Better to be safe than sorry, I guess. We took advantage of the situation. It's what good policing is about."

"Anything come of it, the drug raid?"

"Nope. The intel was stale. The crew had already cleared out. What happened with the Joon kid and one of Roderick Ford's crazies—what can I tell you? It's a violent world where people have access to guns."

"Funny you should mention Roderick Ford."

"Why's that?"

"If one of his crazies was devoted enough to kill people in the stairwell of an NYCHA project, do you think there was another crazy enough to blow up McCann's? Ford is famously no friend to the police. I believe he has often referred to them as 'jackbooted storm troopers in blue,' who carry out the will of the socialist government."

Nick shrugged. "Interesting theory."

"I've done some research on Ford in your absence. Where were you for the last few weeks, by the way?"

"On the International Space Station."

"I can almost believe that, Detective Ryan, because you look as pale and thin as someone who spent two weeks in space. He's an interesting character, Roderick Ford. The man is actually worse than the image he projects. I think he's fundamentally a white supremacist. I tried to get an interview with him. I didn't get it, of course. He considers me beneath him."

"You have lots of company. He considers everybody beneath him." Nick went cold inside. "You might think about staying away from him. Whether he incited that nut to murder or not, he's dangerous."

"What are you implying?"

"Not a thing. I'm saying it plainly. Drop off the man's radar." Nick shifted gears. "You were talking about the murders at the Scarborough Houses."

"Was I?"

"I think so."

"The murders got tied up in a pretty neat package, didn't they?"

"If you consider three innocent people getting the shit blown out of them a neat package, we have different definitions of 'neat.'"

"That's not what I meant and you know it." She moved on. "What about the bombing?"

"What about it? You going to tell me that was a neat package too, with Angeline's naked body out there on Fourth Avenue?"

"You can't intimidate me, Nick."

"I disagree, but I'm not trying to. What is it you think you know, and what can you prove?"

"I'm not sure, but"—she stopped to suck down half her coffee in a single shot—"I can say there's more going on here than a bad drug bust, a crazed racist, and an angry bomber. Somehow, Nick, you're at the center of this. I'm good at my job too." Callie slammed her laptop shut. "I'm also good at reading people. You're hiding something big, and when I find out what it is, I'll write it. Don't worry, I'll call you first for comment."

"Let me help you with that." Nick took a card out of his wallet. "My cell number is right there. If I were hiding, would I give that to you?" He checked his watch. "I have to go."

"Did Mack give you the coat?"

"He did. You know, you didn't have to pretend with me."

"I know that now."

Before she could react, Nick reached into her bag, grabbing her phone. He held it up to his mouth. "According to Ms. Barrows, the preceding conversation was strictly off the record and she recorded me without my consent." He replaced the phone in her bag. "Thanks for the coffee and the company."

Nick had a busy night ahead, but now he had an extra stop to make on the way home.

FIFTY-ONE

Sitting next to Ace in the front seat, outside the Woodhaven Motel on Queens Boulevard, Nick read through the pages he had collected from Lenny Feld on his way home that afternoon. Once Mack had warned him about Callie being a journalist, Nick felt he'd wasted Lenny's time. She wasn't even a very experienced journalist. She was enthusiastic, persistent, and perceptive. He had to give her that. Still, she had slept with a source, endangering the source's career and compromising her own professional ethics. Given the things he had done over the past several weeks, he was in no position to judge her.

Most of what Callie had told him about herself at McCann's was accurate. She came from Glencoe. She had been a track star at UK, a scholastic all-American with an enviable GPA. What he couldn't figure out was why Callie had taken such a half-assed approach with him. Why had she exposed herself the way she had at McCann's before she had more solid footing and a better grasp of the facts? What had she been willing to do to get more space on the front page of a newspaper that almost no one read? He smiled to himself because despite everything, he liked her.

Ace caught a glimpse of Nick's expression. "What are you smiling at?"

"Nothing."

"No one smiles at nothing."

"True. I was smiling at something."

Ace let it go. "Wait," he said, looking into the side-view mirror. "Here they come."

———

Keisha Williams chewed the inside of her cheek so hard, the taste of blood was strong on her tongue. But she was willing to do anything to punish Kenyon Cook for raping her. Worse than the split lip and bruising was the self-recrimination. All she had done for days following the assault was to beat herself up over being so stupid and ignoring the warnings of every other woman in the office. It was turning her stomach that Cook kept his huge callused right hand on the inside of her left thigh, occasionally sliding his fingers up to her panties, the only saving grace being that it was a short ride to the motel from headquarters in East Elmhurst.

"I knew you were a smart girl and that you'd come around," Cook had said to her when she proposed they spend a second night together. "No one with a brain in her head wants to go back in uniform on the block."

He had stood tall over her workstation, gloating, a hungry smile on his face. She wasn't sure whether he called her "girl" because of her Blackness or because he saw all women as less than men, less than human.

"I'll bring the wine. That was the problem last time," she said, fluttering her lashes. "I wasn't loosened up. I like to be a little loosened up first so I can let go."

"I'm not sure I want you loosened up. I like it when they fight."

"I promise you, a glass of wine will help me give you all the fight you can handle."

"I look forward to it. Tomorrow night, then." It was a command, not a question.

As she got out of Cook's car, it was all she could do not to look for

Nick Ryan. This was all his doing. As comforting and reassuring as he had been, she was panicked at the thought of things going sideways. *What if the drugs don't work? What if Cook tries to force me again? What if . . .* So many what-ifs, she was choking on them. But she wanted to hurt Cook for what he had done to her and every other woman who had passed through his office.

They had barely gotten inside the room before he pawed at her, grabbing her breasts, pinching her nipples so hard she wanted to scream. She managed to smile at him as she pushed away.

"Wine first, remember? Then I'll give you a run for your money." She carried the bottles into the bathroom. "Let me get us some cups."

He was already dropping his pants when the bathroom door shut.

———

Ace waved to Nick that they were in the room. Nick popped out of the Ford, a slender piece of shiny metal held against his thigh. He walked around to the passenger side of Cook's classic '71 Bronco. Cook could have had a city car and driver, but he liked to drive on his own. He didn't need a driver who might tell tales out of school. Nick slid the slim jim down between the window and sill. He fished around until the notch grabbed on to what he was feeling for. He gave a sharp tug upward and the door lock clicked open. He gave the come-ahead sign to Ace. Less than three minutes later, their work was done.

———

Nick had made two calls to women in Cook's office before finding Keisha Williams with his third call. He knew he had the right woman because there was dead silence when he spoke his name.

"I wanted to thank you," he'd said to fill the void. "My friend gave me your message, and I know you were trying to warn me."

"Did it help?"

He lied. "It did."

"I'm glad," she said, though she still seemed tense.

"He hurt you, didn't he?"

Silence. Tears. "I'm sorry." Then, she explained what had happened that night at the motel. How she had gone there willingly because she was attracted to Cook. "Then he smacked me around and raped me." More tears. "I overheard a phone conversation he was having about you. That's when I found out your number from a friend and called."

"Don't be sorry. How would you like to help me make sure he can never hurt anyone again?"

"You aren't going to—"

"Kill him? No, not that. What I have in mind would be much worse for a jail keeper than death."

She hesitated. "What would I have to do?"

"It won't be easy."

"Getting raped wasn't easy. What do you need?"

They had met after work the next day.

———

Nick's cell buzzed. He checked his text messages. "He's out."

The deskman, whom Nick and Ace had warned and paid off, said nothing as they strode past him toward Cook's regular room. The door was ajar. Keisha Williams was slipping on her boots at the edge of the bed as Nick and Ace entered. They closed the door behind them. Cook, naked, was on the floor between the bed and the wall. Keisha was panting, her eyes wide with fear and adrenaline.

Nick said, "It's okay. We'll handle it from here."

"But—"

"No buts or what-ifs," Ace said. "Go on, now. Walk a few blocks away and call an Uber. This man is never going to hurt any woman ever again. I promise."

She'd never met Ace, but she believed him. Her breathing slowed. When she stood, her knees were unsteady. She teetered, planting her hand on the bed to steady herself.

"That's the comedown from the adrenaline," Nick said. "Go ahead. I'll call you tomorrow to let you know what happened, but I'm sure you'll see it on the news. Remember your story?"

She nodded. "He threatened me with my job and to hurt me physically if I didn't come back with him, even though he'd raped me. But when he started doing the drugs, I got out of the room and ran."

"That's it." Nick gave the thumbs-up. "Believe me, your role in this won't ever get out. You'll probably never have to tell that story. It's just in case."

She turned and left.

When the door closed, Ace took the baggies out of his pocket with his gloved hands. He wrapped Cook's hands around the plastic bags. When he was sure Cook's prints were all over them, Ace placed them back in his pocket. Nick took out the aluminum foil, matches, a small packet of white powder, and a thin glass tube.

Fifteen minutes later they left the room and went back to Cook's Bronco.

Ace asked, "How long you think he'll be out of it?"

"However long it takes."

————

Forty-five minutes later they watched a disheveled Kenyon Cook come stumbling out of the Woodhaven Motel on unsteady legs. His expression was a combination of rage and confusion. By the time he realized what had happened, he would be on his way to prison. Cook got in his Bronco and tore out of the parking spot. They followed him, biding their time until he got on the Grand Central Parkway. When he did, Nick punched in three digits on the burner phone.

When the 911 operator came on, Nick played a prerecorded message Mack had done for him. "There's some crazy man driving erratically on the Grand Central, heading east between exits fifteen and sixteen. He's in an old blue Ford Bronco with a broken taillight and headlight. When I pulled next to him to alert him, he pointed a gun at me. Hurry. He's apt to kill somebody one way or another."

It didn't take long. Two NYPD Highway Patrol cruisers blew past them, light bars flashing and sirens screaming. One fell in right behind Cook's Bronco. The other pulled alongside, forcing the Bronco to exit. Ace kept a few car lengths' distance, following them all off the parkway and onto the service road. He shut off his headlights and remained close enough to watch the inevitable unfold.

"That was smart," Ace said. "Once there's a mention of a gun, Highway Patrol cops aren't gonna fuck around."

The cops got out of their vehicles, weapons drawn. They approached cautiously from both sides of the Bronco. Cook should have rolled down his window and stayed in the Bronco, both hands on the steering wheel to show he was no threat. Instead, he flung his door open. Big mistake number one. He started yelling at the cops, gesturing with his arms. Big mistake number two. Then, he made the biggest mistake of them all: he reflexively reached for his ID. Luckily for Cook, the cop on his side of the vehicle was experienced and shot him only once, in the abdomen.

After the shot was fired, Ace waved a wallet in the air. "Too bad. Shame we got his ID right here."

"Yeah, a real fucking pity."

"You wanna stay until they find the heroin and the AR-15?"

"Gloating is unbecoming." Nick laughed. "Just drive me back to where we left my car. And thanks again."

"Nah, man, thank you. Good to feel like something more than a chauffeur with a gun."

———

As Nick got out of Ace's Ford and waved so long, his cell phone buzzed in his pocket. A number he didn't recognize showed on his screen. He thought about letting it go to voice mail but didn't.

"Nick Ryan."

"Nick, I'm scared." It was a woman's voice, brittle and barely audible.

"Who is this?"

"Callie."

"What is it?"

"They killed him."

"Who's they? Who did they kill?"

"Murray, my boss at the paper. He's dead."

"Tell me where you are exactly."

"Near Brooklyn College. Under a car."

"I know you're scared, Callie, but you have to concentrate."

"Avenue H, just off Nostrand."

"What kind of car?"

"What!"

"You're under a car. What make of car?"

"Oh, shit!"

"Forget it. I know where you are. It's a short block. Stay put and stay quiet."

FIFTY-TWO

It took only twenty minutes to get there from Queens—an eternity to Callie. In first gear, he rolled the GTO down the short block of Avenue H that led onto the Brooklyn College campus. He hoped Callie would recognize the GTO's throaty rumble and save him the trouble of having to search beneath every parked car on the street. He also kept an eye out for anyone hiding in the shadows, between cars, in doorways, behind hedges. He saw no one. When Callie didn't show herself, Nick feared he hadn't gotten there quickly enough.

He pulled up next to a fire hydrant and reached for the small Glock holstered on his ankle. He also grabbed the Maglite from under his seat. LED technology made it possible for a flashlight the size of his pinky to provide a more powerful beam than the bulky Maglite. What a pinky-sized flashlight couldn't do was help him in a fight. Over the years, that big aluminum tube filled with the weight of three D batteries had been a pretty dependable nonlethal weapon.

Nick kept the Glock at the ready, resting the butt atop the Maglite held out in front of him.

"Callie, it's me, Nick," he called out softly, pausing to listen for a response. "Callie, it's Nick."

When he had finished methodically checking one side of the street without hearing anything but the ambient traffic noise from Nostrand Avenue, he began to worry. He crossed the street. Halfway down the block, his beam caught a dark bulk beneath a new Pacifica minivan.

"NYPD. Get out from under the car, now!" Nick's tone had changed from imploring to I'm-not-fucking-around. "Now means now! Show me your hands first!"

The shape moved. "It's me! Nick, it's me."

Callie slid out from under the minivan. She was shivering. Tears had cut a canal through the grime covering the rest of her face.

"Are you hurt? Do you need medical attention?"

His professional voice seemed to get through to her. "They killed him," she said. "They beat him to death. They were asking him about me and you."

He put the flashlight under his armpit, kept the Glock at the ready, and put his arm over Callie's shoulder. He walked her as quickly as he dared to his GTO, got in, and took off.

"As calmly as you can, Callie, tell me what happened."

She took a few big swallows of air. "Since the bombing, I've been so focused on you and researching Roderick Ford, I haven't done the rest of my job very well. Murray is—was—old, and I was letting him down. I was on suspension for a while, but I would come into the office at night to help catch up for the time I missed. And Murray can't sleep since his wife died, so he comes in at night too, to do work when the phones aren't ringing as much."

Nick could hear her struggling to hold herself together. "Okay, that's good. Keep going."

"When I got near the front door, I heard Murray screaming. I froze. I heard strange men's voices. I got down real low and could see some of it through the glass door. They were big men. One of them kept shouting at Murray, asking him about where I was, how much I had on you, and where my research was. He slapped Murray before he could even answer. Murray kept saying he didn't know what they were talking about or who I was and that a newspaperman never reveals his sources. He laughed at them. That got them really mad and they started breaking Murray's fingers. He couldn't stop screaming, and then he went still."

Nick didn't ask her why she hadn't called 911. He needed her to focus and not fall into the well of guilt. There was always enough time to take that dive later on.

"I should've called the cops, but I was afraid they would hear me, and I didn't want to leave Murray alone. I know that's stupid."

"Never mind that for now." Nick's tone turned more insistent. "You said Murray went still."

"I guess he couldn't take it. He'd had a few minor heart attacks before. It must have given out. The one who was asking the questions told the other guy to feel for a pulse. 'He's dead,' the guy said. They started going through all the files, throwing stuff everywhere. They ripped out the two computer towers. That's when they must've seen me. They chased me down Nostrand, but there was no chance they could catch me. I doubled back twice even after I lost them."

Nick asked her to describe the men, but she said she couldn't see very well through the glass. "They were white—I could see that much—and dressed in suits. I didn't look back when they were chasing me. Look behind you in a race and you lose."

"Okay, we're going to go over there now and—"

"No! No! Please, I can't, and I can't stay in the car. What if they're still waiting for me?"

Nick didn't argue. It didn't take a psychologist to see that Callie was on the edge of snapping. All the reassurances in the world weren't going to help. Murray was dead and whatever evidence his killers had left behind was still there. Nick made his second anonymous 911 call of the evening.

"Please, don't leave me alone, Nick."

"Don't worry about that. I'll take care of you tonight."

That was it. Calista Barrows leaned her head against Nick's shoulder and fell to pieces.

———

He had a drink waiting for her when she came out of the shower wearing Nick's much-the-worse-for-wear terry-cloth bathrobe.

"Sorry," he said, handing her the glass of bourbon. "This stuff's not as good as what I kept at McCann's."

She tried smiling and drank.

"McCann's—that was about you, wasn't it, Nick?"

"Always the reporter."

"Twenty-four-seven. Murray used to say reporters should have real lives outside their work, but he didn't mean it. Tonight he died for his career and to protect me."

Then, she talked about Murray and how he had taken her under his wing. How he treated her like a favorite child. Nick let her talk until she seemed talked out. She wasn't quite done.

"You didn't answer the question about McCann's," Callie said.

"The honest answer is, I don't know." Nick shook his head. "My turn. Who would've known about you pursuing a story on me?"

"Murray and your friend Mack, I guess. Mercy too."

"The three *M*s. There's a pun in there somewhere. It wasn't Mack. Do you think Mercy wanted to hurt you bad enough to—"

"She's hurt because she's a little in love with me. I can't see it."

"Okay, I don't see that either," Nick agreed. "But there had to be someone else who knew."

"That is evidently true, but they didn't find out through me."

Roderick Ford. Nick hadn't worked out how Ford knew about Callie, or the permutations of why he might go after her. But enhanced interrogation techniques—torture—sounded like something Ford's security contractor types would be experienced at. He kept his guesses to himself.

"Finish your drink." Nick stood. "The guest bedroom is—"

"No, Nick." She stood too. "I don't want to be alone tonight. Even if that means you just hold me."

He took her hand and walked her into his bedroom.

They laid there for an hour, Callie resting her head on Nick's chest, his arm over the terry cloth covering her shoulders. She dozed for a bit.

He didn't. She got up to use the bathroom, and when she came back, she was no longer wearing his robe. She hesitated by the side of the bed.

"Is it all right, Nick?"

He reached out and took her hand again. She led; he followed. She gently kissed his closed eyes, his mouth, then stopped and lay on top of him. He wrapped his arms around her back and held her tight to him.

"I've been terribly lonely here," she whispered. "And now I'm scared."

"Easy to be lonely and scared in New York City."

"I used Mercy to get your address, but it was still nice to be held. I liked being wanted. I miss being held."

"I like holding you."

"When I came to McCann's that night we met, I wasn't sure which I was more curious about: you being a detective or you being a detective dressed as a firefighter."

"You're not ever going to get my story, so you're gonna have to settle on me."

She pressed her lips to his and this time there was nothing gentle about it.

FIFTY-THREE

Nick was out of bed, shaved, and showered with the sun. Callie was still dead asleep. Their sex was about all sorts of things, but only minimally about sex. During the night, there had been two tentative attempts, both mutually abandoned and ending in tears. Then, finally, sleep.

Flipping through the channels, Nick saw that both stories were already getting beaucoup coverage. The old saying, "If it bleeds, it leads," was proved true yet again. The torture-murder of Pulitzer Prize–winning journalist Murray Kleinman was the top story on all the six a.m. local news broadcasts. Nick was impressed by Kleinman's accomplishments. The NYPD wasn't saying much, but the press release seemed to imply that robbery was the motive and that things had gone sideways. "A robbery gone wrong" was a time-tested media stall for the NYPD.

The second story on all the broadcasts was the shooting and arrest of New York City Department of Corrections Bureau Chief Kenyon Cook. While the murder story led, the Cook story had more sizzle. All the channels were doing remotes from the scene of the shooting, along the exit of the Grand Central, or from outside the Woodhaven Motel. The deskman was amazingly cooperative with the press.

"Oh, yeah, Mr. Smith—that's the name he always used—he was

here all the time with many different women. He even had a regular room. Paid me extra to make sure it was open for him on the nights he would come in. The cleaning girls, they always complained about how messy it was in the morning. Bottles and drugs and stuff everywhere."

The breathless on-scene reporting also included unconfirmed reports from unnamed sources, regarding drugs and drug paraphernalia found in Cook's room.

Niki Philips, the local NBC reporter, was standing in front of crime scene tape. Behind her were Cook's Bronco, the two NYPD Highway Patrol units, a crime-scene-unit vehicle, and a swarm of activity.

"Department of Corrections Bureau Chief Kenyon Cook, disheveled and unsteady, left the Woodhaven Motel sometime around eleven last evening. Several minutes later a vehicle matching the description of Cook's 1971 Ford Bronco was reported driving erratically on the Grand Central Parkway." She turned. "You can see Cook's Bronco there behind me. The driver of the Bronco was allegedly threatening other drivers with a handgun. When police responded, Cook resisted arrest and made what was described as a threatening gesture, reaching for what responding officers thought to be a weapon. Cook was shot once in the abdomen and was taken to Elmhurst General, where he is reported to be in serious but stable condition. A search of Bureau Chief Cook's Bronco led to the discovery of, what police believe to be, a significant amount of heroin and an AR-15 assault rifle that had been illegally modified to function as a fully automatic weapon."

That was what Nick was waiting to hear. He and Ace had made sure there was so much evidence, Cook's powerful friends dare not try to intervene. Even Houdini couldn't extricate himself from this mess. Cook getting himself shot was just icing on the cake. The cops would eventually track down Keisha Williams, who would in turn lead them to the other women Cook had coerced and raped. He would have to take any deal they offered him. His powerful friends would demand it to save themselves the embarrassment. It didn't take much for powerful friends to become powerful enemies.

Callie was standing behind him when he turned off the TV. She seemed a little shaky but in much better shape than when he found her. Her face, still damp from the shower, glistened.

"There's coffee," he said. "I'll get you some."

"No, Nick. That's okay. The police will want to speak to me, won't they?"

"No doubt. I can find out who caught the case and bring you over there."

As if on cue, Callie's cell phone rang.

Nick wagged his finger. "Let it go to voice mail. You have to think about what you're going to say. You won't be a suspect, but if you say you were at the scene—"

"I understand."

"I can alibi you. This way, whoever did it to Murray will think twice about coming after you or coming at you through me."

Callie thought about it. "Are you sure?"

"I'm sure. This is my fight too."

"What will I say?"

Nick looked at Callie and decided not to overload her with information before she was fully awake. "We'll discuss it on the way to your apartment. You'll need some fresh clothes. No makeup, though."

"I get it."

"Okay, you can call them back now. Don't say anything other than that you just woke up. Be noncommittal about everything else and say you'll be in as soon as you can."

————

Callie lived in an old apartment building in Crown Heights, close to where Ebbets Field had once stood. Like many neighborhoods in Brooklyn, Crown Heights was in the midst of gentrification. For many years, the neighborhood had been uncomfortably divided up between African Americans and Hassidic Jews. A situation that in 1991 had led to the worst rioting in the city since the 1977 blackout. Gentrification was now causing tensions to rise and tempers to flare. Although seemingly unrelated, gentrification had only exacerbated the fallout from the police shootings. Nick got why the African American community felt under siege. Some of it was a matter of perception. Some of it was real.

"This is it," Callie said. "I'm one of the few people in there in a rent-stabilized apartment. They want me out so they can quadruple the rent."

"Welcome to life in New York. Other cities can spread out. Not here. Here, real estate churns and the poor get screwed."

"The poor get screwed everywhere, Nick."

"You weren't poor."

"I wasn't blind either."

"Good point."

He pulled up to the curb right in front of her building.

"Why don't you wait for me here? I'll be down in a—"

"No chance," he said, getting out of the car.

He had his service piece holstered on his hip, keeping his right hand close as he went around to open the passenger door. He saw Callie staring at the bulge beneath his jacket.

"Is that necessary?"

"Part of the complete package. C'mon, let's get this over with."

They rode the rickety old elevator up to the third floor. The thing hadn't been painted or cleaned in quite a while.

"Man, they really do want you rent-stabilized people out of here," Nick said.

"Six months after the last one of us is gone, this place will look like the Taj Mahal and not the men's room at the Port Authority Bus Terminal."

At the door Callie's hands shook so hard, she dropped her keys. Nick picked them up for her and put the key in the lock. She was crying and rested her head on his shoulder.

"I'm sorry," she whispered between sobs. "It just dawned on me again that Murray's dead. I'm never going to speak to him again."

"You ever lose anybody close like this before?"

"Only pets."

"It's going to hurt. Let it. Don't pretend it doesn't. Only makes it worse."

A minute later she had pulled herself together. When Nick tried to follow her into her apartment, Callie turned and put her hand up against his chest.

"Please don't. It's a wreck, and I need a minute, okay?"

"I'll be right here if you need me. And don't worry about what to say to the detectives. We'll go over that again in the car."

She leaned forward and kissed his cheek. "Thank you, Nick—for everything."

"Go on."

As soon as Callie stepped into her apartment, Nick heard someone coming up the stairs. He put his hand around the grip of his gun and turned so that his body blocked the view of his gun hand. The breathless man in coveralls at the top of the stairs eyed Nick with suspicion. He came ahead.

"I'm Pérez," he said. "The super. I have to talk to the lady, Miss Barrows."

"Not now." Nick showed Pérez his shield. "She's grieving."

Pérez was momentarily confused. "Okay. I'm sorry. You tell her something for me?"

"Sure."

"I let the electrician into her apartment. I don't know why she don't just tell me and had to go to the landlord. It makes me look bad. I would fix the electricity for her, but—"

"What electrician?"

"He show me a work order from the landlord."

Nick spun, pushing the apartment door open. "Callie, don't touch anything!"

"What?" Her voice came from deep inside the apartment.

Nick ran to her voice. He found her in front of her dresser, fingers wrapped around the top drawer pulls. "I thought I told you—"

"Stop!"

Annoyed, she tugged at the drawer. "Stop what?"

Nick didn't have time to explain. He grabbed her, turning to keep his body between the dresser and Callie. He pushed her through the bedroom door, then to the side and down onto the hardwood floor. Nick didn't get down in time. The blast blew him out the open front door, into the hallway. His head bounced off the tile floor. When he opened his eyes, Pérez was standing over him. The superintendent's lips were moving in slow motion, and his words sounded like a beehive buzzing a single note.

FIFTY-FOUR

This time when Nick opened his eyes, Joe wasn't there to greet him. The light hit him like a sledgehammer. He grabbed the bedpan, leaned over the bed railing, and heaved. Nothing but mucus and stomach acid came out of him, burning his throat. The heaving made his throbbing head feel as if it might explode. He recognized a concussion. He had suffered one in Afghanistan—the result of a shock wave from a roadside IED. But knowing what it was didn't make anything hurt less. After the heaving stopped, he fell back into bed, retreating into the welcoming womb of unconsciousness.

"Detective Ryan," an unfamiliar woman's voice called to him.

He felt a light touch on his shoulder.

He opened his eyes. The room was relatively dark, the pain in his head not nearly as intense as earlier, whenever "earlier" was. He had no sense of time. Reflexively shielding his eyes with his hand, Nick looked up to see the blurry outline of a woman in scrubs.

"Good to see you're alert, Detective Ryan. I'm Dr. Gupta." She said the South Asian name with a soft Texas twang. "How are you feeling?"

"Like . . ." his voice cracked, his throat raw and dry. Even he could smell his bad breath. "Like my head was a piñata."

"That's funny." She didn't laugh. "You have a concussion."

"How did I get it?"

"You have no recollection of the event?" The tone of Gupta's voice changed from cheery to severe.

"Where am I?"

"Maimonides Medical Center."

"In Borough Park?"

"Yes. I was the neurologist on duty when they brought you in. Before we go any further, Nick, I need to perform some tests."

After the doctor had him do some eye tracking and checked his balance and his cognitive function, she asked him the last thing he remembered.

"I was in my car with Callie," he mumbled, struggling to remember. "Callie! What happened? Did I have a car accident? Is Callie here too?"

"Please calm down, Detective Ryan. There are two detectives outside who wish to speak to you. I will—"

"She's dead."

"Is that a guess or do you recollect something specific?"

"An educated guess, Doc."

"The detectives outside—I will speak with them and limit their time with you. If your pain gets too great or if you feel yourself begin to lose consciousness, press the call button." She placed his hand around the signaling device. "I won't be far away, and I will alert the nurses."

Nick didn't recognize either detective—one white and in his forties, the other Asian and barely thirty.

"Detective Ryan, I'm Detective Park," the Asian detective said. "This is Detective McQuilton. How are you feeling?"

"Like shit."

"That's understandable."

Nick wasn't interested in talking around things. "She's dead—Calista Barrows."

The two detectives looked at each other. McQuilton gave his partner an almost imperceptible nod.

Park said, "Nope. She's down the hall, and from the look of it, she's in better shape than you. A few scrapes and bruises."

"What happened?"

"You don't remember?"

Nick was angry. "Look, I'm not fucking with you. You want me to answer your questions, answer mine."

"A bomb," McQuilton said. "In her dresser drawer. She says you got her out of there just in time. Good move. Our guys say if either of you were any closer . . . well, we wouldn't be talking."

He felt numb. First, the bombing that killed Angeline, and now this. The questions that followed made sense: Did he know who might want to hurt Calista Barrows? *He sure did.* Did he think there might be any connection between the murder of Murray Kleinman and the attempt on Calista Barrows? *Only a fucking moron wouldn't.* Did he think there was any connection between the bombing at McCann's and the attempted murder of Calista Barrows? *Abso-fucking-lutely.* Why was he with Calista Barrows that morning? *Because she was scared and lonely and needed my help.* How well did he know Calista Barrows? *Intimately and not well at all.*

The *only* good thing about the concussion was that it allowed Nick to give vague answers or no answer at all. Every answer he gave was an evasion, because the truth would have gotten Park and McQuilton nowhere. Roderick Ford would never be tied to any of this no matter what Nick answered. Taking down Kenyon Cook was one thing. He had even been given unofficial sanction to do so. Taking down Roderick Ford was another matter altogether. When it came to Ford, Nick intended to take Shana's father's advice. He would ask forgiveness once the deed was done. Permission be damned.

Park seemed to buy most of Nick's bullshit; McQuilton, not so much. McQuilton waved Park ahead, saying he wanted a private moment with Ryan.

When McQuilton was sure his partner was out of earshot, he said, "Chief Joon wanted me to tell you that you have his undying respect. That he is indebted to you and that you would understand. He gave me strict instructions to give you a wide berth. So even though I didn't believe a thing you told us, I figure you've got your reasons. I respect that and what you did at McCann's. You need my help or feel like telling me what's really going on, let me know."

Nick didn't watch him leave. Instead, he closed his eyes and went to sleep. When he got out of the hospital, there was work to be done.

FIFTY-FIVE

At Joe's insistence, he took some time away from his unofficial responsibilities.

"Take a few weeks. The city can hold its breath in the meantime, and you're too good at this for anyone to let you burn out."

Nick didn't argue the point. Owing to the severity of his concussion, he was already on leave from his official duties, the ones that meant following the rules. *The rules.* Nick was no longer quite sure what those were. More clearly than ever, he saw that the rules were intended only for the poor and the powerless and were meant to keep them that way. Regardless of what Joe wanted to believe, it was precisely for this reason that Nick intended to return to the shadows. Until then, he had a lot of catching up to do, mostly with himself.

Since the day he set out to kill Ricky Corliss, his life had changed more than it had since his first few weeks on the ground in Afghanistan. Between the meeting in the tire shop, the mess at the Scarborough Houses, the caper with Roderick Ford, the McCann's bombing, the reclamation of the funds stolen by Aaron Lister, and Nick's return to a hospital bed after the bombing at Callie's, he barely had time to breathe, let alone think.

Ford got what he wanted. Callie wasn't dead, but she was gone, scared off. Nick had just driven her to LaGuardia. They barely spoke during the ride. Most of what they had to say, they had shared while Nick was still in the hospital.

"I'm done, Nick," she had told him, sitting next to his bed. Her face was scraped and bruised. "First Murray and now this. For what? I'm not even sure why. It doesn't matter, because it's not worth my life."

"I agree."

"I'm going back home to Glencoe for a while to get my head straight."

"Then what?"

She formed a *W* with her fingers. "Go Wildcats."

"You're taking the coaching internship."

"Starting in the spring."

"Good."

With tears in her eyes, Callie leaned over the bed rail. "If I leave, will I be safe, Nick?"

He reached through the rail and took her hand. "Leave your notes, photos, and laptop with me. I'll make sure you'll have nothing to worry about—one way or the other."

She opened her mouth to ask him what he meant by that, but the words didn't come out. In the end, she didn't want to know. She just wanted to be safe.

When he dropped her off at Terminal B in front of the Southwest sign, Callie pointed to a cardboard box on the GTO's back seat, next to her carry-on bag. "That's my laptop and all my notes on every story I worked on since I arrived in New York. Even my phone is in there." She held up a new iPhone. "The only thing I have on this is my essential numbers. Nothing else. No photos or data."

"Got it."

"Are you sure I'll be—"

"In the hospital I told you I'd make sure you have nothing to worry about. It was true when I said it. It's true now. Go live your life, Callie. Don't look over your shoulder, because there won't be anything or anyone there to see." He kissed her on the cheek. "Go."

As she pulled the bag off the back seat, she said, "If you're ever in Kentucky . . ."

"You'll be my first call."

It was a fifteen-minute drive from LaGuardia to the cemetery. As he walked to Pete Moretti's grave—he had been to Angeline's a few days earlier—Nick laughed to himself, remembering the two sorry-assed junkies he had stopped from getting themselves killed. Everything else made that confrontation feel as insignificant as a squabble over a pickup basketball game. But it wasn't a game. None of it was.

Detectives Park and McQuilton were about as close to discovering the bomber as Chicago was to New York City. The device used in Callie's apartment was similar in design and construction to the one used at McCann's. Mack had told him that bomb makers often had a signature as unique as their own handwriting.

"Oh, we knew which devices were IRA and which were Unionist. We often knew the builders by name and style. The way they clipped the wires, the marks the nippers left on the wire tips, the method for winding the wires about the contacts, the timer or type of remote they preferred—like a behavioral profile, it was."

Mack had further confessed that his unit had sometimes exploded devices on their own to sow disunity among the factions.

McQuilton echoed much of what Mack had said. "The bomb squad says it was probably the same guy. It was wired the same—same type and amount of explosive. They think it's someone with military ordnance training, but they don't recognize the signature."

Nick could tell there was something McQuilton wasn't saying.

"What's wrong, McQuilton?"

The detective threw his hands up. "I'm no expert, but it seems less like the same bomber and more like someone *copying* the first bomber. The setup was the same, wiring and all, but the wires weren't from the same spool. The explosive was the same type but not chemically identical. I don't know. I'm just frustrated."

Nick empathized. "Easy to get frustrated when you're not making headway."

"The offer I made in the hospital still stands. You need my help, let me know."

Nice try, Nick thought. McQuilton was really aiming for Nick to take him into his confidence and let his guard down. That wasn't going to happen. He knew lots of detectives like McQuilton—people who did their jobs and chafed at the brass for boxing them in; chafed at witnesses who weren't telling all they knew. Nick had other things to occupy his time.

As he approached Pete's grave, Nick took note of the weather for the first time. It was quite the opposite of the raw and rainy day when they planted Pete in the ground. The sun was out and warmer than it had any business being in November. There were wispy white clouds and contrails from a jet that had just taken off from LaGuardia. He wondered if it was Callie's flight. There was wind. There was always wind on Long Island—wind that smelled of the sea. Nick was alone in the endless stone rows. He had caught a glimpse of someone earlier, a woman. Now she, too, was gone.

Nick's thoughts turned to the days immediately following Pete's suicide. The days when he had decided to finish what his old partner had so ham-handedly begun. He caught himself thinking how unjust it was that Pete was dead and that Ricky Corliss had outlived him for even a single minute. He would have none of it. Sometimes, Nick believed that people had created God so there could be a final arbiter about what was right and just and to answer the question, "Why?" Most people needed that. Not Nick Ryan.

He looked down at the temporary marker where the headstone he ordered would soon be installed. "Pete, old buddy, you fucked up. You fucked up and you changed my life, you son of a bitch."

Nick wasn't a grave talker, but felt the need to say it aloud just the same. As he spoke, he felt eyes on him. He noticed a woman in black coming his way. Something about her movements felt vaguely familiar. He couldn't think why. As she got closer, he saw that her hands were hidden beneath a long cloak. That her head and neck were wrapped in a silky scarf so that little more than a few stray blond hairs and her sunglasses were visible. She stopped on the opposite side of Pete's grave and stared at the temporary marker.

"Peter Moretti," she said. "Was he a relative?"

"Best friend."

Nick expected her to utter some meaningless cliché about how sorry she was. She didn't. He might have given her credit for that had he not been so busy racking his brain about why she seemed familiar.

"Why are you here?" he asked. "Relative or a friend?"

"I am here to speak with you, Nick Ryan."

Her English was peculiar in its complete lack of any accent whatsoever. Each letter enunciated. Not foreign. Not flat. Not twangy. Not *anything* to distinguish it. It was spoken as if by an extraterrestrial who had learned it without any cultural influences. Then it hit him. The feline movements of the figure in black across the street from McCann's. *The bomber!* Before he could even think about reaching for his ankle holster, her gloved hand emerged from beneath her cloak. In it was an odd-looking big-barreled pistol that Nick didn't recognize.

"You are aware you would not be able to reach me or access your weapon before I could fire."

"I am."

"Good. You are not only a talented man but a sensible one as well."

"McCann's—that was you?"

She nodded. "Yes, but we have encountered one another before the unfortunate events of that evening."

Nick furrowed his brow, searching his memory. "Where? Afghanistan?"

"Let us leave it at that. I have observed your talents before, so I am not surprised that our paths should cross again under these circumstances." She raised the weapon. "Move on, Nick."

He didn't need to be told twice. "The Ford coupe for Roderick Ford—nice touch."

"I thought so. My assignment was to make certain you paid a price for what you had done to him and to let you know that he held you responsible as the cause of the destruction. He is a man incapable of accepting blame."

"You were also the woman running on the boardwalk?"

"I was." She tilted her head slightly. "It was clever of you to have someone watching your back. You are learning quickly."

"Am I supposed to thank you for the compliment? You're a murderer."

"And you are not?" Her mouth was hidden, but Nick sensed she was smiling. "I am a professional. I perform as I am paid to perform. You, Nick Ryan, are not quite there. You will be, someday. I do apologize about the woman. I now know she was an intimate of yours."

"Which woman? Angeline or Callie?"

Her body language changed. It went from relaxed to angry. "The bombing at McCann's—I was responsible only for that device. I had no part in the device at the journalist's residence. If I had, she would not have survived. Be assured of that. I left Ford's employ before that amateurish attempt on her life."

"I don't believe you," he said, though he did. "The signature is the same."

"Similar is *not* the same." For the first time, there was emotion in her voice. Her professional pride had been wounded. "I have no reason to tell you falsehoods."

"Who then?"

"If I were to guess, the cocky, unsubtle, incompetent fools with whom Ford surrounds himself. Why is it that men are so foolishly trusting of incompetent bullies? I cannot swear to it, however. I would question how they garnered enough intelligence to copy what they believed was my signature. I suppose, with Ford's considerable resources, he has a vast reach."

"Why are you here at all?"

"You intrigue me, Nick Ryan."

"Forgive me for . . ." Nick coughed, quickly bending over to reach for his Glock. He heard the whoosh, felt the sting in his neck. His body went numb as he toppled across Pete's grave. He wasn't unconscious, but he wasn't fully coherent either.

The woman knelt over him, blocking out the sun.

"I assumed you would eventually try some heroics because, in your heart, you are still a policeman above all else. That will diminish with time, Nick." She stroked his face. "It is inevitable. I am going to leave a card in your pocket. There is a phone number on it. If you are in need of my services—and you someday will be—call it. That, too, is inevitable. With the card, I will leave you another useful document. I owe you something for the woman's life and I pay my debts." She buried her hand in the left pocket of Nick's peacoat. Then, she pulled the small dart out of his neck. "You will go to sleep very shortly. It will be a brief, pleasant sleep. You will wake up feeling quite elated. So long, Nick Ryan."

His eyes remained open long enough to see her disappear among the tombstones.

FIFTY-SIX

Nick had been summoned, not by Joe but by Martellus Sharp. He could only imagine what Sean had done this time to require his intervention. He didn't have to imagine, though. His little brother's history of fuckups was legendary. Sean seemed to swim in a world of addictive behaviors, and while it was all well and good to say that addiction was a disease, it was hard for the people close to the addict to see it that way.

Martellus Sharp's family brownstone on Cumberland Street in Fort Greene would have fit perfectly in Brooklyn Heights. Trouble was that for most of their lives, his family wouldn't have. Skin color mattered in New York City, just as it mattered everywhere else in the USA. Always had. Native New Yorkers were first to call bullshit on the melting-pot metaphor. *Maybe someday*, Nick thought, ambling up the damp tan steps to the double front doors. A historically Black neighborhood that had found an uneasy truce with gentrification, Fort Greene gave Nick hope that the melting pot might someday shift from the mythic to the actual.

He pulled the old-timey doorbell. Waiting, he turned and beheld the streetlight shining off the wet blacktop. The raw gray air smelled of snow, still felt like it, though the snow had already come and gone. Snowfall twice this early in fall was a bad omen for the coming winter.

Nick wasn't sure he believed in omens, but the past month had given him pause about a few things he had once been stone-cold certain about. The old London planetree to the right of Sharp's brownstone had refused to surrender its last leaves to the snow or the season. In Brooklyn even the sidewalk-bound trees were stubborn.

He heard the doors pull back. One look at Martellus's weathered, unsmiling face told Nick this wasn't going to be pleasant. Dealing with the fallout from his brother's bad behavior seldom was.

"This is for you." Nick handed him a bottle of Cabernet.

Martellus raised one corner of his mouth and thanked Nick. "You better come in."

"What did Sean do this time?" Nick asked, walking through the vestibule and heading straight into the kitchen. The house was beautifully appointed with vintage period furniture, but they always talked in the kitchen. "Where's Winona?"

"Winnie's upstairs visiting my sister," Sharp said, opening the wine and pouring two glasses. He sat across from Nick.

"Cheers!" Nick drank, put his glass down. "So, Marty, what did Sean do this—"

Sharp pointed at Nick, then at his own chest. "This here, tonight, you and me, got nothing to do with Sean. Far as I can tell, Sean's getting his act back together, going to meetings every day and trying to get Marie to forgive him. And since he heard he'll be getting most of his Lister money back, he's been good to ride with."

"Then what?"

Sharp took a swallow of the red, making a face as if he were impressed. Whatever pleasure there was in his expression faded quickly away. "You were at the Scarborough Houses the night the Joon kid pulled the plug and that couple was killed."

"I was." Nick's detached, take-it-as-it-comes expression remained intact. "How'd you know?"

"There was an NYPD cordon in the courtyard." Sharp finished his wine, refilled his glass. "Two kinds of people get recognized in this world: the famous and the hated. Given your dad's testimony and what you did to that Rasmussen asshole, ain't no one on the job got any love for you."

"Remind me to cry about it later."

"That was some weird shit—you, a detective third working Brooklyn North Narcotics, being at the scene of a triple homicide on the other side of the borough. But that isn't even the weirdest part. Nah. I hear you were dressed up like a firefighter. How you explain that? 'Cause when I try figuring it out . . .'"

Nick pushed his glass aside and leaned toward Sharp. "I'll tell you what I told a reporter who had the same questions. I was working a tip from a CI about a gang slinging H out of one of the project's buildings. We used the gas leak and the fireman gear as cover for the raid. The joke was on us because the gang got tipped off and cleared out."

"Did the reporter believe you?"

"You'd have to ask her."

"Strange, isn't it, how all that stuff came down in the same place on the same night?" Sharp rubbed his freshly shaven face, the peppery scent of Old Spice suddenly filling the air. "Gas leak, evacuations, a convenient white supremacist, a big drug bust gone wrong . . . Man, that's an amazing bunch of coincidences. Gotta be pretty hungry to swallow that load of shit."

Nick shrugged. "We don't believe in coincidences until reality forces us to."

"We've been talking, but neither of us has said much. I'll hand it to you, Nick. You haven't lied, not exactly, but we both know that coincidence line is a crock. Joon killed that couple 'cause he fucked up. Don't even deny it. Dark stairwell, he's all panicked, probably never had his weapon out of his holster before." Sharp paused, sipping his wine. "I talked to some people about the kid."

"You shouldn't have done that, Marty."

Sharp ignored him. "Joon didn't want any part of the job. Fathers and sons, man. You know how that shit goes."

"Better than most."

"I don't know how much you had to do with it or how you managed it, but all that stuff Roderick Ford said—none of it was true. There was no NPLF, no lone-wolf right-wing nutjob named Karl. This is your chance to tell me what really went down."

Nick shook his head. "Can't do it."

"You mean won't."

"I mean can't."

Martellus Sharp slammed his fist down on the kitchen table. "Nick, your family and me, we go back. You got a choice to make."

"You want to talk choices and truths? Here's the truth. The people who were on scene that night had a choice to make. Let's say your intuition is right, that the Joon kid fucked up. That he killed those kids and then ate his gun in shame. You think anyone in this city was in the mood to parse the details of what really happened? We both know that the circumstances in the stairwell that night were nothing like the first two shootings. There was no malice involved, only incompetence. That said, all anyone would hear was that one more bad cop shot down an unarmed Black teenager. The city would have burned. That's the truth. Would you have let it burn?"

"Maybe this town could stand a little burning. Sometimes, that's how things change."

"You really mean that, Marty? You'd let the rage loose knowing that the people who always get fucked worst and hit the hardest when it happens are the Black community?"

"I'll tell you what I know. I know that the truth isn't pliable. The truth isn't the same thing as a lie agreed upon. Lies robbed that dead girl and boy of the only thing left to them. My people have been beaten down, lied to, and lied about for four hundred years. It's hard to tell a person who has only one life allotted to them that change comes slow and it's gonna take more time." Sharp reached across the table and put his hand on Nick's shoulder. "That's what I know. You saw it all for yourself when we were in the same house together. I've been on the job forever and I still get crap from guys ain't fit to tie my shoes. So yeah, Nick, I would have chosen the truth and let whatever was going to happen, happen."

"The people there that night—they didn't have the luxury of time or perspective."

"But they knew right from wrong."

"Once you've been in battle, Martellus, right and wrong . . . their definitions change. Let me ask you a question."

"Sure."

"When you heard Ricky Corliss was dead, how did you react?"

Sharp cocked his head. "I was happy that motherfucker was dead, but what—"

"You were happy because of what happened to Moretti and because Corliss couldn't hurt anyone ever again. Did it matter to you that the Mafiya probably killed him? Would it have mattered if *I* had killed him?"

"Nah, probably not."

"Where's the right and wrong in that? How much did the truth matter then?"

"Apples and oranges. Look, I know you were in battle. I can't even imagine what that shit's like, but right and wrong don't change. If they did, where would that leave us on the street? If truth doesn't matter, what's that say about us?"

"It leaves us alive to fight another day. Caring about the commentary is above my pay grade. And whether we like it or not, the truth sometimes makes things worse."

Sharp shook his head. "You can sleep at night believing that?"

"C'mon, Marty." Nick gave a mournful laugh. "We're NYPD; sleep never comes easy."

"You got a choice, Nick. You always got a choice. I don't know what you've gotten yourself into, but whatever it is, watch out you don't lose who you are in here." Sharp tapped his chest. "Things you got wrong, you can still make right."

Nick stood and shook his old friend's hand. "Thanks, Marty. You're a good soul, but sometimes it's what we do in the shadows that matters."

As he said it, Nick thought about the gun case on the floor of the GTO's back seat, and about what he planned to do in the morning.

FIFTY-SEVEN

The temperature had risen twenty degrees overnight and any hints of snow vanished. The thin predawn light in Bedford Hills was muddy and diffuse in the thick fog. Using a stone wall, Roderick Ford stretched his calves and hamstrings for his morning run. He found comfort in the misty, womb-like shroud. Comfort had been the one thing to elude him in his ascension. Oh, he took full advantage of the many perks that accompanied money and fame: the finest wines, the sleekest yachts, women of other-worldly beauty, the rarest of cars, the most luxurious houses, the most influential allies. Yet, regardless of their number or how he stacked them in combination, they failed to provide actual comfort. *To be comfortable is not to have comfort.* But if the cost of gaining comfort was a return to the anonymity from which he had risen, the price was too steep.

"I would recommend we take it inside today, Mr. Ford, sir," said Powell, his head of security. "The fog makes it impossible for us to do our job effectively."

"You know what I recommend?"

"No, sir."

"I recommend you shut the fuck up and do your job without making excuses. Let's go."

Ford popped in his earbuds and selected his Beethoven-Wagner mix. His romance with fascism knew no bounds. Beethoven would have detested Ford, but the facts never much mattered to Ford. The world was what Roderick Ford said it was. He was strictly a Wagner and Beethoven fan. He considered Mozart, despite his many alleged liaisons with women, entirely too gay.

With the teasing strings and horns of "Ride of the Valkyries" blasting in his ears, Ford took off running toward Mount Kisco. He was flanked by Powell and a larger, younger man named Salzberg. His specially equipped Suburban trailed twenty feet behind the trio, its headlights projecting an eerie glow against the fog. In his mind's eye, Ford envisioned the helicopter attack sequence from *Apocalypse Now*. He imagined himself as Lt. Colonel Kilgore, his lips moving as he spoke the lines Robert Duvall had delivered so brilliantly in the movie. The morning air smelled not of napalm or victory but of dank, rotting leaves.

———

Following the map the woman had left in his pocket, Nick navigated through Westmoreland Sanctuary. He thought about confession. The priest forgave your sins. He did not take them away. The novenas and Hail Marys weren't erasers. They were weights placed on the opposite side of the scale from the sins, as means of balance. As if it mattered. He tried and failed to remember how long it had been since he sat in the box and spoke to a confessor through the screen. *Bless me, Father, for I have sinned . . .* His last confession would be just that, his last.

Nick had fantasized about doing Ford differently—something akin to what he had done with Ricky Corliss. Capturing him, forcing him to confess his sins in excruciating detail. It had all been very theatrical, the stuff voyeurs and movie audiences crave: an explanation of means and motives, a tussle between good and evil. In the end, what he had done with Corliss was a monumental waste of time.

He stopped, checked his watch, his compass, and climbed.

The fog was thicker in Mount Kisco, and though dawn had broken, it was barely brighter than it had been at the beginning of his run. Ford was unconscious of it all, lost in the moment and the runner's high. Beethoven's "Ode to Joy" was filling his head. He knew that the German lyrics had something or other to do with brotherhood and heaven, and he sang them lustily though without a clue to their actual meaning. He just liked how the language sounded. He turned into the sanctuary, where the Suburban could not follow.

"*Freude, schöner Götterfunken, Tochter aus Elysium. Wir betreten feuertrunken . . .*" Here, he stopped singing and hummed along.

Powell dropped behind his employer as the trail narrowed. As he did, he signaled for Salzberg to take up a position in front of Ford.

———

Nick found a comfortable perch and waited. He ignored the birds and the chittering of small animals rustling through the ground cover. He listened for different sorts of sounds—lumbering, awkward sounds made by animals so self-assured, they announced themselves as if with trumpets.

Snipers were a part of war, although he had never been comfortable with them. There was an inherent unfairness in their very nature. Life wasn't fair, war even less so. Whatever saved the lives of your forces and degraded the enemy's forces, whatever advantage, you took it. He looked through the AN/PVS-30 night-vision scope mounted to the rail of the M110. The scope saw through the fog as easily as through pitch darkness. As Nick saw his target come into view, his objections evaporated. He adjusted his scope and measured his breaths so that nothing would interfere with the shot.

———

The bullet shattered Roderick Ford's sternum, tumbling through his heart muscle like a drunken gymnast. Where the bullet traveled after that was moot. Ford never heard the shot over the chorus singing the words to Schiller's poem about God dwelling above the stars. The fog and the trees made it difficult for his men to know where the shot had come from. Nick had no intention of helping them by firing again. He was gone from his shooting position and retracing his steps back to the stolen car before Roderick Ford had finished soaking the ground with his cold blood.

EPILOGUE

Ergo Sum, on the fourth floor of the Time Warner Center, was among the most expensive eateries in New York City. That was saying something. Nick was unimpressed. Life had taught him that quality did not necessarily correlate with price. He was, however, enjoying the views of Central Park as he waited for his lunch partner. It was a command performance of sorts.

He sipped his sparkling water, the tang of squeezed lime perfuming the air. He would have preferred bourbon, but Dr. Gupta had forbidden alcohol until she was 100 percent certain that all the concussion symptoms had fully subsided. He was enjoying the stark truth of the naked trees in the park. Nick had an affinity for trees as they were now: bare, when you could see their complexities apart from the distracting beauty of their leaves.

"Nick." It was a woman's voice, though not the one he expected.

"Shana?" He stood up to face her.

It happened as it always did. The sight of her made him a sixteen-year-old boy again. They moved their heads to kiss, bobbing and weaving until they each picked a cheek. They did not embrace. Even after her recent visit to his bed, even with the discovery of Becky, not much had changed. She was still married. And he was still a kid from Brooklyn.

"I never thought I'd see you here without me," she said, jealousy in her raspy voice. "You said you always hated places like this."

"Hate?" He shrugged. "Not *hate,* exactly."

"Resented, then."

"Much better."

She changed subjects, conscious of how she sounded. "How are you feeling? I read about you in the papers."

"They must not have mentioned the hospital visiting hours in the *Times.*"

She winced. There were weapons that only people connected for life could use against each other.

"I couldn't," she said. "Your bed is one thing; your *sick*bed is something else."

"I get it. We're vampires now, the two of us, never to be seen in the light of day."

"What?"

"Never mind."

"You didn't answer my question, Nick. How are you feeling?"

"I'm okay now. I've got a little more time before I go back to work."

Unconsciously, she raised her hand and stroked his face. "I'm worried about you."

"Don't be, not for my sake. I have someone new to live for." He took her hand and put it gently down by her side. "Vampires, remember?"

She blushed slightly, realizing what she had just done in public—and also how touching him came so easily to her. She leaned in close to him all the same. "I will come back soon."

He wanted to tell her not to but didn't. She couldn't get there soon enough to please him, and he wanted to know everything there was to know about his little girl. Before either of them said another word, Nick's lunch partner arrived.

"Detective Ryan," Senator Maduro called to him, shaking hands as she made her way across the restaurant. When she arrived, Maduro greeted Shana as if they were old acquaintances. Nick shouldn't have been surprised. Money and power. Power and money.

"Won't you join us, Shana?" Maduro asked.

Shana understood the offer the way it was meant: *Nice to see you. Please contribute to my campaign. Then fuck off!*

"So long, Senator. Goodbye—I mean, so long. Never goodbye, right, Nick?"

Maduro didn't bother to watch Shana leave. Nick couldn't help but watch.

Maduro sat across from him. "Unfortunately, Detective Ryan, I can't stay for more than a drink, but please enjoy your meal. Have you ordered?"

"Not yet."

She signaled for a waiter and ordered a Belvedere Bears martini, desert dry. "Just have Henry wave the vermouth bottle at the shaker." She turned her attention back to Nick as the waiter departed. "I wanted to thank you, Detective. I am unaware of the gory details, but I am told I'm indebted to you."

He said nothing. He was being tested again. It never stopped.

She raised an eyebrow. "Nothing to say?"

"Free lunch is nice." He winked. "Porsches are better."

"Resourceful, attractive, and funny."

"I'm here all week, Senator. Try the veal and remember to tip your server."

Her drink arrived. "Cheers." She sipped. "Frankly, Nick . . ." She lowered her voice, leaning toward him. "These places make me uncomfortable."

"Says the woman from Washington Heights drinking a martini made of vodka that costs several thousand dollars a bottle."

Maduro laughed. "Says the man who keeps a private bottle of fifteen-hundred-dollar bourbon at his local bar."

"Touché, Senator. Cards-on-the-table time?"

"Come work for me."

"As what?"

She smiled. "You tell me."

"I don't think so, ma'am."

"But we haven't negotiated. I know several Porsche dealers."

"I like you, Senator. I voted for you and will again, but let's keep it at that." He stood. "What you've been told notwithstanding, you don't owe me anything. Thanks for the sparkling water and the views of the park."

She grabbed his wrist as he excused himself. She stared into his eyes. "There could be all sorts of perks."

"So long, Senator."

————

Restless, Nick stood naked at the window as he had the day he set out to kill Ricky Corliss, only now the landscape before him was bathed in night. The glow outside the window was not from the sun but from ten thousand head- and taillights, from millions of bulbs on the bridge, from the houses across the way in Staten Island, and from the office towers at the fingertip of Manhattan. The city spread out before him was no less busy, no less beautiful, but a little less cruel than it had been on that morning so many weeks ago. Some things had changed. Some had not. He had changed, and he had not.

Lenny Feld, who, besides Ace, had been Nick's only visitor at Maimonides, was ensconced as ever in the basement of a synagogue, waiting patiently for deliverance that he hoped Nick would someday bring. Nick had meted out a form of justice for Keisha Williams, for Angeline and Callie. Revenge was still a pale deliverance. That was a lesson unlikely to be unlearned. It wasn't about the method of vengeance or how you felt in its aftermath. It was about the result. It was about getting rid of the cancer, and he had done that. No one mourns the tumor.

With Mack's help, he had retrieved the stolen money from Lister— even his brother's tiny piece of it. He laughed, remembering who he had once believed Mack to be. Mack, who had already found another Brooklyn bar to hide behind, camouflaged in a red beard and blarney.

But Nick wasn't laughing at the bodies he'd left behind on the gym floor at Riverhead or the stab wound scars in his own flesh.

He caught Shana's reflection in the window and turned to look at her. During their years together as a couple, her vanity had been a point of contention. Not any longer. He turned and kissed her hard on the mouth.

"Mmmmm . . . you taste of me. I like that, Nick Ryan. I always have."

"You don't hear me complaining."

"Come back to bed." She playfully bit his neck. "Vampires can't afford to waste the dark. Then, I'll show you the pictures of our little girl."

"I have to make a call; then I'll be in."

Shana headed back to bed. From the safe in his guest bedroom, he took out a white card with only a phone number on it.

"Hello, how may I help you?" an electronically distorted voice spoke into Nick's ear. It sounded male. Nick knew better.

"I don't believe that people's lives can be traded for favors."

"How wrong you are, Nick Ryan," said the voice. "You will learn as much."

"You said we had met before, but I still can't place you."

"To be accurate, that is not exactly what I said. No matter. Stop trying. It will prove to be a fruitless pursuit."

"Anyway, your map helped me. You knew it would."

"I am aware. Poor Roderick Ford. Few will mourn such a man."

"That's all. I owed you this call."

"We will speak again."

"I don't think so."

"Think what you like. Until next time."

The line made that annoying beeping sound. Nick hung up as well.

He went back to the window. The only thing he hadn't come to terms with was what he had done at the Scarborough Houses. Martellus Sharp's words about right and wrong rang in his head. Ace had described that mess as the offspring of Shitstorm and Clusterfuck. He supposed what bothered him most was that all the victims in that stairwell were innocents, of a kind. Martellus was right about them. Nick had robbed them all of the truth. Still, he—along with Lenny, Mack, and Ace—had kept the lid on things. They had turned down the flame on a pot that was this close to boiling over. Moving forward, that would have to suffice. He had helped push this sleepless city back from the brink of chaos, and its citizens could go about their waking lives a little bit safer than before.

Nick turned away from the window, to the woman in his bed. Before he did, the Joe burner phone buzzed across the top of the guest bedroom dresser. He hesitated before picking up, but he had come too far to think there was any going back.

"Ryan."

"Tomorrow," Joe said.

"Where?"

"Someone will pick you up at the garage entrance of your building at six."

"What's it about?"

"You'll find out tomorrow. Now, get some sleep. You'll need it."

But there would be little sleep for Nick. Shana was right. They had no time to waste.

ACKNOWLEDGMENTS

I owe a huge debt of gratitude to Shane Salerno and his team at The Story Factory, including Ryan C. Coleman and Deborah Randall. Shane has changed my life, and it was his idea that sparked the creation of this novel. I would like to thank my editor, Michael Carr, and everyone at Blackstone, especially Josh Stanton for believing in this project from the very beginning. I would like to thank Stephanie Stanton for the best cover of any book I have ever written and published. She captured everything I could have hoped for and brought the character and the world of the story vividly to life. I'd like to thank Lieutenant Michael Kauke of the New York City Fire Department (New York's Bravest) and John A. Powell MD, PhD, FACP. Thanks also to Erin Mitchell and my friends Tom Straw, Peter Spiegelman, and Ellen W. Schare for their sage advice. But none of this would have any significance if not for Rosanne, Kaitlin, and Dylan. My family were the ones who sacrificed so that I could pursue a career as an author. Sometimes, words fail. This is one of those times.

AUTHOR'S NOTE

Is Nick Ryan a hero? It's not for me to say. One of the reasons I choose to write crime fiction is that it allows me to place my characters in high-stakes situations under stressful circumstances. Situations where they are faced with difficult, sometimes all-but-impossible, moral decisions. I have certainly done that to Nick in *Sleepless City*. And while the main focus of the novel is entertainment, I hope that as you were reading, you asked yourself what you would have done in Nick's shoes.